THE BLOOD SHE LEFT ME

BOOK ONE

DAVID LEE NORRIS

Cover design by Akaimi the Artist: www.akaimi.art

CHAPTER ONE

NYAH

OKLAHOMA CITY

Nyah Carter could think of at least seven different ways to kill the boy sitting in front of her in class without even getting up from her desk, but not a single way to talk to him.

His name was Andre. Sweet, beautiful Andre. The nicest guy in the eleventh grade. Probably the whole school. The boy who smiled at Nyah when everyone else seemed to keep their distance. The boy who once stood awkwardly at the door an extra five seconds just to hold it open for her. The boy sitting so close, she could smell his cologne. So close, yet so far.

Everyone in class was busy talking or scrolling on their phones while they waited the last few minutes for the bell. It was the perfect time. Just tap him on the shoulder and start up a conversation. If not for the whole talking part, it was a pretty good plan. She'd probably end up saying something dumb like "Heyyy," then freeze up. Nyah had her strengths, but conversation wasn't one of them. Throw in a cute boy and things got worse. So much worse. She wasn't sure what Andre was into, but she was pretty sure girls who couldn't form a complete sentence were not on that list.

She decided against it. He seemed to like her, so why screw it up by talking? Besides, she was fooling herself if she thought she had any right to this life. Andre didn't even know her real name. Around here she wasn't Nyah Carter, she was Destiny Claremore. One of hundreds of other girls in this mostly Black school where she could easily disappear in the crowd. That meant no friends and definitely no cute boys. One of the many sad perks to a life on the run. No, Andre was sweet, but relationships brought the kind of attention she didn't need. Best to keep him at a distance.

She was just starting to convince herself she was fine with all that when Andre turned around in his desk to face her.

"Hey, Destiny."

"Heyyy," Nyah said, then froze.

Andre smiled. God, that smile. He looked to be thinking about something. Or maybe he was waiting for Nyah to say something else. She should say something else. Definitely. Maybe about the weather? It was nice out. Or at least it was this morning. She opened her mouth to speak, but Andre beat her to it.

"So um, how'd you do on that test?"

"Her tests are always easy."

That wasn't so hard. Andre even laughed a little. Of course Nyah wasn't sure if he genuinely thought it was funny, or if he was just being polite.

He was wearing a beautiful African Dashiki, mostly white with a blue, orange and green pattern. The boy had an eye for fashion.

"Nice shirt."

Andre looked down as if to remind himself what he was wearing.

"Oh, yeah. Thanks. I picked it up at Lady D's."

Lady D's? Nyah loved that place. She felt the corners of her lips curving into a smile.

"Up on Kelley Street?" she asked.

"Yeah, for sure. You go there?"

"Every chance I get." She couldn't keep the words from coming out. Conversation seemed to flow like honey with this boy.

Andre didn't seem to mind. He just sat there, smiling at Nyah with those beautiful brown eyes that seemed to read her like a book. When she realized she was staring back, her cheeks seemed to catch fire. She broke eye contact and looked down at her desk.

"Okay, yeah. So that's cool," she said, hoping to sound apathetic but more likely sounding desperate.

Nyah couldn't stop herself, even though she knew she had to end this charade. Andre was talking to Destiny, not Nyah. It was time to quit while she was ahead. Tell him she needed to finish some school work or something. He'd understand. He always did. He'd turn around, life would go on and that would be that.

"Look. They got a big sale this weekend," Andre said. "You want to go? It's cool if you're busy or something."

"Sure, that'd be nice," she heard someone say. Or was that her?

"Cool. We can look for some good deals. Maybe get some coffee." He smiled and turned around.

Nyah closed her eyes and finally let herself breathe. Did he just ask her out on a date? Did she just say yes? He did. She did. She thought for a moment, then decided not to change her mind.

Andre surprised her by turning back around. He glanced at the teacher to make sure she wasn't looking, then back at Nyah.

"Maybe we should kiss."

"What?"

"You know, to have something to remember until this weekend," Andre said.

Andre didn't wait to explain. He just leaned in closer, closed his eyes and parted his lips just so. Nyah closed her eyes and leaned forward, giving in to the moment and anticipating the warmth of his breath as it teased her lips.

"Destiny?" Andre's voice startled Nyah back to reality. She blinked and tried like hell to look normal.

"What?"

He handed her a piece of paper. "It's my number. Text me and I'll save yours."

Nyah took the paper, but dared not say another word.

"You okay?" Andre asked.

"Yes. I'm fine. Thanks."

She waited until his back was turned, then closed her eyes and silently pounded her fist on the desk. Had she lost her damn mind? Was sanity just taking a break today? She rested her head on her hand, took a breath and looked down at the paper he'd given her. The name 'Dre' neatly written out above his number. Good handwriting for a guy. She almost crumpled it up. Almost. She looked at the back of his head. How was that sexy too? Maybe she'd hold on to his number for a while. Maybe a little time with a guy like Andre would be...

Motion from the window caught her attention. She turned just in time to see light glinting from what could only be a rifle scope. She launched herself onto the floor, landing in a roll towards the cabinets by the window. Less than a second later, the chair she'd been sitting in made a loud "pop" sound and rocked to one side. The sound of broken glass filled the air along with a few pieces of the shattered chair an instant later.

Before comprehension set in, before the first kid could scream, Nyah finished her roll on the ground and slammed her body against the cabinets, landing in a crouch. She raised her head just long enough to get a look at the shooter positioned on the roof next door. It was a face she recognized, but couldn't remember from where. One thing was for certain, he wasn't some random school shooter on a rampage, he was here for her.

"Oh my God! What was that?" the girl who'd been sitting behind Nyah screamed.

The shooter was still there, but not for much longer. She had to do something now before he packed up and disappeared into the crowd.

"Someone lock the door. Active shooter!" the teacher yelled.

Nyah ignored her. "Stay down!" she yelled as she stood and ran towards the door.

Andre and the rest of the class were up and moving towards the back of the classroom. Nyah pushed her way through the crowd until she noticed the slip of paper with Andre's number on it getting trampled on the floor, no doubt brushed off her desk during the chaos. She looked back at the crowd of students taking cover in the back. They'd be okay, but the emotional trauma from what just happened would stick around long after this was over. Maybe the rest of their lives. All because of her. There was no normal. There was no going back. She refocused, turned and ran out of the classroom, slamming the door behind her.

There was a covered walkway outside where she could make her way to the next building without getting spotted by the shooter. She pushed through the double doors and nearly ran into her math teacher, Mr. Townsend.

"Whoa! Destiny, wha..."

She raced past him, down the walkway and into the building next door. The stairs were just ahead. She slammed open the double doors with her body and raced up the stairs two at a time, stopping just short of the door that opened to the roof to catch her breath and listen for any sounds of movement. She reached down and pulled the dagger from the sheath strapped to her thigh, twirled it and brought it up to a striking position. A bit of the gold etching glinted in the light and caught her eye. Even in this moment of chaos, she couldn't help but admire its beauty.

"Focus," she whispered to herself. "You've got one shot."

Mapping out where she would be on the roof and the shooter's last location in her mind, she took a deep breath, exhaled, then burst through the door.

As she rolled on the ground she saw the shooter already turning towards her. He was quick, damn quick. An instant later and she would have been toast. But this time, Nyah was quicker. And that was all that mattered.

She rolled into a crouch and flung the blade just like she'd been taught. It spun twice then hit dead center in the shooter's chest. He winced and looked down in surprise, then lowered his rifle and fell to the ground.

Nyah stood up and scanned the roof. Thank God, no cameras. She ran to the shooter and rummaged through his pockets for any kind of ID. There, on his belt. A school custodian employee tag with his picture. Now she remembered where she'd seen his face. Smart way to blend in once all hell broke loose. She pulled her knife from his chest, wiped the blood off on his shirt and slid it back into its sheath, then pulled a pack of Spree candy from the pocket inside her skirt and popped one in her mouth. Only then did she notice her hand was shaking. She clenched a fist and ignored it, focusing her attention on the dead man one last time.

"He sent a sniper," she said with a mixture of fear and rage in her trembling voice. "A fucking sniper to kill me. They'll never give up. They'll never give up until I'm dead."

She left the dead man there, raced back downstairs and calmly made her way into the hallway. The classroom doors were all closed and the emergency lights were flashing. The school wasted no time in going on lockdown. She huddled into a corner and worked up her best sobs. She'd tell them she just got hysterical and ran off. It was a believable story.

Later, after the police secured the building and all the kids were escorted out, she noticed Andre running to what looked like his parents. They grabbed him, hugging and crying.

A black Toyota Corolla pulled up next to Nyah and a man two sizes too big for such a car lumbered out. Danny, her adoptive father. He grabbed her in a tight hug.

"You alright?"

"Yeah. I'm fine," she said, without taking her eyes off Andre.

Danny knew right away she was lying. He always did. He followed her gaze and spotted Andre, the boy she'd told him about on more than one occasion. He put his big hand on Nyah's shoulder and gently squeezed. She hated what was coming next.

"We need to go," he said.

Andre pulled free from his parents to look around, spotted

Nyah and smiled. She shouldn't have let her guard down. It was unprofessional and stupid and it nearly got her, and maybe others killed. But damn, the boy could smile.

"Nyah," Danny said, urging her towards the car. "Stop waving and get in."

Not realizing she'd been waving that whole time, she jerked her hand down and reluctantly climbed into the car.

"Okay, I'm ready."

Her cover blown, Nyah knew she'd be gone tomorrow. Some other school, some other town, miles away from this one. She looked through the window and searched for Andre. One last look. One last smile. One last time at pretending to be normal. But he was gone. Swallowed by the crowd. As Danny slowly pulled out and began to drive away, she knew she'd never see that smile again.

CHAPTER TWO

ESI

AFRICA, 1892 - THREE MILES WEST OF AKPA VILLAGE, DAHOMEY KINGDOM

"Have some water," Jean said as he handed his canteen to Leo. Leo was looking a little too worn since their regiment began this march from Poguessa nearly a month ago. "I promise it's only water this time. No whisky."

Managing a faint smile, Leo grabbed the canteen and took a long drink before taking a seat on the large rock next to Jean under a tree.

"Good man," Jean said, taking the canteen back from Leo and twisting on the top. "Rest and get your strength back."

The hike from base camp to the streams was longer than they'd expected, so the group of about twenty men, mostly legionnaires, was taking a short break.

Jean pulled out a cigarette and offered the pack to Leo.

"No," Leo said, waving off Jean's outstretched arm. "They can smell the smoke."

"They? The Dahomey soldiers?" he asked as he lit the

cigarette and took a long, deep drag, then let the smoke slowly exhale from his lungs.

"The women! The Amazons," Leo said as his eyes scanned the patch of trees for signs of danger. "More fierce than the men. They fight to win or they die. No surrender."

Jean exhaled another drag, then picked up his rifle sitting next to a tree.

"Look, my friend," he said, holding up his rifle. "No Amazon can match our guns. These bullets turn flesh to pulp." He brought his cigarette to his lips and let it dangle so he could run a finger along the bayonet. "And our steel reaches further than their dreaded machetes." He leaned the rifle back against the tree. "We are the ones to be feared."

Unswayed, Leo kept scanning the trees and brush surrounding the soldiers.

"The streams are just ahead," Jean said. "There, we will get fresh water, then rejoin our comrades at camp and be on our way again. To Cana, then on to Abomey and finally put an end to all this mess."

For the first time since the hike began, Jean noticed Leo's shoulders relax.

"Comrade," Jean said, putting his hand on Leo's shoulder. "You will go back to France, a hero. A real he--"

A loud cracking noise penetrated the woods around them. Leo and the rest of the soldiers instinctively ducked and took cover. For a moment, he forgot where he'd put his rifle, then remembered it was behind him. Turning back to reach for it, he noticed Jean hadn't moved.

"Jean, get down! Get..."

Jean sat wide-eyed and slack jawed. Blood trickled down from a hole in his forehead. He was still holding the cigarette in one hand when he fell, face forward into the dirt with a thud.

"Ambush!" a soldier cried out.

More shots rang out as puffs of smoke appeared in different spots from the woods straight ahead, hitting at least one soldier who cried out in pain. At once, the soldiers returned fire. A volley of gunshots echoed through the trees and smoke filled the air.

Startled back to reality by the noise, Leo grabbed his rifle and raised to a crouching position next to his dead friend to take aim. Except there was nothing to take aim at.

"Cease fire!" the commanding officer yelled.

The gunfire stopped and the woods fell silent. The smoke cleared as the soldiers kept their deadly aim, ready to fire again at a moment's notice.

Five seconds went by. Six. Seven. A limb cracked in the woods behind them.

"The rear!" someone yelled.

The well-trained soldiers turned and aimed in one quick motion. But the ones they called Amazons, the Agojie women warriors of the Dahomey Kingdom, were quicker. Only a few soldiers managed to get a shot off before the warriors were on them with a blood-curdling battle cry, using their machetes to cut the flesh and bone of the men who would try and take their country from them.

Leo rose and took aim at an Agojie fighting with a soldier nearby. He put his finger on the trigger and was about to pull when he felt someone punch him. Realizing there was no one nearby, he looked down and saw a knife sunk deep into his chest.

He lowered his rifle and fell to his knees. The sounds of battle faded around him and a strange sort of calm began to settle in. He looked up and noticed a woman walking towards him. He made a move to raise his rifle, but she kicked it from his hands.

"Who..." he managed to get out before he fell to his side and rolled onto his back.

The woman knelt down next to him and pulled the knife from his chest. The pain was extraordinary now, yet he couldn't help but notice her face. Beautiful, deep brown skin marred only by a scar from her temple to her chin. It was her, he had no doubt. The one they called Esi. He'd heard all the stories and now here she was, staring down at him with those dark and terrifying, yet undeniably beautiful eyes.

With his remaining strength, he reached up to touch her face, but she was already gone. Off to continue a fight he no longer cared for, in a war that seemed now like a far off dream. He dropped his arm and turned his head to face Jean, his fallen comrade.

"We are gone too soon, my friend," he managed to say. "Are we not heroes?"

Then he closed his eyes and let the darkness take him completely.

CHAPTER THREE

MOVING DAY

HOUSTON

As the movers unloaded boxes and rolled in appliances, Nyah sat alone on her bed trying to convince herself they were safe. The string lights laced through the rails of her headboard and the cherry blossom vine lights on the opposite wall gave the room a warm, comforting glow, but it wasn't enough to keep her mind from racing. She closed her eyes and fought back the familiar fear creeping up inside her.

Houston was a big city and she could disappear here. New city, new hope. Maybe they'd figure this whole thing out. Maybe this time everything would be different. Maybe this time they wouldn't find her. Maybe this time-

"I'm dating someone."

Nyah flinched and opened her eyes to see Danny standing in the doorway.

"Don't do that! You scared me!"

"Sorry. Your door was open."

"For a big guy, you sure are quiet."

He was a big man for sure, but not very intimidating. At least not in outward appearance. Nyah knew his choice in clothes had almost everything to do with it. He could gain high-value intel on the most dangerous warlords, plan and execute a search and kill mission with flawless precision, but he couldn't pick out a decent shirt. Currently, he was wearing his white bucket hat with an oversized pink and green floral Hawaiian shirt. It complimented his light-brown skin tone, but did nothing for his shape.

"I'm dating someone," he said again.

"Next time kno... You're what? How? We haven't even finished unpacking!"

Danny tried to squeeze into Nyah's purple reading chair near her bed. Apparently he felt the conversation would go better if he was sitting down.

"Jada," he said, still trying to get comfortable in the chair.

"My gymnastics coach?" Nyah turned to give Danny her full attention. "What? When?"

Danny settled on an awkward position in the chair, the most comfortable he could manage, then pointed to a Stephen King book sitting on Nyah's dresser.

"That's one of his best," he said.

"Yeah? I haven't started it ye... Wait, don't change the subject!"

Danny sighed, then took off his hat and put it on his knee.

"It started about a year ago," he said.

"What the hell, Danny? A year ago?"

"You were always a little late for your sessions, so we talked a little while she waited for you," he said, fidgeting a little in the chair. "Eventually, we both realized we wanted more. So we went on a couple dates."

Nyah stood up and looked down at the big man. "A couple dates? And you didn't tell me?"

"I was about to tell you when..." His words trailed off.

"When someone tried to kill me?" Nyah finished. She turned her head and closed her eyes as the memory of Andre and the day a man tried to put a bullet in her brain came rushing back.

"Sorry, I know it's still fresh," Danny said. "But things are starting to settle down now and we figured maybe it was time to give it another try."

He turned to make sure none of the movers were within earshot. "Look, it's alright if you want to ditch school tomorrow. You've been through a hell of a lot."

Nyah sat back down on her bed, crossed her legs and rested her head against the headboard. "No, It's cool. I think I need the distraction," she said. Then, looking back to Danny she added, "Where is she now?"

"She was ready for a change too. She's got family not far from here, so that was enough for her. She just signed a lease on an apartment close to them. She's moving down next week."

"How much did you tell her about us?"

"Nothing. She still doesn't know."

Nyah stared at Danny, waiting for the answer to what she thought was an obvious question.

"What?" Danny asked.

"What's she going to think when everyone suddenly starts calling me Trisha instead of Destiny?" Nyah always liked the name Trisha, so she chose it as her new cover name while they were in Houston.

"Right. I told her you wanted to start using your middle name. You know, a fresh new start and all."

"It's not my middle name."

"She doesn't know that."

Nyah leaned her head back and stared up at the ceiling.

"You can't lie to her forever."

"That's another bridge to cross, Nybear. Are you okay?"

Nybear was his nickname for her. Nyah always thought it was a little silly, but she let him get away with it. And deep down, she kind of liked it.

"It's a lot to take in. And you're just springing this all on me now."

Danny sighed. "I know."

She looked back at Danny. "You sure you're not moving too fast with all this?"

Danny thought a moment before he spoke. "Maybe." He shifted in the chair again. "Look, I'm a middle-aged man who knows how to hold a gun better than I know how to hold a woman. I like Jada. She likes me. I gotta take this chance."

Nyah sighed and examined Danny for a minute. Maybe he was right. Maybe the big, sad man had been lonely for too damn long. She leaned over and rested her hand on his knee.

"Just please be careful, right?"

"Always, Nybear."

He grasped her hand with his, engulfing it completely, and leaned over to make sure he had Nyah's full attention.

"You got your mom's strength, Nybear. I can see that. Your mom saw it too. She told me she saw it in your eyes."

The sudden mention of her mom hit Nyah hard, flooding her with emotions she'd been doing a good job of keeping hidden. She stood up, crossed her arms and turned away from Danny, hoping to hide the tears welling up in her eyes.

"Okay. I need to get ready for tomorrow," she said.

"Oh. Yeah, for sure," Danny said, then clumsily got up from the chair, nearly tripping in the process. "You need a bigger chair."

"It wasn't meant for Sasquatch."

"I'll be in the greenhouse if you need me."

Of course he would. If there was anything Danny loved more than cooking, it was gardening and his assortment of herbs and spices he was planting in his new greenhouse.

He was about to leave when Nyah pointed to his outfit.

"Please tell me you didn't wear that on your date."

Danny put on his bucket hat, tugged on the rim and straightened his shirt.

"She likes the way I dress," he said. "And she likes my hat."

Nyah rolled her eyes, grabbed the book from her dresser and collapsed back onto the bed. "Then maybe you two were meant for each other," she said as she opened the book and began to read.

"You got your momma's mouth for sure," he said, then turned to leave, stopping just short of the door. "And her eyes," Danny said without looking back. "She had such damn beautiful eyes."

Then, just as quietly as he'd entered the room, he left.

Nyah smiled.

"You're a good man, Danny," she whispered without looking up from her book.

CHAPTER FOUR

THE AGOJIE

NEW ORLEANS

"Turn here," Gordon said to Jeff as he drove the oversized, black Lincoln down an old street on the city's east side.

Gordon pounded the dashboard with his fist when Jeff missed the turn.

"Dammit! Are you even listening to me?"

"It's too dark out here, Gord. Can't see a damn thing."

It was late and they were supposed to have the package delivered by now. Ordinarily it might not be such a big deal, but this was a special request from the boss. Sitting in the back seat was Felix the Fixer. The man who could fix just about any sticky legal situation except his own. Lately, his extra curricular activities had caught the attention of the Feds, and getting him to the safe house in one piece had suddenly become their top priority.

Gordon glanced back at Felix. His stained, white button-up shirt was tucked into his jeans, but did little to keep his belly from pouring over onto his lap. He was fidgeting with the door handle as if he were about to open it and make a run for it at any moment. Gordon turned back around and chuckled at the thought of Felix stumbling down the street, pushing his glasses back onto his fat face, only to stop and sit down on the curb to catch his breath after about a half block down the road.

"What's so funny?" Jeff asked.

'"Nothing. Forget it," Gordon said.

Jeff shook his head and kept searching for a turn. He was too tall even for this big car. He hunched and peered over the steering wheel, cursing under his breath.

"It's too dark out here," he said again, then jutted his skinny pointing finger to something ahead. "Look, there's another road."

"You guys even know where you're going?" Felix asked.

"Yeah, sure," Gordon said. "We're almost there."

If half the stories Gordon heard about Felix were true, he'd sooner put a bullet in his head than keep him safe. Over the years he'd committed his fair share of sins, but he drew the line at hurting kids. It was no wonder the Feds wanted him locked up. Never, ever hurt a kid. Gordon wished he could yank him from the back seat and beat him black and blue with his bare hands, but then he'd have to explain it to Mr. Montello. Felix was good at his job and the boss needed him alive. Better to just get this over with and be done with it.

Jeff made a right turn, then a left. "See, I told you. There it is just ahead." Jeff sat up straight, the top of his head almost touching the roof.

Gordon checked out the surroundings, scanning for any signs of trouble. "Let's get this done," he said, trying to make his impatience obvious to Felix.

~

This section of New Orleans was still feeling the effects of the hurricane, which the new mayor promised to fix up. That empty campaign promise made this the perfect place to stash this creep until the heat died down.

The small houses along the road were lined with rusting, waist-high chain link fences. Behind the chipped and peeling painted walls of the old homes were countless stories of days gone by. Better days, filled with hope for a future that never came.

Jeff pulled into the last house on the right, the tires crunching the gravel driveway until they came to a stop just short of the closed gate.

"I got the key," he said, then climbed out of the car to unlock it.

Gordon watched Jeff as he stood in the glow of the headlights, fumbling with the keys.

"Come on, you big freak," he mumbled to himself while massaging his bicep with his fingers, still feeling the effects of last night's workout at the gym. He wasn't tall like Jeff, but he was built like a brick house. Unlike Jeff, he worked hard to get his body.

As Jeff tried one key, then another, Gordon glanced around, then turned to look out the back window. Something seemed wrong. He couldn't put his finger on it, but something was definitely wrong.

"What the hell are you looking at?" Felix asked.

"Quiet," Gordon said. "Did you hear something?"

"Hear what?"

Gordon turned his attention back to Jeff, who abruptly stopped fumbling around for the key. Gordon guessed he'd found it, but he was taking his time doing anything else. He reached over to the driver side and pounded on the horn.

"Let's go!" he yelled.

Jeff slowly turned around, wide-eyed, with what looked like a knife sunk deep into his forehead. He stood there for another second or two in the headlights before slowly falling sideways and smacking onto the gravel driveway with a thud.

"The fuck!" Gordon yelled, reaching for the gun holstered under his jacket and fumbling with the door handle at the same time. He swung the door open and nearly tripped trying to get out, but managed to keep his balance. He pulled the gun and crouched behind the door, aimed towards the house and squinted to find his target.

"Come out!" he yelled into the darkness. "You don't know who you're fucking with here. Come out now and I'll kill you quick."

Gordon strained to hear anything that would give his target away. Footsteps, rustling noises, any goddamn thing he heard would end up with a bullet in it. But other than the low rumble of the car's engine, it was silent.

He stayed low, keeping his Glock ready, while moving around the door to the front of the car until he could see Jeff lying on his side. Keeping his gun aimed with one hand, he grabbed Jeff by the shoulder and rolled him over, careful to stay out of the glow of the headlights. The knife, or whatever it was stuck in his head was gone. Nothing but a hole and a small trickle of blood remained.

"It's her," he whispered to himself. "The goddamn Amazon."

He moved backwards until he was back behind the cover of the open door.

"What the hell's going on out there!" Felix yelled.

"Shut up and stay in the car," Gordon said.

He peered once more into the darkness, but still no sign of the attacker.

"I know you're out there," he yelled into the black night. Nothing but a warm, humid gust of wind answered his call. He gripped his gun tighter. Adrenaline rushed through his body and his senses became laser focused. Things were starting to get fun.

After a few more moments of silence, Gordon decided on a different approach.

"You know what? I'll make this easy for you!" He stood up and raised his gun over his head, then slowly set it on the roof of the car. "Look! No gun!" He pulled off his jacket and tossed it onto the passenger seat and closed the door. "I bet you ain't near as tough as they say. Come out and let's see what you got."

He'd heard stories about the woman they called the Amazon. She was a ghost, they said. A killer you never saw coming until it was too late. But Gordon always thought those stories were bullshit. Probably never fought a real man like him before. He was going to take great pleasure in this. All those years of sweating it out in martial arts and boxing classes were about to pay off.

"I'm gonna strangle your neck with my bare hands and watch the life drain from your–"

"Psst," came a whisper from behind.

Lightning quick, Gordon spun to his left, bringing his right fist around and using his momentum to power a punch aimed dead center at the source. It should have nailed her, but she was gone and his punch hit nothing but air. He was trying to recover when someone kicked him hard in the ribs, knocking him sideways into the car with a thud.

"Son of a...!" Gordon pressed a hand to his side and looked up. Standing in front of him was the Amazon, dressed in some kind of red and gold costume with a mask that left the bottom half of her face exposed. Her rich brown skin looked smooth and untouched, like she'd never taken a real punch in her life. Screw the stories, she was just a girl. And it was time to teach her a lesson in real pain.

"Let's do this," he yelled and pushed himself away from the car towards her. Gordon came out swinging with right and left jabs followed by hooks and uppercuts, all the while moving in closer and forcing his opponent backwards. He should have nailed the bitch a dozen times by now, but somehow she dodged every last punch. And worse, she seemed to be doing it with minimal effort.

She ducked another right hook, then sprang up with a stiff-armed push to his chest that knocked him back a few steps and threw him off balance just enough for the woman to finish with a jump kick to his face, sending him sprawling back against the car.

Gordon made an "Umph" sound and looked up just in time to see the Amazon close the gap between them and unleash a series of punches of her own, pounding Gordon's face and body. Pinned with his back to the car, Gordon tried in vain to shield his face from the onslaught with his arms. The woman finished with a solid right hook to Gordon's jaw, followed by a knee to his gut.

Another "Ooomph!" was the only thing Gordon could get out as he clutched his stomach and hunched over.

"I'm calling for help!" Felix yelled from the back of the car.

Gordon grabbed the door handle and pulled himself back up.

"Put the ph- phone down," he said, gasping for breath. "Or I'll put a bullet in you after I finish with her."

He rubbed his jaw and glared at the Amazon. "Now you pissed me off."

Fueled by a fresh wave of anger, he lunged at her again, throwing three more quick jabs, followed by a right hook, but most of his energy was drained and his punches were much slower now. She easily dodged the jabs and ducked the hook. Gordon almost fell over from the momentum, but recovered. To his surprise, she hadn't counter attacked. She just stood there, staring at him in the darkness with those dead eyes. Was she just playing with him? He stepped back, putting some distance between them. Partly to catch his breath and partly to change up his tactic.

"You're one tough bitch, I'll give you that."

Still, she said nothing. She just kept staring at him like a lion toying with its prey. Acting more injured than he was, he stumbled around the woman until she was between him and the car.

"But ain't no woman ever gonna get the best of me!" Gordon yelled, then lunged forward, grabbed the Amazon in a bear hug and slammed her back against the car. He pushed away and rammed his fist twice into her stomach trying to knock the wind from her lungs, then pulled his left fist back to pound her face and knock her teeth out. But the woman jerked her head to the side at the last second and Gordon's fist crashed through the glass of the passenger-side window instead.

"Aahhg," came a guttural noise from Gordon's throat as he pulled his blood-covered hand from the broken window. "You fucking bitch!"

Bloodied and out of breath, Gordon knew it was over. He leaned his back against the car to catch his breath and held out his uninjured hand in surrender, as if to call for a truce.

"Okay, look," he said. "You can have the guy. He's all yours." He moved aside as if to let the woman through. The Amazon stood still with her eyes fixed on Gordon. It reminded him of a goddamn snake, coiled and ready to strike. It was starting to unnerve him. But he still had one play left.

"I don't care what-" He rolled to his right, grabbed the gun from the roof mid-spin with his good hand and brought it around with the barrel aimed straight at her head. He tried to pull the trigger but couldn't. The feeling in his hand was gone somehow. Instead, a new feeling of pain he'd never known before exploded in his gut.

He looked down to see the same dagger she'd used to kill Jeff buried to the hilt in his gut. He lowered the gun, sank to his knees and looked up at the woman.

"You bi...," was all he could manage to get out.

He tried to raise the gun, but the Amazon kicked it from his hand. She stood over him a moment longer, watching him like a hunter admiring her kill. It was over. He'd been beaten by a goddamn woman. Gordon always knew death would come for him sooner rather than later. It was part of the business. But he never in a million years thought it would end like this. Fate had a messed up sense of humor.

His strength gone, he closed his eyes and gave in to the darkness. He fell sideways, landing with a thud on a cold patch of grass next to the driveway, never to get up again.

Felix repositioned himself to get a better view through the window. "I'm calling for help." He grabbed his phone and punched in some numbers. "You better think hard about what you're about to do. Mr. Montello wants me safe!"

Rachel, the one Gordon called the Amazon, pulled open the back door, reached in and swiped the phone from his hand. Felix jerked his hand away and covered his face as he scrambled away from the open door to the other side.

As much as this worthless man deserved death, Rachel promised the mothers of several of his victims thirty minutes alone with him in a dark place where no one could hear his screams. If he was still alive after that, she'd hand him over to the FBI.

She leaned in and grabbed a handful of his hair to drag him out of the car when she heard a clicking sound from the engine, followed quickly by a flash of blinding, white hot light. Then everything went dark.

ACROSS THE STREET, A WOMAN STOOD IN THE SHADOWS, CLOTHED IN A black and green suit from head to toe, almost identical to Rachel's. She was mostly hidden in darkness, except for the faint light of a distant street lamp casting an eerie glow on her mask. Unlike Jeff and Gordon, she knew the true nature of the woman who just gutted them both. She was no mythical Amazon. She was the very real Agojie warrior. One of the last of her kind. As elusive as a snow leopard and as deadly as a carpet viper. And Gordon paid with his life for foolishly thinking she was anything less.

She watched as the Agojie climbed into the backseat to pull him out of the car. She'd wait until he was out and the Agojie was distracted to make her move. She needed every advantage she could get.

She glanced around once more for onlookers, waited for a car to pass, then stepped out onto the street and walked only two steps before she was suddenly assaulted by a white-hot light that filled her vision, followed closely by a loud boom and a shockwave that nearly knocked her to the ground. She shielded her eyes and walked backwards until she was back on the sidewalk.

As car alarms and panicked screams from neighbors filled the air, she took one last look at the now burning car.

"Dammit, Bruno," she whispered. "What the hell were you thinking?"

Then she turned and disappeared into the darkness.

CHAPTER FIVE

TABLE FOR ONE, PART 1

Nyah sat alone in the Fonville High School courtyard during lunch with a cheeseburger, a bottle of Topo Chico, a half-eaten pack of Spree candies and a book placed neatly on the table in front of her. Danny hadn't made it to the grocery store yet, so he swung by the school to drop off lunch from The Burger Melt. A local favorite situated in the corner of a rundown strip center between a barber shop in the space next door and an auto mechanic on the other side of a barbed-wire fence in the adjacent lot. It was the kind of place locals loved and strangers passed by without a second glance. Or even a first glance. Danny and Nyah fell in love with the place after their first bite. And once Danny learned the owner, Lionel, was a fellow former Army Ranger, the love affair was sealed.

The burgers reminded Nyah of nights with her mom. Sometimes, after what her mom called a "hella rough" day of training, she'd take Nyah to a place just like The Burger Melt for a burger and fries.

"There ain't much a good cheeseburger can't fix," she'd always say.

They'd sit there, sweaty and bruised, eating and talking until the sun went down. It was as close to normal as she'd ever felt. So far, it had been one hella rough year, and this cheeseburger had a lot of fixing to do.

Around the courtyard, students grouped together, talking and laughing like old friends do. Friends with memories made from years spent navigating elementary, middle school and now high school together. Spending long summers by the pool talking about the boys or girls they liked and the teachers they loved to hate.

She took a bite and opened her book. People, she'd learned, were much less likely to come up and talk if you were reading a book. Lately, she'd been on a Stephen King kick.

Last year was one she'd rather forget. Her cover had never been blown so soon. But still, she'd been there long enough to make a few good memories. Andre came to mind. A memory she liked to play over and over in her head. If only it hadn't ended the way it did.

She stopped reading, took a sip of her drink and took in her surroundings. Across the courtyard, some teenager in a football jersey stood up on a table and shouted across the crowd.

"Yo Quin!"

A dark-brown skinned, good looking boy on the opposite side of the yard, apparently Quin, also in a football jersey with the name 'Grady' stitched on the back, took his cue and stood up on his table.

"What?" he yelled back.

A bunch of students took notice and stopped talking to see where this was all going.

"Nice shirt! How much you pay for it?"

Quin glanced down at his jersey, then back up. "Yo thanks! About eighteen and some change," he yelled.

Just about everyone in the courtyard broke out into cheers and shouts. Quin took a bow and raised his hands as if all the praise, whatever it was for, was completely unwarranted. Then both Quin and the other boy sat down as if nothing happened.

Nyah wasn't sure what to make of it all, but her mind was already somewhere else. Back in Oklahoma City with Andre and their last conversation.

"Nice shirt," she'd said.

"Thanks. I picked it up at Lady D's."

She pictured how the date that never was might have gone. Maybe after shopping, they'd have gone out for a cheeseburger. Maybe a movie. Then she remembered the sound of cracking glass, the bullet that punched a hole in her desk just inches from Andre, and the chaos that followed. All because of her and the trouble that follows wherever she goes. She shook off the memory, ate some more and tried to read. Never look back, she thought. Always forward.

Her phone buzzed and Jada's name popped up on the display.

"How's my favorite coach," Nyah said, holding the phone in one hand and the cheeseburger in the other.

"Hi Trisha. I really like that name, by the way."

"Thanks."

"Is this a bad time?"

"Nah, just eating lunch with all my friends."

"Your friends?"

"You sound surprised."

"You're alone, right?"

Nyah put her cheeseburger down and closed her book. "Wouldn't have it any other way."

A pause, then Nyah heard Jada sigh. She never had much of a sense of humor.

"So he told you about us?"

"So he did."

"Listen, Trisha. I like Danny. A lot. And we're good together. I haven't felt this way about anyone in a very long time. I hope you can understand."

"I understand he's gettin' it on with my coach. But it's cool. I just want him to be safe."

"He's safe, and he'd never let what we have come between you guys. That man would die for you."

Nyah pulled a mirror from her beige, leather sling bag to check her hair and makeup. She had it in two large Afro puffs today. Not her favorite, but it was quick and easy.

Danny always said Nyah looked like her mom. Looking at the girl in the mirror, she guessed she could see it too. Her mom's smooth, rich brown skin, her full lips and round eyes that narrowed in the corners. Just like her mom. She could see it. Maybe.

"We just wanted you to have some time to recover from all that mess back in OKC," Jada said.

So many lies. Danny couldn't tell Jada the real reason they packed up and moved, so he made something up. They needed to get out of Oklahoma after the school shooting. It was just too much for Nyah, and they'd been thinking about moving away from Oklahoma anyway. It was a believable story. But the very mention of her old school was enough to send Nyah into another spiral. She saw herself plunging her knife into the man's chest. Except this time she didn't throw the knife, she stabbed him from up close. Close enough to see the fear in his eyes as the life drained from his body. She dropped her mirror back into her sling bag. Was that something else she inherited from her mom? The beautiful eyes of a killer? It was scary to think about. But somewhere deep down, she thought maybe she liked it. And that was even scarier.

Movement from the alleyway across the courtyard caught her attention. A place people didn't normally go to eat lunch. She tensed and scanned for any signs of trouble.

"You sound distracted," Jada said.

"I'm okay. Really," Nyah said. "With Danny or whatever."

More movement. This time she glimpsed the long, curly blonde hair of a girl and the figure of someone else, a boy maybe, who seemed much bigger. Maybe two kids in an argument? Not a shooter. Not a threat. She relaxed, but now she was curious.

"I gotta go. We'll talk soon," she said and ended the call without waiting for a reply, just like they did in the movies.

With a practiced calm, Nyah grabbed her sling bag, got up and walked at an angle towards the alley, careful to avoid any sight-lines of potential lookouts. The world around her slowed and she became hyper aware of her surroundings. Two girls to her left. A group of students ahead. Someone walking past, but not looking up from her phone. Rooftops clear. No threats. A worrisome thought popped into her head. She *was* starting to like this.

She stopped at the wall about two feet from the entrance, pulled out her phone and stared at the blank screen while she listened.

"Why you talkin' shit about me?" She heard a guy's voice from around the corner. "Why you talkin' so much shit?"

"Get off me, Clint!" the girl yelled. "Let me go!"

Her voice came off as confident and strong, but Nyah could hear an underlying panic. She dropped her phone back into her sling bag and turned the corner. It was the white girl from gym class with some guy she'd never seen before. There were only a handful of white people at this school, and two of them were in this alleyway. The girl was taller than Nyah and heavy-set, but she looked small next to the guy towering over her. The boy named Clint stood inches away from her, pushing her back to the wall every time she tried to get away.

"Why you going around telling everyone I stole your stuff?" Clint asked, giving her another push. He seemed more agitated than angry, like he wasn't denying he stole anything. More like he just didn't want this girl to accuse him of it.

"Hey girl," Nyah said, like they were old friends. "We need to go."

"Go away," Clint said without looking back. He sounded annoyed, but kept his voice steady and calm. "Whoever you are, go away. She's not going anywhere right now."

"Get off her, Clint," Nyah said, dropping the friendly tone.

Clint sighed, then reluctantly turned around and stepped toward Nyah, presumably hoping to intimidate her with his size. Nyah was surprised to see an innocent-looking face, peppered with light freckles on his cheeks and sporting a pair of black, Clark Kent-style glasses. He was tall, well built and a damn fine dresser. Under different circumstances, Nyah might have asked where he got his Agnona cotton silk stitch polo from. She'd seen the very same one in an expensive catalog recently.

"Look. It's cute that you want to step in and save your friend or whatever, but not today. We have business." he said in the same, calm, almost soothing voice. He made a circular motion with his finger. "Now turn around and walk away while I'm still giving you the chance."

"He'll hurt you! Just go!" the girl behind him yelled.

Clint's calm and collected demeanor was deceiving, but Nyah could see the rage building in those blue eyes of his.

She moved in closer. Close enough to look up at Clint.

"You should let her go, Clint. Do the right thing here."

Clint seemed a bit unnerved by Nyah's sudden invasion of his personal space, but laughed it off and stared back down at Nyah.

"I gotta admit, you've got some balls," he said. "But I'm really close to losing my shit here. Step back. Leave. Now."

When Nyah didn't budge, Clint grabbed her by the shoulder of her black, mock turtleneck and yanked her forward. Her new turtleneck. The one she'd bought to go with her suede miniskirt and black ankle boots. He'd have done better to take a swing at Nyah's face than to touch her new outfit.

Nyah swept her arm underneath and around his and leaned in with all her weight until his arm bent inward and popped at the elbow.

"Shit!" he yelled.

Keeping the pressure on his arm, Nyah moved her right leg behind his and slammed the open palm of her free hand into his nose, using his own weight to do the rest. His glasses flew off as he tripped and came down hard on his back, slamming onto the concrete with a thud.

"Holy shit!" the girl yelled.

Clint arched his back in pain and grabbed his nose with both hands. "Ahh Fuuuck!"

After a quick check to straighten her turtleneck, Nyah picked up Clint's glasses from the ground and knelt down beside him.

"You got some blood on your shirt, Clint," she said, as she slid his glasses back onto his face. "You really shouldn't have worn white today."

"What the fuck!?" he yelled, still holding his nose.

Gently grabbing his wrists, she pulled his hands away to reveal a swollen, broken mess of a nose. "Does it hurt?"

"Fuck you!" he yelled, though it sounded more like "Fud do."

His eyes were filling up with tears. He tried to turn away, but Nyah touched his chin and turned his head back to look him in the eyes.

"There now. It's gonna be okay," she whispered as she ran a finger lightly down the side of his cheek. "So long as you never, ever look at this girl again. Do we have a deal?"

When Clint didn't answer, Nyah tapped the tip of his nose with her finger. "Boop!"

"Ahh! Stop!" He tried again to turn away, but Nyah held his head in place.

"Do we have a deal?"

"Yeah, whatever! Fuck!"

CHAPTER SIX

TABLE FOR ONE, PART 2

Nyah slammed her fists on the table loud enough to attract the attention of people sitting nearby. Her cheeseburger and Topo Chico were gone. Another hapless victim of the dutiful custodian no doubt. Frustrated, she sat down and considered ditching the rest of school to go grab another one.

"What the hell was that?" someone asked.

Nyah looked up to see the girl from the alley, along with the guy from the tabletop yelling match earlier. Quin, or something.

"You're welcome," she said, and looked down at her phone hoping they would go away.

"Look, thanks for helping her out," Quin said after a moment. "I'm Quin, and this is Desiree, but everyone calls her Desi."

Nyah glanced up, but said nothing. Quin was cute, in a classic sort of way. Tall with broad shoulders and black curly hair with undercut sides and a few strands across his forehead.

No doubt a star football player who'd broken a few hearts in his day.

"Yeah. Thanks. I should've led with that," Desi said. "Sorry, I just can't figure out how you did it."

"I'm Trisha. And forget about it. I was just trying to help out."

Nyah hoped that would end the conversation. The awkward silence that followed made it clear they weren't leaving without a little more clarity. She put her phone down and eyed the pair.

"Look. I took a self defense class once. No big deal."

"Bullshit," Desi said. "That was some serious martial arts or something."

"Do you need something?" Nyah was losing her patience. "I'm kind of busy."

"No, no," Quin said apologetically. "Just that we wanted to say thanks."

"Cool," Nyah said, then remembered how hungry she was. "The Burger Melt is close by, right?"

"Yeah," said Quin. "Right up the road. You going? Because I could go for a cheeseburger."

"They have the best cheeseburgers," Desi said.

This was starting to remind Nyah a little too much of Oklahoma City.

"I need to get to class," she said, hoping they would take the hint.

"You still have like 30 minutes left in lunch," Desi said. "Plenty of time. Come on, let us buy you a cheeseburger. It's the least I can do to thank you for kicking the crap out of Clint."

This was something Nyah wanted to know more about. She lowered her phone long enough to ask.

"What was that all about anyway?"

Desi seemed to tense at the question.

"It... It doesn't matter," she stumbled on her words. "Clint's a dick. That's all."

This was the first good look Nyah had of Desi. A bigger girl, with a round, pretty face and blue eyes framed by long, wavy blonde hair with bangs to her eyebrows. A few of her bangs were dyed blue, which made her look even prettier, and her short fingernails were painted to match.

"He stole something of hers," Quin said finally. "Clint and some of his friends have been breaking into cars around the neighborhood. They broke into hers and stole a bunch of stuff. Nobody can prove it was them, but everyone here knows it." He glanced around the courtyard, maybe looking for Clint. "Funny thing is, he ain't poor. His dad made a killing in tech, so they got money. We think he's just bored or something."

Nyah thought it sounded crazy to confront a guy like Clint over something so small, but whatever.

"You two together?" Nyah asked.

"Nah," Quin said. "She's my girl though. We've been friends since we were kids. Come on. Let's grab a cheeseburger."

Nyah considered saying yes. She was even about to mouth the word when an image of Andre flashed in her mind. This time, he was lying on the floor in a pool of his own blood with a hole in his head. Another image. The shooter peering through his scope from the roof with Nyah dead in his sights, ready to take his second shot and end her life. Her hands started to shake. She felt like a sitting target with so many people around. She stood up and grabbed her sling bag and her book.

"No. I have to go. I have to go... somewhere else," she said, and left before Quin or Desi could get out another word.

CHAPTER SEVEN

ESI, NAWI AND URIBI

CANA, DAHOMEY KINGDOM - NOVEMBER, 1892

The trench smelled of sweat, blood, piss and wet clay. The regiment of fifty Agojie women soldiers hidden inside were dressed in hand-sewn, blood-red tunics and headbands emblazoned with golden crocodiles stitched in with a form of appliqué. A technique they'd made into an art form.

Esi's orders were short and to the point. "Hunt the officers," she'd said. "Their heads at all costs."

Another day was about to dawn, and the battles would begin again soon. Until then, they waited, making quiet conversation.

"We will not win this war," Nawi said. "They are too many for us. We will die here in this trench."

Nawi, Esi and Uribi sat side by side in the trench, patching wounds and sharpening knives. Three women bound together in a lifelong friendship beyond that of the already extraordinary kinship of the Agojie warriors. Now in their late twenties, they'd become legendary to the younger recruits. Stories of their heroics in battle were required study for all.

"Then at least we die together," Uribi said.

"The only death for me," Nawi added.

Uribi spit, then paused her work to admire Nawi, who was busy tending to a minor wound. Even covered in dirt and blood she was beautiful. More so than Esi herself if that were possible. When not at war, Nawi designed and sewed gowns from the finest materials to fit her tall, slender figure. And while she kept her hair tied back in battle, at home she let her long braids cascade over her shoulders and adorned her hair with flowers. Had she not chosen the life of service to her king, the men of Dahomey would have lined up for a chance at her hand.

Uribi, short and stocky, never cared about such things. She chose more practical clothes and kept her head shaved and ready for battle. She returned to her work and ignored the nagging sense of doom that was quietly creeping its way into the trench.

"And so together we will die. For our king," said Esi. "But not before we make them bleed."

Nawi finished the bandage, pulled her knife and began to examine the blade. "What do you want?" she asked the other women without looking up. "If we live, what is it you want?"

A short pause, then, "To see my brother again," Esi said. "I've not seen him since..."

"Since your father gave you to us," Uribi said.

"Yes."

"It's hard to think of what we lose to gain what we have," Nawi said.

Esi gestured to the other women in the regiment. "These are my sisters. My body. The Agojie. I would die for any of them," she said, then pointed to Nawi and Uribi. "And you are my heart. We've grown together, trained together and killed together. Without you, I die." She picked up her rifle to inspect and clean it.

A few more seconds of silence passed, then Nawi sheathed her blade and looked up to the sky. "I want freedom." She said, then closed her eyes as the memories of happier times filled her mind. She stretched her arms out wide and Esi had to duck to avoid getting hit in the face. "To spread my arms, feel the sun on my face and dirt under my feet. To look up at the clouds and not over my shoulder."

"Freedom is all you want?" Uribi asked.

"Yes, dear friend. Freedom to live. Freedom to fight another day for our king. What about you?"

"A bottle of whisky and a strong man to serve it to me," Uribi said.

"Now on that, we agree!" Esi said. The women burst into a round of laughter that eased their tensions, if only for a moment.

A rifle shot, followed by a scream sliced through the warm, stagnant air. The trio rose in unison with their heads just above the edge to see the source.

"Arepa!" Someone shouted from down the line.

In the distance, Esi spotted him. Arepa, the man they'd put so much hope in, running for his life towards the trench, slowed only by a limp in one leg.

"Look there, behind him," Nawi said. "Two soldiers. They must have discovered him as a spy."

"Come!" Esi said.

Esi grabbed her rifle, jumped from the trench and landed in an all-out run, with Uribi and Nawi close behind. It was dawn, with the rising sun to their backs. Shadows and silhouettes would be their ally.

They ran silently, using brush and rocks for cover as best

they could until they were no more than fifty yards from the pursuing soldiers.

"Ahhheee!" Esi yelled.

"Ahhheeee!" the other warriors echoed as they ran to intercept.

The battle cry stopped the soldiers in their tracks, but only for a moment. They spotted the women and snapped their rifles up into firing position.

Esi gave the signal and in practiced synchronization, all three fell to a prone position on the ground just as bullets whizzed past overhead. Esi aimed and fired her rifle. She knew they were out of range, but it caused just enough of a distraction for Nawi and Uribi to roll several feet in opposite directions, widening the gap between them all.

"Strike!" Esi yelled.

Before the soldiers could get a fix on them again, Uribi, who was closer and definitely within range, raised to a crouch, fired and struck one of the soldiers. He grabbed his arm and fell to the ground. The other soldier took cover behind a nearby rock, but it was already too late. Using the distraction of gunfire, Nawi anticipated the soldier's next move and flanked him. Her knife was buried in his back before he even realized she was there. He gasped, dropped his gun and fell to the ground.

CHAPTER EIGHT

AREPA THE SPY

Arepa limped his way to the trench with the help of two warriors from the regiment. He'd been shot in the leg and Nawi breathed a sigh of relief when she saw there was an exit wound. Still, he was losing blood fast and the wound needed to be mended.

"Wrap his leg," she said, as they lowered him into the trench.

While the warriors tended to his wounds, Esi knelt down by his side. She knew a French attack could happen at any moment, so she had to act quickly.

"Tell us, old friend, what did you learn?"

"I... they– aghh!" he yelled out as one of the women poured whisky over his wound to disinfect it.

As much as she admired this man, Esi was quickly losing her patience. He was their most loyal spy, but he was no soldier. Pain was something he had little tolerance for.

"Listen," Esi said. "You will be okay. But I need you to tell us what you learned."

Realizing for the first time how he must look in front of

these battle-hardened women, he tried to regain some of his composure. “It will end soon,” he said. “They will-”

He grimaced and clenched his teeth as another woman tightened a tourniquet to his leg. After a few seconds, he continued.

“They will destroy you and the rest of what remains of Béhanzin’s Amazons, then march on Abomey. Your capital will fall and there will be no choice but surrender.”

“We will die fighting,” Uribi said.

“You will,” Arepa said. “They will talk of a truce, but they know Béhanzin will never agree. They will march on Abomey. It has begun. They have already sent someone to kill your king.”

Nawi, who’d been scanning the field that stretched into the darkness for signs of enemy movements, took notice of this last part and returned to Arepa’s side.

“One person to kill our king? Who did they send?”

The women completed their patchwork on Arepa’s leg and moved away. Arepa tried in vain to find a more comfortable position in the trench.

“A damn fool if you ask me,” he said. “What man could possibly get to your king and hope to live?”

“Who did they send?” Nawi asked again.

“A man named Jabari.”

A silence fell over the group. Esi sat down and put her face in her hands. “This cannot be.”

“You know him?” Arepa asked. “This man with a death wish?”

“How can this be?” Uribi asked. “Jabari is long since dead!”

~

Esi leaned back against the trench wall and Nawi cursed under her breath.

"He is no fool," Esi said. "If they have sent Jabari, it is already too late."

Arepa shifted his position once more, but was only successful in aggravating the pain in his leg. He tried to hide it, but Uribi noticed. She reached into her satchel and pulled out a metal flask.

"Drink this," she said, handing it to him. "It's good medicine."

Arepa took a sip then put a fist to his mouth and squeezed his eyes shut. "Whisky. Thank God." He took another sip and waited for the burn to wear off once more. "Who is he?" he asked.

"He was our brother. A soldier for the king," Esi said. "The best. He had no equal."

"Except Adisa," Nawi said. "His love, his fire and his only weakness."

"Adisa?"

"She was our sister," Esi said. "A true warrior. But she fell in love, and love is a privilege we sisters are not allowed. So they planned to run away together, but Adisa died in battle before they could leave."

"Jabari never forgave the king," Nawi said. "He disappeared. We thought he was dead."

"He is not dead," Arepa said.

"Nor his desire to avenge his love," Uribi said.

"It will not end like this," Esi said. "It can't. We must protect our king!"

"Come," Nawi said. "We will go to Abomey and stop him."

"How?" Uribi asked. "Abomey is a half-day's march, and Jabari may already be there!"

"I have a way," Nawi said.

"What way?" Esi asked.

Nawi thought for a moment before continuing. "Yes. I have a way. But only two can go."

"What is this nonsense?" Uribi asked.

"Do you trust me, friend? We need to go now."

Both Uribi and Nawi looked at Esi, their commander, for a decision. Esi hesitated. None of the women in the trench would ever see home again. And if what Nawi said was true, that only two of them could go, this would be the end of the three. A lifelong bond broken forever. But a decision needed to be made quickly. Every second they wasted put the life of their king in more danger.

"Uribi, go with Nawi," she said, finally.

Uribi stood in silence, unwilling or unable to respond.

"Uribi. Did you hear me? Go with Nawi and stop Jabari."

"No," Uribi said.

"What? You disobey?"

"I cannot win against Jabari, you know this." She put her hands on Esi's shoulders and looked her in the eyes. "You must go, Esi. You and Nawi are the only chance we have of stopping him and saving the king."

"What she says is true," Nawi said. "If anyone has a hope of defeating him in battle, it's you. But we must go now!"

Esi looked into Uribi's eyes, searching for another answer she knew wasn't there. She reached out and took Uribi's hand.

"We have fought well together," Esi said.

"We have."

"I hope you find that strong man to serve you whisky."

Uribi smiled. "Go. Save the king. Then find your brother," she said. "Promise me you will."

"It is a promise."

She let go of Uribi's hand and turned to the other sister warriors in the trench.

"We leave you now, sisters. Our king is in danger. Nawi and I will save him or we will die trying."

"Ahheee," the other warriors shouted. "Save our king!!"

"Uribi will lead you now. Follow her as you did me," Esi said, then raised a fist into the air. "Fight well, die well."

"Fight well! Die well!" the others repeated in unison, raising their fists into the air.

After one last look at her sisters, Esi and Nawi climbed from the trench and disappeared into the darkness.

CHAPTER NINE

PAIN SEES PAIN

Never look back, Nyah's mom used to say. Always ahead, never back. Nyah supposed there was truth in that, but looking back always seemed easier. Take last week for instance. Having a panic attack and nearly losing it in front of everyone was a memory she'd love to forget. But it was like a song stuck on repeat in her head. The more she tried to block it out, the louder it played. A constant reminder of why she could never fit in. Never be normal.

She was back in the courtyard for the first time since the panic attack. Never let fear hold you back from doing something you like, was something else her mom would always say. That one was easier. As much as she'd love to hide and never show her face out here again, she loved eating her lunch in the open air of the courtyard even more. So, with her leopard-print top and faux-leather skirt, the cutest outfit she could throw together, she gave it another chance.

No cheeseburger this time. Just a sack lunch, a fresh pack of Spree candies and a book. She'd finished The Dead Zone and was a quarter way through Carrie. Nyah felt a personal connection with Carrie. They might have been great friends.

Desi and Quin were sitting near the fountain with some friends, occasionally stealing a glance at Nyah's table. Quin was sitting in between Desi and another boy wearing a pink Polo and torn jeans with his hair styled into cornrows. He put a hand on Quin's shoulder and Quin smacked it off. Desi reached over and punched him on the shoulder, then all three broke out into laughter.

On the other side of the courtyard, Clint sat with a bandaged nose at a table with three other boys and a girl, laughing and having a good time. Even the bullies had friends.

She looked down at her book. "You see, Carrie? Friends ain't so bad. It's too late for you, but maybe I could give it another try." She opened her bag and pulled out a sandwich. "But if I see one drop of pig's blood, I'll kick all their asses."

"Yo Quin," came a voice from across the courtyard. Just like last week, a boy in a football jersey was standing on a table. "Nice shirt! How much you pay for it?"

Right on cue, Quin stood and hopped onto the edge of the fountain. "I paid eighteen for this one!"

And then, same as last week, everyone in the courtyard erupted into shouts and cheers as Quin bowed.

"But don't forget where it came from," he said, then pointed back to the boy who asked the question.

The crowd cheered some more and the other boy bowed, then sat back down as if none of that just happened.

Nyah couldn't understand why they were so obsessed with how much his damn shirt cost. And didn't schools usually pay for football uniforms? She tried to make herself care, but it was no use. She stopped paying attention and went back to her book.

Later on, she glanced at her phone. 12:15. She'd almost made it through lunch without another attack. Another ten minutes and she'd be fine. As the sun came out from behind a cloud and warmed the back of her neck, she started to think she could make it.

That was until her phone lit up with a message from Danny.

I'll make dinner tonight.

It was code that meant he'd seen or heard something that caught his attention and to be on alert. It wasn't enough to pack up and leave, but it was plenty enough to remind her she wasn't a normal kid having a normal day at school. Her hopes of making it through lunch vanished.

She'd seen this message dozens of times over the years, and not once did it cause so much anxiety as it was causing her right now. She closed her eyes and tried to control her breathing. Slow breaths, in and out. She opened her eyes and told herself it was probably nothing. It was definitely nothing.

She put her book down on the table. Was the courtyard smaller somehow? Were the people closer than before? She scanned the rooftops, realizing for the first time how trapped she'd be if another shooter came to take her out. She got up, grabbed her things and walked away, leaving her unfinished lunch behind. Slowly at first, then fast. Now, she was almost at a jog. It was even harder to breathe.

She ran inside the main building, down the hall to the girl's bathroom. It was quiet. No noise and no one else inside but her. She walked to the first sink on the row, grabbed the edge and focused on her reflection in the mirror.

Concentrate. Think. Calm yourself. Slow and easy breaths. Close your eyes. Breathe out... slow. One, two, three... Now open them. Good. You're doing good.

She looked down at the sink and shook her head. "You're not cut out for this, girl," she said to herself. "You're nothing like your mom."

She closed her eyes and took a few more slow, deep breaths just for good measure. Her panic attacks were coming on more frequently lately. She didn't know why and she didn't care. She just wanted them gone.

The door squeaked open and a woman Nyah didn't recognize walked in. She stopped for a moment and stared at Nyah as if surprised to see someone else in the bathroom, then continued on to a mirror three sinks down. From the corner of her eye, Nyah saw the woman slip a hand into her purse. Instinctively, her own hand moved to the dagger strapped to her thigh under her skirt, then felt almost embarrassed when the woman pulled a tissue from her purse and leaned in closer to the mirror to dab at some eyeliner. Not a gun, not a knife, just a damn tissue.

"Are you alright?" the woman asked, glancing at Nyah's reflection in the mirror .

Realizing she must look ridiculous standing there, Nyah grabbed her sling bag and rummaged through it until she found her half-eaten pack of Sprees.

"Yeah. Fine," she said, then popped a Spree into her mouth, tossed the pack back into her bag and left.

To her surprise, Desi was sitting on the floor in the hallway across from the bathroom when Nyah walked out. Her head was down and a few blue-dyed strands of hair hung over one eye as she scrolled on her phone.

"Waiting for someone?" Nyah asked.

Desi looked up and smiled.

"You," Desi said, sliding her phone into her jean-jacket pocket. "I know a panic attack when I see one. I just wanted to check on you."

"I'm fine, thanks," Nyah said, then turned to walk to class. She'd be early, but standing there any longer would have been painfully awkward.

Behind her, she could hear Desi get up to follow.

"I'm fine," Nyah said, glancing back at Desi. "You can go now."

Desi picked up her pace and caught up with Nyah. "Look, you're new here, right?" Desi asked. "We're just trying to be friendly."

"I don't need any friends. Really," Nyah lied. Years on the run made being honest a luxury she couldn't afford.

The bell sounded and kids crowded the hallway. Nyah stopped and turned to Desi.

"Look, I'm sorry," she said. "I just have a lot going on."

"Let me guess, you got problems at home? Problems with the parents?"

"You don't know me, Desi, but trust me on this. You don't want to be friends with me."

"I don't know you, but I recognize you," Desi said. "You're hurt. You're messed up. You're not normal. Just like me and Quin. Pain sees pain."

Nyah kept quiet, but didn't leave.

"Messed up ain't so bad," Desi continued. "You just can't keep doing it alone. We need each other to get through this fucked up world."

Nyah shook her head.

"It's not about that," she said. "I wish it were that easy."

"No? Then what?"

"You don't quit, do you?"

"Nope. You'll either love that or hate that about me by the end of the year."

"Not feeling much love at the moment," she said, then checked the time on her phone. "I need to get to class."

"Just let me say one more thing," Desi said, then walked to a row of lockers away from the foot traffic and leaned against them. When Nyah didn't follow, she waved her over. Nyah hesitated, then reluctantly agreed.

"Look," Desi said. "You think I risked my life confronting Clint for some spare change and a pair of shades he stole from my car? I don't give a shit about all that. But there was something else he took."

"Something worth getting your ass beat over?" Nyah interrupted.

"Yeah. Something worth getting my ass beat over. It was a quarter my dad gave me when I was four. It was like a reward for not wetting the bed for a week or something. I put it on a string a while back and kept it hanging on my rearview mirror."

"Sorry, but I still don't think that warrants you risking your life," Nyah said. She pulled out her phone to check the time again. "I should really get to class."

Desi looked away. When she turned back, her eyes were wet with tears.

"He died," she said. "Last year in a car crash. He was my everything. Our everything. My little sister is still a mess. Nighttime is the worst. I stay with her most nights, but sometimes she's all alone in her room, crying herself to sleep."

"Damn. I'm... I'm sorry." The only thing Nyah could think

to say. She put her phone back in her sling bag. Since she wasn't sure what to say next, she said nothing.

Desi leaned her head back against a locker and let out a long, deep sigh. "My mom left us years ago. She came around like once a year when my dad was alive." She laughed and shook her head. "When he died, she got the house and moved in, but she's still gone all the time. Now it's basically just me and my sister. It's like that quarter was this little reminder of my dad I kept with me wherever I went. A reminder that I could be something, you know, special."

The hall was mostly cleared out now, but neither of them noticed or cared.

"It's funny," Desi said. "A bunch of relatives stepped up to help us after he died. Aunts, uncles, you name it." She wiped her eyes and laughed once more. Nyah thought it was just to keep herself from crying. "But we found out pretty quick no one would ever love us the way he did. I took that for granted when he was alive. You know?"

"And once it's gone, it's gone forever," Nyah said. "I lost both my parents."

Desi looked at Nyah, then leaned over and nudged her with her shoulder. "You see? Pain sees pain."

"Trisha," came Quin's voice. "Ya'll gonna be late."

Desi and Nyah turned to each other and laughed.

"Why's that funny?" Quin asked.

"It's okay," Desi said. "We just needed a moment."

With an understanding taught by years of friendship, Quin stopped talking and leaned against the lockers next to Desi and Nyah. For the next few moments, all three stood there in silence. The bell sounded and shoes squeaked on the floor as the last few students hurried to class before the doors clicked shut. They were late, but none of them cared.

"Meet us for that cheeseburger later?" Quin asked.

"Yeah," Nyah said. "Sure."

"Cool."

They stayed a few moments longer. Quin left first, then Desi and Nyah in the other direction. For the rest of the day, Nyah thought about Desi, Quin and cheeseburgers, but not her panic attacks. They were gone. At least, for now.

CHAPTER TEN

LAST CHANCE TO BAIL

Nyah sat on a bus stop bench across from The Burger Melt with her thumb hovering over the send button of her phone. She'd been this way for several minutes now, contemplating her message to Danny.

She could leave now. Get up and go home. Desi and Quin would understand. No real feelings hurt. Not yet, anyway. But give it time and they would get hurt. Nyah had no doubts about that. It's why she knew leaving now would be better for everyone. Yet, there she was, sitting at the bus stop, thinking about that cheeseburger. The smells from the restaurant drifted across the street, filling her mind with sweet memories of her mom and the times they'd had together.

She hit send before she had the chance to think about it anymore.

> Gonna skip training tonight, out with friends.

A few seconds later, Danny responded with a question mark. Nyah was quick to respond.

You can have a girlfriend, I can have friends.

A few more seconds passed, then another text from Danny.

Call if you need me.

lol! I'll text.

Text then. Have fun.

Nyah put her phone in her sling bag and was about to get up to walk across the street when her phone dinged again.

Making sushi with Jada tonight. She likes it.

Nyah shook her head and typed out a quick response.

K. Ditch the bucket hat.

A few seconds passed before three bouncing dots popped up, disappeared, then reappeared.

She likes my hat.

Nyah smiled.

lol have fun!

She tossed her phone back into her sling bag a second time and looked up just in time to see Desi and Quin walk inside The Burger Melt.

"Last chance to bail," she whispered to herself.

She stood, took a deep breath, looked both ways and crossed the street.

CHAPTER ELEVEN

BACK HOME

Nine-year-old Rachel sat at the table in her mother's kitchen, watching as she shaped the hamburger meat into patties.

"How many times I gotta tell you, girl?" her mom asked as she placed them neatly into the pan, filling the air with the sizzling smell of spiced meat. "You gotta be careful out there."

She'd crashed her bike on the sidewalk again. Or maybe she'd fallen from the neighbor's tree. Which was it? Why couldn't she remember? She guessed it didn't really matter because she was here now, and Momma was making everything better, just like she always did. The sound of sizzling beef, the spatula gently tapping against the cast-iron skillet, Momma humming some tune Rachel couldn't name. Even the heat from the stove comforted her.

The song shifted and went off key. Eventually, the singing turned to laughter. Quietly at first, then louder. It was a strange, eerie laugh Rachel didn't recognize.

"Momma?"

"You're one tough bitch, I'll give you that," her mom said.

"Momma, what?"

"But ain't no woman ever gonna get the best of me."

Her mom spun around. The spatula she'd been holding was a gun now. And it wasn't her mom, it was a man. Gordon, she thought. But how'd she know that name? Gordon, Gordon, Gordon. She tried like hell to recall, but the memories were paper thin, crumbling to dust with the slightest touch.

He smiled with a wicked, ugly grin.

"I'm gonna strangle your neck with my bare hands," he said. "Watch you di–"

The stove exploded behind him in a flash of light, followed by a loud boom that pounded her eardrums. She felt heat burning her skin and broken glass piercing into her neck and back as she turned to shield herself from the blast. Then nothing.

Rachel opened her eyes and sprang up. A burst of pain shot through her head and she used both hands to press against her temples for relief. None came. It felt as though her skull would crack open. Fighting the pain, she looked around to take in her surroundings. She was on a couch in what looked like someone's living room. A blanket lay across her lap and a pillow was on the couch where her head had been. Slowly, she brushed the blanket aside and waited for the worst of the pain to stop before she tried to get up. She'd been asleep. Or knocked out, more likely. The memory of what happened and how she ended up here was gone. Her mind was a blank slate.

Then the pieces started coming back. Little by little. A fight. A man in the backseat of a car. A flash and then everything went blank. She tried to stand up, but all she could do was hobble and grab on to a nearby chair. She checked her pocket for her phone. Of course it was gone.

She was standing in a small room, possibly in an apartment building. A couple of pictures hung from the wall above a

TV. An easy-chair next to the couch and an end table with a few paperback novels sat in the space between them. She hobbled over to a mirror hanging on the wall, grabbing on to whatever she could to keep herself stable, and was shocked to see the face staring back at her.

Her Agojie suit was torn in several places. The sleeve on her right arm was gone, and the right leg was ripped off below her thigh. Her face mask had also been torn, exposing part of her forehead. She touched her face, hands and arms, but other than some scratches and a killer headache, she seemed fine. She tugged at the torn fabric of her suit. Ruined. She'd have to make a new one for sure. But first she had to figure out where the hell she was and whose ass she had to kick to get out.

CHAPTER TWELVE

THREE BEES

Nyah played many roles during her time on the run. From goth girl to a geeky bookworm. While not all kids in those categories were anti-social outcasts, those particular personalities gave just the right "stay the fuck away" vibe to keep her under the radar and out of the social spotlight.

As she walked inside The Burger Melt, she remembered how closely matched to her personality those characters actually were. The sudden onslaught of people laughing, talking, sometimes yelling, made her want to turn around, run away and hide. She was about two seconds away from doing just that when she heard Quin's voice.

"Hey Trish," he said from across the restaurant. "We didn't think you'd show up."

He was standing with Desi near the front counter, apparently ready to order. Nyah walked over and immediately felt a wave of relief from the extreme anxiety she'd felt creeping up on her a moment before. Something about standing alone in a crowd full of people who all seemed to be having a good time was, as her mom might have said, hella triggering.

"Why not?" Nyah asked, giving Quin's outstretched hand a light tap.

"Just thought you might have a change of heart or something."

"You promised me a cheeseburger," Nyah said. "I take that seriously."

Quin nodded. "I did in fact do just that," he said. "You guys go get a table, I'll order."

The inside of The Burger Melt was almost as unimpressive as the outside. It consisted of two rooms for seating, a front counter and a grill. They'd come just in time for the after-school crowd. A bunch of hungry teens, glad to be out of school and not quite ready to go home.

Desi and Nyah found a table in the back dining area where it was only slightly less noisy. Nyah took her time sliding into the booth, trying to think of something to say. She'd already marked the exits and sized up every customer for potential threats, but coming up with a good conversation starter was something beyond her ability.

"I hate being around this many people," Desi said just as Nyah was about to mention something about the weather. "But Lionel's burgers are worth the noise."

"People suck," Nyah blurted out, then immediately regretted it. "No offense. I mean, not all people. You seem cool."

Desi laughed. "No, I get it. I like birds."

Nyah raised an eyebrow.

Desi seemed surprised at her own words and buried her face in her hands. "Oh God, that sounded so dumb."

Nyah folded her arms and leaned back in her seat. "I feel like there's more to that story."

"Sort of." Desi tapped her blue nails on the table and thought for a moment. "Okay, fine. You may think this is stupid, but a few years back I was really depressed and spent pretty much an entire summer at home. Barely went out at all. I found my dad's old, ratty binoculars and started watching birds in the back yard. It was calming. I couldn't get enough. It was like, damn, those birds have it all figured out, you know?"

Nyah didn't know, but she was curious to see where this was going.

"They just don't care. They don't get sad. They don't get depressed and start watching humans to fill the time. It's because they have it all and they fucking know it. They can fly, they can poop wherever they want and they can sit high up in a tree and watch us down here struggling to get through life. I felt like that was where I wanted to be. I wanted to stop being human and join the birds."

"Damn, girl. You really thought this out," Nyah said, then once again immediately regretted the words coming out of her mouth.

"You see. I knew you'd think I was crazy."

"No. I didn't mean it like that."

Desi looked down at the table, apparently unconvinced. Truth was, Nyah did get it. The need to break free and fly away without a care in the world. Never looking back, never regretting anything anymore. It all made perfect sense.

"I like birds too," Nyah said.

Desi looked up to see Nyah holding out a fist. She smiled and returned the fist bump. "Bird or nothing," she said.

Quin dropped a tray of food on the table and slid into the booth next to Desi. Three cheeseburgers, fries and drinks. Nyah grabbed a cheeseburger and a bottle of lime sparkling water.

"Yo, Quin!" someone yelled from the other side of the room. Quin smiled and nodded.

"Hey Quin," two girls who looked like cheerleaders sitting at a table behind Quin said in unison. He flashed them a quick smile, then turned back to Nyah and Desi without saying a word. Nyah figured this must be routine for Quin. An act he'd perfected ever since he stepped into the role of popular football star. Happy, confident Quin for the crowds, real Quin for people like Desi.

Desi put her hand on Quin's. "Hey Quin," she said in her flirtiest tone.

Quin shook his head and pulled his hand away to grab a cheeseburger. "You didn't tell Trish about your freaky bird obsession did you?"

Desi sighed and slapped her hand on the table. "Would you leave me alone about that?"

"You do know that's why you don't have friends. You can't go around telling people you wish you were a bird."

Desi picked up a fry and threw it at Quin. "I got friends."

"You mean Malcolm?"

"Yes, Malcom. He's a friend."

"He helps you with chemistry. He's more like your tutor."

"Yeah well, people suck," Desi said, then smiled at Nyah.

Quin shook his head and started to unwrap his cheeseburger. Nyah looked down at her food and only then realized she was smiling. She hadn't smiled in months. It made her feel vulnerable, but it was nice.

"People aren't so bad, Desi," Quin said, glancing around the restaurant. "In moderation."

Nyah bit into some fries and thought about this for a moment.

"Seems odd for the star quarterback to say," she said. "I thought you'd like the attention."

Quin grabbed a few fries. "Running back," he corrected. "And believe it or not, I'm more of an introvert. Most people don't know that about me."

Desi tossed a half-eaten fry at Quin. "Most people don't

know that about me," she mocked. "Quin, baby, everyone knows that about you."

"You can stop throwing food at me now, Desi" he said, then leaned in closer. "You really think everyone knows?"

"Yes. But they love you for it. You can do no wrong here, Quin."

"I bet I could do some wrong."

Desi laughed. "I've seen you try to act bad. It's cute, but no."

Still trying to figure out the introverted jock, Nyah tried shifting back to Quin.

"So you'd rather spend your time with Desi and the weird, new girl than the popular kids?" Nyah asked in between bites of her cheeseburger.

"You have friends, and you have real friends. Desi is one of the real ones." Quin said before taking another bite. "The kind your spirit just connects with the moment you meet. Know what I mean?"

Nyah had seen those types of friendships play out over and over again on TV. Friends who never needed a reason to hang out or have something important to say. Friends who were happy just being around each other. But she'd never seen a friendship like that in real life. Until now. Quin and Desi had that kind of chemistry. Watching them together was to witness something magical. No script, no rehearsals, just free-flowing improv at its best. Two spirits connecting in a way that can't be explained.

"So where you live, Trish?" Quin asked.

Normally, this was a question Nyah would avoid by asking a question of her own, but she didn't feel the need this time. Their persistence was annoying, but not the worst thing. Maybe it was the cheeseburger and fries, but she found herself letting her guard down.

"Off Parker Street in an old blue house," Nyah said just before grabbing some more fries. "It must be like a hundred years old."

Quin and Desi exchanged glances.

"What?" asked Nyah. "You know the place?"

"The huge, two-story one"

"Yeah. Why?"

"It's probably haunted or something," Desi said. "Supposedly, a kid died there not long after it was built. People say she's still there, wandering the halls and doing scary ghost shit."

"Well maybe I won't sleep so well tonight," Nyah lied. She was haunted by things much scarier than ghosts.

The owner, Lionel, appeared at their table wearing an apron and a dish towel over his shoulder.

"Quin, Desi and Trisha!" he said in his grizzly voice.

Nyah was impressed that he remembered her name. Even if it wasn't her real name. He pulled the towel from his shoulder and wiped some sweat from his brow. He was a big man with rough, dark skin and a short white beard he had a habit of scratching whenever someone was talking to him. It was obvious time, and perhaps a little too much of his own good cooking had gotten the better of him over the years, but he was still in great shape, with a chest that seemed to strain the limits of his Burger Melt t-shirt and biceps to match.

Nyah wondered if he was this friendly to whoever gave him those scars on his neck and shoulder. Or, like Danny, was there a different side of Lionel that he tried most days to keep locked away.

"Good to see you kids." He pointed to Desi and Quin and spoke to Nyah in a hushed tone. "Don't let these two get you into any trouble, Trish."

"Oh come on now, Mr. Lionel," Quin said. "We were just

about to go kick a few puppies and yell at some seniors over at the retirement home. Why you got to be ruining our fun?"

Lionel burst into laughter and clapped Quin on the shoulder. "You guys enjoy your meal and let me know if you need anything, okay?" And then he was off to the next table.

Lionel wasn't trying to break any stereotypes about men his age and dad jokes, but Nyah didn't mind. It reminded her of Danny and how he always had a dumb dad joke ready for any situation. It was like a warm blanket on a cold night.

THE TRIO SAT IN SILENCE FOR A FEW MINUTES WHILE THEY ATE, THEN Desi leaned over and nudged Nyah with her shoulder. "Admit it, you're having fun with us."

"It's not terrible," Nyah said.

"You know, we're not that different," Quin said.

"You both keep saying that." Nyah took a long sip of her sparkling water. She never got tired of how that first sip tasted.

"Okay, it's like this," Quin said. "You like old songs, right?"

"Mostly old TV shows, but yeah."

"Whatever. You know Blind Melon from the 90s?"

"Blind which?"

"Blind Melon," Quin repeated.

"You might remember the music video," Desi said. "The girl in the bumblebee costume dancing around, looking for other people to dance with?"

"Yeah. Yeah, okay. I remember," Nyah said, putting her drink down so she could finish her cheeseburger. "Bunch of skinny white boys, right?"

"I heard the bass player wrote that song before they formed the band," Quin said. "I think it's about depression and being alone in a new place. Seems kind of relatable for you."

"It's like, he wants it to rain so he can justify staying home in bed all day," Desi said.

Nyah wanted to say it did sound like her. Almost exactly. Sometimes, she wanted nothing more than to hide away in her room and never come out. Was that a bad thing? Was she depressed too? It made sense. But it didn't matter, because right now she felt like she was on the last scene of a feel-good drama. The part where all the problems of the episode are resolved and the actors are laughing and talking their troubles away at their favorite restaurant while the ending credits roll. It was nice, and the last thing she wanted to do was think about how depression could be yet another log to throw on top of a life already engulfed in flames.

"I just remember the girl dancing around in a bee costume," Nyah said.

"She reminds me of my little sister," Desi said.

Nyah took another bite, then grabbed a few more fries.

"So let me guess." Nyah pointed at Desi and Quin with her fries. "You two are the bees who found each other and now dance around all awkwardly in a field together?"

"Something like that," Quin said.

"Except you can't dance for nothing, Quin." Desi said.

"Don't need to dance when I can watch you make a fool out of yourself on the floor. That's all the entertainment one man needs."

Nyah ate quietly as Quin and Desi talked. It was oddly calming. Was this what being a normal kid was like? Maybe this could work. Maybe... As if to remind her of how different she actually was, her brain flashed with memories of Andre, her old school and the bullet that shattered through glass and all her hopes of ever being normal.

She put down her cheeseburger and tried to control her breathing, but it was too late. Her heart raced. The space around her suddenly seemed too small. She was trapped. A sitting duck. For the first time, she scanned the buildings across the street for possible sniper nests and spotted at least three, no four. God, she'd let her guard down again! She thought of getting up and running for the exit. Don't look back, just go.

A warm hand touched hers. Nyah almost grabbed it with her other hand to twist it back and away hard enough to snap bones when she realized it was Desi.

"Hey, hey, hey," she whispered, soft and calm. "It's okay."

"No, it isn't," Nyah said, then abruptly tried to get up.

Desi's hand was soft, but firm. Still, Nyah felt compelled to leave. To get up and run and never, ever look back.

"I gotta go. Sorry!"

"Trisha," Desi said just above a whisper. "Look at me."

Reluctantly, Nyah turned to look at Desi. Her blue eyes stared back, chasing away her fears.

"I'm here," she said. "You see me? Quin is here too."

Nyah glanced at Quin who was busy returning messages on his phone. He hadn't noticed. That was good.

"Let's be here together," Desi said. "Breathe for me. Slow."

Nyah wanted to say her name wasn't Trisha, it was Nyah. Nyah Carter. And for the past several years she and Danny had been on the run from a very dangerous crime family, moving from place to place to try like hell to stay one step ahead of them. But it wasn't working. Somehow, they always found her. And they would find her again. Maybe sooner rather than later. And this time, Quin and Desi might be the ones to get hurt, or even killed.

She wanted to tell Desi and Quin all of that, then get up and do what she did best. Run like hell. But she didn't. Instead, she closed her eyes and tried to breathe. It wasn't working. She tensed and looked outside for signs of a sniper.

"Slow," Desi said. "Think about that cheeseburger in front of you."

Nyah breathed in, then slowly out. Two seconds went by. Three. Nyah felt trapped in a cage with the air being sucked out. Four seconds. She felt the cool air around her, the smell of good food and Desi's hand on hers. Five seconds. Six. She opened her eyes. Desi was smiling. Quin was eating and still responding to messages on his phone. Nyah smiled.

Desi squeezed Nyah's hand and rested her head on her shoulder. "You're a bee, just like us," she whispered, then went back to her food as if nothing happened.

The panic was gone. Just like that. Gone. She breathed in, then slowly out. The restaurant was packed, but no one was looking. Small miracles, Nyah thought.

"I ALWAYS GRABBED MY QUARTER," DESI SAID AFTER A FEW SECONDS of silence.

"What?" Nyah asked. She'd finished her cheeseburger and was working on her last few remaining fries.

"When a panic attack set in," Desi said as she stabbed through the ice in her drink a few times with her straw. "At school, I'd hang it around my neck and hold it tight. Worked every time."

"But you left it in your car," Nyah said.

"One time. I was tired. Wasn't thinking. Wish I hadn't..."

"It's not your fault," Nyah said.

"Yeah, well, what can I do?"

Sensing Desi was ready to change the subject, Nyah turned her attention back to Quin.

"So what's wrong with you, Quin?"

Quin looked up.

"What?"

"Desi said you were broken like us. What's broken about that fine-ass body of yours?"

Quin laughed as he put his phone down to grab a fry from Nyah's plate. "Well if we're being honest. My dad doesn't give a shit about me."

At least you have a dad, Nyah thought.

As Quin spoke, Nyah noticed a dark expression replace his usual cheery one. He lowered his head and kept his gaze fixed on his plate as he mindlessly tapped his fork on the table.

"Doctor Darius Grady puts his work before everything," Quin said. "He's some super geneticist at the university and when he's not in his office working on grants, he's out of town working on some project he won't tell me anything about. He's never been to one of my games. Damn, I'd be surprised if he knew I even played ball."

"Hey Quin. Good game last week," a kid said as he and his friends walked by the table. In an instant, Quin's frustrated and sad expression turned into a smile. His public face was always on call.

"Yo thanks," he said, and gave the kid a fist bump.

"How much you pay for that shirt?" Nyah asked once the group was gone.

"About a..." Quin started, then realized Nyah wasn't being serious. "Oh, that's just how many touchdowns."

"How what?"

"How many points I put on the board, you know? Like if I score two, I say I paid twelve." He took a bite of burger and added. "It's just a thing we do around here."

Nyah was less impressed now that she knew the reason behind it all.

"What about your parents? What do they do?" Quin asked. He was almost as good as Nyah at diverting attention away from himself and onto someone else. She had to respect that.

This was a question she'd never been asked, but the words still came out easily. "Never knew my dad," she said. "And my mom got sick and died when I was 14. A good family friend adopted me and the rest is history." Other than a few details, this was the truth. It felt good to talk about it to someone other than Danny.

"Oh damn," said Quin.

"Sorry," said Desi.

Nyah finished off her Topo Chico and put the bottle down with a little more force than necessary.

"It's okay, really. I guess we are kind of alike. And it feels kinda good to talk to you guys about it."

Quin went back to his phone and Desi focused on her burger. Nyah wasn't used to this part of the conversation. Was she supposed to say something to keep it going? She played with her fries while she thought.

"You don't seem like a shy boy," she said, finally.

"What?"

"Big football star is too afraid to ask a boy to homecoming?"

Quin set his phone down, looked at Desi, then Nyah. "What are you-"

"Trisha!" Desi interrupted, reaching for Nyah's arm in a failed attempt to keep her quiet.

"Just ask him," Nyah said. She looked down at her fries, but felt Quin's stare burning a hole in her.

"Quin, it's all good. She didn't know," Desi said.

"The fuck it is," Quin said. He glanced around to make sure no one was within earshot, then glared at Nyah. "What the hell, Trish?"

Instead of waiting for an answer, Quin abruptly got up and

left, nearly knocking his tray to the floor as he did. A couple of people nodded and waved as he left, but Quin just brushed by and walked out of the restaurant.

Nyah stopped eating and stared at Desi. “What did I say?”

“Fuck, Trisha!” Desi said, trying her best to keep her otherwise calm voice from turning into a yell. She looked around the room, then lowered her voice to a whisper. “You nearly outed him in front of everyone!”

CHAPTER THIRTEEN

WARREN

The pounding headache returned, accompanied by a constant ringing in her ears. Rachel shook it off and leaned with her back against the wall near the entry to the kitchen and listened.

A spatula clinked on a cast-iron skillet and the aroma of sizzling beef filled the air. Someone was cooking hamburgers. She closed her eyes and breathed it in. She couldn't remember the last time she'd eaten.

She reached down to pull her knife, but her fingers touched an empty sheath. A quick scan of the living room and she spotted it, resting on an end table by the couch where she'd been lying. Its golden etchings glinted softly in the lamp light. Whoever brought her here was either careless, or posed no threat. Likely it was the latter, otherwise she'd be dead or tied up somewhere. Still, she had to be careful.

Feeling the strength returning to her legs, Rachel hurried to the end table, picked up her knife and walked back to the open entry way of the kitchen. A man stood with his back to her in front of the stove. He was taller than Rachel, maybe a little over six feet, wearing green scrubs with short sleeves. Whoever he was, he didn't seem the least bit concerned about the unconscious woman on his couch.

She checked the blind spots in the kitchen to make sure he was alone, then made her move. In three quick steps, she was close enough to reach around his neck and press the razor-sharp edge of her blade to his throat.

"Shit!" The man dropped the spatula onto the counter and raised his hands. Rachel noticed a tattoo of a tree on his right arm with long branches covered in bright green leaves that stood out on his chestnut skin.

Rachel leaned in close to his ear.

"Who else is here?" she whispered.

"No one. I swear. It's just me and you."

Rachel considered this, then moved the knife away and stepped back.

"Sit down," she said.

"Okay, sure," the man said without turning around or lowering his hands. "But can I take these burgers off first? I can't just let them burn."

"Do it quick," she said.

In one swift motion, he picked up the spatula, skillfully pulled the patties from the pan and placed them on a plate. They were perfectly browned with a little black searing on the edges. The cheese was melted and dripping from the sides and she could tell he'd sprinkled them with a dash of salt and pepper while they were still in the pan. God, she was hungry.

He put the spatula down, turned the burner off and raised his hands once more.

"Can I turn around?"

Rachel put her hand up to cover the exposed part of her face, then realized he must have already seen her. The pounding in her head returned. She cursed herself for letting this happen.

"That's fine," she said. "Just sit down."

He turned around, giving Rachel her first good look at his face. He had a short, Caesar Cut hair style and a studded earring in one ear. He had no facial hair, which made him look younger than he probably was. Judging from the scrubs, Rachel figured he had to keep a clean-shaven look for work. One look at him made Rachel forget how hungry she was. Strong jawline, smooth skin. And was that a sparkle in his ey-

"Okay, I'm just going to sit down," he said.

When she realized she'd been staring a little too long, she quickly turned away and motioned to the table with her blade.

"Sit there," she said.

He sat down at the table, only lowering his hands once to pull out a chair. It was one of those vintage tables with a grey formica top, wide, chrome edging and four, 1950s-style red chairs.

"Okay, I'm sitting down," he said. "Are you okay? You were pretty banged up."

Ignoring him, Rachel walked to the window and pulled open a curtain to get a look outside. From what she could tell, they were on the top floor of an apartment building. A few cars were parked on the street below and people walked along the sidewalk. She let the curtain fall closed and turned back to the man. He hadn't moved and still had his hands raised. She slid her knife back into its sheath.

"You can put your hands down," she said, pressing her fingers to her temples to try and ease the throbbing. "Who are you and how did I end up on your couch?"

He lowered his hands and rested them awkwardly on the table.

"I'm Warren. And I drove you here in my car. That blast knocked you out cold."

A wave of nausea swept through Rachel's body. She walked over to a chair opposite Warren and sat down at the table. He made a move to get up and help, but quickly changed his mind when Rachel looked up and glared at him.

Broken pieces of memories flashed through her mind, threatening to send her into madness if she couldn't fit them all together. So much of what led up to this moment seemed to be gone.

"I'm a nurse," Warren said. "You have a concussion and you need to rest. Let me get you some water."

"First tell me about the explosion."

"No ma'am." Warren said with a new confidence in his voice.

Rachel looked up. "What?"

"I'm a caregiver first, and you need some care. Let's start with that."

He reached across the table and put a hand on Rachel's arm. She pulled back, but only slightly.

"Look, I can tell you're in a lot of pain right now. I'm going to get up and get you a cold glass of water and some ibuprofen. Now if you want to use that scary dagger and cut me for that, so be it."

Instead of a response, Rachel put her elbows on the table and buried her face in her hands. Reading that as consent, Warren got up and walked to the cabinet where he kept a bottle of ibuprofen, grabbed a glass from another cabinet and filled it with filtered water from the fridge, then cautiously sat both down in front of Rachel and returned to his seat.

"How did I get here?" she asked after Warren sat back down, squeaking his chair on the tiled floor as he moved himself closer to the table.

"Please take a drink. And take two of those pills. From the looks of it, you need it."

Rachel grabbed two pills from the bottle, popped them in her mouth and chased them down with a drink of water. Then took another long drink after she realized how thirsty she was. When she was done, she slammed the glass back down on the table hard enough to shake it and cause Warren to flinch.

"One more time. How did I get here?"

"Your car blew up."

"My car?"

"Fuck yeah. Maybe your car. I don't know. I was on my way home from my shift when I saw you climbing into the back seat like you were looking for something. Then I saw the explosion in my rearview mirror and turned around to see what happened and if anyone was hurt. I saw you laying in some bushes a few feet away. You must have jumped out right before it happened."

Rachel closed her eyes, trying desperately to remember the car and the explosion. At last, the memories came rushing back. They'd found where they were taking Felix the Fixer, the creep who liked to hurt kids. She got there first, ambushed Montello's men, then went for Felix. A clicking sound, then everything went blank.

"You alright?" Warren asked.

"Yes. Keep going."

Warren only nodded towards the glass of water. Frustrated, Rachel grabbed the glass and took another sip.

"Keep going."

"That's pretty much it," he said. "The car blew up and I ran to help. You were out cold. I put you in the back seat of my car and drove you here. You were awake when we got here. At least enough to stagger up to my apartment. You were mumbling something, but I couldn't make it out. I put my jacket around you. I was gonna tell people you'd drank too much, but I lucked out and didn't see anyone in the halls or the elevator. I laid you on the couch, covered you up and came in here to cook you some food. I figured you'd be hungry when you woke up."

"Why didn't you take me to the hospital? You're a nurse, right?"

Warren leaned back in his chair and pounded lightly on the table with his fist as he considered his words. Rachel thought he was about to say something he hadn't planned on confessing.

"Let's just say in my past life I didn't always play so nice with everyone. But I cleaned up and turned my life around." Warren said, then nodded towards Rachel's torn suit. "I don't know what you're into, dressed up like that, but I know when someone's in trouble and doesn't want to be found. So I went with my gut. Took a chance and brought you here."

If what he was saying was true, he'd saved Rachel from a world of trouble. There would have been questions. Questions that could have poked and prodded their way into the secrets of the Agojie legacy. This man had earned her gratitude.

"Thanks," she said. "I appreciate that."

The nausea was getting better, but her head was still pounding.

"Do you want to take that mask off?"

"No."

"You sure? It's all tor-"

Warren's eyes opened wide as if he'd realized something. He leaned in to get a better look at Rachel's suit.

"Oh sweet damn. That suit!" he said, then paused to think it over. "Yeah. I know you. You're the Agojie. You have to be! Oh my God, you 're a legend!"

CHAPTER

FOURTEEN

ESI, NAWI AND THE RIDE TO ABOMEY

TWO MILES WEST OF CANA, DAHOMEY KINGDOM, AFRICA

Nawi sat, slumped by a tree with an empty flask at her side when the two mounted French soldiers on patrol rode by.

"You! Get up!" One of them shouted in broken Fon language.

Nawi picked up the flask and held it up to the soldiers.

"You bring more whisky?" she said, then burst into laughter.

One of the soldiers pulled his rifle from a saddle holster and took aim at Nawi.

"She's drunk. Just like the others," he spoke in French to his comrade.

Nawi held up a hand. "Do not shoot. I think I have something you might want." She clumsily got to her feet and pulled the hem of her battle skirt up a few inches. "Maybe there is a way we can help each other, no?"

The soldier pulled the hammer back on his rifle and aimed for her head.

"Nonsense!" he said. "We don't make deals with Amazons."

"Wait," his comrade said, putting a hand on his shoulder. He dismounted his horse and walked over to Nawi, taking in her strong and slender body with his eyes. "Maybe there is a way," he said in Fon.

Nawi stumbled forward a little, then put a hand to her forehead in a mock salute. "Oui Monsieur," she said, then tripped and fell into his arms.

The soldier tried to push her off, but Nawi leaned in and fell limp.

"You stink of whisky!" He said, still trying to get her back on her feet.

Nawi grabbed the lapels of his coat and pulled him close enough to whisper in his ear. "And you stink of treachery."

She pulled the knife she'd hidden behind her back and stabbed him three quick times in his side.

"And now you stink of death," she said, then pushed him away. He stumbled a few steps before collapsing onto the dusty road.

Before the second soldier's finger even touched the trigger of his rifle, Esi sprang from behind the bushes, launched herself into the air and tackled him. They both came crashing down with Esi landing on top, knocking the wind from the soldier's lungs and the rifle from his hands. Esi stood and pulled her dagger to finish the job.

"Esi, wait," Nawi said. "Let this beast live."

Esi dropped to her knees and pressed the edge of her blade against the soldier's neck.

"Let him live? He and his people have slaughtered thousands of our brothers and sisters. Their spirits demand his blood."

Nawi walked to Esi and put a hand on her shoulder.

"We will never stop fighting. So long as the French dare to set foot on our land, we will cut them down. But is there no room for mercy?"

Esi looked up at her friend.

"This does not sound like you, Nawi."

"I've had time to think. Blood has marred the beauty of our land for too long, Esi. Perhaps it is time to show there is more to Dahomey than this."

Out of respect for her commander, Nawi stopped talking and backed a few steps away to let Esi consider. As Esi's most trusted advisor, she had done her job. Now it was up to Esi to decide.

The soldier's eyes were red with anger, embarrassment and perhaps a little sadness. Esi thought for a long moment. Just when Nawi thought she might slice his neck, she stood and slid her knife back into its sheath.

"Get me some rope," she said to Nawi.

THE SOLDIER SAID NOTHING AS THEY TIED HIM TO A TREE, ONLY grunting when Nawi gave the ropes one last, hard pull. Then both women stood and looked down at him.

"You are Esi?" the soldier asked. "There are so many stories, yet few have actually seen you. There is a very big price on your head."

Esi ignored this and knelt down to look him in the eyes.

"You'll never outlive the ridicule you'll receive when your comrades find you like this," she said. "But you will outlive today. You can thank my friend for that."

THE HORSES WERE NERVOUS FROM THE COMMOTION, BUT THEY WERE accustomed to life on the battlefield and remained where the soldiers had left them.

"Esi, let that horse go free. Someone will find him." Nawi said, pointing to the smaller of the two. "The other is bigger and stronger. We'll have to give him rest along the way, but I think he can carry us both to Abomey."

Still unsure of Nawi's ability, Esi once again questioned her plan. "Can you even ride a horse?" she asked.

Nawi mounted the horse and reached down to help Esi climb onto the back. "Yes, I told you. I took a lesson."

Esi grabbed her hand but stopped short of getting on. "A lesson? You said you were trained."

"A lesson, lessons. It makes no difference. We could run to Abomey, but there is no time for that."

Cautiously, Esi climbed onto the big animal. "We have fought many battles side by side," she said, wrapping her arms around Nawi's waist. "But I do not want to die like this."

Nawi only laughed, and with the confidence of an expert, kicked the horse with the heels of her feet and yelled, "For Abomey!"

The horse, apparently not sharing in Nawi's enthusiasm, remained where it was, eating at a patch of grass just off the trail.

"One lesson?" Esi said mockingly.

"It was a short one. Help me!"

Esi took her right hand from Nawi's waist and slapped the horse on its backside with all the force she could muster as Nawi kicked with her heels and yelled "Go now!"

At once, the horse reared, then launched into a canter, then a gallop. Nawi used the reins and stirrups to guide the horse back onto the trail as best she could. Towards Abomey and their king.

CHAPTER

FIFTEEN

STAY FOR DINNER

The Agojie's kept a low profile, but rumors and stories were impossible to keep hidden for long. It was possible Warren had heard a few of them. The Agojie was a timeless legend. A hero for some, the devil in the flesh for others. But she was also a shadow, and even those who knew of the Agojie would likely go their whole lives without ever even getting a glimpse of her.

"You helped my cousin and her family a few years back when the company she worked for decided they'd rather see her dead than take a chance on her exposing their secrets," Warren said.

Rachel remembered his cousin well. She'd lost all hope and became suicidal. She was on a bridge, about to jump when Rachel stumbled across her. Rachel was also at a low point in life, burdened with bad choices and missed opportunities. So the women bonded over their sorrows. In the end, Rachel offered the Agojie's help.

"How is Janet?" Rachel asked.

Warren shook his head and stared at Rachel in amazement.

"We owe you so much. You have no idea."

Rachel closed her eyes, more annoyed with the pain in her head now than troubled by it.

Warren held up his hands in surrender. "Forget all that. I'm sorry. Just a little starstruck is all. You need to take care of that concussion."

In truth, Rachel would rather listen to Warren talk than think about everything that just happened to her. Had she been targeted? If so, why? And who was responsible? She needed to get out, get better and regroup if they were going to figure this all out.

"Damn, that reminds me," Warren said. Without asking, he got up from the table and left the room. He was treating her more like a house guest than some strange woman who'd just held a knife to his throat. Rachel waited a few seconds before growing concerned. She was about to get up and go look for him when he popped back into the kitchen with a hoodie in his hands. He tossed it on the table in front of her.

"Put that on if you want. It's all I have, but it will keep you warm."

Rachel pushed the hoodie aside. "Where's my phone? I need it now."

"Right! Yeah, sorry." He walked to the counter and unplugged a phone from a charger. "It was a little scratched up and the battery was dead, so I put it on the charger. Should be good to go now."

He held it out and Rachel swiped it from his hand. She pressed the home button and the screen lit up with several missed calls and unread text messages from her partner, Byron.

"What's your address? I need to let someone know where I am."

"1302 Mentone Avenue."

As she entered her passcode and started to type out a message, she could see Warren shifting uncomfortably in his chair from the corner of her eye.

"Something on your mind?" she asked without looking up from her phone.

"Yeah. I mean no. It's good."

It clearly wasn't good. Now he was tapping on the table with one hand like a damn drummer. Rachel stopped and looked up.

"Seriously, what?"

"Okay, look," Warren said, straightening up in his chair. "I know you gotta go and all. Maybe get your head checked out some more. But can I at least make you a cheeseburger before you go? I make a damn good burger. And there ain't nothing much a good cheeseburger can't fix."

Rachel's thumbs hovered over the keypad. She'd already typed "I'm fine," along with cross streets to Warren's address. If she sent it now, Byron would be here in minutes, likely breaking several traffic laws along the way. She considered this for a moment, then remembered her growling stomach and those perfectly-seasoned burgers, the smell still lingering in the air.

She deleted the text and typed "Safe. Call soon," along with "20," a code Byron would know to mean she wasn't sending the message under duress. She sent the message and set her phone on the table.

"You have any onions?" she asked.

Warren's eyes lit up and he smiled.

"Fresh from the farmers market. Maybe you can slice one up with that knife of yours."

~

An hour later, Rachel walked onto the street from Warren's apartment, scanning the surroundings for anything out of place. It was a narrow street, lined with trendy restaurants, bars and parking lots for tourists. Down the road, a small jazz band played, filling the air with the classic sounds of New Orleans street music. She walked about a half block to a blue Lexus parked at the corner and hopped in the passenger seat.

"Nice hoodie," Byron said as she closed the door.

Rachel forgot she'd put on the hoodie halfway through dinner with Warren. Caught off guard, she stumbled to come up with an explanation.

"Found it," she said. "Suit got ripped up good."

No matter the situation, Byron's comforting smile was a permanent part of his persona. A mask to hide his true feelings and fears from the world. He was a big man. Rachel thought he looked like a younger and more muscular version of Sinbad. But his size was more intimidating than his teddy-bear personality. So he learned to hide it. An art he'd mastered in the military to prepare for everything from torture to interrogations. Whether he was the one asking the questions or the other way around. And as far as Rachel knew, she was the only one who could break through that facade and throw him off his game. From the corner of her eye, she saw his smile falter for the briefest of moments when she told him about the hoodie. Byron knew the story was bullshit, but he also knew Rachel would tell him the truth eventually. And he was right. He wasn't just her right-hand-man, he was like a brother to her. So instead of making a big deal of it, Byron put the car into drive, checked for traffic and pulled out into the street.

"I drove by the house. Cops everywhere," he said as they drove away. "Felix was killed in that explosion."

"What the hell happened?" Rachel asked.

"You were ambushed. How'd you get out? When I lost

comms with you, I thought maybe..." He couldn't finish the sentence.

Rachel put a hand on his shoulder and smiled at the big man.

"I'm fine. Really. A little scratched up, but fine."

Byron moved his hand from the steering wheel and placed it on top of hers.

"Good. Don't scare me like that again, okay?"

"No promises," she said, then straightened up in her seat. "But who ambushed us?"

She asked the question even as the answers were forming in her head. Byron filled in the blanks.

"You're not a ghost anymore. They know who you are. They know *where* you are."

"The Montello Family." Rachel said.

Byron nodded. "That whole thing with Felix was just a setup to get to you. A big trap."

"Fuck!" Rachel leaned her head back on the headrest and closed her eyes. "They didn't care one bit about keeping him safe from the Feds."

"We'll lay low for a while until we figure this out." Byron said, then sniffed the air and gave Rachel a judgy look. "Why do you smell like burgers?"

Rachel brought her sleeve to her nose and breathed in. Sure enough, the lingering smell of beef, cheese and onions remained. She wasn't sure what to say, but she knew she couldn't lie. Not to Byron.

"Some guy took me in," she said after a pause. "Pulled me from the bushes and carried me to his house. I was out cold."

Byron pulled the car to the side of the road, put it in park and turned to face Rachel.

"Someone *saw* you like this?"

"I'd probably be handcuffed to a hospital bed right now if he hadn't."

Byron sighed, turned away and rested his hands on the steering wheel.

"Okay. Who is he? And did he make you dinner?"

"He's a nurse, and I was starving. So yeah."

Byron was a laid-back kind of guy who always rolled with the punches, even if he was the one getting punched. But Rachel had known him long enough to tell the difference between big, lovable Byron and Hulk crush, Byron. The latter was reserved for those times when he sensed someone he cared about was in danger. And right now, he had that killer look in his eyes.

They sat there in silence for another few seconds. Rachel thought it best to keep quiet. At least for now. Eventually, Byron let out a long, deep breath, put the car into drive and slowly pulled back onto the street.

"Did you tell him anything?"

Rachel shot him an annoyed look.

"Sorry," he said. "What's his name?"

"Warren," Rachel said, just a little too quickly. "I mean, I think."

Byron turned right onto St. Louis and headed northeast towards Interstate 10. Rachel knew where they were going next.

"Safe point A?" she asked.

"Safe point A," Byron said. Meaning one of several safe houses the pair had accumulated over the years. It helped that Byron worked in real estate as a cover. "We'll figure this all out when we get there."

"How the hell did they find us? How did they find me?" Rachel asked, more to herself than anything.

"Don't know. But Bruno hasn't forgotten about Alaska. And

as long as we're alive, we can talk. And Bruno hates loose ends."

They drove for a few blocks, then Byron started tapping on the steering wheel with his fingers. Rachel knew he only did that when he was thinking about a problem. After a few seconds, he asked, "You hid that formula good, right?"

Rachel tugged the collar of Warren's hoodie tighter around her neck, leaned her head back and thought back to that mission in Alaska all those years ago. It didn't go quite as planned, but she got the job done.

"Yeah," she said. "No one will ever find it."

"Good," Byron said. "We can't let it fall into Bruno's hands again."

They drove for a few minutes in silence. Byron stopped tapping, but Rachel knew something was off. She reached over and grabbed his arm.

"What's wrong?" she asked.

Byron was silent for a moment longer. Almost as if he didn't want to put words to the question running through his mind.

Then, finally, "Is this going to be a problem?"

"Is what going to be a problem?"

"This Warren guy."

"No. Why would you ask that?"

"I just need to know about any changes. You know?"

"Yeah. I know." She moved her hand to his shoulder and squeezed. "Don't worry, big guy. I got this."

She pulled her hand away and turned to look out the window. She closed her eyes and secretly took another long, quiet sniff of Warren's hoodie. This time, other than burgers, cheese and onions, she caught the faint trace of cologne. She knew right then this was definitely going to be a problem. And she liked it.

CHAPTER SIXTEEN
ATTACK THE KING

ABOMEY, KINGDOM OF DAHOMEY, AFRICA - NOVEMBER, 1892

Draped in his ceremonial robe and flanked by the Fanti, his elite female bodyguards, King Behanzin stood with his staff and his pipe, center stage on the rally mound. He took a long puff from his pipe and slowly exhaled as he surveyed what remained of his kingdom.

He waited patiently as the crowd noise died and silence filled the air. Even then, he did not speak for several long moments. A technique his father used to build the tension and anticipation.

"My people. I see you," he said at last. "I see the tears that flow, the hands that shake, the long embraces as if to say goodbye."

The French invasion was imminent, and the people of Abomey needed words from their king. The crowd encircled the rally mound, pushing past the merchant stands and gates. Some smoked pipes, while others stood holding babies on their hips or wrapped in cloth close to their chests. There'd been rumors of abandoning Abomey. Torching the city and destroying everything in it before the French could march and take it for themselves. Most villagers knew the power of the French and any chance of defeating them had mostly faded away.

Behanzin paused to take another puff from his pipe, considered his words, then spoke.

"The French are knocking on Abomey's door," he said. "But there is still today. Today, there is no goodbye. Today, we are free. And though our beloved city may fall, we will leave them nothing to steal."

A lone cheer from the crowd, followed by others until the entire mass of people were shouting and yelling for victory. Behanzin raised his staff to quiet them.

"They have pushed us out of our homes. Soon, they will be standing on this very soil. I say we welcome them with fire!"

Once again, the crowd erupted into cheers.

NAWI AND ESI STOOD IN THE BACK OF THE CROWD, ONE ON EACH SIDE, cloaked in kangas that covered their heads and arms. Both had taken up high positions, Esi on a stack of wood and Nawi on a crate. They shared a quick look of disbelief as the king spoke of burning their beloved city to the ground. Had they fought for so long only to flee? There was no time to worry. They had a mission.

They scanned the crowd, glancing at each other for occasional updates. So far, nothing. Even with all the stops to let the horse rest, they'd made good time. But now they both wondered if it was enough. Jabari was a master of stealth and disguise. He could be anywhere in this crowd.

Esi motioned for Nawi to go warn the king. She spotted the

closest Fanti, jumped down from her perch and began pushing her way through the crowd, but it was slow going. The people packed in tight so they could be close enough to hear the king's words. It would take Nawi time to work her way through. In the meantime, Esi kept scanning the crowd for any traces of the king's would-be assassin.

King Behanzin raised his staff and pointed to the city. "These buildings are just buildings." Then he lowered his staff until the tip was touching his chest. "But Abomey is in our hearts! And so long as we live, so too does Abomey!"

This was the king they'd come to see. Strong and true, brave and strong. A king who would not abandon them even in their darkest moment. The king they knew. The king they loved.

The mood of the people changed. Some began to shout and clap, while others danced in circles, kicking up dirt and singing victory songs.

"I tell you, my people," he shouted. "We will come back stronger than before. Free from fear, free from tyranny, free to live our lives as we wish!" He slammed the end of his staff hard onto the floor. "Free!"

The king had a gift for words. Something Esi always admired. But both Esi and Nawi knew if the king should die here today, on this stage in front of everyone, all the hope he inspired would be lost. And Abomey, along with the entire Kingdom of Dahomey, would fall.

Esi spotted someone in the crowd and pulled the hood of her kanga down to get a better look. He was practically unnoticeable except for his cloak. It was a design she wasn't familiar with. When not at war, she and her sisters took up trades. Esi was a seamstress. She'd designed and sewn many cloaks for men and studied other designs popular in the kingdom. She knew every one of them by heart, and yet she couldn't place this one. There was something else too. Something in the way he walked through the crowd. Deliberate, and slow. Even when the people in front of him didn't move, or someone shouted at him for getting in the way, he never pushed back or raised his voice. It was Jabari. It could be no other.

Nawi was making slow progress, and Esi knew she'd never make it to the king in time. Jabari, on the other hand, was already moving forward with deadly precision. Suddenly, as if he could feel the weight of Esi's stare, Jabari turned and scanned the crowd until he spotted Esi. Her heart sank as he pulled his hood back to reveal his face. The same face she'd come to love all those years ago. He slowly shook his head, as if to warn Esi to stay away, then pulled the hood back on and continued his way to the king.

The element of surprise was gone. Jabari knew they were here and would only work faster to eliminate the king before he could be stopped. Esi pulled off her kanga and let it fall to the ground. No more need for secrecy. In her battle dress, she hoped people would be more likely to move aside as she made her way through the massive crowd towards Jabari. It was the best she could hope for.

JABARI ALTERED HIS COURSE AND HEADED TOWARDS A GROUP OF merchant stands to the right. Esi knew his plan. He would get within shooting range and kill the king with a rifle shot. A French-made rifle, no doubt. Jabari was an excellent shot with any rifle, but a rifle like that in Jabari's hands would make him deadly accurate.

Esi jumped to the ground and landed in an all-out run, leaping over a small fence and dodging people and obstacles in her way, sometimes shouting to get people to move. She turned a corner to a row of merchant stands and kicked up dirt as she forced her body to run faster than it ever had before. The stands were mostly empty, their owners no doubt among the crowd of people listening to the king. She remembered, too late, to check for signs of Jabari.

She saw motion from the corner of her eye and turned just in time to see a figure lunge at her from one of the stands. Jabari slammed into her side and knocked her to the ground. Esi grunted, rolled once then pulled her knife from its sheath and sprang into a crouch, poised to counter attack. But Jabari made no move to fight. He pulled down his hood and looked at Esi.

"Why did you come, Esi? I do not want to kill you."

His face looked different than she remembered. Worn from sadness, anger and years on the run. New scars lined his head and neck.

Esi stood up and slid the knife behind her back.

"What would Adisa say to you now, Jabari? Would she want you here, doing this terrible thing?"

Jabari's face contorted with pain and sorrow at the sound of her name.

"You know nothing, Esi! I loved her!" He pointed to the king. "And he took her away! So today, he dies. Today I avenge my love!"

Using his momentary distraction, Esi pulled the knife from behind her back and flung it at Jabari. Jabari twisted his torso sideways a split second before the knife would have buried itself into his chest. Instead, it whizzed by and sank deep into the wall of the wooden stand behind him with a thud. Before Jabari could recover, Esi charged and rammed her body into his. As they fell to the ground, Esi bent her knee and used the force of impact to drive it hard into Jabari's gut. She followed with several lightning-quick punches to his face.

After the third or fourth punch, Jabari grabbed a fistful of dirt and flung it into Esi's face. Esi tried to ignore the sudden pain and blindness, but it slowed her enough for Jabari to counter attack. He punched Esi in the throat, then clapped his hands hard together over her ears, stunning her long enough to push her off and onto the ground. He stood over her, wiped some blood from his nose and spit.

"You are not my enemy, Esi!"

Esi coughed and looked up, still squinting from the blinding dirt in her eyes. "An enemy of the king is my enemy," she said, then rolled to her side and kicked Jabari in the knee.

He stumbled back from the pain and Esi was up and charging before he could regain balance. This time, she slammed him back against the merchant stand and unleashed a new series of punches to his head and stomach. Jabari took several blows before he regained his balance, ducked a punch and came up hard with his elbow to Esi's chin. She rocked back and Jabari rammed a knee into her stomach. He grabbed her around the waist intent on throwing her, head-first into the merchant stand, but the moment he lifted her feet from the ground, she rammed her forehead into his nose. He dropped Esi and she grabbed her knife from the stand and rammed the butt end into Jabari's head once, then whipped around in a full circle and hit him a second time, cracking his jaw and jerking his head to the side. Jabari stumbled back and fell to the ground, tried to get up, then fell down again.

~

Esi walked to the side of the stand and picked up Jabari's rifle. "We will let the king deal with you, traitor."

Something on the rifle pricked her hand. She brought it up and saw a trickle of blood. Inspecting the rifle, she noticed a tiny pin sticking from the forestock. It looked like something Jabari added to the rifle himself, though she didn't know why. It seemed to serve no purpose other than giving someone an annoying sting.

She set the rifle down and pulled a length of rope she'd tucked inside the pocket of her skirt to tie Jabari's hands together, then dropped it when she realized it was no rope, it was a snake. She pulled her knife, but the snake was now just a piece of rope again. Esi rubbed her eyes and knelt to pick it up. Once again the rope turned into a snake, and this time struck out fast at Esi's hand. She pulled it back an instant before it would have sunk its fangs into her flesh, then brought her knife down hard with her other hand, stabbed through its head and pinned it to the ground. She blinked again and saw she'd just impaled the rope.

"What is this nonsense!" Esi picked up the rope and walked to Jabari, who was still lying face down on the dirt. She knelt down and grabbed his hands to tie them up when the ground beneath her suddenly shook. Esi lost balance and fell on her butt. It moved again. She looked down and noticed she was sitting in water.

"Jabari, what is this..." When she looked back at Jabari, he was standing over her. Next to him was another man. Another Jabari? No, it couldn't be! But there they were standing side by side. She covered her eyes to shield them from the sun. Jabari and his double walked closer. Her knife was on the ground next to her. She must have dropped it. She reached to pick it up, but it turned into a weed. She tried pulling it from the ground, but couldn't. It wriggled in her hand, then quickly wrapped tightly around her wrist and pulled it to the ground. She tried, but could not break free.

Jabari knelt down beside her. It was just him now. His double had vanished. "Did you think I would face the Agojie without a plan, Esi? You see the elephant outside your door and miss the mouse sneaking into your home."

He stood up and grabbed his rifle, removing the pin from the forestock and wiped it clean with his shirt.

"An Ibogaine paste I made. It has healing powers, but the visions... the hallucinations come first. Your mind will clear soon and you will be fine, old friend." He covered his head with his cloak and tucked the rifle inside. "But the king dies today."

Esi tried to get up, but couldn't. The weed wrapped around her wrist grew tighter every time she moved. She watched as Jabari disappeared into the crowd once again.

CHAPTER SEVENTEEN

SONGS OF OLD

Nawi's plan to force her way through the crowd and alert the Fanti of Jabari's presence wasn't working. The crowd surrounding the rally mound was packed too tightly. Jabari could be near the king by now and ready to strike. She had to come up with a different plan, and fast.

She remembered the drums she'd seen stacked under a tree near the entrance and had a thought. She turned and pushed her way back through the crowd until she broke free at the back, then ran to the drums and picked up the biggest one.

She flung the strap over her shoulder and prepared to play. If she couldn't reach Jabari in person before he got to the king, maybe, just maybe, she could reach him through song.

She banged the drum once with her hand. A low, loud and resonant tone echoed from the bottom, but was drowned out by the shouts and yells from the crowd.

She hit it twice more. "Boom, boom!" Then waited for the bass tones to fade and repeated. "Boom, boom!"

Once the second set of tones faded, she began pounding out a familiar Dahomey rhythm, her skilled hands moving from the deep, lower-toned part of the drum skin to the higher-tone, outer edge. And then, she sang

"IF ONE DAY WE MEET
AN ARMY OF MIGHT
WE'LL FEAR NOTHING"

A battle cry of old. A love song for their kingdom. The crowd recognized it immediately.

"We are invincible
We are strong.
We are Dahomey!"

A song of childhood, sang to them by parents who learned it from their parents. A song with the power to unite generations. A song with a special meaning for Jabari.

The crowd began to join in. One, then two, then six or seven. Soon, dozens were singing, dancing and even shouting.

"We fight for our land
We die for our sisters
Our brothers."

Soon, even the king took notice and paused his speech.

"Send us your soldiers
We will fight them back
And they will run like cowards."

The king raised his staff. "Sing!" He shouted. Everyone sing!"

“We sharpen our knives in victory
Our minds in defeat
Together we face lions
Together we are strong”

It was working. Nawi hoped it would be enough. If Jabari was listening, if he remembered the song, it just might be. She closed her eyes, hoped for a miracle and sang.

CHAPTER EIGHTEEN

JABARI

Jabari was surprised when he spotted Esi and Nawi in Abomey. He was told her regiment would be fighting in the trenches and would likely die there. Someone, a spy perhaps, must have told the women of their plans to kill the king. No matter. There wasn't time to think of Esi now. The Ibogaine would soon wear off and she would be fine. By then, it would be too late to save her king. She was foolish to think speaking of Adisa would change his course. It was too late to change anything. He longed to be with his sweet Adisa again. Longed to avenge her death and kill this wretched king where he stood.

He pushed through the crowd to another empty merchant stand. The people around him were so busy listening to the king they didn't notice when he slipped around to the side, out of sight and within firing range of the king.

Behanzin was always good at enchanting a crowd. Jabari wondered how they would react when his magical words were cut short by a bullet. After a quick scan to make sure no one could see him, he pulled his rifle from his cloak, sat down and rested the barrel of the rifle on a crate. It was a clear shot, and he had no doubt his aim would be true. He took a deep breath, carefully moved his finger to the trigger, lined up his target and slowly exhaled.

A drum beat rumbled through the crowd, momentarily breaking his concentration. Too quiet for anyone near him to notice at first, but the drumming grew louder and more rhythmic and one by one, heads turned towards the noise. Jabari froze when he recognized the song. A familiar sound to the people of this city. A battle cry for most. A love song filled with sweet memories for him.

CHAPTER NINETEEN
ROOFTOP ROMANCE

Warren was lounging in a patio chair on the roof of his apartment building with just enough of a cool breeze and beer to push aside the troubles of his day. He'd just finished two non-stop shifts at the hospital taking care of patients, and now it was time to take care of himself.

"Got a beer for me?"

Rachel's sudden appearance startled him back to reality, spilling a little beer on his shorts in the process. But any thoughts of being upset vanished when he saw the woman standing in front of him. The Agojie was a highly-trained weapon with near super-human abilities, but she was also sexy as hell. And Warren couldn't take his eyes off her.

"You look like you just walked out of my dreams," he said.

Rachel pulled off her mask, tossed it on the table and sat down on Warren's lap. After a long kiss on the lips, she put her arms around his neck and rested her head on his shoulder.

"Rough day at the office?" Warren asked.

"Very." She breathed him in, intoxicated by the smell of his cheap cologne.

Warren grabbed a blanket from the chair next to them and wrapped it around Rachel.

"I brought this out in case you showed up in your suit again. What would my neighbors say if they saw me making out with the Agojie?"

"Can't have people talking," Rachel said, then pulled the blanket tight around her shoulders and snuggled closer to Warren. "Can I stay here forever?"

"Might have to do a beer run every now and then, but yeah. I'd like that."

They'd been together for a few months now, but Warren still got a kick out of knowing he was her man. And he still loved being this close to her. Close enough to feel her breath on his neck and her soft hair on his shoulder. For a time, no more words were needed. They sat together in silence, listening to the car engines and honking horns on the street below. There was no reason to move. No reason to talk. No reason to disturb their perfect moment.

"What do you call this place?" Rachel asked.

Warren closed his eyes and thought for a moment. "My escape," he said.

"I like it."

"Me too. Especially right now."

"Gotta admit. It would be better if I had a beer in my hand." Rachel gave Warren another kiss, then slid off his lap, wrapped herself in the blanket and sat down on the chair next to his.

"I get the feeling you're using me for my beer." Warren said as he grabbed a beer from the ice chest, uncapped it with the bottle opener on his keychain and handed it to her.

Rachel smiled. "Your words, not mine."

"I still don't know why you can't just use the elevator."

Warren took another long sip of beer, then motioned to the fire escape on the side of the building. "You shouldn't be climbing that thing. Ain't been up to code since the 80's."

"It's a little rusty, but it works fine." Rachel waved a hand down her suit. "And this has a way of attracting attention in elevators."

"You should be more worried about attracting the attention of people who want to blow you up."

"Apparently so." Rachel held out her beer for Warren to toast. "Here's to another day above ground. Right?"

Instead of returning the toast, Warren gave Rachel a look that said he wasn't about to drop the subject.

Rachel's smile faded and she started peeling the label off her beer. An old, nervous habit.

"Okay, I get it," she said. "But don't forget how it attracted the attention of a certain hot nurse."

"It was a damn good silver lining," Warren said, giving in to the moment. "You reeled me in like a fish."

He reached his bottle across to return the toast. Rachel tapped her bottle to his.

"Best catch of my life," she said.

Day was fading to dusk, the air was growing cooler and the city lights were beginning their nighttime glow.

"So you still have no idea who tried to kill you?"

Rachel pulled her knees up and rested her feet on the ice chest, then leaned back and breathed in the night air.

"Do we have to talk about this now?"

"Yeah, we kinda do."

"It kills the mood, don't you think?"

Warren leaned forward and set his beer on top of the ice chest. "I don't get it. How could you just go on like it was no big deal?"

"It's my job. And right now, I'm off the clock. You know, work-life balance and all."

Warren shook his head and sighed.

"Look," Rachel said, after another long sip of beer. "It's a crime family. The Montellos."

Warren sat up straight in his chair and turned to face Rachel. "The Montellos? What the hell, Rachel?" He stood and paced around, trying to let this new information sink in. "You've known this for a while, haven't you?"

"Does it matter?"

"I guess it kinda does, yeah." Warren shook his head. "I can't believe this. Do you know why? I mean, why do they want you dead so bad?" He shifted his stance and the old roof creaked a little under his feet.

"We had a little run in with them a few years back in Alaska. Apparently they're still not over it."

Warren lowered his head and stared at the ground.

"Apparently not. And it seems like you should be taking this a little more seriously."

"Seems like you should be getting me another beer," Rachel said as she finished off the first.

"Come on, Rachel. This is for real." Warren walked over and rested his arms on the iron railing along the edge of the roof to look out over the city and gather his thoughts. The sun was all but gone now, leaving the world covered in soft twilight. The string lights installed by management flickered on and cast their warm glow across the rooftop.

A group of four people burst through the door that led onto the roof, laughing and carrying a small ice chest. They glanced in Warren and Rachel's direction, then turned and headed to a circle of chairs set up on the opposite side of the roof. Far enough away for Rachel and Warren to continue their conversation without being overheard.

Rachel set her empty bottle down, walked behind Warren and wrapped him in the blanket with her. She exhaled slowly and thought of ways to explain once again to this big, beautiful man the dangers of the life she'd chosen.

"Sometimes it's too much, you know? If I think about it too much, I start to go crazy." Rachel said.

"So the jokes help."

"They do."

"I get that. But it doesn't stop me from being worried."

"Don't. I'll be fine."

"Don't give me that. You know how many gunshot and stab wound victims I see every day who thought they'd be fine?"

Warren turned in the blanket so he could face her. Rachel kept her arms around his neck, keeping a tight hold on the blanket. Anyone watching would think they were just another couple whispering intimate secrets to each other between kisses. Rachel wished that were true.

"They got the drop on you, and you don't want me to be worried about that?" Warren asked.

"God, you're sexy when you get all serious like this."

"Not funny! I don't want you to get hurt. Not the woman I lo..."

Rachel cocked her head. "The woman you what?"

"The woman I like."

"Ha!" Rachel grabbed Warren by his shoulders and pushed him back against the railing. "Don't lie to me. I have a knife."

Warren grabbed Rachel by the waist, spun around and pushed her back against the railing. "Go ahead. Pull it."

Rachel grabbed his shirt with one hand and pulled him close enough to feel his breath on her lips.

"I got a better idea," she whispered.

Warren smiled. "God, you're sexy when you kiss me like this."

As Warren leaned in, Rachel could have sworn she felt a tiny spark jump from his lips to hers.

CHAPTER TWENTY

HIDE AND SEEK

The shouts woke Esi from a dream. She tried to move, but her arm was still entangled in the vi- No. There was no vine. Her arm was free. She raised her arm to examine it. There was never a vine. She'd been lying on her back, staring at the clouds and hallucinating. The Ibogaine's effects were strong, but it was wearing off. Her mind belonged to her again. She forced herself up and stood on unsteady legs.

"I will never stop fighting for you!" She could hear the king shout to the crowd. "We are Dahomey! We are victorious!"

She found her knife still lying on the ground, slid it into its sheath and scanned the crowd for any signs of Jabari. There, near the front edge, about to disappear behind another merchant stand. It was the perfect spot for Jabari to take his shot and maybe even disappear in the confusion that followed. He might just get away with this.

Esi bolted, her feet kicking up dust behind her as she ran. She kept to the back edge of the crowd as long as she could until she was forced to cut through to get to Jabari. She cursed under her breath. The crowd was too large. Too tightly packed.

It would slow her down, and she knew it. There wasn't enough time. But if the king's life was in danger, she would do everything she could to save him.

She hopped a small fence and dodged people walking by. Some stopped to stare in amazement when they realized who she was. Esi was not shy about pushing them away if they didn't move quickly enough. Still, Jabari seemed miles away.

"Move!" she yelled to a group of kids who'd gathered to play a game in the dirt. They scattered just in time for Esi to run past, leaving a cloud of dust in her wake.

The crowd thinned enough for Esi to pick up her pace. She was closer. Almost to the merchant stands where Jabari was setting up. But still not close enough. A small group of people moved aside to sit and rest and Esi shot through the gap, nimble and graceful as a gazelle, controlling each breath as she maneuvered her way through the crowd. Somewhere in the distance, she heard the sound of a drum.

CHAPTER
TWENTY-ONE
ADISA

Jabari sat motionless as the crowd danced. His finger on the trigger and the king in his sights. He could take the shot now. One shot to the chest. It would be over and Adisa would be avenged. The music played on. The people sang. He closed his eyes to listen.

"Together we fight lions
Chase enemies
Dance in victory
Together!"

"Do you remember the first time we sang this song together?"

He opened his eyes. Adisa stood before him.

"My love!" Jabari lowered his rifle.

She turned to the crowd and listened as they sang.

"Together, we are Dahomey!
Fighting as one for our land

Our king
Our love
Our soul"

"It was when we met," she said, turning back to Jabari. "You were trying to impress me."

She was just as he remembered. Beautiful, tall and strong. A long, black and gold dress caressed her body. The gold necklace he gave her draped elegantly around her neck.

"I remember," Jabari said.

"It's love that ignites
Our passion to defend
To fight to the end"

Adisa smiled. A smile as beautiful as the moon on a clear night.

"You were dancing like a big, tough warrior. I was new, so young. You wanted to impress me. Show me how strong you and your men were."

Jabari laughed. "We sang this song as we danced."

"You do remember."

Tears welled up in his eyes. He set the rifle down and stood.

"And then you smiled and changed my world forever," he said. "I knew then, right then, that I loved you, Adisa."

"You danced well. So well."

"Yes," Jabari said. "Until it was your turn. I did not tell you then, but you and your sisters were the better dancers that night."

"That night?"

"Many nights," Jabari said, then laughed. "But not every night."

He stretched out a hand to Adisa.

"I would give anything to hold you in my arms again, my love. Life without you has not been good to me. I cannot let go. I cannot move on. I have tried, but..." Jabari looked down and shook his head, searching for words to put reason to his tortured soul. "I have tried so hard. But I can't. I won't."

Adisa smiled.

"What we had was magical."

"The Gods smiled on us for a time," Jabari said. "For a time I had everything."

Adisa's eyes fell to Jabari's rifle. Her smile faded. She looked to the king, then back to Jabari.

"Do not do this, my love."

Lost in the memory of Adisa, Jabari had almost forgotten his mission. His face grew stern and he knelt down to pick up his rifle.

"He took you from me!" he said, looking up at Adisa.

Gone was Adisa's beautiful smile. In its place was a look of sadness, fear and disappointment.

"But you still live to remember me," she said. "Do not do this evil thing, Jabari."

Jabari stared for a long moment into the eyes of the ghost before him as tears from his own eyes began to smear the dirt on his face. Then, with a new resolve, he raised his rifle and took aim once again at the king.

"Go away, Adisa. Today, I avenge you."

"Today you shame me!" Adisa said. And then she was gone.

Jabari wiped his eyes and put his finger on the trigger. "I bring you vengeance, my love! Vengeance for you and for me!"

THE SONG ENDED AND THE KING STOOD UP AND RAISED HIS HANDS TO silence the crowd. He would speak again. This was the perfect time. He tightened his finger and told himself to squeeze the trigger, but didn't. Couldn't. A second went by. Two seconds. The king moved. Jabari remained still, his rifle now aimed at an empty chair on the stage. He closed his eyes. Three seconds. Four. This was wrong. Wrong wrong wrong. Esi was right. This would only bring shame. He moved his finger from the trigger. Five seconds. "My sweet Adis—-"

His words were cut short by the pain of Esi's blade as it tore through his flesh.

CHAPTER TWENTY-TWO

REUNITED

Esi ran past a stack of crates and spotted Jabari crouching with his rifle aimed at the king, well within firing range. He could have taken the shot by now, but hadn't. Why? There was no time to think, just act. She pulled her knife from its sheath, lunged at Jabari and sank the blade deep into his side.

Jabari dropped his rifle and fell to the ground. His head hit the dirt hard and Esi heard him groan. The Fanti noticed the disturbance and were already moving the king off the mound.

Esi spotted Goutto, her lifelong friend now the Fanti General. Goutto tapped another guard on the shoulder and the pair jumped from the mound and ran towards Esi.

Confusion swept over the crowd. Most were beginning to ask questions about the king, while others, mostly those closest to the merchant stands, noticed Jabari laying on the ground next to Esi and began calling to the Fanti.

Esi knelt down near Jabari. His breathing was ragged and his strength was gone.

"I miss her," he whispered between breaths.

Esi put her hand to his face.

"I miss her too, Jabari."

"You were right, Esi. Killing the king... would have only... brought shame."

Thinking more clearly now, Esi knew Jabari had plenty of time to take his shot. He was in range and ready to fire. The king should be dead now. Yet, he lived. Jabari had chosen a different path.

Esi leaned in closer.

"You honored her today, Jabari," she whispered.

Jabari smiled.

"She always knew better. She... told me. You told me."

"More importantly, you listened, Jabari."

His eyes moved from Esi and fixed on something just past her.

"I... see her now, Esi. I see her."

"What is it you want, Jabari?"

"To... be with... her again."

Esi leaned in and kissed Jabari on the forehead, then wiped the tears from his eyes. The painful look on his face was gone now. Replaced by happiness and the sweet anticipation of reuniting with his one, true love.

"You will be with her again," she said. "Go. Embrace her and be at peace, old friend."

Jabari's breath slowed. A final tear streamed down his face. He blinked once, then no more.

"Esi!" Goutto shouted. She and the other Fanti soldier had made their way through the crowd to Esi.

Esi stood, her gaze still fixed on Jabari.

"Is that... Jabari?" Goutto asked, staring down at his lifeless body. "Why is he here?"

"To settle an old debt," Esi said.

"Esi, are you alright?"

Esi looked at Goutto and rested a hand on her shoulder. "Yes, my friend. I am fine."

"Come," Goutto said. "The king must know you're here."

CHAPTER
TWENTY-THREE
BURN THE CITY

King Behanzin looked slightly disheveled, but otherwise fine. He was watching the remains of the crowd through a palace window, flanked by two Fanti and a servant, when Goutto ushered in Esi and Nawi.

"My King," Goutto said.

The King was surprised when he turned and saw his two finest warriors standing in front of him. "Esi? Nawi? Why are you here? You abandoned your post in Cana?"

Both women were still in their battle dress, covered in dirt and spots of blood from the war. No doubt their stench reached the king's nostrils, but he made no mention of it.

"These women are the reason you still breathe today," Goutto said. "They left Cana this morning to come here and stop Jabari."

"This morning? How did you get here so quickly?"

"We had help, my king," Nawi said. Both Esi and Nawi's heads were lowered before the king. "We came here by horse."

"Horse?" Once more the King seemed genuinely surprised. "You know how to ride a horse?"

"She took a lesson," Esi said, and softly elbowed Nawi. Both women laughed, then quickly regained their composure.

Shaking his head, the King returned his gaze to the dwindling crowd outside. "Once again I owe you my life. This is not the first time, and I am thankful to you both."

He grabbed his pipe from a tray next to his chair, lit it and took a long, slow puff before getting down to business. "I'm sorry, but I cannot stay to thank you properly. We must gather our things... and leave Abomey."

"My king!" Esi said, forgetting the formalities and raising her head to see the man she was speaking to. "Is there no other way?"

"No, Esi. The French are already at our gates. We will leave and rebuild. To do that, I need my strongest warriors by my side. I need you both."

Noticing Nawi's silence, Esi bowed her head and replied.

"We go where you go, my king," she said.

"Good." The king motioned to a door that led to the Agojie wing of the palace. "Go now and dine with your sisters. You must be hungry. Then prepare for our departure. We leave in two days," he said, then left the room, followed closely by his guards and the servant.

After dinner, Esi stopped Nawi in the hallway on their way back to the palace rooms.

"Why did you not speak?" she asked.

Nawi kept her eyes fixed straight ahead, refusing to look at Esi.

"What was I to say?"

The sun was setting and the light grew dim. Servants appeared and began lighting candles that lined the hallway.

Esi paused to let them pass, then lowered her voice to a near whisper.

"What troubles you, Nawi?"

Nawi slumped her shoulders and turned to look Esi in the eyes. "I cannot go," she said.

"You must go with your King, Nawi."

Nawi shook her head and turned away.

"No, Esi. The fires will burn, but they will not destroy everything. The French will rebuild and rule our land. I cannot abandon my sisters and brothers again. This time, I stay and fight."

Esi grabbed Nawi's shoulders and stared into her eyes, searching for meaning and answers that were not there.

"But you will die! Come with us and we will rebuild."

Nawi pulled away and walked to a nearby window. Her eyes took in the city below. The people, her people, were busy moving and packing their belongings, preparing for the mass exodus. Every road and every building she could see held memories. It was hard to imagine all of it would soon be up in flames. The city she called home for so many years. She could not just walk away from it so easily.

"I will not die," she said. "Some of the other sisters also speak of staying behind. We will become assassins. Disguise ourselves as working women and wives during the day, and kill French officers in the night."

Esi joined Nawi at the window and for a time, both stood in silence.

"Then I stay with you," Esi said.

Nawi laughed and turned to lean her back against the wall. "They will recognize you at once, Esi. You would die on the first day."

Esi sighed and leaned next to Nawi. Nawi put an arm

around Esi, pulled her closer and rested her head on Esi's shoulder. "We've said too many goodbyes already, old friend. But this one may be the hardest."

"I cannot lose Uribi and you on the same day," Esi said, holding back tears. The Agojie never shed tears. They were trained warriors, skilled in the art of death and stealth and learned to numb themselves to pain. But while Esi could endure pain that would make most men beg for mercy, she was no good at saying goodbye to old friends.

The candlelights in the hallway flickered as a draft of cool air rushed through.

"I had a dog once," Esi said.

"A dog? When?"

"When I was a little girl. I loved her, but my father hated her. I found her covered in fleas behind the old shops, took her home and cleaned her every day until she shined. One day I came home and she was gone. My father said..." Esi paused to keep herself from crying. "My father said she'd run away, but I knew it was him. I knew he'd taken her away from me."

Now both women were silent. Two childhood friends who were never short on words, stood silent in the now empty hallway with their backs to the wall.

"Take this," Nawi said, breaking the silence. She reached behind her neck, unclasped her medallion. An old piece of jewelry she'd purchased from a roadside merchant a few days after she joined the Agojie sisters. "It has always brought me good fortune." She handed it to Esi. "Take it and remember me."

Esi took the medallion and squeezed it in her hand. "We will meet again," she said. "Our bond cannot be broken, even in death."

"Death? You said you wouldn't die," Nawi joked.

"I was talking about you!"

Both women laughed. A genuine laugh that erased the sadness of the moment, if only for a while.

CHAPTER TWENTY-FOUR

THE DANCE

The smells from the kitchen hit Nyah before she could even open the door to her house. Danny was cooking something, and whatever it was made Nyah question her earlier dinner choice at The Burger Melt. Especially knowing it may have cost her friendship with Quin.

Desi tried to explain why Quin was so upset, but that only made Nyah feel worse. She said Quin was waiting for the right moment to come out. Until then, he had to keep it secret. Nyah of all people should have understood that. She'd been living a lie since birth. She felt like the worst kind of jerk.

Danny was in the kitchen. A sizzling skillet in front of him and a bottle of beer on the counter. Jada was there too, leaning against the counter with a beer in her hand. She smiled when Nyah walked in.

"Hey girl," she said.

Nyah opened the fridge and grabbed a bottle of sparkling water. "What's for dinner?"

"Chicken fajitas with avocado salad and spicy, roasted

potatoes," Danny said. "And I made some of my homemade hot sauce. Grab a plate."

Danny's cooking was her kryptonite. She could try to resist, but there was really no use. No matter how strong she thought she was, one smell and she was gone. She grabbed a plate.

"How'd it go with your friends?" Danny asked.

"You made friends?" Jada asked, then squeezed her eyes shut. "Hold on, I'm trying to picture what that would look like."

"Now you've got a sense of humor?" Nyah snapped back.

"Hey, I'm funny," Jada said, then looked to Danny for reassurance. "Right, Danny?"

When Danny kept quiet, Jada grabbed a dish towel from the counter and threw it at him. Danny made a show of trying to shield himself from the attack.

"Alright, alright," he said, still tending to the sizzling chicken fajitas in the pan. "You're funny as hell."

"Whatever," Jada said.

"Not to interrupt, but I may have lost one of those friends tonight," Nyah said.

Danny put down the spatula and turned to Nyah.

"Damn, baby. You only had two. Was it that Desi girl?"

"Quin," Nyah said as she stepped past Danny to scoop some fajitas onto her tortilla. "But I'm sure Desi will be next."

"Why you being so hard on yourself?" Jada asked.

"Experience, I guess."

With a full plate in one hand, Nyah grabbed her drink with the other and headed for the back patio.

"I'll be out back drowning my sorrows in these fajitas," she said, then slid the door closed behind her.

~

THE MOON WAS FULL AND THE AIR WAS BEGINNING TO COOL DOWN. Two rows of string lights ran from the house to a tree, then back to the house, creating two v-shaped forms in the backyard and casting just the right amount of warm light on the deck where she sat.

The yard was small, but on nights like these, it was her sanctuary. She queued up her playlist and blasted Beyonce's *My Power* through the Bluetooth speaker. Tierra Whack was killing the first verse. A strong, powerful song that always reminded her of her mom. A true warrior. Fierce and deadly, yet soft and gentle when she needed to be.

Nyah was about to take her first bite when her phone dinged with a message from Danny.

> Second chance headed your way now.

Nyah sighed and put down her phone just as the patio door slid open.

"I knew I shouldn't have told you where I lived," she said without looking back.

Quin walked into view and sat down in the chair next to Nyah with a bottle of Topo Chico in his hand.

"No food?" Nyah asked.

"The guy, Danny, offered me a plate, but I wasn't hungry," Quin said. Noticing Nyah's full plate, he added, "I'm surprised you got room left."

Nyah was savoring the taste of the grilled chicken, perfectly seasoned and marinated. She took another bite before responding. Quin didn't seem to mind the wait.

"He's my adoptive dad. And his fajitas will make you lose your religion," she said as she set her plate down on a table next to her chair, then wiped her mouth with a napkin. "You should have said yes."

Quin took a sip of his drink and leaned his head back on the chair. Happy to sit and listen to the music, Nyah did the same. The second verse kicked in through the speaker. It was Beyonce's turn.

"I love this song," Quin said, slowly bobbing his head to the rhythm. "We used to play it in the locker room before games."

Nyah was in no hurry to talk. Talking always seemed to get her into trouble. Better to stay quiet and let him do the talking for now. But even so, she felt the need to apologize. He deserved that much. She took a deep breath, closed her eyes and spoke.

"Sorry I almost outed you in public."

It felt good to say it out loud. Surprisingly good. But instead of responding, Quin just sat there, bobbing his head to the music as if Nyah hadn't said a word. It was unnerving. Until it wasn't. It made sense. He wouldn't have come over if he hadn't already forgiven her. Maybe just saying it was all he needed. All both of them needed.

The third verse kicked in. This time, a South African artist.

"Busiswa!" Quin and Nyah said in unison.

They listened for a few more measures until Quin broke the silence.

"How'd you know?" he asked with his eyes still closed.

Nyah looked at him as if he were joking. "I mean, it was pretty obvious," Nyah said.

Quin opened his eyes and gave Nyah a quizzical look. "Obvious? Like, how?"

Nyah sighed. "The way you looked at him at lunch today," she said. "And when he grabbed your shoulder, I saw how you held on to his hand for a split second before pushing it away."

"Someone was paying attention," Quin said.

"Like I said, pretty obvious."

Quin shook his head, then pulled a fresh pack of Spree

candies from his pocket and tossed it onto the table. Now it was Nyah's turn to be surprised.

"How'd you know I liked these?"

"You're not the only detective. You pop one in your mouth every time you get nervous."

"That obvious?"

"Yeah."

My Power faded out and Ruth B's *Slow Fade* queued up.

"His name's Dustin," Quin said. "And it's not that easy."

"What? Being gay?"

"No. Coming out. I mean, Dustin is ready. He wants to tell the whole world. But he wants me to be ready with him. And I'm just not there yet."

"What they gonna say?" Nyah asked. "Oh damn, our star quarterback is gay! What will we do now?"

Quin laughed. "Running back."

"Whatever. What does a running back even do?"

"Runs and scores." Quin leaned back to gaze up at the stars again as Ruth kicked into the chorus. "I'm feelin' this playlist."

"I never get tired of these songs."

They both stopped talking and listened some more. Nyah unwrapped the pack of Spree and popped one into her mouth, while Quin kept staring up at the sky as if all the answers were right there, just out of reach.

"And Desi was right," Quin said. "I can't dance. So even if I come out and ask him to the homecoming dance, we'll just end up sitting there lookin' all dumb."

A few more seconds, a few more lyrics and a few more thoughts passed before either of them spoke.

"What do you like about him?" Nyah asked. "Other than his good taste in clothes. Another clue, by the way."

Quin smiled. "You're really into fashion aren't you?"

"My mom got me into it. She always said fashion is power.

The right clothes and hairstyle give you strength, and the wrong ones take it away."

"I get that," Quin said, taking another sip of his drink. "I guess it was the way he *didn't* like me."

"Didn't?"

"Yeah. I know it sounds messed up."

"No, that sounds perfectly normal," Nyah said.

"Look, this ain't easy to talk about."

"And I ain't easy to talk to," Nyah said.

"No," Quin laughed. "You're... You're easy to talk to." Again, Quin leaned his head back and closed his eyes. Words seemed to come easier to him that way. "It's like everywhere I go, people act like they know me and want to be my friend."

"Because you're the big man on campus."

A sip from his drink before he said, "Yeah. Except Dustin didn't care about all that. He was just nice, you know. He always smiled, but never acted like he wanted to be friends, or wanted my approval, or anything from me other than a smile and maybe a wave back," Quin said. "I really liked that about him."

"That and an ass that won't quit," Nyah said. "Makes sense now."

Quin laughed and shook his head.

"You know I'm right," Nyah said.

"So one day I caught up with him after school to talk," Quin said, trying his best to ignore Nyah's comment. "You know, like walk right up to him and talk."

"What'd you say?"

"I was like 'Hey.'"

"Did you work on that line in the mirror?"

Quin laughed.

"I was nervous and didn't even know why," he said. "Anyway, he said 'Hey' back and we started talking right there on the steps in front of the school for like two hours. Next thing I know, the sun was setting. Everybody was gone and it was just us, sitting on the steps, talking and laughing. I remember the laughing the most. I hadn't laughed like that in months, maybe years. I knew right then this was something special."

Rihanna's *I Wanna Dance in the Dark* played next. Another one of Nyah's old favorites.

A cool breeze played a soft chorus through the trees as moonlight flickered in and out past the leaves. The string lights, enchanted by the rhythm, danced along, swaying slowly from side to side. Nyah pulled her knees up to her chest and slid down in her chair.

"You want to go back inside?" Quin asked.

"No, I like it out here."

"Me too," Quin said.

Wind chimes played in the distance. Leaves blew in the wind and somewhere far away, a dog was barking.

"What's your secret, Trish?" Quin asked.

"My what?"

Quin leaned back into the chair and let the night air caress his face.

"Don't play dumb. I know when someone has a secret. Game recognizes game."

Nyah took a long sip of her drink, hoping Quin would drop it. He didn't.

"New girl comes to school, doesn't talk to anyone. Throws down on big, bully boy Clint like he was a rag doll and won't say how she did it. You got secrets," Quin said.

Nyah looked at Quin. It was easy to keep secrets from him. From everybody. She'd been keeping hers for so long, it came naturally. Along with the fine arts of distraction and diversion. All she had to do was ask Quin something about Desi or Dustin, or hell, football, and he'd drop it. But in this moment, for all the years of sworn secrecy, she wanted nothing more than to tell him everything. About her life on the run. The countless hours of training to fight. To defend. To become the warrior she never asked to be so she could fulfill a promise to a long-dead king. And then as a reward for it all, she got to watch her mom die. She wanted to tell him everything. Looking at him sitting there with his arm behind his head and his eyes closed, she knew it would be easy. Quin would listen. He may not get it, but he would understand. Or would he?

"I… I just don't get along with most people," she said, then leaned back into her chair.

"Whatever," Quin said. "Your secrets are yours to keep. But Desi and I got you. We're friends now. Believe that, girl."

Rihanna was kicking into the second verse. Nyah clenched her fists and took a deep breath. No, she couldn't tell him. Not now. Maybe not ever. This secret could get them hurt. It could get them killed. It was her burden, not his.

After a few more seconds of silence, Nyah put her drink down, sighed and stood up in front of Quin.

"Come on," she said.

"What?" Quin opened his eyes to see Nyah holding a hand out.

"I'll teach you to dance."

"Nope," Quin said and leaned his head back.

Nyah kept her hand extended. For a few seconds, Quin tried to ignore her.

"You can't teach this," he said finally. "I got no rhythm."

"You think I want those big feet stepping all over my toes? Don't make this any harder than it has to be."

"You don't give up, do you?"

Nyah said nothing, but kept her hand extended.

"Damn. Alright," Quin said, and reluctantly stood up. "We'll see how long it takes you to give up."

Rihanna's lyrics flowed and the music surrounded them.

"You feel that?" Nyah asked. "You feel the rhythm?"

Quin waited a few seconds, then answered "Yeah. Yeah, I feel it."

"Good, now move with it. Like this."

Nyah took a step to the right and let her left foot follow. Then she stepped back to the left and her right foot followed. Quin watched Nyah's feet as she danced and swayed her hips with the rhythm. Eventually, he worked up the courage to try it himself.

"Okay, like this?"

Nyah looked down at Quin's feet. He was doing it. Sort of.

"Not bad. Even with those Sasquatch feet."

Quin smiled, but kept moving. His timing was a little awkward, but he was keeping up pretty well. Nyah moved in time with him.

"See? It's like we're moving together," she said.

"Oh damn. Yeah," Quin said.

Nyah closed her eyes. "Imagine the music is a map to the scoring zone in football."

"The end zone?"

"Whatever," Nyah said. "It's showing you how to get there, you just have to follow."

Quin thought for a moment, then smiled and looked down at his feet as he moved from side to side.

"Oh damn, that makes sense."

"Good. We'll work on your hands next," Nyah said.

Quin was swinging his arms to the left and right, almost, but not quite in time with his feet and the music.

"What's wrong with my hands?"

"Just keep dancing."

And they did. Under the string lights, moonlight and stars, Nyah and Quin danced.

Later, after Quin was gone, Nyah walked into the living room where Jada and Danny were watching a movie, sat down on the arm of the empty love seat and stared at the couple. They were snuggled together, but quickly sat up straighter and repositioned themselves on the couch like two teenagers caught making out.

Danny grabbed the remote from the coffee table and paused the movie.

“You okay?” he asked.

“Yeah. I’m good.” This time she actually meant it. “You two look cute.”

“Okay wait,” Jada said, then grabbed her phone and held it up to record. “Say that again.”

Nyah rolled her eyes and got up to go to her room. “Took you less than five seconds to make me regret saying that.”

Jada put the phone down and smiled. There was a look of relief in her eyes. The kind you get when something finally goes right. She’d been waiting for Nyah’s approval ever since this thing with Danny started, and this was pretty much it. Maybe Danny having a girlfriend wasn’t the worst thing ever.

“Thanks, Trisha,” Jada said, still smiling like she’d just aced a final exam.

“‘I’ll be in my room,” Nyah said, then left them to their movie.

She switched on the lamp on her nightstand, dropped to her knees and slid out a white box from underneath her bed. Inside was her Agojie suit. She pulled it out and laid it across her bed.

Her battledress, as her mom used to call it. She ran her

fingers across the front. The hand-sewn suit felt cool to the touch. She knew every stitch by heart because she'd sewn it herself. The product of countless lessons from her mom. To her, the uniform was just as important as the training. A tradition passed down from the beginning.

Even after all this time, she still marveled at its design. The materials have changed over the years, but the design remained the same. Deep, wine red that faded into rich blacks. The golden flowers sewn into the arms and legs using appliqué stitching. The Dahomey flag sewn into the arm stood in contrast to the dark red background. She'd worn it several times in practice and sometimes, on nights like this one, alone in her room. But so far, never in a real fight. At least not yet. There was power in the suit. An almost uncontrolled power she felt every time she slipped it on.

The choice to become the Agojie was hers, and not a day went by when she didn't feel the weight of it. The line could end with her and no one would blame her, not even Danny. But deep down, she knew she'd never forgive herself.

Nyah pulled the mask from the box and laid it next to the uniform on the bed. This too was made by hand. Deep red and black tones with more flower accents.

The clock on her nightstand read 12:30 a.m. Except for the cool air hissing through the vent, the room was silent.

She sat down on the bed and wondered, not for the first time, how she could let Desi and Quin get so close so fast. Like all the other schools, she'd come to Fonville ready to leave at a moment's notice. But now a quick exit didn't seem so easy. She was stuck between worlds. Old traditions or new friends. Fighting injustice or cheering for the football team. No matter how many times she thought it through, there was no way of having both. Even if that was exactly what she wanted. The warrior was as much a part of her as it was for her mom. And though the connection with Desi and Quin was new, she could feel the strength they gave her growing every day. She knew right then she'd do whatever it took to protect them.

As she glided her fingers along the soft fabric of the uniform, a thought crossed her mind. She folded the uniform, tossed it in the box and carefully slid it back under the bed, then pulled on her light, floral print crop jacket and walked downstairs. The time to start protecting her friends was now. And she could think of at least one wrong that very much needed to be made right again.

"Where you headed to?" Danny asked from the couch.

"Out for a walk. I'll be back. I have my phone."

Without waiting for a response, she stepped outside and closed the door behind her. The air was a little humid, but cool. She closed her eyes and breathed it in, letting the air fill her lungs for a few seconds before slowly exhaling. The night was clear and the stars were out. It was a good night. Avoiding the motion-activated light by the garage, Nyah stepped off the porch from the side, walked through the gate and disappeared into the night.

CHAPTER TWENTY-FIVE
THE AMBUSH

NEW ORLEANS

"How long?" Byron's voice cut through Rachel's earpiece and startled her back to reality.

"For what?" Rachel whispered into the microphone stitched into her Agojie suit. She repositioned herself on the balcony of the old building near the French Quarter where she was currently waiting for her target.

It was a warm night. The light from the full moon was mostly hidden by clouds. The sound of thunder in the distance, followed closely by light droplets of rain tapping quietly on the metal railings around her helped calm her nerves.

Byron was in a rented cargo van about a block away, scanning the video monitors he had set up on a makeshift workbench in the back.

"The tilapia with lemon-caper sauce," Byron said. "You said to pan fry the fish first, but you didn't say how long. You good out there?"

"Fine," she lied. It was happening less often now, but ever

since the explosion she'd sometimes lose focus and drift off to another place for a while. "Can we talk about this later?"

"What? We always talk food during missions."

"Just not feeling it tonight."

"I think you said three minutes." Byron said. Rachel knew he was scribbling down notes. He always did. There was a pause, then "You're thinking about Warren again aren't you?"

"About three minutes, then turn," Rachel whispered into her microphone, hoping like hell to keep the topic on food. "But sprinkle the filets with salt and pepper first, and heat up some butter and olive oil in your pan."

Ever since they'd started dating, Warren was pretty much all she could think about. But Byron didn't need to know that. At least not right now. He'd just get worried and start to think maybe Warren had become a problem after all. Which he wasn't. Not in the slightest. If anything, he was the one keeping her grounded through all this.

She hadn't gone out with a guy in years and was afraid she wouldn't know what to do. But being with Warren felt natural. Easy. Almost like coming home. They made the rooftop their usual meeting spot. She'd bring take out, he'd bring the beer, and together they'd sit, talk and laugh until the sun went down. Sometimes, much later.

Even better, there were no secrets between them. Warren told Rachel all about his life in the gang. The people he hurt and the lives he helped destroy were always eating away at him. He became a nurse so he could try and give back a little of what he took. But no matter how hard he tried, no matter the lives he saved and the families he kept together, it was never enough. The guilt he felt deep down lingered.

And since they'd met in the middle of an operation, Rachel couldn't exactly keep that part of her life secret. He knew everything. The Dahomey legacy, the fighting, the suit, Byron, all of it. No secrets. It was dangerous, she knew, but it felt good to have someone else to talk to at the end of the day other than Byron.

Movement from inside the restaurant across the street caught her attention.

"I see something," Rachel whispered into her mic.

Byron grabbed a small joystick and panned one of the cameras to the right, then zoomed in. Someone was walking near a front window of the restaurant towards the front.

"I see him. He's leaving," Byron said.

A well-dressed man, flanked with two bigger men, walked outside. The smaller man, Vincent Gallo, was the target.

Known as the Consigliere, Vincent was one of the most powerful figures in the New Orleans Crime Family. An advisor to the boss himself. He'd have the answers they needed. Now they just had to catch him.

Vincent pulled a cigarette from his coat pocket and lit it, while the other two scanned the area. He liked to walk a few blocks after a big dinner, which made security tough. So to keep things fluid, Vincent kept two cars with drivers parked in different locations ready to go at all times. And since he was the only one who knew which car he'd choose, this part was a guessing game. After a couple of puffs on the cigarette, Vincent turned and walked to his left, followed closely by his two guards.

"He's taking the sedan," Byron said. "Two blocks away."

"I'm on it," Rachel said.

"Don't be runnin' off again like last time," Byron said.

"I was carried off, remember?"

Using the cover of darkness and practiced stealth, she flipped over the railing of the patio and lowered herself quietly to the ground. She ran to the opposite side of the block Vincent and his men were on, turned the corner and ran parallel to them.

"So what's next?" Byron asked.

"What?"

"After you fry up the fish, what's next?"

"Kind of busy here," Rachel said, avoiding street lights and keeping to the shadows as she ran. This street was mostly empty, save for a few small clusters of drunk and wandering tourists and the usual outcasts who made this street their home.

"Okay."

"Put the fish on a plate," Rachel said. "Then add the wine, lemon, tomatoes and capers to the pan and simmer it for like, two minutes."

"Got it," Byron said. "I'm taking notes."

"You could just get takeout."

"I can cook."

"Instant soup. And even with that you read the directions."

"I'm getting better," Byron said. "Besides, she likes a home-cooked meal."

Byron had many talents, but cooking and women were not among them. He'd dated several women since he and Rachel teamed up. Several he really liked. But the only thing Byron ever loved was the job, so it always ended the same.

He'd been seeing Sarah for about a month now and according to Byron, things were going good. But Rachel wondered how good things would be when Byron missed three dates in a row because he was researching clients, or on a job with Rachel. Byron would apologize, then cancel another date. Rachel had seen it too many times to count. The cycle would continue until Sarah had enough and decided to get out.

"You're a brave man," Rachel said. "If she doesn't leave you after tonight, it must be love."

Rachel turned right onto a street. It was a straight shot from there. If she timed it right, she'd meet up with the trio at the next intersection, one block away from his car and the waiting driver. She pulled her knife and bolted. No time to plan, she had to hit them fast and hard before Vincent's driver got suspicious and called for help.

"I'm almost there," Rachel said.

Just before Vincent and his guards walked into view, Rachel leaped onto the bed of a truck parked by the curb and crouched down to listen. She heard footsteps. They were nearly there. She closed her eyes and counted. "One, two..." The rain was a soothing, steady drizzle now. A few drops trickled down her mask and onto her cheek, cooling her skin.

"Three."

She climbed onto the roof and launched herself into the air just as the men came into view. With less than a second to react, she hurled her knife through the air towards one of the guards. It spun twice before it slammed, butt-end first, into his temple and knocked his head to the side. Rachel raised her fist and brought it down hard into the second guard's jaw as she landed on the sidewalk.

The first guard had collapsed from the blow to the head and was struggling to get back up. Rachel kicked him once in the face, grabbed her knife and used the butt end to crack him over the head. He fell flat on the ground again, and this time he didn't move.

The second guard was recovering and already reaching inside his coat for his gun when Rachel jump-kicked him in the face, whipped her body around and snapped the heel of her foot across his jaw. His head jerked to the side and he staggered back a few steps before falling to one knee. The big guy was stubborn, but far from invincible. Before he could get back to his feet, Rachel closed the gap between them and rammed her knee into his chin, sending him sprawling backwards onto the wet pavement with a smack.

By this time, Vincent was making a break for his car on the next block. Rachel raised her knife and hurled it towards him, sinking the blade deep into his right shoulder. Vincent stumbled and fell hard into a parked car on the side of the road.

"Ah fuck!" he shouted as he tried in vain to reach for the knife.

Rachel pushed him back against the car, grabbed a handful of his hair and slammed his head onto the roof and held it there.

"Let's talk," she said.

"Go to hell!" Vincent spat out.

"I'll send you there first," she whispered into his ear, then slowly pulled the knife from his shoulder, forcing another string of grunts and cuss words from Vincent.

Rachel spun Vincent around and slammed his back against the car. She leaned in close, her blood-red and black mask partially lit by streetlights, partially covered in shadows. To Vincent, she looked like a demon.

"Oh God! It's you!" he said. "They're looking for you. They're all looking for you!"

"How did they find me? What do they want?"

Suddenly, Rachel heard the sound of engines, likely SUV's, roaring in the distance.

"Dammit, Rachel," came Byron's voice into her ear. "They're on to us. Must have been another setup. Get out now!"

CHAPTER TWENTY-SIX

QUARTER FOR YOUR THOUGHTS

Shade is a scarce commodity in the south. From Oklahoma City to Houston, it didn't matter. The summer heat had a way of lingering around long past its welcome. Nyah thought of this as she sat with her gym class on the bleachers in the only spot not shaded by the school building behind them. A price she paid for showing up late, she supposed.

She tied the side of shirt into a knot, partly to help keep cool, but mostly in a futile attempt to add a little fashion to the ridiculous white with yellow-trimmed gym uniforms the kids in this class were forced to wear. She was jealous of Quin down on the field, practicing with the football team. At least they looked good while they sweated it out on the field.

"Good morning, class," came a voice from the bottom deck of the bleachers.

Nyah was surprised to see the woman she'd almost pulled her dagger on in the bathroom the day before.

"I'm Coach Michelle Stasney, your new gym coach," she said. Nyah never met the old coach, but heard she'd left for a head soccer coaching job in another district.

Coach Stasney made some gestures with her hands that Nyah recognized as American Sign Language.

"In this class, you're gonna sweat and learn a little sign language along the way," Coach Stasney said. "It gets loud in the gym and out here. And since I don't like to yell, we're going to learn a few words in sign language."

Some of the students groaned, but Nyah didn't mind. She trained hard at home with her instructors, and anything that lessened the amount of physical activity she did at school was welcome.

A girl sitting next to her leaned over and said "What's sign language for dumb?"

When Nyah didn't respond, she repeated the joke to another girl who seemed to think it was funny.

Coach Stasney held two fingers upside down with one hand and tapped them twice on the palm of her other hand. "That means stand up. Remember that."

She waited a few seconds. When no one stood up, she repeated the motion. This time, they got the message.

"Great! You're learning already. Now get on the track and run a mile." Not waiting around for questions or protest, Coach Stasney picked up her clipboard and walked down the short flight of stairs to the field. A no bullshit kind of move Nyah couldn't help but respect.

After looking at each other for answers and finding none, the students began to get up and walk to the track. Some took the time to stretch, while others started to run as soon as they set foot on the track. And still others, like Nyah, who had no intention of running, simply started walking around the track. Coach Stasney was talking with another teacher and didn't even seem to notice.

Desi got onto the field last, picking up her walking pace just long enough to catch up to Nyah.

"Hey," Desi called out from behind her. "Slow down."

Nyah glanced back. "Hey."

"Notice anything different?"

Nyah gave her a quick once over. "You dyed a streak of your hair pink instead of blue today?"

Desi touched the pink strands of her hair. "Well, yeah. But not what I was talking about. Look closely."

"Okay, I give up. What?"

"Got my quarter back."

Sure enough, the quarter her father gave her when she was a kid was tied to a string and hung around her neck. Back where it belonged.

"How'd you do it?" Desi asked.

"Do what?"

"Come on, Trisha! How the hell did you get it back?"

Nyah's silence only agitated Desi.

"I found it in my locker this morning," she said. "And when I saw Clint in the hall, he turned and walked the other direction like I was the Grim Reaper."

"Maybe he felt bad and decided to give it back."

"Bullshit. I know it was you. I just don't know how you did it."

Nyah shrugged. "Look Desi, I don't know what to tell you."

"So that's it? No explanation?"

More silence.

Desi raised her hands to the clouds and shouted, "What's with you and your secrets!"

A few kids nearby turned back to look. Desi smiled and waved and waited until they lost interest before she went on.

"Whatever," she whispered. "But thank you. Thank you so much." She gripped the quarter in one hand. "I can't tell you what this means to me."

"I think you can't stop telling me," Nyah said, flashing a quick smile in Desi's direction.

Desi gave Nyah a playful slap on her shoulder. "Whatever, punk."

Nyah spun when she heard footsteps behind her. Quin, startled by Nyah's sudden move, held up his hands in surrender.

"Whoa. Damn, Trish. It's me," he said. "How'd you even know I was here?"

"You have big feet," Nyah said, returning to her walk with Desi.

"She's not wrong," Desi said.

Quin glanced down at his feet, then jogged a little to catch up to the pair. He was in his football gear, holding his helmet in one hand. Apparently, he'd taken a break from practice.

"I'm gonna ask him," he said.

"Who?" Desi asked.

"Dustin. I'm going to ask him to the homecoming dance."

Desi stopped and turned to face Quin.

"You're coming out?" Desi asked with a mix of disbelief and joy. "You're freaking coming out?"

"Your quarter." Quin pointed to her necklace. "How'd you get it back?"

Desi grabbed the quarter in one hand.

"Never mind that right now. You're gonna do it for real?" she asked, then wrapped Quin in a bear hug and squeezed him tight. "I feel like a proud momma bear!"

"Hey girls!" came Coach Stasney's voice. For the first time, Nyah and Desi realized they'd made an entire loop around the track and were back near where the coach was standing. She held up her hands in an L shape and hooked one of her pointer fingers around the thumb of the other hand. She moved both hands forward and wiggled her extended pointer finger.

"That means run," she said. "Now stop flirting with Mr. Football and run."

Desi let go and the trio continued, with Nyah and Desi making an effort to run until they were far enough away to walk again.

"What the hell, Quin? I thought you weren't ready," Desi said.

"Come on, Desi. What are people gonna say? Oh damn, our star running back is gay? What will we do now?" Quin said, flashing a quick smile to Nyah. "I'm going to ask him after the game on Friday."

"And you're sure he's, you know, okay with this?" Desi asked.

"Yeah," Quin said. "Hell, if it were up to him, I'd make some big, romantic gesture in front of everyone, but that's not really me."

"You do you, Quin. I'm happy for you." Desi nudged Nyah with her elbow. "You know we're both going to the game, right?"

"I don't do sports," Nyah said.

"I don't either. It's why I need you there with me."

"I wouldn't mind if you were there," Quin said. "You know, for support."

Nyah sighed and the three kept their pace around the track for a second time. Coach Stasney was too busy talking to notice.

"I'll think about it," Nyah said, even though she already knew the answer.

CHAPTER TWENTY-SEVEN

ESI AND THE KING

ATCHERIBE, AFRICA, 31 MILES NORTH OF ABOMEY, 1893

Esi was dressed in a full-length, red gown with gold trim and a gold silk band around her head. It felt good to be rid of the stench of war and death. Good to feel pretty once more. If only for a little while.

She stood in the King's room, surrounded by carvings and paintings. King Behanzin was a lover of art and spent years collecting pieces from around the kingdom. All of which he went to great lengths to ensure came with him from Abomey.

Her attention turned to a wooden carving sitting alone on a pedestal. She traced the contours with her fingers. Smooth and solid, expertly crafted by a master's hand. It brought her both joy and sadness.

"The Crowned Eagle. One of the most powerful birds of prey in the world," came a voice from behind her. The king's voice. "Your father was a fine craftsman."

Esi turned and knelt before the king. "My king. I did not hear you come in."

"Rise, Esi. You have earned the right to stand in my presence," said King Behanzin. He walked past Esi and picked up the carving to study it. "He gave this to me when he brought you here. A little bribe to make sure we treated you well, I suppose. But it was I who should have paid him."

"My father abandoned me," Esi said. "I begged him not to."

"Had he relented, you would not be here now."

"For that, I am thankful," Esi admitted. "My brother was all I had left outside the palace walls, but now he is gone too."

"For that, I am sorry."

The king gently placed the carving back on the pedestal and walked to a nearby window. For a few moments, they both stood in silence. Esi was about to say something when the king finally spoke.

"I never wanted to be king, Esi," he said. "I told my father I wanted to fight."

Esi paused to consider this. "You would have given up your place on the throne to fight?"

"I was young and tired of politics. I wanted to fight alongside the soldiers," he said, then laughed to himself. "I demanded my petition be granted with all the authority of a young boy with all the answers."

"Had he agreed, you would not be here now," Esi said.

The King smiled at Esi, then turned his attention back to the window.

"We are far from home now, Esi."

"We will return."

"No."

"My King?"

"No, Esi. We will not."

Esi stepped forward then stopped herself before going any closer to the king.

"My King. We are rebuilding our forces. Soon we will be stronger-"

He turned to face Esi, and for the first time since she'd known him, she saw tears forming in his eyes.

"They have a new King," he said.

The news stunned Esi into silence.

"The French have appointed my brother, Goutchili, as king of Dahomey. It is over. There is nothing left for me to do but surrender."

"Goutchili is a puppet for the French. He will do whatever they ask of him," Esi said. "We will fight!"

"No!" he shouted, alarming a Fanti guard who appeared from the shadows with her machete drawn. The king waved her off and she disappeared as quickly as she'd appeared.

"I watched as my father, Glele, sent our men and women to be slaughtered against the French with their big guns," the King continued in a much softer voice. "I thought I could do things differently, but the French and their allies are too strong. We are done fighting. I will not sacrifice any more of my people."

He walked to a chair across the room and sat. Esi, stunned by the king's confession, remained silent.

"Do you remember when I gave that to you, Esi?" the king asked, pointing to Esi's knife strapped to her hip. Esi pulled it from its sheath and rested the steel blade on her palm. The deep, rich color of the wooden handle was engraved with flowers on a vine covering the entire surface. A symbol of unity among the warriors and their kingdom. A family of one. The weight was perfectly balanced, and the steel blade was razor sharp.

"Of course," Esi said, admiring the blade. " It was a gift from your father. And you promised it to the fighter who could prove the strongest in battle."

"It is a thing of beauty."

"I never grow tired of gazing at it," Esi said.

"You were always the finest, Esi. You earned that knife, and you earned my respect."

"Thank you," Esi said. Sensing the King was leading to something more, she returned the knife to its sheath.

"But your loyalty will cost you. The French do not care about the other warriors. But you, they want you dead. And they will not rest until they see your head on a spike."

The King stood and walked to Esi. Esi lowered her head, but the king gently lifted her chin.

"Look me in the eyes, Esi. You cannot stay here, and you cannot go back to Dahomey. You know this, right?"

"My King. I will go back to Dahomey with you. If I die, I die."

"No. You will not do this."

He grabbed Esi's hands and cupped them with his own.

"You will live, Esi. You will carry on the name of the Agojie. Go from this place tonight. You must make your way to Whydah and the port. There is a man there named Louis. An Impresario with plans to display some of your sisters to the world. He is not a good man, but he owes me."

"To display them? Where?"

"He will take them to Paris, then America. He says people will pay a high price to see the famous Amazons of Dahomey."

"No!" Esi said, looking up at the King. "My home is here with you and my sister Agojie!"

Behanzin let go of Esi's hands.

"You would defy your king's wishes?" he asked.

Once again, Esi turned her eyes downward. "No, my king. It's just..."

"You have no home, Esi! Your brother is dead, your sisters in battle are dead, our kingdom has fallen." He picked up and lit his smoking pipe, took several short puffs, a long one, then picked up a small stack of papers as smoke drifted into the air.

"These are your papers," he said, handing them to Esi. "With these, you will have no problems in America."

"My papers?" Esi asked as she took the documents from him. "How?"

"I may no longer rule this land, but I still have influence." He took another long puff. This was his way when he was thinking. "We have done bad things. Terrible things," he continued as he exhaled smoke. "But we have also loved and fought for our kingdom. Our people. You will not let the good that we have done be forgotten. And you will fight to make right any wrongs we may have done. They must remember Dahomey this way. Promise me you will carry out this last order."

"But how? I do not know America. I will be lost there."

The king put a hand on Esi's shoulder and looked her in the eyes. "You are my fiercest warrior and bravest leader, Esi. No matter the odds, you always manage to find a way."

She turned so the king would not see the tears now forming in her own eyes. He was right, and she knew it. There was nowhere she could go where the French would not find her. This was truly the end. Dahomey had fallen.

"My King. I have no money," she said, remembering everything she owned was in Dahomey. A place she now realized she'd never see again.

The king took another puff, grabbed a ledger from his desk and sat down on his chair.

"Do you think I would not take care of you, Esi?" He tore a page from the ledger and handed it to her. "Remember this name and this number. It is a bank in Harlem, New York. And those are the numbers of an account. There is a man by the name of Morris. He's a good man. He knows our language and he will get things in order for you."

"I don't understand."

"My fathers before me knew our allies would one day betray us, so they set up a way to keep our money safe. We have business relations in America and used their help to set up an account. I have switched control of the account to you."

"I cannot..." Esi started to protest.

"Take it. You'll find there's enough money there to last for generations," he said. "But you must first make your way to Whydah and find the Impresario. It will not be an easy journey. Can you do it?"

When Esi hesitated, Behanzin added, "Please, Esi. Dahomey will live because of you."

Esi stood at attention and took a quick breath. "Yes, my King. But what will you do?"

The king sighed and looked away.

"I will surrender to the French."

"No!" Esi said, shocked at this proclamation.

"It is what's best for my people. And I am done, Esi. I am ready to live in peace."

Esi had never seen the king like this before. This once great king who led thousands into battle, now sat alone in his chair, staring through the window with an unfamiliar look of defeat in his eyes. She wanted to say more. To do more. Surely there was still fight in him. In Dahomey.

"Yes, my King." was all she managed to say.

As she stood at attention in front of him, she knew it would be the last time she'd utter those words. It was too much even for a warrior to bear. Too many goodbyes and too many tears. The life she'd known and loved for so long was at an end.

CHAPTER
TWENTY-EIGHT
COMING FOR YOU

"Get out! They're almost on you!" Byron's voice shouted through Rachel's earpiece.

Vincent, confident in his imminent rescue, remained defiant and laughed at Rachel.

"Sweetie, you'll never get away," he said. "I don't know how you survived that explosion, but next time they'll make sure you're good and dead. They even got the Angel hunting for you."

Sensing an opportunity, Vincent tried to sucker-punch Rachel in the jaw, but she caught his fist with her hand and rammed her forehead into his nose to return the favor.

"God damn!" he shouted as he grabbed his nose with his free hand.

"How did they find me!" she demanded. "What else do they know?"

"You broke my fucking nose!" Vincent yelled. "You broke my..."

"I'll break more than that if you don't talk. What else do they know! Who is the Angel?"

Vincent spit, then pulled a handkerchief from his pocket and held it to his nose.

"They know everything, sweetie. And the Angel? She's just like you. And she's coming for Byron and that nurse boyfriend of yours too."

Rachel felt her heart sink. She took a step back and stumbled on the curb. "What..." she started to say. "How..."

"Rachel!" came Byron's voice from somewhere in the distance.

Thinking he could take advantage of Rachel's confusion, Vincent pushed himself away from the car and walked so close to Rachel she could feel his breath on her face.

"That's right. They're coming for you and your boyfr-"

Rachel brought the butt end of her dagger around and slammed it into Vincent's jaw before he could finish the sentence. He spun halfway around, then fell hard to the ground. A split-second later, two SUVs skidded around the corner and braked just short of Vincent and his guards. Several men got out with guns drawn, but other than a few footprints on the wet pavement, there were no signs of anyone else.

"Byron! Go! Go!" Rachel yelled into her earpiece as she ran down the sidewalk. This time not giving a damn about being seen. "They're coming for you too!"

"Check," Byron said, and immediately began shutting down monitors and powering off equipment.

"No time to get back," Rachel said. "Get to safe point B."

"You going too?" Byron asked.

When Rachel didn't respond, he asked again.

"Rachel?"

"I gotta warn him first," Rachel said.

"Negative," Byron said. "I'll call him. Get your ass to safe point B."

"No, he just pulled a double shift and he'll be sleeping now. He turns his phone off when he sleeps. I have to get there!"

Rachel pulled the earpiece from her ear and stuffed it into a small pocket on the waist of her uniform.

"Rachel. Rachel!" Byron called, but there was no answer. "Dammit, Rachel!"

CHAPTER TWENTY-NINE

FRIDAY NIGHT LIGHTS

The game was already well into the second quarter when Nyah and Desi showed up. Desi's car, a Corolla almost as old as her, needed a new battery. Or maybe it was the alternator. Either way, it was down for the count, so Nyah and Desi met at The Burger Melt and walked to the stadium after a cheeseburger and fries.

They paid for their tickets and headed towards the shouts and cheers in the stands. A few feet from the entrance, Nyah slowed her pace, then stopped. Without missing a beat, Desi walked back to Nyah and wrapped her in a big hug.

"I told you, you look fine," she said, then pulled away to look Nyah in the eyes. "You're killing it in that outfit."

Having never been to a football game, or even watched one on TV for that matter, Nyah wasn't sure what to wear. After some time, she decided on her Bohemian-style floral print beanie cap to go with her retro, red faux leather slim-fit jacket, white sleeveless top, black polka-dot skater skirt and black, hightop Converse. Desi on the other hand kept it simple like always with a pink, tie-dyed T-shirt, jeans and her pink and white Vans.

But it was more than Nyah's choice in clothes that bothered her, and Desi knew it. Nyah didn't like big crowds, and until now she'd managed to avoid them altogether. It was easy before she met Desi and Quin. Lots of things were easier. But this was something she had to do. Wanted to do. So for the first time in her life, she was going to walk herself into a football game, sit with dozens of other people she didn't know and act like she was having a good time.

"I feel like I overdressed," Nyah said.

Desi grabbed Nyah's hand.

"It's perfect," she said as she turned and began walking with Nyah towards the entrance. "You're perfect. I'm perfect. And this moment tonight for Quin will be perfect. But only if we're there. Without us, he'll just crash and burn."

Nyah smiled. "He is pretty helpless sometimes."

"Right? Now let's go show him some love."

THEY SPOTTED DESI'S FRIEND MALCOLM SITTING ON THE FRONT ROW of the stands and made their way over to him.

"Hey Malcolm," Desi said, then made a quick introduction. "Trish, this is Malcolm. Malcolm, Trisha."

When Desi said they were meeting Malcolm at the game, she hadn't prepared herself for this. He was beautiful in every sense of the word, and Nyah suddenly wished she hadn't skipped on the lip gloss. He stood to greet them and Nyah had to look up to make eye contact. He was a good seven inches taller than her.

"Hey, Trisha." Malcolm said.

His voice was deep and silky smooth like melted dark

chocolate poured over a scoop of ice cream. And Nyah was the ice cream. He took her outstretched hand and shook it gently. His grip was strong, his hand smooth, his gaze intense.

"You can just call me Trish."

He smiled. "Okay, Trish. Nice jacket."

Desi gave a thumbs up behind Malcolm and Nyah had to force back a smile.

"Thanks," she said.

Malcolm was a contrast in style. His short-cropped afro and his square, black-rimmed glasses gave him that classic nerd look, but his T-shirt did little to hide his well-defined chest and biceps. Gym muscles, Nyah thought, but damn good ones.

Nyah could spot Malcolm's weak points in an instant. Everything from his stance, to his close proximity to her left him open to an easy attack. But when it came to making some kind of conversation, her brain checked out and left her standing there alone. So instead, she blurted out the first thing that came to mind.

"You should sit in the middle," she said, then immediately regretted it.

So much for first impressions. Her random 90s TV show reference sounded more like a girl desperate to sit close to a guy she'd only just met. Desperate and pathetic.

"Um, Malcolm is in my Chemistry class," Desi said, stepping in to put the wounded conversation out of its misery. "He's always bailing me out of jams."

And there it was in perfect Nyah form. A trained killer of people *and* relationships. This one before it even got past hello.

The trio sat down on the front row with Desi in the middle. Nyah closed her eyes and thanked the gods for small miracles. Maybe if she just kept quiet for the rest of the game she could keep from digging her social grave any deeper.

Not even a minute went by before Malcolm leaned forward and looked in her direction. Nyah tensed. Was he going to say he needed to go sit somewhere else? Worse, tell her she was weird and ask *her* to go sit someplace else? At this point she would. Why not? Just get up and-

"Francis was the unsung hero of that show," he said, then quietly leaned back to watch the game.

The crowd erupted into cheers as the Fonville Jaguars scored another touchdown, but all Nyah could hear were Malcolm's words playing over again in her mind. He actually picked up on the reference. And better yet, he thought it was funny. A small victory, but she was going to savor every last bit of it.

"Yeah, he really was." Nyah said, fighting back a smile.

"Who was the hero?" Desi asked.

Malcolm and Nyah just laughed.

"What's the score?" Nyah asked, trying to change the subject.

"We're up by six. About to be seven after this extra point." Malcolm said. "Quin just ran in a fifty-yard touchdown."

Desi leaned over and nudged Nyah with her elbow.

"That's what all the cheering was about," she whispered, picking up on Nyah's distraction. "I told you he was cute."

Nyah pushed Desi away with her shoulder, but couldn't keep a smile from betraying her illusion of indifference.

THEY WATCHED IN SILENCE AS THE SOUTH HOUSTON BOBCATS FOUGHT their way downfield to try and counter Fonville's last score with one of their own. Desi was leaning forward with her arms resting on her knees, which put Malcolm in better view. Nyah suspected this was on purpose, but she couldn't very well call her out on it. So she let it go and tried her best to act interested in the game.

"This your first year here?" Malcolm asked eventually, still keeping his attention on the game.

Nyah did the same, though she had no idea what was going on.

"Yeah."

Malcolm put two fingers to his lips and whistled when a player from South Houston running downfield with the ball was taken down by a faster player from Fonville. The player recovered and lined up with his teammates for another try.

"You like it here?" he asked.

She was starting to like it more with every passing second.

"It's alright."

On the next play, a player on the Fonville team grabbed a guy who looked like he was about to throw the football and pulled him to the ground. The crowd went crazy, so Nyah assumed it was a good thing. Malcolm clapped and whistled, and Desi stood up and yelled something about a sack.

"Well if you ever need help with chemistry," Malcolm said after the crowd calmed down. "Or..."

He paused for a moment, almost as if he were thinking of something, then turned to face Nyah.

"Or anything else," he said.

Those words, or something about the way he said those words drew her to him. Before she could stop herself, she turned and found herself staring into his eyes. She looked away, then down and then both of them almost turned their attention back to the field again. The game again. Anything but each other again. But again, their eyes met. And this time, neither of them looked away. In that instant, she saw him. The real him. A kid just as scared as she was, trying like hell not to mess things up with life, school, friends, everything. A boy hoping to find something in Nyah's eyes just as much as she was hoping to find it in his. And in that moment, that microsecond in time, they found it.

The crowd erupted into a frenzy of cheers and shouts that startled them both back to reality. They turned away. Back to the game, back to the real world where a player from Fonville was running down the field with the ball.

"Interception!" Desi yelled. "Go, go, go!"

She and just about everyone else were on their feet jumping up and down, shaking the stands from the impacts. Malcolm stood and clapped, but seemed distracted. Nyah sat and watched as the player crossed into the scoring zone, or end zone as Quin called it. Desi grabbed Malcolm in a hug, then turned to Nyah.

"Did you see that?" she asked, then turned back to the game without waiting for a response, oblivious to whatever the hell just happened between Nyah and Malcolm.

Or maybe nothing happened. Maybe she just wanted something to happen so her brain made the whole thing up. Maybe he was actually creeped out when Nyah looked into his eyes like that.

Malcolm glanced over and smiled. She pretended not to notice, but she did. Yeah, something definitely happened.

THE CROWD QUIETED AND THE GAME WENT ON. DESI WAS TALKING TO Malcolm about something that happened on the field, and Nyah was finally relaxed enough to look around and take everything in. The people, laughing and talking. The smell of cheap food. It wasn't bad. Not great, but not ba-

Movement from the top of the visitor stands caught her attention. A man with a rifle! She almost jumped from her seat when the rifle took the shape of a camera. A fucking camera. She tried to laugh it off, but her mind would not give up so easily.

A quick scan of the stadium and she spotted another man standing alone on the ground just next to the visitor stands. Almost out of sight, but not quite. A glance behind her revealed at least two more photographers in the press box. Any one of them a potential sniper. People in the crowd could be in danger. Desi could be in danger. What the hell was she thinking?

Her heart pounded against her chest and her hands began to shake. Desi, noticing something was wrong, leaned back to block Malcom's view of her. Nyah would have to thank her for that later. No way she wanted Malcolm to see her like this.

Nyah closed her eyes and tried to shake off the anxiety, but her mind filled with another vision of Andre. The bullet. The broken window. The screams. The blood. She shook her head. No no no no. Not now. But it was too late. Her mind was back in Oklahoma City, in class with a boy named Andre. This time it was raining. Drops of water turned into blood as they streamed into the classroom through a bullet-riddled window.

Nyah turned from the window to Andre. He smiled, but there was a gaping wound in the center of his forehead. Blood trickled down to his nose and slowly dripped onto the floor.

"What's wrong, Nyah?" he asked, then his smile turned into a wicked grin. "That's right. I know your real name. Why did you lie to me? Why couldn't you just leave me alone? Why-"

"I'm sorry!" Nyah shouted.

"Trish, what?" Desi asked with a look of both confusion and concern.

Oh God. Had she just yelled that out loud? The looks on both Desi and Malcolm's face told her all she needed to know.

"Sorry. Nothing," Nyah said, trying hard, but failing once more to seem like everything was normal.

Nyah tried to force herself back to reality. Back to the game. But it was no use. She looked around. People were everywhere, trapping her in. She couldn't get out if she needed to, and right now she needed to more than anything. Her breathing was short. Her heart raced. A hand touched her wrist. Desi's hand. Desi's big, strong, soft hand.

"I got you," she said softly. "You got this."

Nyah closed her eyes.

"You got this," Desi repeated.

"I... got this."

"Breathe. Just breathe."

"Like the damn song?" Nyah was joking, but now it was all she could hear in her head.

"Yeah. Good song. Just breathe like that."

She breathed. Once. Twice. Three times. Slow and smooth. Steady and calm. She felt the cold metal of the bleachers beneath her. The chatter of the crowd and warm breeze around her. She opened her eyes, took another slow breath, and relaxed.

"You good?" Desi whispered.

"Yeah," Nyah said. "I think." Even though inside she was furious for losing control again.

"I know exactly what you need," Desi said. "Cheesy, crunchy, no good for you nachos. A guilty pleasure guaranteed to calm your nerves."

Nyah was about to protest, but Desi had already pulled some cash from her purse and handed it to Malcolm.

"You mind?"

Malcolm smiled and pushed Desi's hand away.

"I got you," he said. Then to Nyah, "You need anything else?"

She needed lots of things. A normal life that didn't involve getting suspicious anytime someone looked at her just a little too long, or when Danny didn't return a text right away, or when a car drove by just a little too slow, or hell, when someone pointed a camera in her direction. All of that would be just perfect.

"Maybe a Pellegrino if they have any," she said.

"Got you," Andre said. And then he was off.

NYAH WAS WATCHING THE GAME AS IF SHE'D SUDDENLY GAINED interest until she could no longer ignore Desi's intense stare and the big smile on her face.

"Shut up," Nyah said. "Just, shut up."

"I didn't say anything." Desi leaned over and bumped shoulders with Nyah. "But I *saw* everything."

After a few seconds of trying to ignore her, Nyah gave in. Anything to keep her mind off her panic attack.

"Okay, what?" she asked.

"Did you hear how he said that?"

"Said what?"

Desi worked up her best leading-man smolder and lowered her voice. "You need anything else?"

"Come on. He was just being nice."

Desi raised her eyebrows.

"Okay, fine," Nyah said, then looked around to make sure no one else could hear. "It was kinda sexy how he looked right at me when he asked, right?"

"Oh hell yes," Desi said. "He wasn't just asking about snacks, baby girl."

Both girls laughed and Nyah pulled the half-eaten pack of

Spree candy Quin had given her from her sling bag and popped one in her mouth.

South Houston scored a touchdown. People on the visiting side cheered and the South Houston band broke out into a rendition of R-O-C-K in the USA. Nyah was steadfast in her dislike for large crowds, but she had to admit there was something energizing about it all. The lights, the cheers, the warm night air. It was nice. So long as she didn't freak out again.

"I told you you'd have fun," Desi said.

"It's not terrible."

A buzzer sounded.

"That's the two-minute warning," Desi said, pointing to the scoreboard. "I think Quin's gonna find Dustin and ask him to the dance at halftime."

"Half time of what?"

"The game. Damn, Trish. You really don't know sports."

"I told you that."

"Anyway, it's the halfway point of the game when the teams regroup and the band plays on the field. That's when he's going to ask Dustin. I want to go see him and wish him luck."

"You sure he wants you to do that?"

"Why wouldn't he?"

"I mean, he may be nervous."

"Of course he's nervous. Damn, Trish. You aren't too good with people either."

"I'm pretty sure I told you that, too."

"Friends are there for each other. We need to be there for him. You know?"

"Okay. Sure."

Nyah scanned the crowd and spotted Dustin in the stands sitting next to some of his friends. She suddenly felt a little nervous herself. Almost like she was the one about to ask someone to homecoming.

THE BUZZER SOUNDED AND THE PLAYERS LEFT THE FIELD TO SHOUTS and cheers just as Malcolm came back with the nachos.

"No Pellegrino, but I got you a Perrier," he said as he gave her the drink, then handed the nachos to Desi. "I hope that's okay."

"It's fine, thanks," Nyah said.

"Sup, Quin?" Someone shouted from the stands.

Both Nyah, Desi and Malcolm turned to see Quin walking back onto the mostly empty field. He stopped at the mid-field sideline, still in his uniform, holding his helmet to his side and turned to face the crowd.

"What's he doing?" Desi asked.

"You think I know?"

A few more people yelled out to Quin, including Malcolm, but he remained silent and motionless with his head bowed down.

The crowd grew curious. Some shouted "You okay?" and "Ya'll got this, Q!" Still, Quin waited.

"A little dramatic, don't you think?" Nyah asked.

"Shhh. He's about to do something," Desi whispered.

Quin waited for everyone to quiet down, then took a long, deep breath, exhaled, and opened his mouth to speak.

"It's time!" he yelled.

The snap of snare drums filled the air. A marching cadence, crisp and clean, broke the silence as the drum line marched onto the field and lined up just behind Quin. The crowd leapt to their feet. The cheerleaders rushed out, each holding a cardboard square.

Someone else came onto the field and handed Quin a microphone, then rushed off. Quin let the drum line beat out a few more measures before slowly raising it to his mouth. The drumming stopped. Then the cheering. Silence and anticipation filled the stadium.

"Oh hell no," Desi said. "No, no, no."

"What?" Nyah asked. "Is this part of the game?"

"No. He's about to ask Dustin to homecoming right here. In front of everyone!"

CHAPTER THIRTY

TWO TO THE HEART

Byron cranked the engine, shifted into drive and slammed on the gas. The tires spun on the wet pavement, then gripped the ground and jerked the van forward out onto the street.

A blur coming at him from his right. He turned just in time to see a truck speeding towards him and t-bone his van, sending it sliding to the other side of the intersection with bits of shattered glass slicing into his face. The van slid, tipped over and fell onto its side. Byron coughed and tried to move, but his legs were pinned underneath the dashboard. He heard car doors open, then slam shut. He peered through the shattered front windshield and saw two distorted figures walking his way.

He managed to pull one leg free, but the other wasn't so easy. Something sharp had dug itself in, and pulling it only made the pain worse. The men were getting closer now. He gritted his teeth and pulled one last time. The pain felt like a hot iron digging into his leg. He let out a short scream as it pulled free, then launched himself head first into the cargo area of the van just as bullets pierced through the windshield and punched holes in the front seats. That famous picture of Bonnie and Clyde's car shot up by Texas Rangers flashed in Byron's mind. But unlike Bonnie and Clyde, Byron planned to make it out of this one alive.

He rolled to the back and took shelter behind the desk that once held the TV monitors, then pulled his Sig Sauer P226 from its holster. Another round of gunfire pierced through the windshield, bullets tore through the seats and shattered the back window. Using the gunfire to mask the noise, he kicked open the back door. What was now the bottom half of the two doors swung open and hit the pavement. Byron waited for the gunfire to stop, then crawled out and limped his way around the van until he was halfway to the front, just out of sight of the shooters. He heard one of the men kick in the shattered front windshield.

He closed his eyes to listen for the second shooter and pinpoint his location. "Say something. Say something," Byron whispered to himself.

"Check the back!"

Bingo! In one, swift motion, Byron raised his Sig Sauer and moved from behind the shelter of the van. The first man was kneeling down, peering into the van. The other still had his gun drawn, but was pointing it down. Byron shot him first. The bullet pierced his forehead. His head rocked back and he fell to the ground.

"Fuck!" the second guy yelled as he scrambled to get up and aim his gun. Byron put three bullets in him. Two through the heart and one through his head for good measure. His gun fell from his hand and he crumpled to the ground like a rag doll.

Sirens wailed in the distance. Byron checked the SUV to make sure it was clear, then holstered his weapon and quietly limped away, disappearing into the cold, rainy night.

CHAPTER THIRTY-ONE

MEANT TO BE ALONE

Rachel burst through the door to Warren's room, not bothering to catch it before it slammed hard against the wall, waking him from sleep. On instinct, he rolled and reached for the Glock he kept in the nightstand drawer, but a hand caught his wrist before he could pull it open.

"Warren! Get up!"

It was Rachel's voice.

"Rachel?" It was dark and his vision was still a little blurred from sleep, but he could tell Rachel was in her Agojie suit. "What the hell?"

Rachel yanked open a dresser drawer and started pulling out clothes. "We need to go, now!"

Warren knew Rachel well enough not to ask questions when she was like this. When the Agojie Warrior was at the wheel and Rachel was just along for the ride. He pulled off the covers and got out of bed.

"Must be bad if you're putting those shorts together with that shirt. What's going on?"

"I'll explain later. We have to go. Now!" Rachel tossed him the mismatched outfit. "We'll buy more clothes later."

Rachel peeked through the window blinds while Warren changed. The street below his apartment was empty, but that meant nothing.

"Come on. We'll take the fire escape down. Stay away from the windows."

"What about my shoes?"

"Just carry them for now. Put them on later."

"Stop," Warren said.

Rachel moved from the window towards the door. "No! Follow me. We have to get out."

"Look," Warren said, grabbing Rachel's shoulders to get her attention. "I don't know what's going on or what's about to happen, but I trust you."

"Good, now let's g..."

"And I love you, Rachel."

For the first time since she'd entered the room, she stopped and looked Warren directly in the eyes.

"I've known it for a while now, just didn't tell you," He let go of her shoulders, but Rachel didn't move. "I... I just wanted to say that before we walk through this door to whatever hell you're about to lead us into."

"Okay," Rachel said, more stunned than anything.

"You've given me so much in these past few months. Things I never thought I could have again. I'm happy now. Thank you for that."

"Okay," Rachel managed to say again.

"Okay," Warren said. "Now, can we go?"

"Sure."

"Okay," Warren said. He smiled, kissed Rachel on the lips and turned to walk into the living room.

"Wait," Rachel said. "I... I love you too," she said.

"I know," Warren said. "Now come on."

THEY'D JUST MADE IT TO THE LIVING ROOM WHEN THE FRONT DOOR crashed open. Rachel caught a glimpse of a canister tossed inside, but before she could get to Warren it exploded with a loud bang and a flash of light. It was enough to stun Rachel, but only for a moment. A man appeared in the doorway through the haze with a gun pointed straight at her face. Rachel sidestepped and slammed her body against his, knocking him off balance just long enough to pull her knife and drive it deep into his side three quick times. He grunted, stumbled backwards until he tripped over a chair and fell onto the floor.

More gunmen burst through the doors.

"This way!" she yelled to Warren, motioning towards the guest room. There was a window in there that led to the fire escape. If they could get to it, they just might have a chance.

Scattered gunfire broke out just as she slammed her body through the door and fell onto the guest room floor.

"Get down!" she yelled to Warren. But Warren was silent. She looked back and saw him lying face-down on the living room floor.

"Warren!" She got up and ran to his side, ignoring the room full of gunmen now surrounding her. She fell to her knees and rolled him onto his back. His shirt was covered in blood and his eyes were staring past Rachel to the ceiling.

"Get up! Get up, baby!" she yelled, knowing deep down he would never get up again. "No, no, no, no... not like this!"

Something cracked against the back of her skull and everything went dark.

CHAPTER THIRTY-TWO

HOMECOMING KING

This was a bad idea. A very bad idea. Probably the worst idea he'd ever had. But it was too late to go back now. Too late to find some other way to do what he was about to do. He'd look like a damn fool if he walked away now. As his coach always said, win or lose, he was in it to play so he might as well play to win. Still, it felt like a very bad idea.

Quin squeezed the mic so hard he thought it might break, but it was the only way he could keep his hand from shaking.

The cheerleaders flanked him on his left. Silent except for the faint rustling of mylar pompoms in the breeze. The drum line stood at parade rest behind him like statues, waiting for Quin's cue. If it ever came.

Win or lose. Too late to go back now.

He found Desi and Nyah in the crowd and nodded. Desi gave him a thumbs up and smiled, while Nyah just looked at him like a mom watching her kid at his first piano recital. Nervous, a little scared and ready to protect.

He couldn't let them down. Not after all this.

In it to play.

"You got this, Quin!" Desi yelled from the stands. A few others from the crowd echoed the sentiment.

Quin smiled and raised the mic to his lips.

"Hey, I'm Quin." His voice echoed through the speakers, across the field, into the stands.

More cheers. Quin held up a hand to quiet them.

"There's someone..."

He stopped before his shaky voice revealed just how nervous he was. Nyah's words from The Burger Melt echoed through his mind. Big football star is too afraid to ask a boy to homecoming? Damn right he was. Bad idea, Quin. Very bad idea.

Calm, easy, you got this. Desi said so.

He took a breath, then exhaled slowly. After this, things would be different. People would be different and nothing would ever be the same again.

His coach and the rest of the team were lined up in front of the bleachers on the track, waiting like all the rest to see what he was about to do. Coach only let Quin take up time during the half because they were up by so many points. But by the way he kept shifting his weight from one foot to the other and checking his watch, it was clear his patience was about to run out.

People were staring. Of course they were. Curious and patient, but that would soon turn to frustration if he didn't do something soon. Say something soon. But the words weren't there. Just not there. This was a very bad idea.

Coach looked at the other players, shook his head and started towards Quin. It was over. Coach would put a hand on his shoulder, take the mic, tell Quin it was okay and usher him off the field. There'd be some awkward clapping as people looked at each other for answers that weren't there, and life would go on. Just like that. Maybe it was for the best. Maybe people would understand.

He needed to say something. Maybe apologize and say he just wasn't feeling it. Sure, they'd understand. He raised the mic to speak when a memory swept over him like a warm breeze. He closed his eyes and he was there again. One week before the game, lying side by side with Dustin on a soft, grassy hill at Burke Park. They held hands and watched the last rays of sunlight slowly disappear over the horizon, leaving behind a bright red and pink fire in the sky.

"We do this. We go all in like this, and we win," Dustin had said to him. "No more hiding, no more games. Whatever the world has to say, whatever the fuck they throw at us after that, we win because we'll be free, Quin. That's everything. That's the game right there."

He opened his eyes and saw his coach was halfway across the track. A few more seconds and it would be too late.

He wouldn't walk away from this. No more hiding. It was time to be free. Time to go all in.

Quin raised a hand to stop his coach. Whether it was out of respect for Quin or just plain curiosity, he did. But probably not for long. Coach was ready to end this thing. But that was okay, because so was Quin.

"As you can tell, I'm a little nervous," Quin said into the mic.

Laughter from the crowd, then someone whistled.

Quin looked at Dustin sitting on the third row and smiled. Dustin smiled back.

Might as well play to win.

"Listen, there's someone in the crowd tonight. Someone special."

~

Nyah was both amazed and concerned at how nervous Quin seemed on the field. This was his home, the place he felt most comfortable. Yet there he was like a frightened little boy, almost too scared to speak. She wanted to help, but there was nothing to do but watch. And maybe protect if she had to.

"I bet it's Jasmine," a girl behind Nyah said.

"Oh God, yes," her friend responded. "He's always talking to her in Biology class."

Realizing this could go one of two ways, Nyah clenched her fists, ready to throw down on anyone who laughed, or worse, yelled out some slur when Quin made his announcement.

"Someone I'd very much like to ask to the homecoming dance," Quin said. "It may be a surprise, but..." Another pause, then, "I want you to know, this is real. This is me."

He looked down again, as if to contemplate his next move, then turned and pointed to the line of drummers behind him.

A lone snare drummer kicked into a crisp, tight drum roll, and one by one the cheerleaders began turning around their cardboard squares.

The first sign read "How about," the next four were the letters H-O-C-O.

"Who is she?" Someone yelled from the stands, followed by a few more cheers and screams. The last cheerleader turned her cardboard square to reveal Dustin's name.

The snare drum stopped, and for a few seconds, there was silence. Nyah heard one of the girls a few rows back gasp. She was about to get up and head her way when Desi stood up first.

"We love you, Quin!" she yelled.

Then someone else shouted in agreement, followed by another. Then the entire crowd was on their feet, cheering and shouting. A sound so loud, Nyah thought people could hear it from blocks away. She stood up and looked around. Everyone was cheering. Actually cheering for Quin.

Then, all at once, they started chanting Dustin's name.

"Dustin! Dustin! Dustin!"

Nyah spotted Dustin, still sitting down, and for a moment thought he might run away. But he didn't. After a few more chants of his name, he stood up and made his way down to the field. He turned and waved at the crowd, and the cheers kicked into high gear.

Dustin took the mic from Quin's hand and stood silent until the crowd noise died down. Then slowly raised the mic to his mouth.

"Yes!" Before he could say another word, the crowd lost their collective mind. Dustin handed the mic to someone and hugged Quin. The cheerleaders were waving pompoms, jumping and shouting and the drum line broke out into a hip-hop rhythm. Desi held out her hand, palm up, to Nyah. Nyah smiled and slapped it.

"I'm so proud of him right now," Desi said, clearly holding back tears.

"Desi, are you crying?"

"Don't judge me," Desi said, wiping her eyes. "See. I told you we'd have fun tonight."

CHAPTER THIRTY-THREE

WATCH YOUR BACK

Quin was named Homecoming King. A moment made more special after confessing his deepest secret to the crowd. Even Nyah gave a little shout when they called his name.

After the game, he invited Dustin and a few friends, including Desi, Nyah and Malcolm, to The Burger Melt, then to watch a movie at his place. Quin always liked to wind down after a game with a quiet night. It sounded nice, but Friday nights were reserved for Danny. It was their pizza and movie night. A tradition Danny and her mom started when she was pregnant with Nyah. After her mom died it seemed more important than ever to keep it going. So every Friday night, Danny and Nyah would relax on the couch with some good pizza, a movie and a framed picture of her mom sitting on the end table. It was an exclusive event. Not even Jada was invited.

Desi caught a ride with Dustin. He offered to give Nyah a ride home, but she didn't mind the walk. It was only about two miles to her house from the school, and she needed the time to decompress from the game. It was a lot to take in.

Quin's surprise homecoming proposal, the unexpected and complete acceptance from the crowd. And of course Malcolm and that... What even was that? A moment? Yeah, that felt right. A damn nice one too. Who knows, maybe he'd ask *her* to homecoming.

She took the same route back as she and Desi took to get there, cutting through smaller neighborhood roads when she could. She was halfway down one of those roads and still lost in thought when she realized the lone streetlight, which was on when she and Desi passed by earlier, was out now. Something else was off too. It took her a second, but then remembered the damn dog. It was barking its head off on their way to the game, but not a peep now.

She'd let her guard down. It seemed to be happening more often these past few days. Maybe having friends did that to you. Looking around, she realized this would be a perfect place to set a trap. Even the older-model Lexus parked just to her left in front of an empty lot could serve as good cover for an ambu-

A blur of a figure launched itself from behind the car. Nyah turned and instinctively raised an arm just in time to block a punch just inches from her face, but wasn't so lucky with the second one. A blow to the ribs that knocked the wind from her lungs.

"Unph!" was all Nyah could get out.

The pain distracted Nyah long enough to miss a quick and powerful uppercut to her chin. Stars filled Nyah's vision and before she could recover, the figure followed with a left hook to Nyah's jaw that snapped her head to the side. She stumbled back a few steps in front of the car, tripped on the curb and fell onto the grass.

Nyah pushed herself to her knees, but a kick to her injured ribs sent her back down to the ground with waves of pain shooting through her mid-section. Nearly unconscious, Nyah looked up just in time to see her attacker raise a foot to stomp Nyah's head and finish the job.

Nyah's training kicked in. She caught the foot in both hands and twisted with all the strength she had left. Her attacker grunted and fell to the ground face first.

Nyah rolled and sprang to her feet, still trying to catch her breath. She reached for her knife, then remembered she'd left it at home. The attacker seized on Nyah's distraction, twisted on the ground and kicked the side of her leg, sending a bolt of pain through her body. Nyah stumbled, giving the attacker just enough time to get up and deliver a jump kick to Nyah's chest, pushing her back towards the drainage ditch that ran alongside the road, then finished with a strong right hook that connected with Nyah's temple. Nyah spun to her right, then fell face first to the grass and rolled limply into the ditch.

This time, she didn't get up.

NYAH WAS STILL CONSCIOUS, BUT JUST BARELY. THE ATTACKER standing over her on the road looked like a blurry, shadowy figure of death. And for the first time, she could make out the shape of a woman.

After a quick check to make sure no one was watching, the woman walked down the slight embankment and knelt by Nyah's side.

"Hey, Nyah," she said while trying to catch her breath. "You put up quite the fight there!"

This close, Nyah could make out more details. She was wearing a bodysuit made from a deep green and black fabric with a matching mask that covered most of her face. A black skull was sewn into the side of the neck.

Paper-thin memories danced through her mind. Names

she could almost make out, but not quite. Covered by a thin veil. Montell- something. Bruno maybe? The.... The Angel. That one she remembered. She'd found them. But how?

The Angel pulled what looked like a knife from behind her back. Nyah made a move to get up, but the Angel grabbed her shoulder.

"No, hun. You're coming with me."

"Hey!" came a voice from somewhere in the distance.

"You need help?" Another voice yelled out.

A group of teens, likely coming home from the game, were walking towards them. The Angel stood and slid her knife back into its sheath.

"Lucky night, I guess," She said to Nyah, then jumped out of the ditch, hopped into the Lexus and sped off into the night.

The teens came into Nyah's view a few seconds later. She tried asking for help, but could only silently mouth the word. Even if Coach Stasney from gym class had taught it to her in sign language it wouldn't have made a difference. Nyah could barely open her eyes, let alone raise a hand to sign.

"Damn, she's beat up bad! Call for help," she heard one of them say just before the world around her went dark.

CHAPTER THIRTY-FOUR

THE IMPRESARIO

WHYDAH, AFRICA - DECEMBER, 1892

The looming clouds teased, but failed once more to bring the relief of rain to the dry and dusty afternoon. Esi sat alone with a glass of sodabi at a table in the back of a run-down shebeen. In a coastal city like Whydah, one could find all types of imported liquors, but Esi preferred the sweet taste of local sodabi.

She knew these types of establishments were forbidden in Dahomey, yet they thrived. No matter where you go, people always need a drink. And no matter how hard you try, you can never keep them from finding one.

The cool dirt beneath her feet and the darkened room were comforting after such a long journey. She sipped her drink and waited for the impresario. A man named Louis who was determined to make money from putting her sister warriors on display in Paris and then America. She did not like the man for this, but she needed him to get her to America and fulfill her final promise to her king. And from what she'd gathered, he came here just about every day for a drink.

The journey to Whydah had been long and treacherous. The king was right, the French wanted her dead, and it was hard to go a day without seeing at least one sketched picture of her face nailed to the side of a building or post. But she knew the land well. Much better than the French. She'd stuck to back trails and roads during her walk and used disguise and subterfuge, old tricks perfected by the Agojie warriors, when she needed to stop at a village or town to resupply. Even now, she dared not pull back the hood that covered her head for fear of being recognized.

A tall, skinny man dressed in a tan suit and derby hat entered the Shebeen. His pale complexion, reddened from the African sun made him stand out among the other patrons. He was accompanied by three women dressed in deep red and blue striped dresses with flowered headdresses. Agojie attire. Two of the women were muscular and tall, while the third resembled more beast than human. She was maybe twice Esi's size in both girth and muscle mass. Her hand alone was the size of Esi's head. All three women carried machetes on their belts. There was no doubt this was the impresario with the women he intended to show.

The small crowd of people cleared a path as the newcomers made their way to two tables near Esi in the back. Most turned or bowed their heads as the women passed, knowing it was forbidden to look at an Agojie warrior.

They sat at two tables. One for him, the other for his companions. He yelled for whisky and a woman across the room immediately got up from her chair to fulfill his order. Apparently, he was accustomed to having his way in this place. Esi took another drink of her sodabi and watched as he pulled a stack of papers from his bag and began rifling through them, not even bothering to look up when the woman set his drink down in front of him.

A minute later, a young woman no older than eighteen, stumbled and bumped into his table, splashing a bit of his whisky from his glass.

"You stupid fool!" he yelled. "Look what you did."

She grabbed a cloth and clumsily tried to clean up the mess. "I am sorry, sir," she said in slightly slurred speech.

Annoyed, the impresario delivered a back-hand slap to the woman's cheek, sending her sprawling to the floor. A man a few tables down stood and ran to her side.

"Afia!" he said as he knelt to help her back to her feet. "Are you hurt?"

"No. I am fine," she said, pressing one hand to her cheek.

Esi could see tears in her eyes. Formed partly from the sting of the slap, and partly from the sting of embarrassment.

The man turned to the impresario and pounded his fist on the table.

"Do not touch her again!" he shouted.

The impresario, already back to his papers, did not look up. When the man persisted, one of the three women he'd come in with stood up and touched her hand to the hilt of her machete. The man's eyes widened.

"My apologies," he said, as he held his hands out and backed away. A few steps back, he turned to the young woman and helped her back to their table.

ESI HAD SEEN ENOUGH. IT WAS TIME TO TALK BUSINESS. SHE FINISHED her drink, stood up and walked to his table.

"Louis?" she asked.

Louis sighed and shook his head, then slammed a fist down on the table.

"Will you people not let me rest? Go away! I am busy."

Esi put a golden coin with the king's seal on the table and Louis looked at it with moderate interest. He'd heard of these coins, but had never seen one in person. He put his papers aside and ran his fingers across the engraved image of the king's face. They were special coins, handed out by the king himself to his messengers. Anyone presented with one knew immediately the person presenting had a message from the king himself.

Louis picked up the coin, examined it for a moment, then tossed it back down on the table and leaned back in his chair to look up at Esi.

"What do you have for me?" He took a small sip of whisky and dabbed the corner of his mouth with a handkerchief. "Make it quick."

Esi sat down in the chair across from him.

"Did I ask you to sit?"

"No," Esi said.

Louis shook his head, looking both annoyed and partly astonished at Esi's bold move.

"What is it you want? You have a message? Quick with it. And take off that hood. I demand to see who I'm talking with."

"I am the message," Esi said, without removing her hood. "The king wishes you to transport me to America."

Louis only laughed and slid the coin back across the table to Esi.

"The king? What king? Have you not heard? Your king is finished. You have a new king now." He flicked a hand at Esi as if to shoo away a bug. "I suggest you go away before you get into trouble here."

Esi picked up the coin and slid it back into her satchel.

She'd anticipated this. Why should a Frenchman like this, loyal only to money, be willing to do a favor for a fallen king?

"I can see you are a man of business," she said. "Why do something if there's nothing in it for you, no?"

"Exactly," he said. "And by the looks of it, you have nothing to offer me."

He picked up his glass and examined the color of the whisky for a few seconds before taking another sip. He pursed his lips from the sting, then placed it neatly back onto the table. Esi waited patiently. The three women at the next table glared at Esi as they whispered to each other and drank. Louis glanced up and smiled. It seemed he was enjoying the power he held for the moment.

"And yet, she remains!" he said, then leaned in closer to Esi. His cheeks were pitted with pockmarks and his breath smelled of whisky and stale smoke. "As a favor to your king, I will let you walk out of here unharmed. But my kind offer will end very soon. Go now."

He stared at Esi for a moment longer. When she remained seated, he smiled, leaned back in his chair and swirled the whisky around in his glass.

"You are a stubborn woman. Fine. Then I shall enjoy watching you di-"

Esi reached across the table and grabbed Louis's wrist, splashing whisky onto his hand. Louis tried to pull away, but her grip was a steel trap. Esi pulled him closer and leaned in until their faces were mere inches apart. Her cold, dark eyes, visible from underneath her hood, sent a shiver down his spine. A look of fear and uncertainty flashed across his face.

"You may fool a few French and Americans with these women," Esi said, then looked to his companions sitting at the next table. "But not many will pay to see such cheap imposters as these."

At once, the three women stood and grabbed the handles of their machetes. Esi let go of Louis's wrist and he immediately pulled it to his chest like an injured animal. His confidence shaken, concern and fear challenged the superiority he'd assumed until this moment.

"How dare you make such an accusation!" Louis said as he gently massaged his injured wrist. "I can assure you, these women are some of the finest Amazons Dahomey has to offer. And now I will sit and watch with pleasure as they prove it by breaking you into pieces."

Esi knew well the name of Amazon, given to her people by European missionaries who were fascinated with their abilities. She and her sisters loathed it, but could do little to stop the white man's fascination with the name.

"These women are no more Amazons than you are," she said. "They are not worthy to clean the feet of a real Agojie warrior!"

The big woman stepped forward and glared down at Esi.

"You will pay for these insults!" She said, her voice as deep as any man's.

She tried to pull her Machete, but only got as far as touching the handle before Esi grabbed her hand and jerked the big woman forward and off balance. Esi stood and pivoted around her, wrenched the woman's arm behind her back and pushed it high up towards her neck. The woman gritted her teeth and whimpered. With her free hand, Esi grabbed a handful of the woman's hair and slammed her head onto the table hard enough to shake more whisky from Louis's glass.

Esi gave her wrist another hard yank towards her neck and this time the woman cried out in pain. Silence swept over the shebeen as patrons stopped to watch the spectacle. Most with great satisfaction. The other two women moved in to help their comrade, but stopped short when Esi pulled the hood of her cloak back just far enough to reveal her face. They recognized Esi at once, and for a moment, stood frozen in disbelief. Slowly, without turning away, they backed up to their table and sat down.

Esi pulled her cloak back over her head and leaned in close to the big woman, whose face she still kept pinned to the table.

"If I ever see you or your friends in Agojie dress again, I will slit your throats and let you bleed out on the dirt while the dogs circle and wait for you to die."

"Yes, Agojie Esi! So sorry! We did not know it was you." the woman said through clenched teeth. "Please let me go!"

Esi released her grip and the woman stumbled to her feet. Her look of disdain now replaced with fear as she stared, wide-eyed, at Esi. Without turning around, she cradled her injured arm, bowed her head and backed up to sit down with her friends.

"Good God," Louis said, nervously looking around the room. Most everyone who stopped to witness the commotion was now going about their business as if nothing happened. Esi had no enemies here. The ones who saw her face would keep it to themselves for now, only to tell stories of it for years to come.

"What on earth? Esi? It's really you?" Louis asked. "What are you doing here?"

Esi picked up Louis's whisky, finished it off in one drink and slammed the empty glass back down onto the table, startling Louis.

"That's how you drink a whisky," she said. "Now, can we talk business?"

Louis only gaped at Esi, still stunned by her presence.

"Here is my offer, Louis. Take me with you and I'll give the Europeans and Americans a show they will not forget," she said. "Nor will they forget the name of the man who brought it to them."

The sound of money and fame was enough to shake Louis from the temporary shock of seeing Esi in person. And more than enough to dissuade him of any thoughts of turning her in for a small reward. He pushed his papers to the side and gestured for Esi to sit back down.

"It seems we'll be doing business together after all," he said with a smile.

CHAPTER
THIRTY-FIVE
FIGHT OR HIDE

Danny, Desi and Quin waited patiently in the hospital room for any signs of movement, noise or hope from Nyah.

Quin sat on a tiny couch reading a book. His tall, muscular frame made the couch seem more like a toy than actual furniture. Desi stood by the window looking out, turning back to Nyah every time she stirred or made a noise. Danny sat in a big chair next to Nyah's bed, drifting in and out of sleep to the quiet rhythm of the beeping monitors.

After what seemed like hours of waiting, Nyah's voice cracked. "Dan. Danny."

Everyone got to their feet and surrounded Nyah's bed.

"Call the nurse, Quin," Danny said while getting up. Quin darted from the room with all the agility of a high school running back.

Danny walked to her side and took her hand. "Hey..." Desi was standing just behind him, so he stopped just short of calling her Ny-bear.

Nyah's eyes flickered, then opened halfway.

"What the hell happened?" she said in a gravelly voice.

"You're in the hospital. You got jumped," Danny grabbed a cup of water sitting next to her bed. "Your throat's dry. Drink."

Nyah tilted her head up just enough for Danny to put the cup to her lips and drink. Then her eyes shot open wide and she tried to sit up, spilling a little water on her gown in the process. Danny tried to calm her as best he could.

"You gotta rest," Danny said. "You were out for a while."

"It's her!" Nyah said. "It's-"

"Easy now," Danny interrupted.

Nyah spotted Desi in the room and got the message. She repositioned herself in the bed to get a better look.

"Hey, Desi. Wha... what are you doing here?" she asked.

"You're serious?" Desi laughed. "Trish. I'm your friend. Remember what we talked about?"

"Sorry. I told you I was bad at this."

"You'll get used to it. How you feeling?"

"Like I got hit by a bus."

Quin walked back into the room, followed closely by the nurse.

"Hello, Trisha," she said, walking over to Nyah's bed and checking the monitors. "How are you feeling?"

"A little nauseous and I have a bad headache, but I guess okay otherwise."

"You took one hell of a beating."

Nyah shifted in her bed again. "Can we raise this thing? I feel like you're all standing around at my funeral."

"Of course." The nurse pressed a button on the bed and raised Nyah to a sitting position. "Better?"

"Yeah. Thanks."

The nurse checked Nyah's eyes and blood pressure, asked a few more questions, then scribbled a few notes on her chart.

"I'll have the doctor come check on you soon," she said.

"We'll see what we can do about that headache." And then she left.

For a while, everyone just stood around Nyah's bed, thankful for the moment, but unsure of what to say next to their beaten and bruised friend. Things like "Are you okay," and "Is there anything we can do?" seemed meaningless. She'd just been beaten nearly to death, then left alone in a ditch. Of course she wasn't okay.

"Oh damn, almost forgot," Quin said finally.

He sprinted to his backpack sitting by the tiny couch, pulled a Burger Melt bag from one of the pockets and walked back to Nyah's side.

"You hungry?" he asked.

She was starving, but hadn't thought about it until now.

"Yeah. Pretty hungry."

"Cool. I know they're gonna feed you here, but we brought you this." He sat the bag on her lap. "Cheeseburger and fries. It may not be hot anymore but..."

Nyah opened the bag and took the food out, then pressed the bag flat on her lap and sat the cheeseburger and fries neatly on top. For a moment, she said nothing. Did nothing. Her eyes, fixed steadily on the food, were moist with tears.

"I could heat it up," Quin said after a few moments.

Nyah looked up, seeming only now to remember the small crowd of people standing around her.

"No. It's... It's perfect," she said, wiping the corners of her eyes. "Thank you."

"Damn, girl. It's just a cheeseburger," Desi said.

"With no drink," Nyah fired back. A joke funny enough to ease the tension in the room and give everyone a moment to remember everything was okay. Even if it wasn't.

"There's a cafeteria," Quin said to Desi. "Let's get the girl something to drink."

DANNY WAITED FOR THE ROOM DOOR TO CLICK SHUT, THEN SAT BACK down in the chair near Nyah's bed and began fidgeting with his bucket hat. Nyah tried to ignore him, but it was no use. He had something to say. Something she didn't want to hear. But putting off this conversation any longer would only make it worse. Might as well rip off the band-aid and get it over with.

"What's on your mind?" Nyah asked in between bites of cheeseburger.

Danny looked almost surprised at the question.

"Nybear. You know what's on my mind." He paused for a moment as if waiting for Nyah to tell him. When she said nothing, he sighed and rested one of his big hands on the bedrail. "We have to leave. We have to cut and run."

Nyah sat her cheeseburger down on the bag, closed her eyes and leaned her head back.

"Tomorrow at the latest. Maybe Florida this time," Danny said. "You gotta say goodbye."

Danny waited a beat. When Nyah didn't respond, he said, "Look I know this is hard-"

"You don't know!" Nyah shouted, filling the quiet room with her voice, then immediately grabbed her throat from the pain it caused.

Dany raised his eyebrows, but waited to speak until Nyah had her say.

"How could you?" She continued, this time almost in a whisper. "Desi and Quin are my friends. Actual friends! I can't just leave them."

Danny stood and walked to the window to gaze out at the traffic below. It always amazed him how the world just kept spinning no matter what hell someone might be going through. A life-changing injury, a terminal diagnosis, or in their case, a mob contract that kept them forever on the run and always looking over their shoulders.

"Sorry, I didn't mean to yell," Nyah said.

"Do you know what makes the Angel so dangerous? What makes her Bruno's number one assassin?" Danny asked, still watching the traffic pass by below. "She's patient. Likes to take her time on jobs. Always waiting in the shadows, calculating her next move, waiting for her target to slip up just once and fall into her trap. The Angel loves playing the long game."

Nyah shifted in her bed, suddenly feeling anxious and a little uncomfortable. Danny left the window and went to her side.

"She didn't just show up tonight, Nybear. She's been here, hiding in plain sight, waiting for you or me to slip up." he said.

"Like tonight, walking down that dark street with my head somewhere else," Nyah said.

Danny nodded.

"You got lucky this time, but she's patient and she won't make the same mistake twice. Listen to me Nybear. She'll kill you. Hell, she might kill your friends too just for fun. The Angel loves this shit. Some people play golf or do puzzles. She likes to kill. It's who she is."

Nyah suddenly lost her appetite and set her cheeseburger down on the paper bag next to the half-eaten bag of fries.

"How did they find us this time, Danny? And so fast. We haven't even been here that long."

Danny shook his head.

"They've done this before, and they're getting better. But so are we. Listen, I know this sucks, but we have to go. I promised your mom I'd keep you safe, and that's what I'm going to do."

Nyah closed her eyes and fought back tears as thoughts of

her mom rushed into her mind. It was no use. The tears flowed. Danny pulled her close and hugged her.

"Will we ever be safe?" she asked.

Danny was about to say he didn't know. That he'd been asking himself that same question ever since the Montello family put the contract out on the Agojies. But so long as they stuck together, they would be fine. And one day, maybe sooner than later, they would figure a way out. He opened his mouth to speak when the door clicked open and Quin and Desi walked in. Danny let go of Nyah and sat down in his chair.

"We had to search around for this," Desi said, putting a cold bottle of mineral water on Nyah's table. "Not as easy as you might think."

Noticing the odd tension in the air, she added "Did we interrupt something?"

"No," Nyah said, still looking at Danny. "We were just talking about when I could go home. Thanks for the drink."

CHAPTER THIRTY-SIX

I NEED WORK

HARLEM, NEW YORK - 1901

Esi sat in a chair across the desk from a man named Morris. She wasn't sure what he did at the bank, but judging by the fine material and stitching of his suit, he was probably someone important. He was a big man, almost too big for his clothes, with thin, wire-framed glasses that he only wore when he was writing or reading.

"I will need work," Esi said.

"No," Morris said without looking up.

"No?"

Since leaving her homeland, Esi learned enough English to understand people and hold simple conversations, but it was nice to meet someone who spoke the Fon language. Though she wished he might speak a little more.

Morris slid a piece of paper across the desk. "Sign here, please," he said in Fon.

"No."

"No? You will not sign?"

"No. I mean yes." she said, reaching for a pen and signing the paper. "When I'm not fighting, I work. I always work. So I need work."

Seeming to ignore her, Morris pulled the paper up and slid it in with the others, then tucked them all neatly into a folder.

"Do you understand me?" Esi said.

"Yes. Very well."

Esi's patience was wearing thin with this man. Was he not listening or was he just dumb?

"Do you have work for me?"

He put down the file, pulled off his glasses and looked Esi in the eyes.

"Esi, as of now, you have more money than your great-grandchildren could spend in their lifetime, should you have any. You are a wealthy woman. Look, I will show you."

He pulled the top page from the folder, slid it across the desk to Esi and pointed to a number at the bottom.

Esi glanced at the number, shook her head and slid the paper back.

"The king promised me money, but so much?"

"So much. And with the interest it will earn in the account I've set up for you, it will grow to be much, much larger."

"So much," Esi said. "Too much."

"Not enough," Morris said, taking the paper and returning it to the folder.

"Too much."

Morris sighed and looked around the room to make sure no one was within earshot.

"I know who you are, Esi of the Agojie. In Dahomey, everyone knows your name. You are the hero of our kingdom."

"I fought for my kingdom, but I do not ask for gifts in return."

"This is no gift, Esi. You've given so much to your king and the kingdom. It's time we pay you back."

Esi leaned back in her chair, resigning herself to lose this argument with Morris.

"Still, Mr. Morris. You see, I need work."

"No."

Esi held out her arms in frustration, "Again with no!"

"Tell me, do you have accommodations?" Morris asked, once again ignoring Esi's protests. Noticing her confusion, he added, "A place to live."

"No. The man I came here with paid for my room, but he is gone."

"We have apartments above the bank. We'll set you up on the top floor. The largest and most grand. It comes fully furnished, so you won't need to worry about anything."

Morris stood up, but Esi remained seated and looking down at the desk.

"Esi. There is no more fighting for you. No more killing. You can live the rest of your days in peace and luxury."

He waited a moment, noticed Esi's solemn look, a look of disappointment, then slowly sat back down.

"And that's precisely the problem, isn't it?" he asked.

"I need work," Esi repeated.

Morris nodded his head. "You need work."

Morris leaned back in his chair and chewed on the end of his glasses. For a time, he seemed to be lost in thought. Esi was about to say something when Morris spoke up.

"I may have some work. Something perfectly suited to a woman such as yourself."

For the first time since she'd met the man, Morris had her full attention.

CHAPTER THIRTY-SEVEN

MOVING DAY, PART 2

Nyah sat on her bed, thankful to be home, but sad to know it might no longer be her home tomorrow.

She knew the rules. If your cover is blown, it's time to go. No goodbyes, just pick up and go. The longer you stayed, the more you put yourself and the people you knew in danger. The best thing to do for everyone was to follow the rules. Better for her, better for Danny, for Desi and Quin. But she was tired of being scared. Tired of starting over. Tired of running. She wanted to stay. To fight. To live her life. But if she stayed, wouldn't things only get worse?

A text message from Malcolm sat unanswered on her phone.

> Hey Trish. Heard what happened. Hope you're feeling better. Maybe we could get a burger sometime?

She typed out a response.

Hey, I'm okay. Thanks for asking! A burger sounds 🔥

She considered sending it. Her fingers hovering over the keypad mere inches from the send arrow. Her thoughts raced. Or was that her heart?

She deleted the message and tossed her phone on the bed. She thought of Quin and Desi and realized how selfish it was to consider staying. She had to do what was best for them. Before she could change her mind, she picked up her phone and typed out a quick text to Quin.

Can you talk?

It only took a few seconds for his response.

About to call dad. Talk after?

So Quin would have to wait. She sighed, then sent the same question to Desi. A few seconds later, Nyah's phone buzzed.

"Hey," Nyah said.

"Hey Trish. What's up?"

"So it's like... We're..." Nyah couldn't bring herself to say it.

"You're what?"

Nyah kept quiet, unable to respond, unable to say a damn thing without breaking down and crying. Why did it always have to come to this?

"You still there?" Desi asked.

"Damn it, Desi. Why'd you have to be my friend?" Nyah asked, breaking her silence.

"What?"

"Why couldn't you and Quin just leave me alone?" Nyah hadn't expected to start crying, but here she was.

"What the hell, Trish? You okay?"

"Sorry."

"What's going on?"

"We're moving."

"What? Where?"

"California," she lied. "Danny got a new job there."

"The fuck?"

"Sorry."

"Stop saying sorry."

"I am. I don't want to go."

"Damn. When?"

"Tomorrow."

"What? When did he get the job?"

"Yesterday. They needed him quick." The lies were well practiced and flowed easily from her lips.

Nyah heard Desi exhale into the phone, followed by a few seconds of silence.

"The hell, Trish?" Her voice now a little choked up. "How we gonna go to the dance together and watch Quin trip over his feet when he tries to dance with Dustin? And I think Malcolm is going to be there too."

"Why would I care about that?" Nyah managed a small laugh.

Desi brought back her leading-man deep voice again, a flashback to the game. "You need anything else, sweet thing?"

"If he called me that, he'd be the one in the hospital."

Now both girls laughed, but it was short lived. The threat of tears that never seemed to run out waited in the shadows. Even now they loomed. Waiting to take over and confess the emotions they both wanted so badly to keep hidden. Nyah took a breath and slowly exhaled, trying desperately to control the sadness, the pain, the regret.

"I guess you'll have to laugh at Quin without me."

"God damn!"

"God damn."

"Can I at least help you pack?"

"Already done," Another lie. "We're leaving in the morning."

"That's just not right. You can't just leave us like that, Trish! Does Quin know yet?"

"No. He hasn't called me back. I wish I had a choice, Desi. I do. But I don't. I never have a choice."

"What do you mean, never?"

"It's nothing."

"Look, let's at least meet up with Quin at The Burger Melt one last time. You gotta be hungry, right?"

"Okay," Nyah heard herself saying.

"Okay?"

A pause, then "Yeah, I'd like that."

"Great! What time?"

Nyah cracked open her door and heard the sounds of a movie playing in the living room. Danny and Jada taking a break from packing. She closed the door and leaned with her back against it.

"How about now?"

"I'll call Quin," Desi said. "See you there."

Nyah ended the call and grabbed her sweater. This was wrong. So wrong. Danny would have a fit if he knew. But right now, she didn't care. Right now, she wanted to be a normal, teenage girl one last time before her life was turned upside down yet again. Right now, she would have a damn cheeseburger and fries with the only two friends she'd ever known. Right fucking now.

Her plan might even work. If she slipped out through her window, she could get to The Burger Melt and back before the movie ended. Yeah, she could pull this off.

She was about to open the window and jump outside when she remembered her phone. Slow down, slow down. Get the phone, leave the house, come back before anyone notices you're gone.

Just as she was sliding her phone into the pocket of her sweater, it buzzed. She pulled it out and saw a text message from an unidentified number. Her heart sank when she read it. The feeling rushed from her legs, forcing her to sit down on the edge of the bed.

> Bang bang, the football star is dead. Run away from me, and Desi will be next. 10 tomorrow night, bayou trails at Elm under the bridge. Come alone. I'll know if you don't.

CHAPTER THIRTY-EIGHT

WORK FOR A WARRIOR

After the paperwork was finished, Morris had someone escort Esi to her new apartment on the top floor of the bank building. He hadn't lied. It was grand and beautiful and reminded Esi of the king's palace back home. But she was not ready to rest, so she put on some clothes provided by the impresario, and set out to meet the woman, Izara. The one Morris said was in need of help.

She knew the way. Morris had shown her on a map. But navigating the streets of Harlem, with so many buildings and people, was no easy task. In Dahomey, people would clear a path wherever she and her sisters walked. Here, they didn't even seem to notice her. Esi could walk over thorns without flinching, but she found the streets of New York tested her patience in ways she had never known.

About a half hour after she set out from the bank, she found what she was looking for. The shop Morris told her about. A sign hung crooked on the doorway with the words *Threads and Fabrics* written in English. Esi recognized it from a picture Morris had shown her. She crossed the street, nearly avoiding a collision with a horseless carriage, and stepped onto the curb. She was about to walk into the store when two men with long, blue coats and funny hats stopped her. One of them had a strange-looking mustache that rolled upwards on either end.

“Where you goin’ in such a hurry?” the man with the mustache asked.

Not quite understanding them, Esi only shook her head. But this seemed only to agitate the men.

“Can’t speak English?” the other man asked. Each of them carried sticks and wore badges on their jackets.

Another blue-coated man joined the group, positioning himself behind Esi. Esi glanced back, shifted her weight and turned her body slightly towards the newcomer.

One of the men touched Esi’s medallion on her necklace with his stick.

“What’s this? Looks expensive. Did you steal it?”

Esi pushed the stick away, which only angered the man. He stepped closer to Esi. So close, she could feel his breath on her face.

“We gonna have a problem here?” he asked.

The plan formed quickly. She’d ram her forehead into his nose, grab the stick from his hand, turn and crack the jaw of the man behind her, duck a blow from the man with the mustache and finish with a foot sweep to knock him to the ground. This would stun them all just long enough for Esi to pull her knife and finish the job.

“Hello!” came a voice from the shop just as Esi was preparing to ram her head into the man’s nose. “So sorry!”

A woman emerged from the shop and stepped between Esi and the first man in blue.

“She’s my friend and she’s still learning the language,” the woman said.

The man with the mustache looked at his friends, then at the new woman.

"Keep a better eye on her," he said. "She almost got herself into some trouble."

"Yes sir," the woman said, grabbing Esi by the elbow and urging her to follow her inside. "Thank you for your help."

She smiled and gave a wave to the men, then whispered in the Fon language, "Come inside with me."

Esi pulled her arm away. "You are Izara?" she asked, relieved to meet someone else who spoke her native tongue.

The woman stopped and turned to Esi. She was tall and slim with long, dark braided hair held back with an African boho-print headband. Judging by her smooth, bronze skin Esi guessed her to be no more than twenty years in age.

"How do you know me?" She asked.

"Morris told me of you."

"Morris? From the bank? Why?"

"He says you need help."

Izara looked around to make sure no one was listening. "Who are you?"

"I am Esi of the Agojie."

Izara froze and stared, wide-eyed for a moment before regaining her composure. "Please, Esi. Come inside so we can talk."

THERE WERE SIX OR SEVEN RECTANGULAR TABLES INSIDE THE SHOP. Each covered with fabrics of different materials and colors. More materials hung from racks along the edges of the shop. Esi had never seen so many different types all at once.

"You are a seamstress?"

"Yes. And I design," Izara said, motioning to several dresses hung in the back of the store.

Esi walked over to one and ran her fingers along the material. It was soft, smooth, yet sturdy.

"This is fine work."

"Thank you. Not as fine as the work I've seen from you and your sisters, but I try."

"This is as fine as anything we've done. I commend you. How old are you?"

"I turn twenty next month."

"So young, yet such beautiful work." She let the dress fall back into place and turned to face Izara. "So this is what Morris was speaking of when he said you needed help."

Izara smiled. "You are disappointed?"

When Esi didn't answer, she held out a hand and gently touched Esi's arm.

"Esi, I know why you are here."

"You do?"

"Yes. I believe I do," she said, then walked to a nearby table to fold and rearrange some of the fabrics. "Dahomey is your heart. You would never have abandoned your kingdom. So I can only guess you were sent here by the king himself."

Esi regarded her for a moment, then joined Izara at the table. She picked up some materials that had no doubt been handled by customers and left in a heap, and began to fold.

"We do things differently in America, Esi."

"Differently? How do you mean?"

Izara sighed. "You can't just go around killing people, Esi." She motioned to the front door. "The police here will find you and put you in jail. You are unknown here. No one is looking for you. You must keep it that way. I don't know what promise you made to the king, but you can do nothing from jail. You must disappear."

Esi scoffed and tossed a freshly-folded piece of fabric to a new pile. "And die?"

Izara stopped folding, closed her eyes and thought for a moment.

"I am happy here, Esi. America has been good to me. It can be good for you, too."

"I am sorry, Izara," Esi said. "I am not like you. I love fabrics and needles, but I need more. I need blood. I am a warrior."

"A mighty warrior. This I understand." After a pause, Izara added, "I knew your brother."

Esi stopped folding and turned to Izara. "You knew Dialo?"

"Yes. Well, no. My brother Amadi knew him. They were friends. When the French invaded Abomey, they fought together. And... died together."

Esi said nothing. The pain of losing her brother still cut more than any she'd endured from her enemies.

"My brother wrote a letter. Let me find it," Izara said, then walked to the counter and began rummaging through some papers in a basket underneath. After a few seconds, she found what she was looking for and held it up for Esi to see.

"Here. Here it is."

She handed a folded piece of paper to Esi. Esi opened it and took her time reading each word with care. When she was done, she set the note down and stared straight ahead.

Izara broke the silence. "He said Dialo fought because of you, Esi. Dialo said he wanted to be brave like you."

A knife to the gut would have hurt less than those words. She closed her eyes to fight back the pain and the lump forming in her throat.

"Forgive me, Esi. I only wanted you to know."

Seeing Esi like this was enough for Izara to drop the formalities and approach Esi. She put a hand on her shoulder.

"Your brother was proud of you," she said.

"Why are you telling me this?" Her voice cracked.

"I think your brother would be happy, Esi. I think..." Izara's words trailed off.

"You think what, Izara?"

"I think he'd want you to be happy. To stop fighting. To live a good life."

Esi brushed Izara's hand away. "You do not know this."

"Aren't you ready? Aren't you ready to rest?"

A pause, then, "I... can't-"

THE BELL ABOVE THE ENTRANCE DOOR JINGLED AND TWO WELL-dressed men wearing bowler hats stepped inside. One of the men was tall and muscular with a pockmarked face and looked to be a size or two too big for his suit. The other, shorter and more portly than his companion, wore a pinstriped suit and held a half-smoked cigar between his chubby fingers.

Izara's face grew pale. She turned to Esi with a look of both fear and determination.

"Please, Esi. No matter what you see here, do nothing," she whispered. "It would only make things worse for me."

This was a look Esi had seen many times on the faces of many frightened villagers during wartime when their homes and families were threatened by invading forces. She knew right away these men were somehow connected to trouble. But Izara was right, causing a disturbance before she could assess the situation would be folly on her part.

"I will do as you say," she said.

"Thank you." She grabbed a broom and handed it to Esi. "Here, act as though you work here."

Esi took the broom and began sweeping the floor, but stuck close to Izara.

The muscle-bound man was eying the material laid out on the tables, picking up a piece every now and then with his large hands to examine it, then tossing it back onto the table. The fat man kept his eyes on Izara as he made his way across the shop towards her. The smile on his face didn't match the malice in his eyes, and only made Izara feel more uncomfortable.

"Been a while," he said.

"Yes, Mr. Richey," Izara said, keeping her eyes fixed on the floor. "It has been a month."

Richey moved in closer, forcing Izara backwards until she was pinned against the front counter. The smell of cigar smoke and tuna fish on his breath invaded her nostrils.

"We need to talk business, sweetie." Richey closed his eyes and breathed in Izara's perfume, then put a hand on her hip. "But then, what's the rush? There's something else I've been missing too."

"Uh, Richey," the man by the door spoke up. "Boss said—"

"Shut up, Lou," Richey said without looking back. Lou fell silent and went back to examining the fabrics.

Richey pulled the cigar stub from his mouth and leaned in.

"Now, where were we?"

Izara turned her face away and closed her eyes. He grabbed her chin and turned her face towards him.

"Don't be shy. We both know that won't get you anywhere," Richey said.

He was about to plant his lips on hers when Esi swept a pile of dust onto his shoes. He stepped back to look down at the mess, then up at Esi. Esi made a quick bow, then continued sweeping.

"What the hell do we have here?" Richey asked, pointing to Esi with the cigar stub. "Business must be good if you can afford to hire some help. Maybe we need to start charging more for our services."

"She is my cousin from Dahomey," Izara said. "She works for a place to live and some food, nothing more."

He shook his head. "Well she needs to watch where she's sweeping." He took one last puff of the cigar, then tossed it to the floor in front of Esi. "You missed something, baby."

Lou snorted a chuckle, while Richey kept his eyes fixed on Esi, looking for any signs of disrespect from this new woman. For a moment, Izara thought Esi would go back on her word and attack this man, but she only looked down and swept up the cigar.

Not quite finished with Esi, Richey pointed to the scar on her face. "Where'd you get that from, sweetie? Some guy put you in your place for talking back?"

"She speaks no english sir," Izara said. "She-"

Richey glared at Izara who quickly lowered her head and looked once more at the floor.

"Where's our money, Izzy?" A nickname Izara was not fond of, but she was glad to draw Richey's attention away from Esi.

She rushed over and opened the register, thankful to put some distance between her and the fat man.

"This is all we have for the week," she said, pulling a handful of cash from the drawer and handing it to Richey.

He grabbed it from her hand and counted it before stuffing it into his inside coat pocket.

"The boss don't like it when you're short," he said.

"I will have the rest next time."

"Plus interest."

Izara lowered her head. "Yes, Mr. Richey."

Richey stared at Izara for a long moment as if considering whether to beat the shit out of her or stop wasting his time and come back later. He shook his head and laughed.

"You're lucky I'm such a nice guy," he said. "We'll be back next month. If you don't have what we need, I can't be responsible for what might happen to your pretty little shop."

"Yes, Mr. Richey. I will have it for you."

"Let's go, Lou," Richey said as he turned to leave. Esi had to side step to avoid getting pushed aside by the big man. Lou dropped the cloth he'd been holding and followed Richey out the door.

"THANK YOU FOR NOT CAUSING A SCENE," IZARA SAID, SWITCHING back to their native Fon language.

She took the broom from Esi and began sweeping up.

"Those men. They take your money?" Esi asked.

"They call it protection money, but the only thing it protects me from is them," she said. "They take from everyone on this block." Izara put the broom aside, pulled her sweater closed and looked down shamefully. "And sometimes, more than money."

Esi walked closer to the window and watched the men as they crossed the street and out of view. She knew exactly what Izara meant, because she'd seen it before. Warlords back home, terrorizing villages and the people. Stealing money and whatever else pleased them.

"Who are they?" she asked.

"The Montello crime family. They run things around here and the police cannot touch them."

"This family has a boss?"

"Yes. Nick Montello."

Once again, Esi turned her attention to the dresses hanging on the wall. They were exquisite. She ran her hand along the lace trim and down the sleeve.

"I need work."

"What?"

Esi turned to Izara and walked closer. "You asked me if I was ready to rest."

"Yes, but-"

"Hear me, Izara. War is my business. Fighting is my business. I need work, not rest."

"So... you must help."

"I must. I will."

Izara considered this for a moment. "I can't afford to pay them. And when the money runs out, they will tear down my store."

"They will not get the chance. We have one month, no?"

"Yes. They'll be back in a month."

"Then we have a month to prepare. I need you to tell me everything you know about them."

"I cannot pay you."

"I don't need money, Izara." Esi touched some fabric on the table as a thought formed in her head. "Will you teach me English?" She asked, then in English added, "I know a little. You teach more?"

Izara smiled. "I will teach you more. It would be an honor."

"And one more thing," Esi said, switching back to Fon. She held up a piece of fabric to the light. "If, as you say, I am to remain unknown, I will need a disguise."

CHAPTER
THIRTY-NINE
THE ANGEL

Something bumped Rachel's head. Then again. Twice this time. It was too dark to see anything.

"Wha-"

She couldn't get the word out.

Then a voice from somewhere in the distance.

"Wake up, Rachel."

Was she sleeping?

"Wake up, my little Agojie."

The memories were fuzzy.

"The sooner the better."

Faint outlines surrounded her.

She bumped her head again. What the hell?

"Wake up!"

Wake up? She was sleeping. But why?

Why, why, why, Warren!

No! Not sleeping. She was dying. Or about to.

Wake up! Get up!

She shouted.

"Warren!"

Her eyes shot open. Two, no three men standing around Warren's living room. Three men and one woman kneeling next to her.

The ambush. The flash bang. The bullets. Warren!

Clear now. Focused now.

The woman was dressed in a black and green bodysuit with a matching mask that covered the top half of her face. Her curly black hair was tied back in a bun. Bruno Montello's Angel? The assassin she'd heard so much about? It had to be. She had a knife in her hand. Rachel's knife. She'd been using the butt end to tap Rachel's head. She made a move to get up, but her hands were tied behind her back.

She saw Warren lying on his back in the middle of the living room floor.

"Warren!" she yelled as tears welled up in her eyes. "No! No! No!" she cried.

His head cocked to one side, his eyes open in a lifeless stare. They hadn't even bothered to cover him up. Rachel tried to push herself over to him. To be by his side. To...

The Angel put a hand on her shoulder to stop her.

"There, there," the Angel said in a mothering tone. Glancing back at Warren, she added, "Doesn't he look peaceful though?"

She put the knife down, grabbed Rachel underneath her arms and pulled her up to a sitting position. Rachel noticed her Agojie mask lying on the floor next to her and suddenly felt more exposed than ever.

"I'm so glad we finally got the chance to meet," she said as if this were a parent - teacher meeting.

The Angel knelt down and gazed at Rachel with all the amazement and wonder of a kid who'd just caught her first fish. The part of her face that wasn't covered by the mask looked young and smooth. Rachel figured her to be no more than 19 or 20.

The designs along the sleeves and mask of her suit bore an eerie resemblance to her own. Another time, another place and Rachel might have asked about it. Not today.

"We need to talk," the Angel said.

"Why did you kill him?"

The Angel answered with a soft chuckle, then gently touched Rachel's face and ran a gloved finger down the side of her cheek. She was lost in some kind of world of her own. Too caught up in the moment, too enraptured by Rachel to care about anything else.

"I'm your biggest fan, Rachel. But I'm also your nemesis. Every superhero needs one of those, right?"

"I'm no hero."

The Angel frowned and looked away to consider this for a moment.

"No. I guess you're right. Well, not anymore at least," she said, then stood up.

"How are we doing on the cops?" she asked the men without taking her eyes off Rachel.

"Still no cops," one of them said. "Neighbors around here must be used to this kind of noise."

The Angel put her hands on her hips and smiled.

"Do you know how long I've been waiting for this moment? How much I planned for this moment? God, this is so fucking sweet," she said, then to the men behind her, "Give me the room."

The men glanced at each other, unsure of what to do or say.

"But ma'am. The boss wants her-"

She turned and gave the men a look that said she wasn't asking. Reluctantly, they stepped out through the now broken front door and closed it behind them. She waited until the last one left before picking up the knife again.

"Such a thing of beauty," she said, holding it up to the light.

All Rachel could do was stare at Warren, dead on the floor not more than fifteen feet away. Her will to listen, to care or even fight died with him.

The Angel knelt down and used the edge of the blade to turn Rachel's face away from Warren.

"Over here, sweetie. Try and stay focused."

"Go to hell," Rachel said.

"That will have to wait."

Rachel locked eyes with hers.

"Then kill me, bitch. I know Bruno sent you. That's what this is about, right? Revenge for destroying that psycho's plans to unleash hell on earth?"

The Angel grabbed a fistful of Rachel's hair and slammed her head against the wall hard enough to crack the sheet rock.

"Don't talk about him like that!"

She was trying to stay in control, but Rachel noticed a brief look of anger flash across her face when she mentioned Bruno and his plans. Anger and... confusion?

"You have no idea what I'm talking about do you?" Rachel asked. "I guess your employer doesn't tell you everything. Go ahead, ask him about Alaska. It's a great story. Left him with a pretty good scar too."

"Shut up! Just stop talking!"

The Angel slammed Rachel's head against the wall two more times. This time hard enough to punch a hole through the sheet rock, sprinkling dust onto Rachel's hair and face. To the Angel's dismay, Rachel seemed unfazed and even a little amused by the punishment.

"You're pretty quick to defend him. Maybe you two have a

little something going on," Rachel said. "Good. That will make killing him in front of you so much more satisfying."

The Angel slapped Rachel hard across the cheek, then jerked her forward by her hair and pressed the blade of the knife against her neck.

"Unless your Agojie strength can strike out from beyond the grave, you'll have a hard time killing anyone. Now let's get down to business."

She pulled the knife away and waved it in front of Rachel.

"The account number engraved on this pretty knife is good, but I need the password. And I need it before I let those men out there take you to Bruno."

So that was it. They didn't just want revenge, they wanted the money. All of it. And with it, there'd be no stopping the Montello family from ending Rachel, Byron and the entire Agojie legacy.

The Angel leaned in close to Rachel's face and whispered into her ear.

"You haven't lost everything yet, bitch. We've got eyes on Byron. Tell me the password and maybe we'll forget all about him. Don't tell us and, well, I have a few fun things planned."

Rachel had been so caught up with Warren, she'd forgotten all about Byron. She cursed herself for such a mistake. She knew the Angel was bluffing about Byron. He wouldn't let himself be found so easily. But he couldn't hide forever. They had the money, the resources and all the patience in the world to keep looking. And they would find him eventually, just like they found her. She had to get out and warn him.

RACHEL EXTENDED HER FINGERS AND TOUCHED THE ZIP TIE THAT bound her wrists behind her back, then reached for the small, retractable blade she kept hidden inside a special pocket sewn into her sleeve. Byron's idea. She'd have to thank him later.

"Time's running out," the Angel said. "Tell me the damn password now. Last chance."

"Seems like you're trying hard to keep your boss out of this part," Rachel said, trying to buy a few more seconds.

"He only has eyes for revenge. The car bomb was his idea. I'm more of a big-picture girl." She leaned in close and whispered. "Password plea-"

Rachel rammed her forehead into the Angel's nose, then brought her now free hands around and clapped them hard against her ears.

The Angel grabbed her ears and fell back onto her butt. In an instant, Rachel was on her feet. The Angel opened her mouth to yell for help, but was cut short when Rachel drove a knee into her nose, followed by a powerful right hook to her temple. She fell to her side, grasping her nose with both hands.

Rachel spotted her knife laying under the couch and made a dash for it, but the Angel recovered enough to spin her body around and kick Rachel's legs from under her, knocking her to the floor. The Angel rolled over and straddled Rachel, pinning her to the floor, then pummeled her with a series of right and left hooks. Rachel took a few punches, then bucked her torso up, throwing the Angel off balance just enough for Rachel to wrap her arms around the Angel in a bear hug, twist and slam her onto the ground hard enough to shake the floor.

Before the Angel could recover, Rachel rolled to the couch, grabbed her knife and lunged. The Angel cried out and feebly tried to shield herself with her hands. An instant before Rachel's blade would have torn into her flesh, the door crashed open and the men who'd been waiting outside stormed in with guns drawn. Rachel pulled herself into a tight roll and launched herself into the guest room just as gunfire broke out and bullets pierced the floor and door frame where she'd been just a split-second before.

She got up and ran to the window, slid it open and climbed onto the fire escape, then disappeared into the night before her pursuers made it into the room.

The Angel followed the men into the room, pushing them out of the way as she made her way to the open window.

"Fuck!" She punched the window frame. "Fuck, fuck!"

She pulled off her mask and threw it to the ground. "Fuck, fuck, fuck!"

The men lowered their guns and stared. "Ma'am. Are you alright?" Realizing her face must look a mess, she turned and headed for the bathroom.

"We'll go after her!" One of them said.

"No," she yelled back. "You'll never find her. She's a fucking ghost."

She slammed the door behind her, leaned over the sink and stared into the mirror at her bloodied and bruised face. Some of her hair had pulled free from its bun during the fight and now hung over one eye. She turned on the faucet and splashed her face with cold water. Droplets of water mixed with tears of rage glistened on her cheeks. She grabbed a hand towel from a stack next to the sink and wiped them dry.

"Damn, damn, damn, damn, damn!" She accented the last damn with a punch to the mirror, shattering it and sending pieces of broken glass clattering into the sink.

She pulled her fist back. A half dozen broken images stared back at her now. She screamed at the top of her lungs like a spoiled child who lost her favorite toy.

"I'll. Fucking. KILL YOU, bitch!"

CHAPTER
FORTY
THE SUIT

"Let's try some English," Izara said in their native Fon language. "Pay me a compliment on my outfit."

Esi sighed and thought for a moment, then straightened in her chair and cleared her throat. "Good afternoon, ma'am. Your dress is like the sun. It burns my eyes."

"Close, Esi. So close."

The sun had long since disappeared, and candles now lit the corner of Izara's shop where the women worked. Carefully and meticulously stitching and sewing Esi's design for the suit. A new symbol for the Agojie warrior. Fierce, bold, strong and beautiful. Izara worked on the wool gabardine pants, dyed a deep red with black accents, while Esi worked on the imported-cotton top, dyed to match. Because of the extraordinary amount of stress Esi would no doubt put the suit under, a bias cut would be essential. Rips and tears were simply not an option.

"Let's try again," Izara said.

Letters and phrases written on pieces of paper hung from walls, while stacks of note cards with even more phrases and words sat in neat piles on tables. Izara's shop looked more like a teacher's classroom than a fabric store.

"This language is too confusing," Esi said in her Fon language. Then, in English, "I see the sea. Do not flee from a flea. What is the sense?"

"Very good, Esi! You are learning!"

"Tell me. How did you learn this language so quickly? Is it because your mind is still young?"

"You are but 30, Esi. Not old."

"Old enough to know when something is foolish!"

Both women laughed and Esi began the work of setting and sewing the gussets under the arms. The suit needed to be snug, but maximum range of motion was critical.

"Tell me, Esi. When this suit is finished, what will you do to the men who threaten us?"

"I will do what I do best. They will not threaten you any more, Izara."

Izara set the material down and rested her hands on the table.

"What bothers you, Izara?"

"I only wish there could be another way. Is there no room for mercy?"

Esi placed the unfinished shirt on the table and took Izara's hand in hers.

"A dear friend once asked me the same thing. I'm starting to believe I should listen." She let go of her hand and returned to her work. "Things are different here, Izara. But some things do not change. Some men are evil. And with those men, there is no other way. They are beasts, devouring the weak. They will only stop when a bigger beast threatens them."

Izara smiled. "The gods have granted me a bigger beast."

Esi held up one of her needles and smiled. "Just as fierce with a sewing needle as I am with a knife."

“I am not so sure about that, Esi.” Izara nodded towards Esi’s work. “You call that a top stitch?”

Esi playfully slapped at Izara’s hand. “Come now! You will see.”

For a few moments, the women worked in a silence that calmed Esi’s nerves just as much as the conversation. It was like spending time with an old friend. Something she hadn’t felt in the years since she'd left Dahomey.

“Amadi was strong in the head,” Izara said. “If he was friends with your brother, he must have been so too. No?”

Esi smiled. “It is true. He argued with everyone. If a merchant charged my father too much for something, Dialo would march straight there and bargain for a better price. No matter if the deal was already done. Dialo would fight for justice, no matter how small.”

Izara held up the pants for a quick examination, then returned to her sewing. “I find I cannot stop thinking of him, Esi.”

“I also find this true. Maybe we never will.”

“But here we are. You and I. Together. Do the gods find this funny?”

Esi paused to think. “Maybe they find it merciful.”

“I like that, Esi. Merciful.”

Esi pulled the sleeve of the shirt and held it up. “We need a mark here. Flowers from home so new warriors will remember Dahomey was also a place of healing and beauty, not just war.”

“New warriors?”

“I will not be the last,” Esi said.

“But... how?”

“I promised King Behanzin I would carry on the name of Dahomey and keep the Agojie warrior alive.” Esi put the shirt aside and held up the mask she’d sewn. Blood red and black, with holes cut for the eyes, leaving the bottom half of the face exposed. It was fearsome, yet beautiful. "And we will live. Even if only in the shadows, Dahomey will be remembered."

"And when you grow old and can no longer fight? What will become of the Agojie then?" Izara asked.

Esi set the mask down, touched Izara's hand and looked her in the eyes. "When I am done, I will find another to replace me," she said, keeping her gaze fixed on Izara.

Esi's implication was not lost on Izara. She thought to protest, but decided against it. At least for now.

She thought for a moment, then reached over the table and touched the sleeve. "The Gbehutu flower," she said. "Known for its beauty and healing powers."

Esi closed her eyes and breathed in the memory of the flower. Its sweet, subtle fragrance, striking beauty and hidden strength. "It is a fine choice, Izara. How can we fit it into our design?"

The women made eye contact and smiled. "Applique!" they said in unison.

The candles were low and the sun would be coming up soon, but neither woman cared to stop. Stopping would bring an end to this magic. This moment. For now, it belonged to them and only them. And for two women torn from their homes and thrown together in this new land, it was enough. Together, they found refuge. Solace. Peace. Doing what they loved and sharing stories of old from a homeland they both knew they'd never see again.

Izara nodded towards a note card lying on the table near Esi.

"I saw you writing on this last night. What is it?"

Esi put her fabric and tools down to pick up the note. "It is a promise to a new beginning."

She handed the note to Izara. Izara placed her tools down, took it and began to read out loud.

"I am Agojie. A priestess of pain, a warrior for the weak..."

"A legacy of blood," Esi continued. "Handed down from our mothers."

Izara looked up at Esi, who sat with her eyes closed. She continued reading, and Esi silently mouthed the words in unison.

"I am Agojie. The blade of Dahomey. The lion of Africa. The last of our kind, until I choose another."

She placed the card on the table and thought for a moment.

"It is powerful, Esi. Your words, they have power."

Esi opened her eyes, picked up her fabric and tools and continued her work on the suit.

"People will know our name, Izara. The bad will fear it and the good will cherish it."

Now both women were working again, carefully cutting and sewing the fabric in the silence of the room.

"The only thing *I* fear is that last stitch you made, Esi," Izara said, pointing her needle to Esi's work. And with that, the still darkness that seemed to settle over the room for a moment was gone, replaced once again with laughter.

CHAPTER
FORTY-ONE
OBSESSION

Since relocating to New Orleans, the Montello family restaurant business struggled to regain the power and influence it once held in New York. Other than the financial trouble this presented on the public side of things, mixing dirty money with the clean became increasingly more difficult.

Always putting the business first, Vincent Montello decided it was time to step aside and bring in new talent with fresh ideas and a face the public would love. So at 25, his son Bruno became the youngest Montello to ever take over the family business.

Vincent took a backseat and watched as Bruno stumbled his way around in the beginning. The business suffered, but Vincent's confidence in his son's ability to steer the ship was steadfast. His gamble paid off when Bruno decided to focus in on what he knew best. Public relations. What he lacked in leadership skills, he more than made up for in self promotion. Always ready with a smile and a clever sound bite for the cameras, Bruno brought star power to the family name.

In a somewhat controversial move, the newspaper named Bruno as New Orleans' sexiest single on his 29th birthday, and a photo of his best smolder was plastered onto the front page. The masses adored him. An everyday man in an Armani suit and a thousand dollar haircut.

The tables were full and the waiting list was long. It seemed to be working. For a while. But after a sex scandal with a married high school teacher and an unfortunate incident with a homeless veteran who was denied a meal by a manager, the restaurant's popularity began to fade once again. Years after Vincent's death, the business still suffered.

There were many who quietly believed Bruno needed to be replaced. Including Fiona, AKA the Angel. As she sat across from Bruno at his desk, watching him sketch out another drawing on his pad, she thought about how he was more likely to run the family name into the ground than bring back the glory it once held in New York.

She was still wearing her Angel suit, minus the mask, inspecting a broken nail while she held an ice pack to her nose. Before coming to visit Bruno, she'd pulled her curly-brown hair back into another bun, leaving a few loose strands to frame the sides of her face, and touched up her makeup as best she could. She may have felt like she'd been hit by a truck, but she didn't have to look like it. At least not with the parts she could control.

"You fucked up," Bruno said without looking up from his drawing.

His therapist said drawing would help with the anger, but so far it only succeeded in turning him into an ill-tempered artist. His preferred method of anger management came in liquid form, and judging from the decanter of whiskey on his desk, Fiona guessed he was about to begin another session.

"You got greedy and you fucked up. Simple as that," he said.

He was leaning back in his leather chair as he sketched, ignoring the strands of his slick black hair that rebelled against his part and hung freely over one eye. He kept his focus on the drawing, softly shading and outlining, occasionally accenting his work with bold, slashing lines.

"There's more to life than revenge," Fiona said. "I'm thinking big picture here."

Bruno slashed a few more heavy strokes on the paper.

"Did that big picture include getting your ass handed to you by the Amazon?"

He still hadn't looked up, but Fiona noticed the corners of his lips curve into a slight smile when he said that last part. He was enjoying this moment of control.

"You're obsessed," he said. "And those big schemes of yours are gonna get you killed someday."

"Those big schemes are gonna get us rich someday. So long as you stop getting in my way. And I'm not the only one with an obsession."

Bruno slammed his sketch pad onto the desk, grabbed the decanter with his scarred, left hand and poured another drink. Fiona smiled. Underneath that pretty-boy exterior was a spoiled, rich brat who still couldn't control his anger no matter how many pretty drawings he made. It scared the hell out of most people, but Fiona knew how to draw him close to the edge without pushing him over.

"You have no idea the depths of my obsession, little sister." Bruno said. He took a long sip of whiskey, thought for a moment, then continued. "That woman. That tribe. The Amazons..."

"Agojie warriors. Have some goddamn respect, dear brother."

For a moment, Fiona thought Bruno was going to hurl the glass of whiskey across the room, shattering it into a million pieces against the wall. But to her surprise, he took a long, deep breath and gently placed it back on the desk. Maybe the drawings were working.

"Don't interrupt me, Fiona. You know I hate it when you do that. I fucking hate it."

He paused to gather his thoughts, unconsciously rubbing the scar on his left hand. An old, nervous habit of his. He told Fiona the scar was from an accident at the restaurant, but after what Rachel said about Alaska, she was starting to wonder if his dealings with the Agojie went far beyond what she'd been led to believe.

"They killed two of our family, Fiona. Two! Dead because of those fucking Ama... Agojies. More importantly, the Agojie and Byron know too much about the project," Bruno stopped short and took another sip of whiskey.

"What project?"

Bruno flashed a warm smile, but his eyes remained ice cold.

"Never mind that, little sis. Let's just say there's a lot you don't know, which is why you need to play by my rules on this."

Fiona tossed the ice pack onto the desk, leaned forward and looked Bruno in the eyes.

"Does it have anything to do with Alaska?"

His smile faded and Fiona noticed a very brief look of surprise flash across his face. Rachel was right. Something did happen in Alaska. Something big.

"Stay out of things that don't concern you!" His voice raised, but not quite a yell. Bruno never yelled. "You made the choice to stay out of management so you could chase your dreams of becoming...” he waved a hand at Fiona’s suit. “Whatever the hell you’re supposed to be.”

“The Angel,” Fiona said.

“Whatever. I let you do that because you’re good at what you do. The best. But stay out of things that don’t concern you.”

Bruno picked up his sketch pad, leaned back in his chair and returned to his drawings.

Figuring it would be better to stay focused on the mission, Fiona decided to drop it. For now.

“She’s rich, Bruno. I read Nicky Junior’s notes too. She’s living off that old king’s money. He must have given Esi millions. By now it’s probably triple that. If we could get that money, we could change things around here. We’d have power in this town again. Real power.”

“Brilliant.” Bruno said, then lowered his sketch pad and leaned in over his desk. “Now if we just had the Agojie.”

Fiona uncrossed her legs, sat up straight and looked around the room.

“I’d ask Byron where she is, but I don’t see him either. Oh that’s right, he killed two of your men and slipped right through your fingers.”

Bruno jerked his sketch pad back up and slashed two more deep marks across the page.

“Dammit, Fiona! If you weren’t my sister-”

“You’d what?” Fiona stood and motioned to the two men standing silently in the back. “You gonna send Stevie and Rick to get her? They wouldn’t stand a chance against her. You need me!”

Bruno didn’t bother to look up.

“I need you to do your job, Fiona. Just do your damn job and get them here. Hell, at this point I don’t care if you kill the Agojie and Byron yourself. I just need them gone.”

"Then stop jumping the gun and let me do it."

Fiona grabbed Bruno's half-empty glass of whiskey from the desk, relaxed back into her chair and took a long sip. Bruno paused from his sketch to watch.

"Don't worry, big brother." She held the glass up to the light and swirled the liquid inside. "I'm the Angel. No one gets away from me forever."

CHAPTER FORTY-TWO

A BEAUTIFUL MONSTER

Byron instinctively went for his gun when he opened the door to the safe house, then relaxed when he realized the figure sitting on the couch in the darkened living room was Rachel.

"You good?" he asked as he closed the door behind him and limped his way to the window to peek through the curtains. The wind was picking up. Brilliant flashes of lighting lit up distant clouds and thunder rumbled not long after. A hard rain was coming.

"You got here safe? No one followed?" he asked, still scanning the road outside for any signs of trouble.

The safe house was a run-down, three bedroom on the northeast side of town. No central air, but the window units in every room kept it cool enough to survive the blistering New Orleans summers. Byron thought the noise from the units made it difficult to hear any approaching threats, which is why he never liked this particular safe house, but the nights were cooler now and the units were off. The house was quiet and calm.

"He's dead," Rachel whispered. "He's... gone."

"Oh sweet Jesus." Byron dropped the curtain and ran to Rachel's side, ignoring the pain in his leg. "Warren?"

Rachel was wrapped in a blanket, sitting in darkness. Byron wondered for how long.

"She killed him. The Angel. Bruno Montello's Angel. We were trying to get out when they busted in. They knew. They've known."

A flash of lightning lit up the dark room, revealing the dried tears that streaked Rachel's face. Her blanket fell open enough for Byron to see she was still in her Agojie suit.

"You were right. I should never have gotten involved with him. He's dead because of me."

"No Rachel." Byron wrapped an arm around Rachel's shoulder and pulled her close. "He knew the risks. He knew the danger involved. Yet he still chose to be with you. He chose love over his own safety. Not even the Agojie could stop love like that."

Rachel sat motionless and unresponsive, staring at the floor. Byron got the hint.

"I'll make some tea," he whispered. "Stay here, I'll be back and we can talk."

For the next hour, Byron and Rachel sat in the living room, sipping tea and listening to the rain as it burst free from the clouds and pelted the roof and windows of their safe house, unconcerned with the sadness and heartache of the people inside.

Absent was the talk. What was there to say? For all the years the Agojie project existed, they were never the targets. The ones on the run. The hunted rather than the hunter. Someone out there knew who they were, what they were, and wanted them dead. And they were quite capable of making it happen.

Bryon spoke first.

"We gotta regroup. Lay low for a while until we can figure out how to hit them back with-"

"I'm pregnant," Rachel interrupted.

Byron nearly choked on his tea.

"You're what?"

"Pregnant." Rachel finished her tea, sat the cup down on the coffee table and wrapped herself up in the blanket again. "I was going to tell Warren tonight. Before all hell broke loose."

Byron sat his cup next to hers, took a breath and slowly exhaled while he thought. Lightning flashed, followed by a rumble of thunder that shook the windows and caused the old house to creak.

"We'll figure this out," he said.

"No."

"No?"

"I've got to go away. I can't do this now."

"What do you mean?"

"Disappear. I've got to disappear. Staying here will put my baby in danger," Rachel sat up straight and turned to face Byron. "Come with me, Byron. We'll change our names. I'll be the single mom with a devoted brother. Maybe together we can give this baby a normal life somewhere."

"You don't have to do this," Byron said. "We don't have to run."

Rachel leaned back and covered her face with her hands.

"I know. But I also know if I stay, we'll find them. I'm not doing this just to keep them from us, I'm doing it to keep me from them. If I stay, I'll find her and I'll kill her, Byron. I'll kill them both. But that would put my baby in danger. I can't do that. I've got to get far, far away from here."

Byron knew she was right. Rachel would hunt the Angel and Bruno down and show no mercy. It was her nature. At his core, it scared the hell out of Byron. Rachel was a monster hidden inside a beautiful frame, and it was one of the reasons her predecessor chose her to be the next Agojie. Rachel was born for this.

"Where you gonna go?"

"I don't know. Someplace far. Mexico maybe. I know someone there. He owes me a favor."

Byron put his arm around Rachel again and she leaned in and rested her head on his shoulder. They sat in silence as the storm played a symphony outside, blending the quiet rhythm of rain with accents of lightning and thunder.

There was no going back. Warren was gone and he'd never get the chance to meet his baby and be the amazing dad Rachel knew he would have been. Rachel hated the Angel for that. She hated Bruno. But most of all, she hated herself. If only, if only, if only.

Her eyes grew wet and tears streamed down. Along with the baby, a sense of fear she'd never known before grew steadily inside her.

"I think I'll go with Danny," Byron said, mostly to try and distract Rachel. "It kind of suits me, don't you think?"

Rachel squeezed his arm. "I like it."

"What about you?"

"Haven't thought about it yet. Been kind of distracted."

"Right," Byron said. He thought for a moment, then asked, "What about the baby? Have you thought of a name?"

"Warren," she said without hesitation.

"Figured that. And if it's a girl?"

Rachel put a hand on her belly, closed her eyes and thought for a moment.

"Nyah," she said. "I've always loved that name."

CHAPTER FORTY-THREE

A TIME FOR WAR

Izara was working with a client when the bell over the door to her shop jingled and Richey and Lou walked in. Another stubby cigar hung from Richey's fat lips, and this time Richey was in a solid black suit with a matching hat.

They'd come sooner than expected. Tuesdays were their normal collection day. Richey must have been growing impatient.

Lou took up his post by the door, once again feigning interest in the materials laid out on a table, while Richey walked over and shoved his big frame between Izara and her client.

"Where's the money, Izzy?"

Izara leaned around to address her client. "So sorry, Margret. Can you come back later?"

After a brief look of concern, Margret hurried out, keeping her head down to avoid Lou's intense stare as she passed him by.

"Where's the money, Izzy?" Richey repeated.

Izara clasped her hands together to try and keep them from shaking.

"I... don't have it."

Richey pulled the cigar from his mouth, blew a puff of smoke into Izara's face and laughed.

"Jesus! Did you hear that, Lou?" he said, glancing back at his big friend. "She says she ain't fucking got it."

"Ain't got it." Lou said. "That's a good one, Richey." A piece of fabric Lou was handling slipped from his hands onto the floor. He didn't bother to pick it up.

"Yeah, that's a real fucking good one," Richey said, turning his attention back to Izara. He put the cigar back between his lips and moved closer to Izara, forcing her back until she was once again pressed against the register.

"Thanks for the laugh, Izzy. Now go get me my money or there's gonna be trouble."

"It is no joke, Mr. Richey. I do not have your money today. I'm sorry. It was a very slow month."

"Wrong answer."

Richey slapped Izara across her cheek, jerking her head to the side so hard she lost balance and had to grab the counter to keep from falling. She put a hand to her cheek and fought back tears from the stinging pain and humiliation.

"One more time. And I'll speak slowly so your little brain can comprehend the words. Where - is - my - money?"

Izara looked down at her shoes, squeezed her eyes shut and prepared for another slap.

"Sir, I am sorry."

"Dammit, Lou!" he shouted back to his friend, startling Izara. "Looks like we're gonna have to look around for the money ourselves. No point in being neat about it neither."

This time Lou didn't respond.

"Lou?"

Richey turned, but Lou was gone. He was about to call out again when he noticed Lou's feet laying prone behind the table where he'd been standing.

"What the..."

Richey pulled a pistol from the shoulder holster inside his jacket and ran to the table. The big man was out cold on his back.

"Christ! Get up, you big oaf! What'd I tell you about drinking on the job?"

He knelt down and shook him. Nothing. He pulled his jacket back to check for a heartbeat and recoiled when he saw wet blood blossoming on his white shirt.

"Goddamn!"

Richey stood and aimed his pistol at Izara, but she was gone.

"What the hell is going on here?" he yelled to no one.

He walked back towards the register with his pistol raised, ready to shoot the first thing that moved. He'd kill her for this. No. Burn her fucking store to the ground first, then cut her fucking throat.

"Where'd you go, Izzy! Don't play games with m-"

"Hi Richey," came a voice from behind him. Richey whirled around with his pistol raised. His eyes caught a glimpse of someone a split second before the figure punched him in the solar plexus with enough force to knock the wind from his lungs and drop him to his knees. His jaw fell slack and the cigar dangled from his lips for a second, then fell to the floor. He looked up and saw a woman standing over him wearing some kind of black and red costume, with most of her face hidden behind a mask.

Gasping for breath, Richey remembered his gun. He tried to raise it, but the woman kicked it from his hand, sending it sliding across the floor until it bumped into the wall.

She knelt down and looked him in the eyes. Her mask faded from black to a deep red, half-covered in what looked like flowers.

"Who... who are you?" he managed to ask.

"Tell Nick it is over," she said. "No more money. The whole block is done with you. He will threaten these people no more."

Richey's curiosity turned to rage. This broad thought she could come in here with her costume, sucker punch Richey and scare Nick Montello out of this neighborhood. He'd heard a lot of funny stories, but this one took the whole fucking cake. It would take a hell of a lot more than a scary costume to intimidate Nick. And it would take a lot more than a lucky punch to keep Richey down. The spasms in his gut were easing, and the pain was mostly gone. It was time to show the bitch who runs this street.

"Okay. Let's talk," He said, holding up his hands in surrender. "I'm sure we can work something out."

When matched with a woman, men rarely admitted defeat so easily. In Dahomey, such pride usually cost them their lives. But it was Richey's lucky day. He would leave this place with only a few broken bones and a bruised ego.

"No need to get violent," Richey said as he shifted from his knees to a kneeling position. "Let's just have ourselves a little tal-."

Richey launched himself upward and tried to grab Esi in a bear hug, but Esi swiveled right, punched him twice in the ribs then rammed the palm of her hand into his nose, snapping his head back and sending him stumbling to the counter.

"Shit!" he yelled, putting a hand to his nose. "You..." He

pulled his hand away and saw blood on his fingers. "You fucking broke my nose!"

He wiped the blood off onto the counter, snarled like a rabid dog and charged at Esi.

"I'm gonna rip off your fucking hea-"

Esi sidestepped and gave Richey a slight push as he rushed past, using his own momentum to do the rest. Unable to stop, he tripped and crashed onto a table, breaking it into pieces as he fell hard onto the floor.

He grunted and slowly forced himself back to his feet, almost tripping over some fabrics as he did. He was moving slower now, trying to catch his breath. Richey was not accustomed to such resistance from the people he was paid to intimidate. His indignation was mixed with confusion over the situation he suddenly found himself in.

"Enough of these games," Esi said. "Go now while you still can."

"Honey, you don't know what you got yourself into." He pulled off his coat and tossed it to the side, then spotted a broken table leg on the floor in front of him and picked it up. "Let's see what your brains look like splattered all over the floor!"

He spit, then charged at Esi, putting all his remaining energy into this next attack. He swung right, left, then right again, moving in closer and growling with rage with each swing. Esi dodged his first three swings, caught the leg in her left hand on the fourth and wrenched it free from his grip. Before Richey could react, she flipped the leg and caught it in a two-handed grip, then cracked Richey across the jaw with a home-run-style swing. The big man twisted around, dropped to his knees, then fell face first onto the floor.

~

A SPLASH OF COLD WATER STARTLED RICHEY AWAKE. HE SPIT, coughed and wiped his eyes. His head was pounding and his body ached. The side of his face throbbed and his jaw hurt like hell.

The world was slowly coming back into focus. He startled when he saw the woman in the costume kneeling next to him, staring down at him with those dark, threatening eyes. He made a move to get up, then froze when he noticed the blade in her hand. It looked razor sharp with some kind of fancy design on the handle.

She sighed and sat down on the floor next to Richey. Looking almost bored, she began rotating the knife in her hand, admiring the light as it glinted off the blade into her eyes. Richey made no attempt to move or get up.

"One more time," the woman said after a few moments of this. "And I'll speak slowly so your tiny mind can keep up. No - more - money. Is that clear?"

Still fixated on the knife, Richey only nodded.

"Good."

She stood, sheathed her knife, then reached down and pulled Richey up by his ears.

"Aahhhggg!" He yelled out. "Fuck!"

Before he could fight back, the woman turned Richey around and pushed him towards the door. Richey caught a glimpse of Lou still laying on the floor as he passed by.

She pulled the door open and shoved him through. Richey stumbled a few steps on the sidewalk, then tripped and fell into a muddy puddle of water on the street.

"You are no longer welcome here, Richey," the woman said from the doorway. "Tell your boss the devil has found him. And she is angry."

~

Richey's face flushed with both anger and embarrassment. He gritted his teeth and tried to yell back, but the woman slammed the door, cutting him off mid obscenity.

He thought of grabbing the shotgun from his car, then going back inside and cutting the broad down. But the shooting pain he felt in his body when he tried to move made him rethink that plan. Better to tell the boss about all this and come back with reinforcements.

He slowly got to his feet and straightened his wet and muddy suit jacket with as much dignity as he could muster. A small crowd of onlookers stood gawking at him from afar. Too many to chase away.

"What the hell you looking at?" he yelled, then grabbed his hat from the street, limped back to his car and took one last look at the shop before climbing in and driving away.

Izara emerged from her hiding spot in the back, slowly shaking her head and marveling at the damage to her shop as she made her way to Esi. She gasped at the sight of Lou's body on the floor and turned away.

Esi was looking through the curtains at Richey as he drove away. She seemed somehow relaxed after all the chaos. More relaxed than she'd been since she first arrived. It was true. This blood work was Esi's world, and she could never leave it behind.

"What is next?" she asked Esi.

"You did not even compliment me on my English."

"Esi. This is serious. What you have started is serious. What is next?"

Esi let the curtains fall back and turned to face Izara.

"Now I finish this," she said. "The Dahomey way."

CHAPTER

FORTY-FOUR

NO MORE SECRETS

Ever since he was a kid, Quin remembered people hating on Galveston Island and its beaches, but he never understood why. It wasn't as nice as other beaches, and sometimes there'd be so much seaweed washed up on the shore you had to use a rake to clear out a space to sit, but Quin liked it just fine.

Sometimes when his dad was away on business, his mom would pack up the car and take him on the one-hour trip down I-45 to spend the day there. He loved crossing the big bridge that separated the island from the mainland. So much water all around. So different from home. Quin always liked to pretend they were on a tropical vacation.

His mom would take her time finding just the right spot, which always drove Quin crazy. When they finally parked, Quin would be out of the car and in the water before his mom even opened her door. He'd jump and splash in the shallow waves that made their way to shore, while his mom sat up the chairs, spread out a blanket and sat the ice chest full of drinks and snacks on top to keep it from blowing away in the wind.

Eventually, Quin would get to work on his sand castles while his mom watched. Sometimes she helped, other times she'd just sit and read a book, looking up at Quin every now and then with a smile and a compliment on his work. There they would stay until the sun dipped below the horizon and the sky turned a deep, fiery red.

He wasn't a kid anymore, but the beach still had a way with him. Anytime he needed to get away, it was the only place to be. As he sat with his eyes closed in his mom's old chair, listening to the waves roll in and the distant squawk of seagulls, he could almost hear his mom's voice.

"Quin, baby. Let me take a picture of you next to your castle."

Soft waves trickled up to shore and tickled his feet. He slowly worked his toes deep into the wet sand until the next wave rolled in and swept away his progress, forcing him to start over.

There on that lonely section of beach, no one knew his name, recognized his face or for damn sure asked how much he paid for his jersey. He loved his school and the people there, but sometimes he needed the solitude and comfort only his beach could offer.

He held his phone in one hand with a message typed out and ready to send to his dad. In the other was a scrap of paper with the words "You got this" written on it. A note Dustin slipped into Quin's pocket before a big game once. Quin noticed it when he was suiting up. Perfect timing too. Up until then, he'd been having a bad day, and the note gave him the confidence he needed to run in a few touchdowns later that night. He was hoping it would work that same magic again.

His dad was supposed to be home from New York, but he decided to stay another few days to finish up a research project that just couldn't wait. Same old story. So instead of coming out to him in person, he'd have to do it over the phone. He gripped the note, took a deep breath, slowly exhaled, then sent the message.

Got time to talk?

And just like that, a weight lifted from his shoulders. No more secrets, not even from his dad. This was the right thing to do. His dad may not understand, but Quin needed him to know.

He closed his eyes and let his thoughts drift to Dustin once again. Lately it was pretty much all he could think about. What would Dustin wear to the dance? Would they dance or just stand around the whole time? So many questions, but God, it felt good knowing they'd be there together. He wiggled his toes in the wet sand and dug his feet in a little more. Quin would wear a black tux. No, gold for sure. With a black and gold paisley bow tie. Showing up with Dustin on his arm wouldn't be the only reason he turned some damn heads.

His phone dinged and Trish's name popped up.

Can you talk?

Quin thought it over. His dad was never quick to respond to a text. Maybe he still had time to talk a little homecoming fashion with Trish. He was about to give her a call when his dad surprised him with a response.

Certainly. I have some time now if it's convenient.

Always so formal.

He thought about calling Trish anyway. He could definitely use the confidence boost. But time was always limited with his dad, so it was now or never. He texted "About to call my dad. Talk after?" to Trish, then mentally prepared himself for his dad.

No more secrets.

~

Something about the feel of Dustin's note calmed him. The wrinkles, the edges and how it tugged and fluttered in the wind, trying to break free from his fingers and fly away. It was all the confidence boost he needed.

He raised his phone to call just as a shadow appeared from behind, blocking the sun around him. Quin turned and squinted, then smiled when he recognized the face.

"Hey. What are you doing here?" he asked.

Everything next happened in slow motion. He registered a gun in her hand an instant before it flashed and jerked upward. Something like a sledge hammer pounded his chest, followed by a white-hot heat that burned from the inside out. His phone dropped from his hand. His strength left him. His breathing was labored. His hands tingled and his arms felt numb.

Dustin's note pulled and tugged harder in the wind. He tried to hold on, but it was no use. It tore free from his grip and fluttered its way down to the wet sand. He put a hand to his chest and felt something wet. He tried to look down, but darkness overtook him and swept away his consciousness.

~

A COLD, WET SLAP TO HIS FACE. FOLLOWED BY ANOTHER. QUIN coughed and spit out water and sand. He'd fallen down. The splashing waves pulling him back from the darkness. The woman stood over him. She smiled and knelt down.

"Welcome back," she said.

Quin tried to ask for help, but no words came out. His chest was on fire. The water around him was red. The woman touched a gloved finger to his lips.

"Shhh," she whispered. "Nothing personal, Quin. I was really starting to like you. But your friend was trying to disappear again, and we just can't let that happen."

She pulled out a phone, typed something, then slid it back into her pocket. For a few seconds, she just stared down at Quin, watching him like a beached fish gasping for air. Then she grew bored.

"Well, I'd love to stay, but I've got a busy day tomorrow."

Quin watched helplessly as she stood and walked away. Calm and easy, like someone out for a casual stroll on a sunset beach.

His phone began to buzz and his dad's picture appeared on the screen. Dustin's note floated in the shallow water just out of reach, the ink already smeared. Quin reached for it, hoping to at least touch the edge one last time. His fingers were almost there when a mocking wave swept in and claimed it for its own.

The sound of the wind, waves and seagulls seemed far away now. A tear rolled down his cheek. He closed his eyes and thought of Dustin, the dance and the memories they'd never get the chance to make. He thought of his dad, Trish and Desi. He thought of his mom. And then he thought of nothing at all.

CHAPTER FORTY-FIVE
THE DEVIL OF DAHOMEY

PRINCE STREET SALOON - NICK MONTELLO CRIME FAMILY HEADQUARTERS, NEW YORK CITY

"So let me get this straight," Nick Montello said to Richey as he sat across from him at a table in the Prince Street Saloon. Richey held a bag of ice to his nose. "She short changed you, and when you went back to collect the rest, a woman in some sort of costume appeared out of nowhere, killed Lou, took your gun and broke your nose before throwing you out on your ass?"

Thunder rumbled and the first drops of rain began to tap lightly on the windows. Finch the Capo and Christopher sat playing cards at a table behind Richey. Mikey and Tommy the Bite, a nickname he'd picked up after he bit the ear off a guy who tried to stick him with a knife during a deal gone bad, sat at another table closer to the front of the saloon. And as usual, Sickle Sully sat alone, sharpening the curved blade he affectionately called Fang while reading another one of his horror novels.

Richey never liked Sully, and just being in the same room with the psycho made him nervous. He wore the same old black trench coat everywhere he went, no matter the weather, along with a beat up western-style fedora he took off some poor schmuck who owed Nick money. He never spoke unless he had to, never smiled unless he was about to off someone, and never laughed unless a character in one of his books met with some kind of brutal demise. He gave everyone the creeps. Including Nick. But he was loyal to the family and deadly with a knife. And that was all Nick cared about.

"Sure, boss," Richey said. "But she was like no woman I ever seen. She was like some sort of devil woman." He glanced over at Sully, then lowered his voice. "You know, like in one of those books Sully's always readin'."

"Devil?"

Richey tried to gather himself and look somewhat calm in spite of his situation.

"Yeah boss. She was stronger and goddamn faster than any man I've come up against."

Nick waved two fingers in the air to the bartender, who nodded and immediately began pouring two whiskeys.

"You know, Richey. This looks bad."

"Yes sir."

From across the room, Sully burst into a sudden fit of laughter that nearly caused Richey to jump from his seat, then turned the page and kept reading as if nothing happened.

The bartender set the two glasses in front of the men. Nick smiled at Richey and motioned for him to drink. Richey set the ice bag aside and picked up his glass, trying without success to keep his hand from shaking as he took a sip.

"There you go, Richey," Nick said. "Drink up."

A flash of lightning lit up the saloon, followed by the loud crack of thunder. The rain began to pour. Nick took a sip from his own glass, set it back down and ran a hand through his curly hair, which he always kept short and neat.

"But you know, Richey, this looks bad."

"Yeah boss. Sure."

Nick was smiling, but his eyes were ice cold. Richey had to look down at his whiskey to keep from crumbling under the pressure of his intense gaze.

"I mean, what will happen if word gets out that my guys were roughed up by a woman?"

"Sir, she was no -"

Nick raised a hand to stop him. "I know, I know. She was quick and strong, right?"

"Right. Like no one I've ever seen."

Nick took a long sip of whiskey, then pulled a cigar from his coat, which Christopher immediately jumped up to light with the Zippo he kept in his coat pocket. Nick took his time savoring the first few puffs while Richey nervously fidgeted with his whiskey glass, almost spilling some onto the table when another loud crack of thunder rattled the windows.

"Still, the problem remains," Nick said as he exhaled smoke and examined his cigar.

"Give me another guy," Richey said. "We'll go out and double down on everyone. Get tough, get more money. We'll put the fear of God in all of 'em."

"But what about the woma... I mean, the devil?"

"Give me three guys. Hell, send Sully too. If she shows up again, she'll wish she hadn't."

Neither Sully nor anyone else in the bar showed any interest in speaking up for Richey.

"That didn't work out so well last time," Nick said.

"She surprised us last time, boss. This time we'll be ready."

"You know somethin'? I believe you," Nick said. He took another long puff and slowly blew smoke into the air. "She got the jump on you, but I think you'll be ready next time. She'll show up and bang! Just another dead broad. Right?"

"Yeah, sure boss. That's it." Richey seemed to loosen up a bit. He took another sip of whiskey.

"And then all will be good again. Like it never happ..."

Nick leaned his head back and burst into a fit of laughter, then slapped a hand down on the table and wiped a tear from his eye.

"Sorry, I can't say it with a straight face," he said, then pulled a gun from inside his coat and shot Richey in the head.

The glass fell from Richey's hand to the table, then rolled off and crashed onto the floor. For a moment, his face was frozen in a shocked expression of horror and disbelief, until he slowly fell sideways from the chair and hit the floor with a thud.

"I had him going for a while though, right?" Nick said as he reholstered his pistol and looked around the room. "I mean, that look on his fucking face!"

"Yeah, boss. You sure did," Finch said without looking up from his card game.

"Good one, boss," Tommy the Bite said from his table near the door.

Undisturbed, Sully flipped a page in his book and continued reading.

Nick took another puff from his cigar, smashed it into the ashtray, then got up to straighten his coat.

"Get someone to clean this mess up," he said to Finch. "Then I want you to take some guys and show that shop owner and her friend who runs this neighborhood. I want you to make them watch as you burn that shop to the ground. When you're done, stuff their bodies in a barrel and leave it in the middle of the street for everyone to see."

"On it, boss." Finch said.

Nick turned to walk to his office in the back and was surprised to see Nicky Junior, his ten-year-old son, standing by the door to the kitchen with his sketchbook in one hand and a bundle of pencils in the other.

"Nicky! You're supposed to be back in the kitchen."

"I... I got bored," he said, staring past his father at the body on the floor.

Nick moved to block Nicky Junior's view of Richey, then turned back to his men. "Clean that up now!"

"Yes sir," they said, almost tripping over themselves as they jumped from their chairs.

Nick pointed to Nicky's sketch pad. "What'd you draw this time, little Nicky?" he asked, hoping to distract the boy.

"Um..." Nicky looked down at his pad, then back up. "Just some flowers."

"Flowers? Flowers ain't something a boy should be drawing." Nick reached out and ruffled Nicky's hair. "Why don't you draw a bull fighter or a cowboy?"

"I... I like flowers," Nicky said, clearly still focused on the body.

"I blame your mother for that." Nick glanced back to see his men tossing a white sheet over Richey's dead body. "Speaking of your mom, she'd kill me if she knew I let you see this. Come on, let's go to the kitchen and get something to eat."

"Boss!" came a voice from over by the door. "We got trouble!"

Nick turned to see Tommy and Christopher looking out through the front window with their guns drawn.

"What?"

"It's Rudy! He's down!"

"What the..." Nick walked to the window and saw Rudy, one of his best and most trusted men for nearly ten years, lying face down on the sidewalk as the rain pelted his body. Nick cursed under his breath, turned to his men gathered behind him and jerked a thumb over his shoulder.

"Get out there and find out what's going on! Bring whoever did that to me. Alive."

He pushed past the men and walked over to Nicky, still standing by the kitchen door. He calmed his voice and put a hand on his shoulder.

"Look, little Nicky, there may be some trouble going on. Why don't you go back into the kitchen and hide out in the pantry for a little while?"

His father didn't know it, but Nicky loved hiding out in the pantry. It was quiet and dark, but with just enough light through the slats in the door to make sketches. It was the only place he could get away from all the noise from the kitchen and his dad shouting from the saloon. And now this. A dead man on the floor and who knew what outside. The pantry was exactly where he wanted to be.

CHAPTER

FORTY-SIX

TROUBLE AT PRINCE STREET

Rudy Carmona tried to squeeze his large frame underneath the small canopy just outside the Prince Street Saloon, but it was no use. Wind drove the rain in like bullets, pelting the side of his trench coat and drenching his shoes. Even so, he stood his post, ready for trouble wherever it might pop up. After everything Mr. Montello had done for Rudy over the years, he wasn't about to let a little bad weather stand in the way of keeping him safe.

Still, things weren't looking so good. Between the pouring rain and the darkness, he couldn't see a damn thing past the street. And standing in the dim glow of the only street lamp left him feeling exposed to anything that might be hiding out there in the shadows. But he wasn't without some help. The sporadic flashes of lightning turned night into day and gave him just enough time to check for any surprises. It wasn't much, but he appreciated any help he could get.

The skies refused to let up, sending rain down in sheets. It wasn't unheard of to attempt a hit in this kind of weather. Wait until their guard was down, then bam! Rudy had seen it before. It's why he didn't relax. Couldn't relax. Not even for a minute.

Lightning flashed, and for the briefest of moments Rudy thought he saw someone standing across the street. He wiped away the water dripping from the brim of his bowler hat, fixed his eyes on the spot and waited.

Seconds went by. It was all he could do to keep from blinking. Pretty soon, doubt started to creep its way in. Maybe his mind was just playing tricks. No one would be crazy enough to stand out in this rain. But his gut told him otherwise. So he kept his focus, steadied his breathing and waited. Something was out there. Something worth his attention.

Another flash and Rudy saw it. A woman standing on the other side of the street next to a pile of trash bags. She was there, then gone. Hidden again in the darkness. He pulled the gun from his shoulder holster.

"Who's over there?" he yelled, trying to raise his voice above the sound of the rain. "I'll give you about three seconds to scram."

Nothing. Not a peep. Was this broad playing some kind of game?

He spread his feet apart and aimed his gun in a two-handed grip. He was done with this. He'd given her plenty of warning. Next flash of lightning and Rudy would put a bullet in her just to be safe. He could figure out who she was later. Probably just another one of those dumb shop owners coming to beg Mr. Montello for more time on the security payments. They never learned.

Lightning lit up the street. Rudy squeezed on the trigger, then hesitated. The woman was gone. The hell? He stepped back and swept his gun from right to left, searching for any signs of movement. Nothing.

He considered crossing the street to go take a look around.

Rain or no, she needed to be dealt with. He took a step towards the street when he caught movement from the corner of his eye, then felt something cold and wet slide across his throat.

"Ack!" was all he managed to get out. He grabbed his throat and turned to see the woman. She was standing in the rain just a few feet away with a knife in her hand, dressed from head to toe in some red and black costume. Rudy thought it might be some kind of joke until he pulled his hand away and saw the blood. Lots of blood. Too much blood. He stumbled back and made a move to raise his gun, but fell to his knees instead.

He stared up at the woman. Rain dripping from the brim of his hat made it hard to see, but the street lamp cast just enough of a glow to make out the features of her suit. Yellow flowers blending into deep reds and blacks. Part of him wanted to jump up, grab her by the throat and squeeze the life out of her, but the other part felt strangely at rest. He was starting to understand now. She was no woman at all. She was beauty and death rolled up into one. A mistress of souls come to claim his for her collection. He wanted to fight back, but deep down he knew hers would be the last face he'd ever see in this life. And somehow, that was okay. No need to fight. No will to fight. Just a desire to give in and sleep. If hell had come calling for Rudy, who was he to refuse?

The last of his strength left him and he slowly crumpled to the ground like a rag doll. His hat fell off, rolled, then tumbled away in the wind until it was stopped by the street lamp. Rain slapped at Rudy's face and carried his blood away in a slow, red stream down the sidewalk to the street and into the gutter. Through fading vision, he watched as the woman stepped over him and disappeared into the alleyway next to the saloon.

CHAPTER FORTY-SEVEN

ROOM FOR MERCY

Mikey and Tommy the Bite walked outside into the pouring rain with their guns drawn. Mikey knelt down, grabbed Rudy by this trench coat and rolled him onto his back. Blood covered his throat and smeared the front of his coat.

"Jesus!" Mikey said, almost tripping over Rudy as he got back to his feet.

Tommy lowered his gun and stared down at the big man. His oldest friend left for dead on the sidewalk like some kind of animal. He'd seen a lot of death in this business, but this one hit home. Tommy and Rudy started with the family together when they were nothing but a couple of young hoodlums. They came up together. Side by side, rising through the ranks. Rudy was like a brother to him. Tommy couldn't remember the last time he cried, but now it was all he wanted to do. Just let it all out right then and there in front of Mikey and the whole fucking world. But this was no time for tears. He pushed them down and away and let anger take their place. A deep rage he'd never known before coursed through his veins. He would kill whoever did this. Kill them slow.

"Tommy, you okay?" Mikey asked.

Tommy shook his head and forced himself to turn away. Fueled by hate, anger and a deep need for revenge, he aimed his gun towards the alleyway.

"Let's check the back," Tommy said. "Whoever did this is gonna pay."

Quick bursts of lightning gave the knife hurdling towards him from the alley a strobe-like effect before the butt end smacked into his forehead and filled his vision with stars. He stumbled back a few steps in a daze as a woman appeared from the darkness, leapt into the air and kicked him square in the chest, sending him crashing down off the curb and onto the street. The back of his head smacked the pavement and Tommy the Bite fell into a world of darkness.

"What the hell!" Mikey yelled.

He swung around to shoot, but the woman kicked his hand just as he pulled the trigger. The bullet zipped by and struck the saloon, taking out a chunk of brick from the wall.

"Shit!"

Before he could fire off another shot, she closed in and punched him in the throat, then wrenched the gun from his grip and cracked him over the head. Mikey fell to the ground next to his friend and didn't get up.

With all the quickness and precision of a calf roper, Esi pulled a length of rope from the pocket sewn into her suit and bound both men back to back by their wrists. Giving the rope an extra tug to make sure escape would be difficult.

She stood and looked down on the men. It didn't feel right

to leave them with breath in their lungs. Especially when there was more work to be done. She remembered the soldier in Dahomey and Nawi's plea. Is there no room for mercy? Words echoed by Izara. Esi still did not like it. Mercy could get you killed. But she made a promise to Izara, and she intended to keep it. At least try to keep it. So far, the big man guarding the door had been her only exception, but as she headed into the darkened alley to finish her work, she knew there would be more. Some beasts cannot be tamed.

NICK WATCHED THROUGH THE WINDOW AS TWO MORE OF HIS BEST men were taken down in less than thirty seconds. This had to be the woman Richey couldn't stop blabbing about. Damned if she wasn't as quick as he said. He holstered his pistol, locked the front door and marched towards the back.

"It's her. That goddamn devil woman. Go make her disappear!" He yelled at the remaining men before he slammed open the kitchen door and disappeared inside.

Finch and Christopher gave each other a look, then hurried to the front window. Sure enough, Tommy, Mikey and Rudy were all down. Finch shook his head.

"You tellin' me a woman did all that?"

"That ain't no regular woman," Chris said.

"Don't let her get into your head, Chrisy. She ain't nothin' special. Just a goddamn woman gettin' lucky is all. And if she comes in here, her luck's gonna run out real quick."

The lights in the saloon flickered, then clicked off, leaving everyone inside stranded in darkness.

"Shit! She cut the goddamn power," Finch turned and marched to the bar to grab his Winchester shotgun. "She'll probably try to get the jump on us from the back." He chambered a round and put a box of extra shells on the bar. “Sully, go check on Squigs at the back exit. If he’s not dead yet, tell him about the girl and be ready. Make her dead. And have fun with it. The girl needs to be taught a lesson.”

Sully, who hadn’t moved an inch since the drama began, set his book aside, picked up his blade and smiled.

CHAPTER
FORTY-EIGHT
SHADOWS IN THE DARKNESS

Thunder rattled the walls of the old saloon as Sickle Sully crept his way through the dark hallway towards the back exit. His coat hung open, giving him easy access to the Bowie knife on his hip, but he wouldn't need it. As always, Fang would be enough. A hooked, eight-inch sickle blade with a hand-carved, wooden handle he designed himself a few years back. Razor sharp and always hungry for another bite of flesh, Fang was a trusted and reliable old friend.

Dim light from the back exit window wound its way around the corner of the hallway, making it possible to see shadows and silhouettes, but not much else. Sully preferred it that way. Darkness and shadows were his ally. The dark corners and closets of his home brought him comfort as a child. Comfort he never found in the daylight. He could hide in the darkness when his father beat his mother in another drunken rage. Eavesdrop in the darkness when she cried and cursed the day she married. And walk undetected in the darkness into his parents' room the night he used a kitchen knife to put an end to both their pathetic lives.

He took a few more steps down the hall, stopping at the turn. Around the corner was another hall that led to the back door where Squigs was supposed to be standing guard, but chances were good he was already dead. That meant the woman must be inside.

The floor creaked behind him. Sully spun and swung Fang through the air, slicing deep into a framed picture of Dogs Playing Poker and into the wall. He pulled it out with a 'thunk' and waited for another sound. But other than the tapping of rain on the roof, the hallway was silent. He must be on edge. He turned his attention once more to the hall around the corner. No doubt the woman was lying in wait for him there. For the first time in his life, Sully felt as though he were the one being hunted. He smiled. This was a game he thoroughly enjoyed.

Once again, the darkness watched over him. If the woman was around the corner, the light coming in from the back window would be just enough to reveal her location, while he remained hidden in the shadows. He moved quietly to the other side of the hallway, pressed his back to the wall and waited. This woman was a worthy opponent, he had no doubt, but even she couldn't fight blind. Sully was a spider, silently waiting for his prey to get stuck in his web.

Lightning flashed and she was there. Not down the hall, but right in front of him. She grabbed him by the lapels of his coat, pulled him around and threw him against the opposite wall. His back and head slammed hard into the wood. He opened his eyes just in time to see the woman in a red and black mask coming for him again. When she was almost on him, he lashed out with Fang in a quick, upward slash meant to cut her from gut to chin. But instead of flesh, it clanged against her own blade, knocking it off path and swishing through the air. Not missing a beat, Sully slashed again. Two quick strikes, right, then left. The woman dodged the first, then blocked the second with her blade. Clang!

Sully saw an opening and thrust Fang towards her chest, but the woman pivoted and cracked his jaw with a wicked left hook. Sully shook it off and swung Fang upwards, certain she wouldn't anticipate a counter attack so soon, and certain he'd cut her to the bone this time. But somehow he didn't. Fang swished through the air once more. Now he was getting angry. He tried to bring Fang up for another attack, but pain shot through his arm when he moved. He looked down and saw the woman's blade sticking through his wrist to the other side. Unable to hold on, Fang dropped from his hand and clattered on the wooden floor. The woman pulled her knife from his wrist, sending new bursts of pain shooting up his arm to his shoulders, then used the butt end to crack him once more across the jaw, followed quickly with a fist to his gut. The wind rushed from his lungs and Sully dropped to his knees.

She kicked Fang out of his reach, then knelt down and used her blade to push his chin up so she could look him in the eyes. Sully couldn't help but admire the cold, dark way she looked at him. Ever so slowly, he moved his good hand closer to the Bowie knife hidden under his coat.

"You can thank my friend for your life tonight," she whispered to him. "You will bleed to death if you do not get help soon. Go. Leave this place and do not look back."

Then she got up and left him there. Alive. Any admiration he may have held for this woman was gone. Never leave someone alive. Very sloppy. It looks bad and it will most certainly get you killed. A lesson this woman was about to learn the hard way.

He waited until her back was turned and she was about

halfway down the hallway, then quietly got to his feet and pulled the Bowie knife from its sheath. He was invisible again. Hidden in the darkness. The woman was so focused on Finch and Chris in the saloon that she'd forgotten all about him. Like a spider ready to feast on its prey, he quietly made his move.

CHAPTER FORTY-NINE

BROKEN FANG

"Somethin' ain't right," Finch said. "It's too quiet. We should've heard from Sully and Squigs by now."

Finch was in position behind the bar with his shotgun, while Chris kept watch near the front, pistol drawn, looking for any signs of trouble outside. The only light in the room came from a few candles and the soft glow of streetlight through the window.

From where he stood, Chris could see Tommy and Mikey. Both men were still knocked out cold on the sidewalk in the pouring rain. Tommy stirred once or twice, but Chris didn't think they'd be getting up anytime soon.

"Let me go check on the guys," Chris said. "We could use the extra help in here."

Finch almost laughed.

"We can handle one little girl. Besides, you'll be a sittin' target out there. Go check on Sully. Ain't no way that bitch got to him. He's probably back there sucking the marrow from her bones right now."

Chris took one last look outside, then pulled a second pistol from inside his coat and walked cautiously to the hallway entrance.

"Sully. What's goin' on in there?" he shouted.

When no one answered, he aimed both pistols into the darkness.

"Sully! You oka-"

Something slid from the darkness across the floor and bumped into his feet. He looked down and saw the curved blade of Sully's Fang, broken from its handle.

"Son of a bitch!"

WHILE CHRIS WAS MOMENTARILY DISTRACTED, ESI SHOT OUT FROM the darkness with the bat she'd found hanging on the wall and swung down hard on his wrists, knocking both guns to the floor. Chris had no time to react before she swung the bat a second time and connected with the side of his face. Chris stumbled back, lost balance and almost fell when Esi dropped the bat, grabbed him by the lapels of his coat and marched him backwards into the saloon towards Finch.

Finch aimed the shotgun at Finch and Esi.

"Let him go. Don't think I won't shoot you both to put an end to you," he said.

Chris was mostly unconscious and could barely stand on his own, but Esi held tight and kept marching him backwards.

"Fuck this," Finch said. "I'm gonna fill you full of holes!"

The sound of the shotgun blast echoed off the saloon walls. Chris's body jerked and then fell limp. Before he could chamber another round, Esi pushed Chris to the ground, pulled her knife from its sheath and flung it towards him. It spun twice in the air before sinking deep into his chest.

Finch fell backwards and smashed into the shelves full of liquor lining the back wall of the bar, then slowly slid to the floor as the bottles came crashing down on top of him. Esi hopped the bar, pulled the knife from his chest and turned her attention to the kitchen.

CHAPTER
FIFTY
THE BEST MISTAKES

If Nyah could take it all back, she would. Every last bit of it. Go back in time and leave Desi to fight her own battles. She could handle Clint on her own. Maybe. Better to get punched by a bully than lose a friend like Quin. If not for Nyah, Quin would still be walking around thinking about football, Dustin and homecoming. Things a normal kid should be doing. Instead, he's just another victim of gun violence. Another victim of the Angel.

But there's no going back. Like they say, what's done is done. Which was just too horrible for Nyah to think about. So she sat on the couch with her arms wrapped tightly around Danny's waist and her head on his shoulder, trying not to think about what was done. It hurt too much to move, or think, or breathe, or exist.

Thunder rumbled in the distance and tiny drops of rain tapped on the window in a quiet, sad rhythm, taming some of the chaos in Nyah's trapped soul.

"It's not your fault," Danny said again.

He'd already said it a dozen times, but he could say it a dozen more and it wouldn't change anything. As far as Nyah was concerned, it *was* her fault. All the things she shouldn't have done. All the things she wished she hadn't said. Everything was playing on an endless repeat in her brain. Still, she was thankful for Danny. Big shoulder to cry on and all. Without him, she knew she'd fall right over the edge.

Nyah guessed this was an all too familiar scene for Danny. All those years ago when her dad was gunned down by the Angel. Her mom curled up on the couch next to Danny much like she was now. Shattered and broken, pregnant and scared as hell on a night just like this one. Nyah wondered what it must be like to once again be comforting someone he loved from an unimaginable tragedy.

"Do you want some tea, Nybear? I can make some."

Nyah gripped Danny's arm. "Can you just stay right here?"

"Okay." Danny rested his head on Nyah's, content to let her cry all night if she needed to.

Danny's phone buzzed. He slid a free hand into his pocket and carefully pulled it out, trying not to disturb Nyah. He opened the security camera app and saw Desi walking to the front door. A second later, the doorbell rang.

"It's Desi," he said softly. "Did you invite her over?"

For the first time in what must have been an hour, Nyah lifted her head from Danny's shoulder.

"No," she said, wiping her eyes with the sleeve of her cardigan. "I didn't know she was coming over."

"Want me to tell her to come back later?"

Outside, the rain was picking up, pelting the house and windows. Nyah could only imagine what it was like for Desi standing outside. Why had she come here? Did she want to yell at her? Tell her she knew this was somehow all her fault?

Whatever. She deserved that and more. And she couldn't just send her home in this rain. What if she got into an accident? What then? Would that be her fault too? God this was all too much. She took a deep breath and readied herself .

"No, it's cool. Let her in."

DANNY SAW A DIFFERENT DESI WHEN HE OPENED THE DOOR. HER T-shirt was wrinkled, her hair was a mess and it looked like she'd been sleeping on someone's couch for a week.

"Hey, Desi. Come on in out of this rain. Trish is on the couch."

"Thanks," Desi said.

Nyah didn't get up. She just sat there with her hands between her knees, staring down at the floor. Without saying a word, Desi walked to the couch and sat down next to her.

"I'll make us all some tea," Danny said, thankful for an excuse to leave the girls alone. He was in the kitchen before anyone had a chance to protest.

A bolt of lightning struck close enough to send a shockwave of thunder through the house, shaking its old frame and rattling the windows. Nyah and Desi were unmoved. Both were beyond shock at this point. A moment later, the wind and rain unleashed fury outside, seeming to forget all about its earlier attempts to comfort Nyah's tired soul.

For a while, they sat quietly on the couch, listening to the rain and the growing awkwardness of the moment. Desi was the first to break the silence.

"So why'd you leave the hospital?"

"Nothing I could do there," Nyah said. "No one but family in the ICU."

"His dad's there now. I don't think he likes me. I don't think he likes anyone."

"What did the doctors say?"

Desi took her time responding. Either she had to think about how to word the answer, or what the doctors said was too painful to talk about. Or both.

"It's not good," she said. "He... he lost a lot of blood on the beach. It took a while before someone spotted him. If he survives, recovery will be a bitch. And that's IF he survives."

"Fuck."

"Yeah. Fuck."

Desi leaned over and rested her head on Nyah's shoulder. Both girls in silent agreement that more words were pointless. After a minute or two, Desi began to sob. Nyah put her hand on Desi's head and tried to fight back her own tears, but it was no use. Desi sat up and pulled Nyah close.

"This is really, really fucked up, Trish."

"I know."

They gave in and let the tears fall. For a while, the room felt cold and dark, without a trace of hope. When the worst of the tears were gone, Nyah pulled some tissue from a box, then offered the box to Desi.

"He's gonna be okay, right Trish?" Desi asked after grabbing a tissue for her eyes.

"He's Quin Grady, Desi. He's gonna beat this. Then he's gonna hold up the shirt he was wearing when he got shot and tell everyone he paid way too damn much for it."

Both girls laughed. A welcomed relief to the agonizing pain they'd both been feeling since this nightmare began.

"There's a big crowd of kids from school outside the hospital," Desi said. "The football team, cheerleaders, just about everyone came out for some kind of vigil."

"No surprise."

Desi punched the arm of the couch. "Just so random," she said. "Makes no fucking sense. The cops are saying on the news that it might be drug related. Can you believe that? Probably because he's black and he goes to an inner-city school. I don't like the way this feels, Trish. It's not right."

"I know. I'm... sorry."

Desi went quiet, and Nyah knew from experience something else was on her mind. After a few seconds, she looked back to make sure Danny was out of sight, then turned to Nyah.

"Look. There's something I need to ask you. Something else that's been on my mind. And now with all this, I really need to know."

"What?"

Without warning, Desi swung an open hand as hard as she could towards Nyah's face. In a blur of motion, Nyah's own hand shot up and caught Desi's just inches from her face. Desi's eyes opened wide.

"What the hell, Desi? Where did that come from?" Nyah asked.

Desi stood and took another look towards the kitchen.

"I should be asking you that!" she said in an angry whisper, not wanting Danny to overhear. "How did you do that? And don't say you took a self defense class!"

"Desi, listen..."

"No, Trish. You listen. Who the fuck even are you? I've been thinking about this ever since that ordeal with Clint. You're not who you say you are, and don't tell me I'm wrong. Because I'm not."

Trish looked up at Desi, not wanting to get up from the couch. Not able to get up. Desi's words cut deep. Her heart sank, her hands began to shake.

"What are you talking about, Desi?"

Desi sighed and slowly sat back down. Nyah noticed she put a little more distance between them. She took a few seconds to gather her thoughts, brushed a few strands of her curly bangs from her face and turned to Nyah.

"See, I'm a curious girl, and I wonder about things sometimes. Like this mystery girl who comes to town with a sketch past and kicks the hell out of one of the meanest boys at school. Then another mystery woman shows up and sends the girl who fights like Jason Bourne to the hospital. And now, my best friend gets shot and ends up fighting for his life. So I'll ask you again, Trish. Who - the fuck - are you?"

Nyah closed her eyes and looked down, clasping her hands tightly together to keep them from shaking.

"Desi, please. You don't understand. I can't-"

"No, I think I do." Desi got up and grabbed her coat from the rack, then turned back to Nyah.

"Trish, or whoever you are, let me know when you're ready to be real with me. Until then just... just stay away."

Before Nyah could respond, Desi stepped outside into the rain and slammed the door behind her.

"OKAY, I GOT CHAMOMILE AND..." DANNY'S VOICE TRAILED OFF THE moment he stepped back into the living. "Um... where's Desi?"

"She's gone."

Danny considered this for a moment, then decided it was best not to ask any questions. He sat the tray of tea on the coffee table, grabbed a cup for himself and sat down next to Nyah.

"Well okay then. Damn. Are you good?"

"No." After a pause, Nyah sighed and leaned her head once

again on Danny's broad shoulder. In the distance, thunder rumbled. Further away now. The storm had done its damage and moved on.

"I have to tell her, Danny."

"Tell her what?"

"Who I am. Who we are. What we are. Everything."

Danny took a sip of tea and thought for a moment.

"We don't do that, Nybear."

"Momma did with Dad."

"That didn't go well."

Outside, the wind picked up. Nyah could see faint flashes of lightning through the window, followed by more distant thunder. More rain was predicted to head their way later that night, but for now, the quiet hiss of air rushing through the vents was the only sound in the house. Nyah leaned over and grabbed a cup of tea, then scooted back on the couch with her knees pulled up to her chest and her tea cradled in both hands.

"Did she regret it?" Nyah asked as she blew gently on the tea. "Telling dad the truth?"

"That's a mixed bag." Danny leaned back on the couch. Both he and Nyah sipped on their tea as they watched the lightning dance on the horizon through the window.

"Your mom fell in love with a man and told him the truth about who she was. It got him killed, and believe me, she never stopped blaming herself for that."

"So she did regret it."

"No. Not for one minute. She fell in love with a good man, and then she had you. And you brought her a new kind of happiness. Sometimes bad decisions turn out to be our best mistakes."

"This may not be a bad decision," Nyah said. "If I don't tell Desi, she could get killed."

"Nybear, we don't do that. We can't risk exposing what we do."

"We also don't make friends and then almost get them killed."

Instead of responding, Danny took another long sip of tea.

"She's in danger. If we leave now, she'll be killed. She's smart, Danny. She already knows something is going on here. If I tell her, maybe I can earn her trust back. Maybe I can tell her to lay low until we figure this out."

"Or maybe she'll call the cops and this whole thing ends," Danny said.

Nyah took a sip. "She wouldn't do that. I know her."

Danny shook his head and laughed.

"You're just as stubborn as your momma."

"Thanks."

"It wasn't a compliment."

"I took it as one."

Danny massaged his temple with his free hand and thought carefully about his next words.

"Look, if you trust her. I mean really trust her, then you do what you gotta do, Nybear. I'll back you all the way."

Nyah sat her cup on the table, pulled a blanket up to her neck and rested her head on what was becoming her usual spot, so long as Danny didn't move.

"How come you and Momma never got together?"

Danny nearly spit out his tea.

"No, Nybear. That wasn't us."

"Yeah, but why?"

Danny considered this for a moment as if it were the first time he'd given his relationship with Rachel any thoughts beyond what it had always been. Friendship. Deep, lasting friendship.

"First off, your mom was too good for a broken-down

soldier like me. But second, our friendship just worked." He took another sip of tea. "And sometimes, I guess that's all you need."

Nyah smiled and snuggled closer to Danny.

"Still, I'm glad you're here," she said.

"I'm glad you're here too, Nybear. So glad."

CHAPTER FIFTY-ONE

A DEAL WITH THE DEVIL

Esi pushed through the swinging door and walked cautiously into the kitchen with her knife ready. The kitchen was dark, except for what looked like the faint glow of candlelight from around a corner in the back. Esi moved quietly along the wall towards the light until she heard the sound of a man humming a tune she'd never heard.

After a moment's pause, she turned the corner. The man stood near a desk in the light of three candles sitting on a rack meant for pots and pans. His back was turned to Esi as he lit a fourth candle on the desk.

Esi held her knife to her side and stepped closer to get a better look. As if expecting her, the man casually turned around and shook out the match. A gun holstered in a shoulder harness hung alongside a jacket on a rack near the back wall. This was Nick Montello, she had no doubt. Only he would be so bold as to stand there so casually after such chaos.

His eyes took in Esi's suit. "What the hell do we have here? On your way to a costume party, sweetie?"

Esi moved closer and glimpsed an unmistakable flash of

fear in Nick's eyes before he turned his head. The desk he was standing in front of was cluttered with papers. A framed photo of an older woman hung on the wall behind it. She stood wearing a dark skirt and a light-colored blouse with a high-fitted collar. A string of what looked to be imitation pearls graced her neck. She wore them beautifully. She stared emotionless into the camera. Her face reflected the wear of a hard life, but her lasting beauty could not be erased. There was an unwavering strength in her eyes. A woman who did what she had to do to make her way in a man's world.

"That's my mom," Nick said, noticing Esi's gaze. "She brought us here from Sicily to start a new life. Her name was Caterina, and she was one tough broad." He walked around the desk and sat down in a big leather desk chair. "I'm Nick. And you must be the little miss who's been giving me and my men so much trouble lately."

Esi turned her gaze to Nick, but said nothing.

"I figured from all the commotion, either my men got you or you got them. If Finch had come back here instead of you, I was gonna give him a raise."

"And what did you plan for me?"

Nick smiled and pulled a cigar from a box on his desk. "I was gonna ask you to work for me."

"I make no deals with the devil."

"Well that's not very nice," Nick said while lighting and puffing his cigar. "We just met. And from what I hear, you're the devil in the flesh."

Esi sheathed her knife and walked closer to Nick. The flickering shadows from the candlelight cast ghostly images across her blood-red mask.

"For you, this is true," she said. "The devil of Dahomey."

Nick blew a long stream of smoke into the air and grinned,

savoring the control he still had. This conversation would go at his own pace.

"Look, I don't know what this is all about, but I can make your life very comfortable, or very miserable. It's your choice. I'm guessing you took down Sully. That ain't easy to do. I could really, and I mean really, use someone with your skills on my team."

Esi sat down in one of the two chairs across from Nick's desk and folded her arms. She could feel Caterina's gaze. Steady and strong, questioning Esi's motives while she kept a careful watch over her son. She ignored it and pressed on.

"Do you like my English?" she asked Nick.

Nick said nothing.

"A friend taught me," Esi continued. "A friend you stole money from."

Nick laughed. "Is that what this is about, sweetie?"

"No. It is about everyone on that block. The ones you steal from. You will do this no more."

His smile faded and his rage, the thing Nick was known for, was beginning to show. He slammed his fist on the desk.

"You think you can walk in here and tell me how to run my business? Listen, honey!" He stood up and shoved a finger at Esi's face. "You don't come into my office and make deals with me. You have no idea the amount of hell I can bring you!"

Esi stood and pulled her knife faster than Nick could react, then stabbed it down between his fingers into the desk. Nick flinched and jerked his hand away.

"Your men cannot protect you now, Nick. It is just you and me here. You can sit and listen to my offer, or I can gut you like a pig and watch as you try to keep your insides from falling to the floor."

Nick stood silent and red-faced as if he were about to

explode, then glanced at the knife and slowly, reluctantly, sat back down.

"That's a good boy," Esi said. She pulled the knife from the desk, twirled it once and skillfully slid it back into its sheath. After a quick glance up to Caterina, she sat down.

Nick went back to puffing his cigar. "Alright, let's hear it."

"I know you, Nick. There is no stopping a man like you. But my friend thinks there is another way. A way of peace. A way of reason. So let us reason."

"You killed my men! You call that peace?"

"Not all your men. I call that a start."

Nick snorted and shook his head. "You got some balls, woman."

Ignoring this, Esi pulled a stack of folded bills from her pocket and tossed them onto Nick's desk.

"There is more money there than you can make in a year from shaking those poor people down, Nick."

Nick picked up the cash and thumbed through it. "How in the hell did someone like you come into so much cash?"

"It is a business proposition, Nick. I'm paying you to stop stealing from my friends."

Nick scoffed. "And if I refuse?"

"Then you will join your men in death."

Nick slapped the stack of cash down onto the desk.

"You don't threaten me, lady. I'm starting to lose my civility here."

Esi stood and leaned in with her hands on the desk. "And my tongue grows weary from so much talk. Take the money and live. Reject my offer and we can finish this now." Her right hand moved from the desk to the knife on her thigh.

Nick held up his hands in surrender. "Alright, alright. Damn, lady." He picked up the money and thought for a moment. "It's just one street. I got plenty more."

"So we have a deal?"

"This money clean?"

"Clean?"

"You know. Legit. Did you knock over a bank?"

"It is clean."

Nick counted the cash. Mostly as a way of buying some time to weigh his options. He took another long puff from his cigar and slowly exhaled.

"Okay. Why not? You got yourself a deal. I'll leave your little friends alone and you get the hell out of my office and never come back."

Esi smiled, but her eyes remained dark and cold.

"A wise choice, Nick."

"Now get the fuck out of my office," Nick said, pointing past Esi towards the kitchen door. "I don't ever want to see you again. You may be tough, but you ain't bullet proof. You decide to pay me another visit, and we'll be ready."

"Stick to your word and you will be free of me," Esi said. "For now, at least. Goodbye, Nick."

Nick watched as she turned and began to walk away. He rammed the cigar into the ashtray on his desk and clenched his fists. No way was she going to just walk out of here like that. Not after what she did. Dumb broad should have never turned her back on him. Big mistake. He grabbed the gun he kept stashed in his desk drawer, stood and aimed it at Esi.

"On second thought, how about I keep your money and put a bullet in your head. I'd call that a win, win."

Before he could pull the trigger, a searing pain exploded in his chest. Suddenly out of breath, he looked down to see a knife buried deep inside.

"The fuck did that come fro..." he tried to finish his sentence, but there was no more air to do it with. He dropped the pistol and grabbed the desk for support, but it was no use. He slowly sank to his knees, then fell sideways to the floor.

Esi walked around the desk and knelt down next to him.

"Some beasts cannot be tamed, Nick." She said, then grabbed the knife and yanked it from his chest. Nick let out a soft "unh" sound.

She wiped the blade clean on his shirt, then stood and caught Caterina's gaze one last time. It seemed to be fixed on her now. Her eyes filled with a mother's rage.

"I gave him the chance to live, Caterina. He chose death."

She stood locked in a staring match with Caterina for another long moment, then grabbed the money from Nick's desk and left. As Nick lay gasping his last remaining breaths, he watched as Esi walked beyond the reach of candlelight into the darkness. A few seconds later, the squeak of the swinging door as Esi left the kitchen would be that last sound to ever reach his ears.

CHAPTER FIFTY-TWO

NICKY JUNIOR

Nicky Junior never wanted to be like his father. He was just a kid, but he was old enough to know his father was a mean man who liked to hurt people. Not Nicky. Nicky wanted to make people smile and feel happy on the inside. And he knew he could do it. He saw it in his mother's eyes every time he drew a field of flowers, or a sunset over the beach. Her face would light up and she'd smile the prettiest smile he'd ever seen. He wanted to make the world smile like that. At least, until now. Now, things were somehow different. Something felt broken inside him. As he watched his father die through the slats of the pantry door, the only thing he wanted to do was scream, cry and hurt the woman who did this to him. Hurt her badly.

He sat quietly in the pantry as his hands moved the pencil with skill and ease on the pad, drawing light and shadows, lines and curves. Slowly, the woman in the scary costume came into focus. The woman he'd be seeing in his nightmares for years to come. He colored in the reds and blacks of her suit.

Every detail, down to the flowers on her mask, arms and legs. He wanted to remember, because he knew he'd find her again one day. And when he did, the woman in the costume would pay for what she did.

CHAPTER FIFTY-THREE

ASK ME ANYTHING

Desi stood in line at Burger Melt, ready to drown her sorrows in a plate of chili fries, when her phone kicked into the No Rain intro and Trish's picture lit up the screen. She considered ignoring the call. But only for a moment.

"Hey Trish."

"Nyah."

"What?"

A pause, then, "My name's Nyah, not Trisha. Nyah Carter. My mom's name was Rachel Carter."

Desi stood in stunned silence, not sure what to say next.

"Can I help you?" a teenage employee Desi had never seen before with "Christie" printed on her name tag asked.

"What? Oh... yeah," Desi said, her mind somewhere else completely now.

"Desi, you okay?" Nyah asked.

"Did you want to order something?" It was a busy day at the Melt and Christie was growing more impatient by the second. As were the people in line behind Desi.

Lionel the owner was working the grill with another

employee and waved when he saw Desi standing at the counter, but the look on his face told her he knew something was off.

"I... I gotta go," Desi said to Nyah.

"Look. Before you go, I want to talk. I'm... ready to talk. There's more I need to tell you. Come over. Please."

Desi took a breath to speak, hesitated, then ended the call.

"You need to order or step out of line," Christie said, motioning to the person behind Desi to step forward.

Lionel's smile faded and Desi could tell it was only a matter of seconds before he left his station to come check on her.

"Ma'am?" came a voice from behind her. "Are you-"

"Yeah... Sorry," Desi said finally. "Can I get a large order of chili fries?"

Christie sighed and began punching a few buttons on her register.

"For here or to go?"

Thoughts whirled through Desi's head, too fast to keep up. She tried to focus, concentrating on where she was, what she needed to do. It was no use. Nyah? More to tell? Was this some kind of joke?

"For here or to go?"

Forget it. Just order your damn fries, sit down and think it through. Trish... Nyah... whoever she is, she's trouble. Stay the hell away from her. Don't go. Remember Quin.

"Look, if you need more time..."

Christie must have noticed the distressed look on Desi's face because she eased up on her tone. Lionel set the spatula down and was about to make his way to the counter. Desi needed to do something. Anything.

She closed her eyes, grabbed the quarter hanging from her neck and squeezed it tight.

"To go," she said, then smiled and waved to Lionel before

he could take off his apron. Satisfied by this, he smiled and waved back.

“Got some fresh fries coming up just for you, Desi,” he shouted, then returned to his station.

“Thanks, Lionel,” Desi shouted back, then to Christie, “Oh, and two bottles of mineral water, please.”

One hour later, Desi was sitting next to Nyah on her bed with a mostly-empty basket of chili fries on the nightstand and Nyah’s Agojie suit laid out in front of them. The cherry-blossom vine lights on Nyah’s wall bathed the uniform in a warm and mysterious glow. To Desi, it was a thing of beauty. And if everything Nyah just told her was true, it was also something to be feared.

“So, you’re rich?” Desi asked, without taking her eyes off the suit.

“Is that all you got from this?”

Desi was mindlessly swirling the last bit of her drink around in the bottle, thinking more than talking. Nyah waited patiently for the questions she knew would come. And they did.

“So let me get this straight. There was an army of badass African women warriors called the Agojie?”

“Yes. In the kingdom of Dahomey, which is now Benin. European missionaries practically wet themselves when they encountered them. They were so freaked out by their strength and fighting ability, they compared them to Amazons.”

“Like Wonder Woman.”

“Yeah, sure. Minus the invisible jet.”

“But one day the French sailed in and conquered them?”

“Yeah.”

"If they were so tough, how'd they lose?"

"The French had better guns."

"And that was the end of them?"

"Mostly. But some kept fighting"

"Where? How?"

"In secret. They blended in with the villagers. Some seduced the French officers and killed them later."

"Brutal bitches."

"They'd cut your throat, then make a sandwich while you bled out on the floor."

"Fuck." Desi sat up straighter. "But one of them... Eso?"

"Esi," Nyah corrected.

"Yeah, Esi. She was friends with the king?"

"He loved her and he loved Dahomey. He trusted Esi to somehow keep the Agojie warrior alive."

"So she comes to America, starts kicking bad-guy ass until she gets too old, then finds and trains someone to take her place? All in the name of Dahomey?"

"Something like that."

"Something?"

"Exactly like that."

"And each new recruit swears to keep the line going?"

"Yup."

"And now you're the latest Agojie superhero?"

Nyah laughed. "No, not a superhero. No superpowers."

"Ever heard of the Black Widow? The Punisher? Hell, even Batman didn't have any superpowers." Desi had been into comics since she was little, so Nyah wasn't surprised when Desi made the connection and ran with it.

"I always thought of my mom as a superhero, but not me. I didn't even ask for this."

"The Agojie. Sounds like a superhero name to me," Desi said, clearly getting caught up in the Marvel theme. "I can almost see the comic book in my head now. Maybe a graphic novel."

"Damnit, Desi. This is fucking real life!" Nyah said, then immediately regretted it. "Sorry. I'm just a little stressed."

"Shit. No, I'm sorry. I got caught up."

"It's cool."

Desi repositioned herself on the bed to face Nyah more directly. "Okay, so how does Danny fit into all this?"

"Everyone needs a Danny," Nyah said. "And every warrior had one. Danny and my mom had a long history together, so it made sense to recruit him after her training ended."

"But then the mafia figured out your mom was the Agojie and killed your dad?"

Nyah took a second to respond. "Yeah."

"Sorry."

"It's fine. That's where everything kind of went south. The Agojie went underground and hasn't reappeared since."

"So, you. You're the last?"

"Yep. When I turn eighteen, I'm supposed to decide whether I want to carry on the tradition or run away. Choice is mine."

"So why you? Sorry, but it seems messed up that your mom recruited her only child to become the next Agojie warrior."

This was the source of way too many sleepless nights for Nyah. Why her? Her mom chose this life, not Nyah. She resented her mom for taking away any chance of being a normal kid, and she was never shy about reminding her of it. But now she could see her mom was only trying to protect her. A lesson learned too late. She'd never get the chance to tell her, and that kind of regret sticks around forever.

"She didn't have much of a choice. Some pretty dangerous people wanted us dead," Nyah said. "And I needed to learn how to protect myself in case... in case my mom wasn't around."

Desi drank the last sip of her mineral water and slammed the empty bottle down on the nightstand. Nyah understood why. She and Desi were different on some things, but on this they were the same. The pain of losing a parent never goes away. You never stop hurting, you just learn to deal with it a little more each day.

Desi waited a few seconds, then continued with her interrogation, twisting the ends of her blonde curls around her finger as the questions came to her.

"What for?" Desi asked. "I mean, isn't that what the cops are for?"

"Spoken like a white girl."

"Point taken."

"There's all kinds of bad things happening around you that the police can't or won't touch. Sometimes the police are the ones doing it. My job... or at least my mom's job, was to make them reconsider their life choices. You know, protect the oppressed and shit. A warrior for the weak."

"Who trains you to fight?"

"My mom. She taught me the Agojie fighting style. After she was gone, Danny recruited trainers. Senseis, coaches, people like that. Jada is one of them."

"Danny's girlfriend?"

"Don't get me started." Nyah grabbed her drink from the nightstand. "Fighting styles are added and changed over time, but the core fighting style, the one of the Agojie, stays the same. My mom spent years teaching it to me. Instead of hanging out with friends, I was learning how to break someone's arm in two moves."

Desi leaned forward and ran her free hand along the

uniform, feeling the material and touching the patterns. There was something hypnotic about its design.

"So why the uniform?"

"So we don't get recognized," Nyah said.

Desi gave Nyah the side-eye and smiled. "Like Clark Kent? Peter Parker?"

"Fine," Nyah couldn't help but laugh. "Like a super hero. You happy?"

Desi picked up the suit and held it out at arms length. "Yeah, I bet it makes your ass look good too. Tell me I'm wrong."

Both girls broke out into some much-needed laughter. Something neither had done in a long while. It felt like sitting down to a favorite meal after a day without food.

Nyah grabbed the sleeve of the suit. "There's something powerful about wearing it. Like all the tradition and power of the Agojie warrior transfers to you once you put it on."

"And you, like, made it yourself?" Desi asked as she gingerly laid out the suit across the bed.

"This one, yeah. My mom taught me. She was taught by the one before her. And so on and so on. The materials have changed, but the design is the same. Esi and Izara's design."

Desi traced the flowers along the sleeve with her finger.

"The Gbehutu flower," Nyah said.

"Okay. So, what's the point of flowers on your suit?"

"Esi said it was to remind us that Dahomey was also a place of healing and beauty, not just war."

Nyah could tell Desi was lost in thought, thinking of ways to put her questions into words. She gave her time to do it. All the time she needed.

"So, do you even want to be the next Agojie?" she finally asked.

"No. I mean... Damn!" Nyah closed her eyes and banged the back of her head lightly against the headboard. "I used to think, hell no. Once I'm free from this bullshit, I'm gonna disappear and never look back. But now..." She gripped the sleeve of her suit like a security blanket in one hand. "I guess I'm not so sure anymore."

"But like, doesn't the whole damn thing depend on you now? Like, wouldn't it end with you?"

"Yeah. Maybe. Danny could find someone else. But maybe it's time, you know? Things went a little haywire when the crime family figured out who my mom was and put out a hit on her. I'm just sayin'. Maybe it's a good time to disappear and never look back."

"You mean run away?"

Nyah didn't respond. She recognized the look on Desi's face. She had more questions, tons more, but she wasn't sure how, or what, to ask.

"I tried like hell to keep you and Quin away from me," she said, trying to change the subject.

"Really? You were so friendly, I didn't even notice."

Nyah leaned over and nudged Desi with her shoulder. "Yeah well, I got to be honest, I'm glad you pushed your way in. Ever since I met you and Quin, life has been... different. It's been good."

"We're good together," Desi said, and reached out her fist. Nyah returned the fist bump. "Like dancing bees."

"Right. But then I got Quin shot and put you in danger. Why are you even talking to me right now?"

"Because that's what friends do. You'll learn that someday," Desi said.

Desi grabbed Nyah's arm. "Look, I know you feel like shit right now, but this whole thing wasn't your fault. And I know Quin would agree."

Quin's memory and their whole messed up situation

flooded into Desi's mind. She suddenly felt like she'd been punched in the gut. She leaned her head back and covered her face with her hands.

"But what the hell are we gonna do? It's not like we can just go on with life as usual while that Angel bitch is out there," Desi said. "What kind of name is that for an assassin anyway?"

"My mom said she stole it from a famous French assassin. I guess even villains have heroes."

"So the Angel works for the mob?"

"More than just works for. She's Fiona Montello, Bruno Montello's sister."

"The crime boss?"

"That's the one. When they were kids, Bruno spent his time learning the family business, but Fiona was more into hurting people. She hung out with all her dad's hitmen, learning the tricks of the trade. My mom figured all this out while we were on the run."

"Damn."

"Not many people have seen her face. Unlike her brother, she stays out of the spotlight. She's somewhere close, but I don't know where. And she said she'll kill you next if I run."

"And that's why you're still here."

"And why you're still alive."

Desi took a deep breath and slowly exhaled. "You're not going to actually go meet her, are you?"

"I have to."

"She kicked your ass."

"She ambushed me."

"You need a plan."

"I have a plan." That was a lie, but Nyah didn't want Desi to get more worried than she already was. She'd think of something. She had to. More than ever, she wished her mom were here. She'd know exactly what to do.

"Bullshit. I know that look. You have no idea what to do."

Nothing got past Desi. It was a little annoying, but Nyah respected her for it.

"Fine. But I'll figure something out."

Desi picked up Nyah's sheathed knife sitting on the bed next to her suit and read the words engraved on the handle. "Victory sharpens the blade. Defeat sharpens the mind."

"It's sort of an Agojie creed. It's older than Esi."

"So why don't you just do one of those ninja rolls and hurl this into her chest?" Desi asked, still examining the knife.

"She'd see it coming a mile away."

Nyah reached over and took the knife from Desi. "Besides, this is what she's after." She traced the string of numbers engraved along the side below the creed with her finger. "These numbers could give her access to our money. And she'll kill me to get it."

"So you think facing her head on will change that? Can't you at least get Danny's help? He was some kind of commando or something, right?"

"If I told him, he'd just try and keep me away. I can't do that. I have to finish this myself."

Nyah pulled the knife from its sheath and twirled it once in her hand. A trick she'd practiced thousands of times over the years, and came as naturally to her now as walking. She turned the blade over in her hand while she thought, the light from the lamp reflecting off the blade into her eyes with each rotation. After a few turns, she froze on the Agojie creed. She stared for a few moments as a plan finally began to form in her mind.

"I know how to beat her," she said, then re-sheathed the knife and tossed it onto the bed.

Desi sat up and looked Nyah in the eyes. "Oh shit. You mean it this time!" After a pause, she added, "You gonna tell me or is it top secret?"

Nyah picked up her suit and stuffed it into her sling bag, then grabbed a notepad from her desk and wrote Danny a note.

Going to the hospital. I'd text, but I know you'd try and stop me.

Be back later.

Love you.
Nybear

"I'll do it my way. The Agojie way," Nyah said as she folded the note and wrote Danny's name on it.

Desi sprang from the bed. "What do you need from me?"

"Drop me off at the hospital, then stay there with Quin," Nyah said.

"They won't let me in. I'm going crazy, Trish. I mean Nyah. Standing around, wondering if Quin's gonna die on that hospital bed. I need this. I want to help you take this bitch down."

"No." Nyah stood up and grabbed Desi's hands, much the same way Desi held Nyah's hands in the hallway that day after the panic attack. "Look at me. You are an amazing friend. It's what you do best. Go do that for Quin. He needs you. And please, let me do what I do best."

Desi pulled her hands away and turned to the window. "Dammit, Nyah. You're not gonna go and get yourself killed are you?"

"Wasn't planning on it."

She turned back to Nyah, her eyes moist with tears. "Promise me!"

"I... promise." Nyah knew this could go either way, and

chances of her getting clipped were pretty good, but what was the point? Desi needed to know she wasn't about to lose another friend, and Nyah understood.

"I'll come back in one piece."

Desi wiped her eyes and grabbed her keys from the nightstand. "Good. Then let's do this."

Nyah turned to leave, then hesitated. "Wait." She grabbed her phone, typed out a message and sent it.

"Who'd you message?" Desi asked.

"Malcolm."

Desi's jaw dropped.

Nyah flashed a slightly devious smile. "We're just talking, okay?"

"Girl! I knew you two might hit it off."

Nyah shook her head in mock protest. "We're just talking."

"Talking about gettin' it on!"

Nyah pushed past Desi towards the door.

"Oh my God. Let's just go."

Desi smiled as she followed. "We're *so* gonna talk about this later."

CHAPTER FIFTY-FOUR

THOUGHTS AND PRAYERS

Desi got lucky with a parking spot just a few feet away from the crowd. She pulled her faded green Toyota in and killed the engine, then both she and Nyah sat in silence, watching the crowd. Many brought flowers and balloons, some held up signs showing their support, while others just hugged and cried.

The rain thinned out the crowd a little, but not much. Nyah couldn't help but admire their dedication. TV news crews were there too, hoping to grab a sound bite or two from a close friend or relative. Nothing got ratings like a local football star falling victim to gun violence.

"Oh look, there's Dustin," Desi said, pointing to the crowd.

He was standing alone by the curb with his hands in his pockets. He spotted Desi and Nyah, waved and walked over. The rain was down to a light drizzle, so Desi and Nyah got out to greet him.

"Hey, Dustin. You okay?" Desi asked.

"Yeah. I mean no. I mean, goddamn," he said.

His eyes were red from tears. He wiped the corner of one eye and looked down.

"I don't even know what to do," he said. "Feels dumb just standing around here."

"You're doing all you can," Desi said. "Just be here for him."

Dustin shook his head.

"Have you eaten?" Nyah asked. She knew how easily it was to forget about things like eating when you lost someone close. She'd gone two days without food when her mom died. Danny had to practically force her to eat some soup he'd made.

"No."

"Let's go get a cheeseburger," Desi said. "I'm buying."

Dustin glanced at the crowd, then looked back down at his feet.

"He'll be here when we get back, Dustin. There's nothing you can do. And Quin would want you to take care of yourself." Desi said.

"Okay. Yeah, sure. I guess I am kind of hungry."

"Good. Now get in the car."

Desi waited for Dustin to get in and shut the door, then wrapped Nyah in a tight hug.

"Don't get killed. I will never forgive you for that." She held on a little longer, then let go and looked her in the eyes. "Promise me."

Nyah smiled. "I'll be okay."

Desi kept staring into Nyah's eyes for a few more seconds, then smiled. "Yeah, I know you will. You're a badass Agojie warrior. Kick that bitch's ass for me."

Nyah grabbed her sling bag from the car, then put her hand on Desi's shoulder. "Thanks for being my friend."

"I'm buying you a cheeseburger after this shit is all over."

"I could use that."

The car door opened and Dustin jumped out. For a second, Desi thought he'd changed his mind.

"Damn, Trisha." He said, holding out a hand. "I was so caught up in all this, I forgot to say thanks."

Nyah gave Dustin's hand a slap. "For what?"

"Quin told me what you did. He said you gave him strength to come out and ask me to the dance."

"He would have done it on his own. Eventually."

"Anyway. Thanks. You're a good friend."

Nyah wished she could believe that. Dustin smiled, held her gaze a second longer, then hopped back into the car and shut the door.

Desi walked to the driver's side and leaned over the roof to whisper, "Don't. Get. Killed."

Nyah clutched the strap of her sling bag. "I need a place to change."

Desi smiled. "Like a phone booth?"

"Oh my God."

Desi pointed to the hospital. "Try the bathroom in the lobby."

Nyah watched as Desi hopped into the car, cranked the engine and drove away. Down the lot to the exit, onto the street and into the night. The rain picked up and the cool, wet breeze chilled Nyah to the bone. For a time, all she could do was watch. A small part of her wanted Desi to come back. Maybe together they could come up with a better plan. Maybe something just clever enough to work and beat the Angel. Maybe. Or more likely, the Angel would make Nyah watch as she killed Desi right in front of her. No, this was the right way. The only way.

Nyah closed her eyes and turned away. To the phone booth, to the super suit, to destiny and maybe her own death.

But no matter her fate, she knew this was right. Fonville, the Burger Melt, her friends, all of it. Houston wasn't just another stop, it was home. And she wasn't about to let the Montello family take that away from her. Not again. She was done running. Tonight, she would fight and defend her friends, even if that meant she'd never see them or Danny ever again.

CHAPTER FIFTY-FIVE

THE ANGEL

Fiona Montello, known to everyone at Fonville High School as Coach Stasney, walked quietly along the hike-and-bike trail parallel with the bayou, towards a section beneath a bridge still under construction. She'd gotten there early, parked the rental close by and took her time walking the trail to make sure Nyah wasn't planning any surprises.

Underneath her long coat she wore the Angel suit with the mask tucked away in a pocket. For the money transfer, she brought a laptop and a portable WiFi device in a bag slung over her shoulder. She was done taking chances. She would get the money and finally put an end to this.

So far, nothing seemed out of place. The four, homeless drunks clustered together under a bridge they no doubt called home, the convenience store owner sweeping up the front lot before closing up shop, and a bicyclist riding in her direction. She lowered her head as he rode past, glancing up just long enough to size him up. He was in incredible shape and looked to be training for a race, but he wasn't a threat. One of the many advantages of working at Nyah's school was knowing all of her friends, and Mr. Iron Man was not one of them.

The question of how Fiona came to be working an assignment at the same school Nyah was enrolled in still bugged her. After Oklahoma City, Nyah and Danny dropped out of sight completely. Word went out and the price for information doubled, but still nothing. Until Fiona just happened to stumble across Nyah in the school bathroom that day. Just dumb luck maybe. Except Fiona didn't believe in luck. Especially with those odds. She was certain someone was working to bring them together, but her questions would have to wait. Getting to Nyah and taking the Agojie down was all that mattered. So she went off grid to keep Bruno out of it and came up with a plan to catch Nyah on her own. She could figure out who to thank, or kill for the chance encounter later.

This was a moment years in the making. She'd always wanted to get to the Agojie before her brother fucked things up. And yes, this was personal. It turned personal years ago when Rachel embarrassed her in front of her men at Warren's apartment, then slipped right through her goddamn fingers. She'd spent too many good years of her life trying to track Rachel down after that for it to be anything less than personal.

Fiona fell into a slump after Rachel's death. Nothing felt right anymore. She still did jobs for Bruno, but her heart was never in it. That is, until she learned Rachel had a daughter. A daughter who would carry on the Agojie legacy. It was like a slap in the face to Fiona, but it also gave her new hope. And now, after all those years of tracking, mapping and planning, the time had finally come. She shook her head and laughed to herself. Life definitely had a sense of humor.

Maybe it was luck after all. Maybe their meeting was inevitable. Maybe fate had smiled on Fiona for once in her screwed-up life. She liked that explanation, even if her gut told her it was bullshit.

Her plan hinged on Nyah not getting stupid and calling the cops, of course. If she did, Fiona had a pretty simple alternate plan. Disappear and kill Desi as a message. A small setback, but she'd find Nyah again. In the end, Fiona always got what she wanted.

Her phone buzzed. It was a number she recognized. She hesitated, then answered.

"How'd you get this number?"

"Where the hell have you been, Fiona?"

Fiona sighed. She'd hoped to avoid Bruno until after Nyah was caught and the money was safely transferred to her account, but once again her big brother proved more resourceful than she gave him credit for.

"You sent a sniper to kill Nyah," she said. "At her school. Are you fucking stupid? You're begging to get the cops crawling up our asses. And I can't get her knife if the cops get to it first."

"I told you he did that on his own. Stupid move." Bruno said, then paused as he put the pieces together in his head. "Did you find her? Did you find the Agojie and not tell me? Is that why you disappeared? You're trying to do this all on your own again aren't you? Just like with Rachel."

"Sorry big brother, but I just don't trust you with this job." Fiona regretted bringing up Nyah, but she supposed he had to know the truth eventually. She turned to make one last visual sweep of the trail before settling in and waiting for Nyah to show up.

"You're lucky I found her again," she said.

"Where is she?"

"About to walk into my trap."

"Enough with these games!"

The store owner was lowering the roll gate in front of his store and locking up.

"I'm not playing any."

"Tell me where she is, Fiona. I'll send some guys to help. Look, there's a lot on the line here. A lot you don't know about."

"That's what you keep telling me. But I'm working solo this time."

Another guy on a bike. This one was shirtless and riding on the street with one hand on the grip and the other carrying two plastic bags loaded down with groceries.

"Look, little sis. After dad died, we promised we'd be in this together. That we'd stay in this together."

"We still are. Once I get that knife and the numbers, I'll make the transfer, then take care of her."

Bruno exhaled into the phone. Fiona knew he was trying to control his anger. She could picture him at his desk with his eyes closed and pinching the bridge of his nose while he tried to slow his breathing.

"Shouldn't you be sketching something?" Fiona asked. He'd become quite the artist after all these years.

"Like I said before, I need them both gone," Bruno said, ignoring Fiona's question. "There are bigger things at play here. Things that could change the trajectory of our family for good. And as long as those two are alive, they could be a problem."

"You think I'd let Danny walk away after all this? Brother of mine, I thought you knew me better than that."

A loud noise on the other end. Fiona thought maybe it was a chair crashing to the floor, or Bruno's fist pounding on the desk. Either way, he was angry.

"Dammit, Fiona! Give it up! What's your plan here anyway? You think Danny's just gonna make a wire transfer for all that cash? You know how many red flags that would raise at the bank?"

The three homeless drunks talked and laughed while they set up their makeshift beds for the night.

"You leave that up to me. I have a secret weapon."

Fiona heard a glass clink and what sounded like liquid pouring on the other end of the line. Therapy time.

"Gotta hand it to you, Fiona. You don't give up easily. If you can actually pull this off, maybe you should consider management when you get back."

"I prefer the field."

"Whatever. But I got to be straight with you, sis. I can't let you embarrass me again without consequences. People are watching and I've got to look strong. Family or no, you fuck this up again and you better disappear for good this time."

"I love you too, big brother."

FIONA ENDED THE CALL AND SLIPPED THE PHONE BACK INTO HER inner-waistband pocket, then turned the corner to the decommissioned part of the trail. About a hundred feet in was a bridge. No traffic above, no lights below and best of all, no witnesses.

She lifted the construction tape and crossed underneath. The storms had filled the bayou to its brink. Darkness made it difficult to see, but she could hear the low rumble of rushing water as it swept away anything unlucky enough to fall into its path. She'd have to be careful not to slip on the wet concrete and tumble down the steep embankment just off the trail's edge.

This time, her plan was as solid as they come. After the transfer, she would kill Nyah and toss her body into the bayou where the water would carry her for miles before anyone found her. Then she'd just need to get to Danny before he could disappear again. Everyone is happy and Bruno still looks like a goddamn hero to the family. Too bad he wouldn't be able to enjoy it for long.

Her plan for him was almost as flawless as this one. Kill Bruno, pin the murder on their rivals and take over the family business. Bruno had run the family's name into the ground long enough. It was time for a woman to take the lead. With Bruno out of the picture and the Agojie bankroll, she'd be able to bring real power and respect back to the Montello family.

She'd just made it to the bridge when she realized her mistake. Weren't there four homeless bums? She cursed herself for letting Bruno distract her from the job. She set her bag down next to a bridge pillar, turned around and came face to face with the Agojie.

"Hey coach." Nyah said, then rammed her forehead into Fiona's nose.

Fiona stumbled back a few steps. Nyah, dressed in her Agojie suit, closed in and clocked her with a right and left hook, then finished with a jumping roundhouse kick to her jaw that knocked Fiona off balance just enough to lose her footing, slip on the wet pavement and fall to the ground.

Nyah, not Nyah now but the Agojie, rushed in before she could recover and kicked her twice in the ribs. Fiona grimaced and rolled to her side, looking up just in time to see the Agojie reaching for her blade. She kicked out hard with her left leg and swept the Agojie's feet from under her, sending her crashing down to the ground. The impact jarred the knife from her grip and it skidded out of reach.

Lightning fast, the Agojie rolled and rammed an elbow into Fiona's gut, forcing an "Oof" sound from her mouth as the wind rushed from her lungs. Nyah jumped on top and used her legs to pin down Fiona's arms, then unleashed a series of right and left-hooks to her face, fueled by anger, hatred and sadness.

"You... killed... my... dad!" Each word punctuated with another blow to Fiona's face while she peered down through her mask with steel, cold eyes. "You should have... stayed... away!"

Teetering on the verge of unconsciousness, Fiona forced herself awake and waited for an opening. It didn't take long. When the Agojie pulled her fist back for a finishing blow, Fiona bucked her hips, throwing her off balance just enough to pull her arms free, grab the Agojie's head in both hands and ram her forehead into her nose, returning the earlier favor. The Agojie's head jerked backwards and Fiona slung her to the ground.

She scrambled to her feet, ripped off her jacket to reveal the Angel suit and reached for the Sig Sauer P365 holstered at the small of her back.

NYAH'S MIND SLIPPED INTO PANIC WHEN SHE SAW THE GUN.

Oh God it's a gun, it's a gun, it's a gun! I'm dead! Momma help!!

No. Focus. fight. Kill her!

Nyah charged Fiona and wrapped her in a bear hug, intending to pick her up and slam her to the ground. But Fiona was ready this time. Something hard cracked against the back of Nyah's skull and everything went dark.

CHAPTER
FIFTY-SIX
DANNY

"You've got to stop pacing, baby," Jada said. She was leaning forward on Danny's couch with her arms resting on her knees, watching as Danny wore down the rug between the couch and the window. "She just went to check on Quin. She'll be fine."

Danny knew Jada was right. He needed to calm down. But he also couldn't help but wonder if the note Nyah left was bull-shit, and the thought of where she might actually be scared him to death. He wanted so much to tell Jada the rest of the story. The part where Trisha was actually Nyah, a kid burdened with an ancient warrior legacy, and right now she could be out there somewhere trying to stop the mob's deadliest assassin on her own. But he knew she'd have questions he couldn't answer. At least not yet.

"Yeah, you're right," Danny said.

He gripped his phone and considered calling Nyah one more time, then forced himself to slip it into his back pocket and leave it there.

"She'll call when she's ready," Jada said, as if reading his thoughts. She stood and put a hand on Danny's shoulder. "I don't like seeing you like this. Seriously, what's bothering you? I know when something's on your mind."

Instead of answering, Danny turned and walked back to the window to look for any signs of Nyah. The rain was picking up again, tapping on the window like tiny rocks. Flashes of lightning lit up the night sky, followed by the low rumble of thunder. He closed his eyes and tried to fight off thoughts of everything that could go wrong.

After losing Rachel, Danny fell into a world of depression. He might have ended it all if not for Nyah. She became his focus. She was the only thing that kept him going. Raising her and keeping her safe was all that mattered. If anything happened to her...

He felt Jada's arms wrap around his waist and her head lean against his back. She was warm and comforting, calming his nerves and easing his fears with just a touch. It was all he needed.

"Come to the kitchen with me, babe." she said. "I'll get you a beer and we can make some dinner. That always helps to get your mind off things."

Danny turned around and pulled her close. Her hair smelled of vanilla with hints of coconut. It was in two-strand twists, pulled back in a ponytail. He always loved how it accentuated the natural beauty of her face.

"I don't know how I got so lucky," he said.

Jada looked up at him and smiled. "You waited long enough. Maybe it was just your turn."

Danny wondered if she would feel the same if she knew the truth about who he was and the things he'd done. The Agojie was a way to make amends for all that. A way to take back some of the hurt he'd caused, even though he knew deep down the guilt would never really go away. He was a different person now because the Agojie gave him a second chance on life. Would Jada be so forgiving?

Danny's gaze drifted from Jada back to the window. "It's just this thing with Trisha-"

Jada put a finger to his lips. "Dinner," she said. "You need a distraction, and I'm hungry. Win, win. And I'll bet Trisha walks through that door before you're done cooking."

Dinner was the last thing on his mind, but once again Jada was right. Danny's troubles could be forgotten in the kitchen. And there were plenty of troubles to forget at the moment. He'd racked his brain thinking of all the places Nyah might have gone, but kept coming up empty. All he could do was sit and wait and hope like hell she'd call.

"What sounds good?" Danny asked as Jada led him into the kitchen by the hand.

She nudged him towards the stove, then grabbed two beers from the fridge, popped the lids and gave one to Danny.

"Hmm. Surprise me," she said as she hopped up onto the counter behind him and took a sip of beer.

Danny thought for a moment, then smiled. "Ever had tilapia with lemon-caper sauce? It's quick and delicious."

"Oh sweet damn. You had me with lemon-caper sauce."

"You'll love it. Can you grab the capers from the pantry?"

A few minutes later, with the help of a beer, a cutting board, a hot skillet and Danny's playlist streaming in the background, his mind was at ease. At least for a while.

He was slicing cherry tomatoes with his favorite knife when a new message alert dinged on his phone. It was in his hand before the text tone could fade. He opened the message and froze, kitchen knife in one hand, phone in the other.

Jada immediately set her beer aside and hopped down from the counter.

"Is it Trisha?"

"What the..." was all Danny could get out.

As Stevie Wonder sang Superstition through the speaker on the counter, Jada pulled the Glock 43 hidden inside her purse and aimed it at Danny's back.

He was still frozen in place, back turned to Jada and staring at the message when Jada spoke again.

"I think it's time to put that knife down and turn around, Danny."

CHAPTER
FIFTY-SEVEN
REVELATIONS

"Good goddamn!" The sound of Fiona's voice woke Nyah from a dream. She was in her Agojie suit, lying face-down on the concrete. Her body ached all over and her head was pounding. She remembered ambushing Fiona, then the gun, but nothing after that. She tried to move, but her hands were bound behind her back with what felt like zip ties. They clenched tightly around her wrists, cutting off the circulation to her hands. Fiona was sitting next to her, dressed as the Angel and typing something out on her phone.

"I guess I underestimated the hell out of you," she said when she noticed Nyah was awake. "Let me guess. You got here early, recognized your coach walking around on the trail and put two and two together. And blending in with those homeless dudes! Respect, girl. Maybe there's more of the Agojie warrior in you than I thought."

A clap of thunder, then the downpour. A hard, steady rain. The kind that floods the streets and keeps the TV news on late.

Nyah rolled onto her back and tried to sit up, but couldn't. It hurt just to move. She tried to settle into something similar to a comfortable position, but even that seemed impossible. She closed her eyes and ignored the pain like she'd been taught. Forcing herself to remain calm and wait for her chance to get out of this mess. If it ever came.

Oblivious to her struggle, Fiona finished typing on her phone, then put a hand to her ribs and grimaced.

"Damn, that's gonna hurt tomorrow. Your mom taught you some good moves, girl."

From her bag, Fiona pulled the laptop and WiFi device and set them down next to her. She typed something in, then turned back to Nyah.

"I sent Danny a nice text. In ten minutes, my phone will ring and we're gonna have a little chat about a certain password I need." She pointed to a window on her computer filled with lines of numbers. "And this program will do the rest."

Nyah's eyes widened. "You stay the fuck away from Danny!" she yelled. "Don't touch him!"

Fiona reached over and patted Nyah on the head.

"There, there. Try to relax, Nybear. You'll need your strength."

A flash of lightning, then thunder. Nyah felt a heavy weight pressing down on her chest. The rain turned into impenetrable walls on either side of the bridge, imprisoning her forever. The oxygen seemed thinner now. It was harder to breathe. She could feel herself beginning to sweat underneath her suit. Another goddamn panic attack. She had to break free and warn Danny. She had to get out. Had to, had to, but she couldn't! She reached for her phone tucked away in a pocket on the thigh of her suit, but it was no use. She closed her eyes and cried silently. Damn damn damn damn! Stupid, stupid, stupid! Danny and the entire Agojie legacy was in danger and it was all her fault!

CHAPTER FIFTY-EIGHT

BETRAYED

"Jada, what are you doing?"

"About to get rich," she said. "What did the text say?"

When Danny hesitated, Jada raised the gun higher to remind him who was in charge.

Danny shook his head. "It... it just said to call this number in ten minutes if I want to see Ny- I mean Trisha again."

"It's okay. You can say Nyah." Jada kept the gun aimed at Danny and used her free hand to push a few buttons on her phone. She turned the screen for Danny to see a timer set for ten minutes.

"We're going to sit here and wait for this timer to go off," she said, then set the phone down on the counter next to her laptop. "When it does, you're gonna call that number."

"Who am I calling? Was that the Angel?"

Jada smiled. "Your favorite arch enemy."

Danny took a step forward and Jada raised the gun. "Don't, Danny. Just don't."

"Jada... I-"

"Look, I know you got a million questions running around

in that big ol' head of yours," Jada interrupted. "But first I gotta get some things ready."

Jada glanced at her watch. The watch Danny bought her on the anniversary of their first date. How could he have been so stupid? She opened her laptop and began punching keys with one hand, holding the gun steady on Danny with the other.

He did have a million questions, but they'd have to wait. This was a job now, and he needed to focus. He obviously didn't know who the woman in his kitchen was, but he was pretty certain she wasn't a pro. Too many tells, down to the way she held the gun in her left hand so she could type with her dominant right hand. But the biggest was how she left Danny standing by the stove within easy reach of all sorts of potential weapons. Including his favorite kitchen knife he'd been using to slice tomatoes. He'd have to bide his time and wait, but he might be able to turn the tables if he could get to that knife.

"Can I at least take the pan off the stove?" Danny asked, motioning to the sizzling skillet.

"Sure."

Danny turned and moved the skillet from the burner with one hand and reached for the knife with the other.

"Stop!" Jada yelled. "You moved the pan, now put your hands up and turn around. I don't want you trying anything funny."

The knife was almost within reach, but stretching his hand out any further could make Jada nervous enough to accidentally fire off a shot. He raised his hands and slowly turned around.

"Not doing anything funny," he said. "Just me, turning back around."

Jada examined the laptop screen for another moment, then turned to Danny and leaned on the counter. Without saying another word, she picked up her phone from the counter and began to scroll, still pointing the gun at Danny in a lazy, one-handed grip, allowing it to lean slightly to the side. Danny couldn't figure out if she was looking at something on her phone related to the plan or just scrolling social media.

After a minute or so, Danny broke the silence.

"Look, while we're waiting for this phone call, can you tell me what this is all about?"

"You always were so impatient," Jada said without looking up from her phone. "Now keep your hands where I can see them."

Danny sighed. "Okay, so at least tell me who you really are. You owe me that much."

Jada looked up and raised her eyebrows.

"Come on, Jada. I mean, is that even your real name?"

She smiled. "No, but I've always liked it. Kind of cute, don't you think?"

"Who even are you?"

Ignoring him, Jada glanced at her watch once more. Danny sensed she wanted to get this over with as quickly as possible. Her eyes still had that warm glow he loved, but they were narrowed and focused. She had the look of someone on the verge of losing control of the situation.

"Here's the deal, Danny. When the Angel calls, she'll have Nyah with her," Jada said, still looking at her phone. "She'll kill her if you don't give her what she wants. And she'll do it. I should know. She and I have a very long history together."

CHAPTER FIFTY-NINE

THE TIME TO FIGHT

Nyah had to calm herself if she wanted to get out of this alive. What was it Desi said? Just breathe. Like the damn song. Breathe in. Slow. Breathe out. Slow. It was working. Sort of. Her heart slowed a little. Her breathing calmed. She felt the cool breeze on her face. She listened to the rain as it poured and dripped from the bridge and tapped on the paved trail below. It was working.

Fiona, apparently oblivious of Nyah's struggle to breathe and regain control, pulled her mask from the pocket of the coat she'd been wearing, slid it on and held her hands out to the side in a mock pose.

"There. Now you get the full effect. Remind you of anyone?"

Nyah blinked. Between her blurred vision and the dark, she couldn't make out much. Until another flash of lightning lit up the sky enough to see every detail of her suit. It was so much like her own, with enough slight variations on the design to make it different. Deep green fading into black instead of the blood-red and black of Nyah's suit. She remembered the feeling she got when her mom first showed her the Agojie suit. She was mesmerized by its beauty, yet somehow terrified at the same time. Though not the same, the Angel's suit had its own element of mystery and fear.

Fiona leaned back on her elbows like she and Nyah were just two friends enjoying the evening.

"So was this your plan? Sneak up and kill me?" She laughed to herself and shook her head. "You're clever, I'll give you that. You got me good. But I've been doing this a hell of a lot longer than you, kid."

Nyah glanced back at her knife, still laying on the ground near the embankment.

"Your knife," Fiona said, knowing right away what drew Nyah's attention. "The Agojie's blade! That's mine now. I need the account number. And I think I'll keep it for a souvenir after this is all over. The dagger of the last Agojie warrior."

She sat up long enough to take another look at her phone, then leaned back on her elbows.

"So, you were asking about my suit?"

"No." Nyah shifted and tried in vain to get comfortable. "Can I at least sit up?"

"Oh!" Fiona said, as if she'd forgotten Nyah was still lying on her back. She got up, reached under Nyah's shoulders and pulled her up to a sitting position. The task sent a fresh wave of pain through Fiona's body. She groaned and put a hand to her side.

"I think you broke some ribs," she said.

Nyah ignored her and tried to twist her wrists. The zip ties were tight, but she could move them a little. With her right hand, she reached for the small dagger tucked inside her sleeve. It was slow going and she needed to keep Fiona distracted.

They sat facing the bayou, watching as the rain poured down into the dark, concrete channel. Occasional flashes of lightning revealed the murky water below as it rushed past, threatening to overflow the banks if the rain kept up for much longer.

"So why does it look so much like mine?" Nyah asked, hoping to buy some more time. It was a stab in the dark, but she guessed that Fiona would jump at the chance to talk about her suit and its background. Something she probably didn't get to do very often. It was a good guess.

"I knew you were curious," Fiona said, then winked and leaned over to give Nyah a playful push with her shoulder. It made Nyah sick to her stomach, but she had to play along.

"Okay, where do I start?" Fiona closed her eyes to think. "Of course. The beginning. Back to when the Agojie killed Nick and this whole shit storm started. You remember Nick, right? Anyway, his son, Nicky Junior, was hiding in the pantry. He was scared to death, poor kid. So instead of making a run for it, he stayed and sketched out a picture of the Agojie. He was quite the little artist."

Fiona paused to check the time on her phone once more. She was nervous. Fiona was a pro, but this was a big job and there was a lot on the line. Nyah wondered how furious Bruno would be if she messed up again.

"Little Nicky Junior never got over it," Fiona continued. "He grew up hell bent on tracking his father's killer down. Spent the rest of his goddamn life doing it and got pretty close, but that's another story."

"You people love your grudges," Nyah said.

"Of course we do! It's about respect." Fiona's smile disappeared and she slapped the back of Nyah's head. "Now don't interrupt me again or I'll tape your goddamn mouth shut."

To Nyah, this seemed like an overreaction. But then,

Fiona's whole life had been built on one big overreaction after another. It was a good reminder that she wasn't playing with a full deck.

The smile returned and Fiona the college dorm-room buddy persona was back.

"So where was I? Oh right, Nicky Junior. He didn't get his revenge, but he found out a lot about that first Agojie and what she was doing here. He wrote it all down and stuffed it into a hidden safe along with his drawing before he died. My brother and I stumbled across it one day when we were playing hide and seek. It took a while to get it open, but once we did we couldn't stop reading. Eventually, we developed our own little obsession."

"I'd say it's more than a little," Nyah said, nodding to Fiona's suit.

"And you're more than a little bitch! What did I just say?" Fiona reached into her bag, pulled out a roll of duct tape and tossed it onto the ground in front of her. "Go ahead. One more word. See if I won't."

When Nyah said nothing, Fiona shook her head and continued.

"So at first, Bruno was fixated on pure revenge for Nick, while I was more interested in the money and the story of the Agojie warriors. But mainly the money. We needed it."

"Revenge for Nick?" Nyah asked. "You sure it wasn't about what happened in Alaska? Maybe to keep my mom and Danny quiet?"

Fiona leaned her head back and shouted to no one, "Fuck! Why does everyone know about Alaska but me?"

"It's a long story," Nyah said.

"We don't have time for more stories," Fiona said, then grabbed a handkerchief from inside her coat pocket and pulled her mask back to wipe some blood from her face. "Anywho, that brings us here. Under this dark and dirty bridge in this pathetic excuse for a city. Why would anyone want to live here?"

"You done?"

Fiona raised her hands to the sky, exasperated. "You see? That right there is the trouble with kids these days. Always so impatient and no fucking respect for their elders."

"Respect is earned, and we don't do bullshit." Nyah repositioned herself and winced from the pain in her bruised side. "You should have used sign language for that monologue so I could have tuned you out easier."

Fiona burst into a fit of laughter and immediately hunched over and grabbed her side from the pain it sent shooting through her ribs.

"Stop making me laugh! It hurts," she said. "Damn, I like you! I hate hate hate that I have to kill you."

Once the pain subsided, she picked up a small rock from the ground and tossed it into the water.

"You sure you don't want to just join up with me? I could teach you all sorts of dirty little tricks."

"Go to hell, Fiona."

"I'm afraid you'll have to go first. Do me a favor and tell your parents hello for me."

Nyah swiveled and kicked her right foot towards Fiona's face, but Fiona caught it in her hand just inches from her jaw. She pushed it away and shook her hand in the air.

"Goddamn that stings," Fiona said. "You're like a little Jackie Chan over there."

"Cut these zip ties and I'll show you the real Karate kid," Nyah said.

"She knows her movies!" Fiona put a hand on Nyah's

shoulder and looked her in the eyes like a mother giving a stern talk to her child. “But as fun as it would be to kick your ass all over again, I’m done taking chances with you, sweetheart. Now sit tight and let’s wait for that phone call.”

CHAPTER SIXTY

JADA

Danny felt as though he'd been punched in the gut. The blood rushed from his legs and his head felt light.

"You worked with Fiona? You worked with the Montello family?"

Jada put her phone on the counter and let out an exasperated sigh.

"You just won't quit with the questions will you?" She shook her head and considered for a moment. "Okay, why not? We've got time. But you better pay attention because I'll only say it once. The Montello family knows everything about the Agojie legacy. How they operate, where the money is, everything. That kind of knowledge takes lots and lots of time and research. You think Fiona or Bruno are capable of that kind of digging? No. But I am. Computers are my thing."

Ignoring her half-empty beer bottle still sitting on the counter, she walked to the fridge and grabbed a mineral water, then slammed the door shut.

"I was their research girl. I spent years putting all the pieces together and doing the groundwork for them. And that means I know everything too. Like how Fiona has been planning to steal all that Agojie money stashed away in your bank and use it to gain more power in New Orleans and beyond. Things haven't been so easy since the family left New York."

She leaned back against the counter and set the gun down long enough to twist the cap off of her drink, then immediately picked it back up. The fact that she put it down at all meant she was growing more comfortable with the situation. A mistake Danny intended to capitalize on.

Danny shook his head. "Good Goddamn," he said. "So you got greedy and hatched a plan to get the money for yourself before Bruno and Fiona could get to it?"

Jada laughed. "Why not? Why the hell not? I know how you recruit Nyah's trainers, so I left the Montellos and disappeared. I have a background in gymnastics. When I was safe, I made a little fake profile of my own and put it out there for you to see. I knew all the keywords you were looking for. Discreet, home training, things like that. And I made sure to include a picture of my lovely face. You're a lonely, middle-aged man. I knew you'd take the bait." She raised the gun and her drink into the air and looked around. "And here I am." She took another swig and chuckled. "Pretty fucking genius, right?"

"So you only got close to me so we'd keep you around?"

"Exactly!" Jada pointed at Danny with the gun. "You're quick! I know everything, remember? Like how you cut ties with everyone when you relocate. Including all Nyah's trainers. If I was your girlfriend, I figured you'd make an exception for me. And of course I was right. You ate it up when I said I was ready for a change too and asked to come with you."

Danny closed his eyes and lowered his head. Jada hopped up onto the counter and set the drink down next to her beer. Maybe it was to fill the silence, or maybe just to help calm her nerves from the stress, but Jada decided to keep talking.

"I knew their plan, but after Oklahoma City, they lost track of you two. And since I couldn't call Fiona up and tell her where you were, I needed a way to get the Angel to Nyah. I remembered Fiona talking about a target Bruno wanted her to capture and bring back from Houston. Some kid he needed for leverage. When I found out he went to Fonville, the rest was easy."

Rage flooded through Danny's body. He made a move towards her, only to stop short when Jada raised the gun.

"Danny, come on. Please don't make me shoot you in the leg." She held the gun with two hands, pointed it towards Danny's leg and shut one eye. "I'm not a pro like you, but I bet I could get you from here."

Danny backed up to the counter again and took a moment to let everything sink in.

"So that's why you suggested coming here?" he asked after a few deep breaths. "All that stuff about your family and your old stomping grounds was a lie?"

"I told you a lot of things to make sure you moved to Houston and enrolled Nyah at Fonville. I knew once Fiona spotted her, she'd forget all about the target and go after Nyah instead. All I had to do was sit back here and wait for her to make her move."

Years of training had made Danny into an expert at keeping his fears at bay and focusing on the mission, and this was no different. No matter what, he would see this thing through. Nyah would live to see another day, even if Danny had to give up his own life to make that happen.

"You sure that thing is charged?" Jada asked, nodding towards Danny's phone on the counter.

"You've seen me check it every two or three minutes since Nyah turned up missing," he said. "It's on and it's charged."

He thought for a moment, then added, "You pitted Nyah

against the Angel, but did you ever think what would happen if Nyah got the upper hand? Maybe Nyah was more than she bargained for."

Jada thought for a moment, then shook her head. "No, no, no, that won't happen. It can't. We're talking about the Angel. Nyah is good. I mean her back handspring is a thing of beauty. But she's just a kid."

Danny learned a long time ago never to underestimate Nyah. She was capable of things he never imagined possible and she was always full of surprises. Just like her mom. And in spite of her denial, Danny could see a flash of fear in Jada's eyes when he suggested the plan might have gone wrong. The seed of doubt had been planted.

CHAPTER SIXTY-ONE

VICTORY SHARPENS THE KNIFE

"I didn't know you were at Fonville until I ran into you in the bathroom that day."

"What?" Nyah had almost reached her hidden knife with the tips of her fingers, but paused to listen to Fiona's latest revelation.

"I was at the school for a different target. Then you showed up out of nowhere and bam, early Christmas."

"What do you mean, another target?"

"You weren't the reason I was sent to Fonville. That's all you need to know about that." Fiona reached over and patted Nyah on the back. "You're more important to me than anyone. You should feel special."

The rain returned to its slow and steady pace. The shelter of the bridge still kept them dry enough, and Fiona seemed unconcerned with the rising water in the bayou below.

"So you think in a city with millions of people and dozens of high schools, you just happened to have an assignment at the very same school I was going to?"

Fiona tossed another rock into the water.

"I'm not an idiot, Nyah. Seriously. I just didn't have time to deal with it. Like I said, you're my priority, Nybear."

"Don't call me that."

Fiona glanced at her watch. "It's almost showtime!" She got up, walked to Nyah's knife and stood over it for a while. "You have no idea how long I've waited to have the Agojie blade in my hand. I was trying to soak the moment in, you know?" She glanced over at Nyah who didn't seem to be paying attention. "Hello? Special moment happening over here."

She reached down and grabbed the knife, only to immediately drop it.

"Shit!" she yelled as she shook her hand in the air. "Something poked me!"

She looked at her hand and saw a thin trickle of blood streaming down her palm.

"What the hell was that?" She turned back to Nyah for an answer, but she was gone. Only a cut-up pair of zip ties remained in the spot where she'd sat.

"You bitch! You little bitch!" Fiona screamed like a child throwing a tantrum. In an instant, she'd gone from a woman in control of everything to someone who'd just lost it all. She pulled her Sig Sauer and aimed into the darkness. "Stupid girl! Stupid stupid stupid! Where are you? Your friends are so fucking dead if you run! Dead dead dead dead dead!"

CHAPTER SIXTY-TWO

A BITCH OF A BUG

Danny inched closer to the knife, biding his time until he felt comfortable enough to make a move. In the meantime, he tried to keep the conversation going.

"So how is this gonna work? What's your big plan here?"

Jada smiled and seemed to relax a little. "Now you're asking the right questions."

She rested the gun on her knee, but kept it pointed at Danny with her finger on the trigger guard. She was an amateur, but she wasn't stupid. Danny was a caged tiger, and she wasn't about to let her guard down.

"By now, Fiona has Nyah. When you call, she'll demand the password to the Agojie account."

"The password? What good will that do? Those funds are in the same New York bank they've been in since the beginning. The people there know me. I have failsafes in place. Not even I could transfer all that money to another account without showing up to the bank in person. They get the least bit suspicious and that account will be locked down tight."

Jada hopped off the counter and laughed. She was fidgety. Another good sign.

"God, Danny. You think we're stupid? Fiona knew all this from the beginning. It's one of the reasons she hired me. I'm the best around. I developed a little bug that allows us to make under-the-radar transfers from any account. All we need is access to the account." She pointed her gun at the computer screen. Danny could see numbers, but couldn't make out anything else. "It's a bitch of a bug. Took years to develop. I could sell it, but after this I won't have to worry about money ever again."

"So all you need is the account number and password?" Danny asked.

"It transfers the money to an off-shore account without alerting anyone. The numbers stay the same for a couple days, then bam, the bug dies and they revert back to the actual balance. Which will be zero. Pretty badass, right?"

Jada examined Danny's face for any signs of surprise, clearly hoping to relish in the moment. When Danny's expression remained unchanged and she realized it wasn't going to be the jaw-dropping moment she'd hoped for, she frowned and continued.

"Anyway, Fiona has a copy and she'll use it to get your money. But what she doesn't know is that I'm going to use that same bug to steal it from her after she steals it from you. I secretly made myself an authorized user on her account before I disappeared. She's never been good with computers, so that part was easy."

"You pull this off and you're as good as dead, Jada. Trust me, they're good at finding people."

"Fiona already messed up once with Rachel. She does it again and Bruno is gonna be pissed. She'll be too worried about saving her own ass to worry about me. At least long enough for me to get far, far away."

"So the Angel does your dirty work and then ends up being the fall guy."

"Bingo. And the best part is, no one will ever know I was behind it all."

"You really thought this through."

"You have no idea. Pretty good plan, right?"

It was a good plan. It must have taken years to create. As Danny mapped out his own plan to end this whole thing, his heart sank as he realized the odds of success were in Jada's favor.

CHAPTER
SIXTY-THREE
DEFEAT SHARPENS THE MIND

Fiona swept her gun from side to side, aiming at anything that moved or made a sound.

"I know you're still here, Nyah. Come out and I promise I'll leave your friends alone."

Except for the rain tapping on the pavement, she heard nothing. Saw nothing. She was about to lose hope when Nyah's voice echoed off the bridge.

"Victory sharpens the knife!"

The echo, combined with the pouring rain made it all but impossible to pinpoint Nyah's location.

"Victory? What are you talking about?" Fiona shouted back. "Listen, Nyah. You can't run away and you can't beat me. I know where Danny is. I know where your friends are. Come out and we can talk."

"Defeat sharpens the mind."

The voice was behind her now. She spun and aimed, but there was nothing but more shadows and darkness.

Just keep her talking, Fiona thought. She'll slip up sooner or later.

"What the hell are you talking about, Nyah? What do you want?"

"You studied the Agojie, but you learned nothing!"

"I learned enough!"

"You learned from our victories, but you never learned from our defeats."

"I don't have time for these games, Nyah. Come out now. Last warning."

She kept her finger on the trigger guard and rested the butt of the gun on the palm of her left hand to keep it steady as she moved from pillar to pillar in the shadows, checking every possible hiding spot. Personal feelings aside, this was still a job and she needed to stay professional.

"Coach, coach, coach. You were a bad student. You missed a very important lesson."

For the first time in her career, Fiona felt like she was losing control of the situation. It was time to end this little game and show Nyah what the Angel was really capable of. She pulled her mask back down over her face, slid into the darkness and waited.

"Esi once faced a man named Jabari," Nyah said, her voice still echoing from the bridge. "He was one of the king's fiercest warriors, but still no match for Esi. So he used his wit to beat her. It was a hard lesson, but Esi let it sharpen her mind. She wrote it down and I learned too."

"Story time is over! Come ou-"

Fiona's vision suddenly blurred. She wiped her eyes, but that only made it worse. She stood up, stumbled and put a hand on the pillar for support, then pulled it back in shocked terror. The pillar was a tree now. Had it been a tree all along?

She looked at her hands, then at the tree. No. It was a pillar again. Her head spun. Her knees felt weak.

"What the hell did you do, Nyah!?" she yelled into the darkness. Then to herself, "What the hell did you do?"

"It's called Ibogaine." Nyah's voice was coming from all directions now. "Not exactly legal, but Danny uses it to help with his addiction. He grows and mixes it himself."

"So you're a witch now? Well, I… I have a gun. That will beat your little potion ever… every time," Fiona said, but she could already feel her grip on the pistol loosening.

Her breathing was labored and her heart began to race. She had to focus. Had to stay in control. Had to. She held the gun in one hand and leaned on the tree, no, a pillar with the other hand to steady herself.

"As you can tell, it sometimes comes with some pretty trippy side effects. Like hallucinations."

"Shut up!" Fiona screamed. "Shut up, shut u–" She shrieked when a snake coiled itself around her ankle. She tried to kick it off, but it wouldn't budge. "I hate snakes! Get it off!" She aimed her gun and squeezed the trigger, but the snake disappeared and the bullet ricocheted off the concrete.

"Boo," Nyah whispered, seeming to appear in front of Fiona out of nowhere.

She punched Fiona in her injured ribs, stunning her just long enough to kick the gun from her hand and send it tumbling down the embankment into rushing water below. Fiona tried to bring her fist around, but Nyah punched her in the throat before it could connect, then grabbed her shoulders and rammed a knee into her gut. Fiona hunched over and dropped to her knees, gasping for breath and clenching her side.

Nyah stared down at her for a few moments to make sure she wasn't getting back up, then left her there to get her knife, still laying on the ground where Fiona dropped it. She picked it up and carefully removed the needle she'd installed before leaving the house.

"Right here." She held it up for Fiona to see. "That's how I got it into your system. I just had to be careful when I was handling it."

Fiona sat down and pulled her knees up to her chest. Aside from the pain, the ground seemed to be moving up and down like waves in the ocean. She closed her eyes and tried to focus.

"You killed my dad. You ruined our lives," Nyah said, taking a step closer to Fiona. "I should kill you right now."

Nyah's suit seemed like another shadow in the darkness. She stood over Fiona, staring down through her mask with cold, dark eyes. It reminded her of the last time she confronted an Agojie. But unlike her mom, Nyah was too confident in her situation. Too caught up in the belief that she'd already won. Fiona was shaky, but had some strength left. She held up a hand to hold Nyah off, while discretely sliding her other hand to the knife strapped to her thigh.

"Okay, okay," Fiona said, buying some time to get back on her feet. "I give up! You got me!"

She stood on shaky legs, ignored her pain and dizziness and waited for Nyah to take another step towards her. When she did, Fiona whipped the knife around and stabbed it into Nyah's gut. But the blade passed through her body like she was a ghost and Fiona's momentum pulled her forward until she lost balance and fell once more to the ground.

She grunted, rolled over and sat back up to see not one, but two Nyahs standing side by side.

She tried rubbing her eyes again, but now there were three Agojie warriors. All of them wearing that damn blood-red and black death suit.

She squeezed her eyes shut and shook her head. "What the

hell?" She slowly got back to her feet, holding her knife out while trying to make sense of what she was seeing.

"Ibogaine can mess with your head in large doses," Nyah said. "I was never good with measurements, so I may have given you a tad too much."

"God d– da– God," Fiona tried to talk, but her tongue felt numb.

For a brief moment, the other two Nyahs disappeared, leaving only the one. The real one. It was all Fiona needed. She brought her knife up and charged again, but the drug had taken its toll. Fiona was clumsy and slow and barely managed to hold onto the knife. Nyah grabbed Fiona's arm, spun and pulled it over her shoulder, then rammed her free elbow into Fiona's nose. Her head knocked backwards and the knife dropped from her hand.

When Nyah turned back around, she saw a broken and beaten woman standing in front of her. Fiona's arms hung limply to her side and her knees were slightly bent. There was no more fight in her. The Angel was done. It was time to finish this.

CHAPTER SIXTY-FOUR

NOTHING TO LOSE

Danny learned more than just culinary skills from Rachel. With her help and years of practice, he'd become deadly accurate in the fine art of knife throwing. And with every distraction, he moved closer and closer to the knife sitting on the counter.

When Jada glanced down at her laptop, he moved closer. A check of the timer, closer still. He was almost within reach, but he couldn't get impatient. Not now. Jada still had a gun pointed at him and it wouldn't take much to startle her and fire off a shot. At this range, she could easily get lucky.

His plan was garbage and he knew it. A knife to a gunfight. For real? But it was all he had. And if there was any chance of turning this thing around, he had to take it.

As the timer continued its relentless countdown, Danny clung to hope. Hope that the Angel failed. Hope that Nyah escaped. Hope that she was still alive and out there somewhere. Hope that he'd see her again.

He could almost touch the knife. One more distraction and he'd make his move. Maybe the last move of his life.

CHAPTER
SIXTY-FIVE
A STORM WITHIN

Fiona sank down to one knee, waiting for the damn hallucinations to stop and the pain that racked her body to subside.

"I guess you got me good, Nyah. What you gonna do now? kill me?"

"Nothing would give me more joy." Nyah said, staring down at the injured woman in front of her.

She could have finished the job by now. Fiona, better known as the Angel, should be dead and the nightmare that plagued them for so many years should be over. But she couldn't do it. Not like this. It was pure instinct and training with the sniper, but now she had time to think. Way too much time. Nyah was no killer. Not like the Angel. Not like her mom. She was just a kid who wanted to go back home and think about prom dresses, final exams and maybe even college. Anything but killing the woman in front of her. She squeezed the handle of her knife and tensed. There was no going back. Not without finishing this. Not without blood.

"Aren't you supposed to be the good guy here?" Fiona asked. "What would your mom say?"

Fiona covered her eyes with her hands, trying to force the hallucinations away. Nyah suspected she was also trying to buy more time.

"My mom would have ended you by now." Nyah stepped closer and raised her blade.

Fiona held up her hands in surrender. "Whoa! Hold on, Nyah. I'm drugged and defenseless. Show some decency."

"You're about as defenseless as a wounded tiger. Get up."

"Kind of on a mind trip right now," Fiona sat down and leaned back on her hands. "Mind if I rest here for just a minute."

"Get up. I won't tell you again."

"Okay, okay. Just give me a second." Fiona slowly got to her feet, wobbled a little, then bent over and rested her hands on her knees. "Is the world spinning for you, too?"

"You killed my dad. You ruined my mom's life. You tried to kill my best friend. You're a monster." Nyah's voice was calm, but a storm raged within her. Her mother always told her to keep cool during a fight. Emotions could prove a greater opponent than your enemy. But right then, all she could think about was the loss. The heartache. The years of running. The utterly messed up childhood and the people hurt along the way. All because of the woman standing in front of her. She should kill her. Lunge and stab, just like she'd been taught. She could, but she didn't.

"Look, when are you gonna get over the whole I killed your daddy thing?" Fiona said. "It's getting a little old."

All at once, anger, rage and sadness took over. Without thinking, Nyah lunged.

"You're so fucking dead!"

A split-second too late, she noticed Fiona raising a

clenched fist. The story of Jabari flashed into her mind. Oh damn! Same trick! Damn, damn, damn! Nyah closed her eyes and turned her head just as the mud Fiona picked up from a patch next to the pillar hurled through the air towards her. She shielded her face with one hand, but specks of mud still managed to get into her eyes.

Squinting through blurred and stinging vision, she saw Fiona, already on the move, coming in at her fast with something in her hand. Her knife! Nyah's training kicked in. She twisted her torso and leaned back just as the knife swished past, missing her chest but cutting into her arm above the elbow.

Nyah shook off the pain and tried to slash up with her knife, but Fiona was ready. She twisted out of the way, then rammed the butt-end of her own knife into Nyah's head with all the strength she had left. Nyah stumbled back and fell to her knees.

"Your little potion wore off quicker than you thought it would, Nybear." Fiona pulled two more zip ties from her waistband pocket, knelt down behind Nyah and pressed her knife against her throat. "And now I'm really pissed off. Give me your damn hands."

She grabbed Nyah's injured arm and twisted it behind her back, sending a shockwave of pain through her body.

"Stop it! That hurts!" Nyah screamed through clenched teeth.

"Oh please. Can't even handle a little scrape on your arm? You're nothing like your mom, Nyah. She was a real warrior. You're just a kid in a Halloween costume." She slid her knife back into its sheath and pulled Nyah's other arm behind her back. "You should have killed me when you had the chance."

When Nyah tried to pull her arm free, Fiona yanked her wrist up higher towards her neck. Nyah grimaced, but forced herself not to cry out again.

"Now, Nyah! I'm done playing games with you."

Nyah's eyes filled with tears. There was nothing to do. No way to win. Her plan was shit. She had her chance and she let it slip away. There was no backup plan. No more surprises. She'd been beaten. She lowered her head and gave in.

CHAPTER SIXTY-SIX

SECOND CHANCES

"You're in over your head, Jada. Or whatever your name is. You know that, right?"

Jada had gone back to sitting on the counter with the gun resting on her knee, unconsciously kicking her left foot against the cabinet.

"You gotta take big risks to make big gains," she said. "Don't you worry about me, big guy."

It wasn't what she said so much as how she said it that made Danny suspect she didn't totally disagree. But they both knew it was too late to turn back now. She was in this for the long haul, no matter what happened next.

"Goddamn, Jada. Was any of it real?"

"What do you mean?"

"Us," Danny said, putting one hand over his heart. "Don't tell me it meant nothing to you."

Jada's smile faded and her gaze shifted to the floor. It was the opening he needed. He could have gone for the knife, but he hesitated. Maybe it was his feelings for her, or maybe he was getting soft, but he decided to give her one more chance to be human. If he could get out of this without killing her, that would be a win.

"It was good. Real good," she said finally, looking back up at Danny. "There aren't many men like you out there, Danny. I mean that."

This surprised Danny, but he went with it.

"So why do this to me? To Nyah? You know somewhere deep down you care about her too."

"Of course I do!" Jada almost yelled.

Danny held a hand out. "It's because you're human. You're good at what you do, Jada, but you can't fake that. You care about us and you know what you're doing is wrong."

"What if I do? What if... It doesn't matter though, does it?" Jada seemed almost in tears now. This was good. "Fiona has Nyah and she'll get your money. I can't stop her. If I walk out of here now, I'll be back where I started. And as a bonus, I'd have the Agojie hunting me down."

"We wouldn't-"

Jada raised the gun and pointed it at Danny.

"Please don't give me that bullshit. I know how you operate, remember? You'd never leave me walking around out there after all I've done."

Danny took a second to try and ease the tension of the moment. Jada lowered the gun and looked down at the floor as if ashamed of what she was doing.

"Jada, it's not too late. What we had was real, even if you were living a lie. You walk out of here now and you're a free woman. You have my word on that."

Now Jada was silent. She relaxed a little and rested the gun on the counter. When she looked up, Danny saw tears forming in the corners of her eyes. She opened her mouth to speak.

"Danny, I–"

The phone timer chimed, cutting her off mid sentence. She picked it up and stared at the screen for a few moments, then slowly put it back down on the counter. She wiped her eyes with one hand, then raised the gun and pointed it at Danny.

"It's time to call the Angel."

CHAPTER SIXTY-SEVEN

THE PRIESTESS OF PAIN

"One more time."

"What?" Nyah opened her eyes to find she was no longer on the trail beneath the bridge. She was... at the gym. Her mom's gym. The place they'd spent hours upon hours training together.

"One. More. Time," the strangely familiar voice repeated.

Nyah looked over her shoulder and saw her mom, drenched in sweat, standing behind her.

"Momma?"

"Yeah, babe?"

"It's you?"

"Yeah."

"Why are you here?"

Rachel smiled and put a hand on Nyah's shoulder.

"Did I ever leave?"

"Um, well yeah."

The smile faded. Without warning, Rachel grabbed Nyah's arm and twisted it behind her back.

"Ahh! Momma please!"

"You know what to do, baby. We practiced this move a hundred times."

"Aggh! I can't," Nyah said, squeezing her eyes shut. "I'm too tired. Let's go home. I just want to be with you again."

"You can't. Not yet."

"I'm not like you, Momma! I'm no warrior!"

Rachel let go and Nyah stumbled away, holding her injured arm.

"I love you, baby, but these people don't care about you. And they won't stop until you're dead. You've got to fight!"

"I know that."

Rachel stepped closer. "Look at me, child. Say it with me. I am Agojie. A priestess of pain."

"I am not-"

"A warrior for the weak. A legacy of blood."

"Handed down from our mothers," Nyah finished.

"Handed down from our mothers," Rachel repeated. She held Nyah gently by the shoulders and looked her in the eyes. "I'm so sorry for all this, baby. So, so sorry. But you know deep down you were born for this. Just like I was."

Nyah pulled free and turned so her mother couldn't see her tears. "But what if I wasn't? What if I'm just some stupid kid trying to play superhero?"

"I am Agojie." It was a different voice now. Rougher, more intense than her mom's. Nyah turned and saw a tall woman, lean and muscular with a scar running down the side of her face, dressed in the Agojie warrior suit. It was an older design, but still the same in so many ways.

"Esi?" Nyah asked.

Quicker than Nyah could react, Esi moved behind her, grabbed her arm and twisted it behind her back so hard it felt like it was going to break. Nyah screamed in agony.

Esi leaned in. "Do not give in to this pain, child."

"I'm just a... kid."

Esi whispered in Nyah's ear. "No. You are Agojie. The blade of Dahomey. The lion of Africa. Fight, Nyah. Our memory does not die tonight. Fight, my child and discover who you are. Who you were born to be."

CHAPTER SIXTY-EIGHT

A KNIFE TO A GUNFIGHT

Danny gave it his best shot. Any hope that Jada might be persuaded to put down the gun and walk away vanished when that timer went off. He knew she had no intention of letting him walk out of here alive. And if he did what she wanted, Nyah was as good as dead too. The time to act was now.

It didn't take long. Jada was preoccupied with making sure everything was ready to go. Danny watched and waited patiently for his chance. One second. Two. She opened her laptop and put the gun down to type something in. Danny spun to his right the instant her hand left the gun, grabbed the knife and turned back to throw.

He saw Jada raising the gun from the corner of his eye. Her reaction time was quicker than he'd expected. The barrel was pointing towards him. There wasn't enough time. A flash of light filled his vision followed by an ear-deafening blast.

CHAPTER SIXTY-NINE

THE BLOOD SHE LEFT ME

Drops of rain pelted Nyah's face. She blinked and found herself back on the trail, kneeling down on the wet concrete. The rain and rushing water in the bayou seemed to be in a shouting match, drowning out all other sounds.

The wind picked up, strong enough to blow rain under the once dry shelter of the bridge they were both under. Fiona tightened her grip on Nyah's injured arm and leaned in closer.

"You want to do this the hard way? Fine!" She jerked her arm up even further, but this time Nyah made no sound. "You should have never put on this suit, Nyah. You're not ready for it."

Something was different now. Nyah could feel it in her bones. No longer a kid on the run from danger. No longer afraid, no longer willing to hide. No longer capable of feeling the pain Fiona wanted to inflict. Nyah was something more. She was a warrior. The blade of Dahomey. She was the Agojie.

She thought of Danny, Desi, Quin and Malcolm. She thought of her mom. She thought of Esi. And then she thought of nothing at all. Her mind was at ease. Her body felt no pain. She was ready to end this. She was ready to fight.

~

"I AM AGOJIE," NYAH WHISPERED.

"What?"

Nyah raised her head. A flash of lightning lit up her cold eyes.

"A priestess of pain. A warrior for the weak."

"Enough of this." Fiona leaned in to grab Nyah's free arm. "Give me your arm!"

"And tonight, you will know it."

Nyah jerked her head back and rammed Fiona's injured nose, then twisted and used her free arm to crack Fiona's jaw with her elbow two quick times.

"Ack!" Fiona grabbed her jaw with one hand. Just enough of a distraction for Nyah to break free, jump to her feet and put all her power into a jumping front kick to Fiona's chest that knocked her back on her heels.

"A legacy of blood, handed down from our mothers, bitch!" Nyah screamed into the night.

Nyah was unforgiving and relentless. She moved in, landing blow after blow, stepping forward with each hit as Fiona was knocked back, closing the distance and keeping Fiona on her heels. Fiona managed to dodge a left hook, then a right, then countered with a right of her own, but Nyah ducked and punched Fiona in the solar plexus, then came back up hard with an uppercut to her jaw.

Fiona stumbled back and nearly fell over the edge of the embankment, but caught herself at the last second. Nyah came in hard with another swing, but Fiona pulled her blade and lashed out before she could connect. Nyah jerked back, missing a slash to her face by mere inches, then twisted her torso to miss a stab to her chest.

Fiona was close and coming in for a third attempt when Nyah jumped into a backwards handspring, landing on her hands and launching herself back onto her feet. She pulled her own knife just in time to block another downward slash from Fiona as she charged towards Nyah with everything she had.

"Fuck you and you're fucking legacy! I'm going to cut you!" Fiona screamed. "Cut, cut, cut you!"

Fiona's eyes filled with rage as she forced Nyah back. Their knives clanging together again and again as the pair fought.

Nyah backed up a few steps, blocking blow after blow. The sound of metal on metal louder than the pouring rain.

Clang! Clang!

Nyah side-stepped a jab from Fiona's blade then punched her in the face with her free hand and followed closely with another downward slash. Fiona pulled back, but not fast enough. Nyah's blade sliced into her face, cutting her from cheek to chin.

She grabbed her cheek and cried out in anger and pain. Blood covered her hand and dripped down her face.

"You little bitch!" She yelled, then charged. "You're fucking dead!"

This was Nyah's game now. Of all the Agojie warriors, only Esi was better with a knife than Rachel. And Rachel taught Nyah everything she knew. She stood her ground and waited.

Fiona came in hard, slashing and stabbing. Nyah blocked and countered. Stepping forward with each strike, forcing Fiona back. Her eyes were cold and dark, without feeling or mercy, lit up occasionally by the sparks that flew from the clashing knives.

The embankment was only a few steps away. Fiona glanced back and planted her feet, but Nyah's attack was too vicious. Too quick. Too deadly accurate. Fiona took another step back. Another.

Clang! Clang!

"I am Agojie," Nyah said, almost in a whisper.

Clang! Clang! Slash!

Nyah could see the hatred and anger in Fiona's eyes slowly turning to fear.

"The blade of Dahomey."

Clang!

"The lion of Africa."

Clang! Clang!

From somewhere deep inside, Nyah let out a scream. Dark and chilling. The Agojie battle cry. "Aaiiiieeee!"

Nyah fainted a stab, launched herself into the air, spun and snapped the heel of her foot across Fiona's temple. Her head jerked sideways just as Nyah landed and drove the blade of her knife deep into Fiona's shoulder.

"Believe that, bitch!" Her scream echoed from the bridge.

Lightning flashed from far away, followed later by the quiet rumble of thunder. The storm clouds had moved on, as if scared away by the battle far below.

Fiona's eyes opened wide in a look of pain, shock and disbelief, but she refused to give up. She switched the knife to her left hand and stabbed out. Slowed by her injuries, Nyah easily caught her wrist in her hand and twisted until Fiona cried out and dropped the knife.

Weakened and defeated, Fiona gave in and sank to her knees.

Nyah sheathed her knife and almost reached for the phone tucked in her side pocket to call for help. Almost. Instead, she knelt down to look Fiona in the eyes. Even through her pain and fear, Nyah could see the hatred still raging within.

"You won't quit, will you?"

Fiona stared back, defiant, angry and silent. Nyah stood and looked down at her.

"You can't quit. Chasing me and Danny is what you live for. And you won't stop until we're both dead."

The look on her face was answer enough. No regret, no remorse, not even in defeat.

Instead of begging for mercy or trying to talk her way out of the situation she found herself in, Fiona looked down, slowly shook her head and began to cry. Quietly at first, then more intense. Deep sobs shook her body, accompanied by a sad, almost wicked-sounding cry. Nyah couldn't see her face, but guessed it was smeared with tears and blood.

Even for a woman like this, Nyah couldn't help but feel sad. Once again she considered calling for help. This time her hand was touching her pocket when she realized something was off. Something not quite right about the way Fiona was crying. Almost as if she were... of course. She wasn't crying, she was laughing. Almost uncontrollably. Nyah felt like a fool for thinking this woman was capable of shedding tears.

"What's so funny?"

"You're right. I'll never quit, Nyah. Not until you're nothing but a bad memory." She looked up at Nyah. No tears, just dirt, some drying blood from the cut on her face and a wicked grin. "But still, here we are. I'm still alive and you're still just a pissed off little girl acting like a warrior."

"I'll show you-"

"Please," Fiona interrupted. "You won't finish this because you can't. You don't have the balls to put an end to me." She lowered her head and coughed, then laughed some more. "Well, let me show you how it's done."

In a flash, Fiona grabbed her knife from the ground with her good hand, sprang to her feet and stabbed towards Nyah's chest.

"Die, you bi- You bi-" Fiona couldn't seem to get the words out.

Her stomach felt like it was on fire. She looked down and saw Nyah's blade buried deep inside her gut. She looked back up at Nyah in disbelief.

"How did... you..." Her knife suddenly felt too heavy to carry. It slipped from her grip and fell to the ground.

Nyah leaned in close and gripped the handle of her knife.

"Balls are overrated," she said, then yanked the blade free.

The energy drained from Fiona's body. She tried to say something, but no words came out. She sank to her knees again and gave Nyah one last hateful look before slowly falling backwards onto the slanted embankment. Nyah instinctively reached a hand out to help, but it was too late. Fiona tumbled twice down the slope and fell into the dark, merciless, rushing water below and disappeared.

CHAPTER
SEVENTY
NO MORE PAIN

Nyah stood motionless, peering into the water, as if Fiona would suddenly spring out like a crocodile and charge. Ten seconds went by. Fifteen. The rushing water, the drizzle of rain, the occasional passing car in the distance and a strange ringing in her ears were the only sounds she could hear. Her breathing calmed and her heartbeat slowed its rapid pace.

Fiona was gone. Actually gone. And this time, she wasn't coming back.

Nyah watched for a few more seconds, then spun the knife in her hand like a skilled gunslinger and sheathed it. She pulled a Spree from the pack in her pocket, popped it in her mouth and took a moment to study her hand. Steady and calm. Not the slightest bit shaky.

Then reality hit. Danny! She dropped the pack of Sprees and grabbed her phone from her pocket. Seventeen missed calls from Danny. She tapped his name. It rang once. Twice. Pick up, pick up!

~

A click. A pause. Some rustling sounds.

"Nybear," Danny's voice was calm, but urgent. "Please tell me you're alright."

"Yes! God, Danny!" She turned away from the water to hear him better. "I'm fine, I'm fine! Are you okay?"

"You got away from Fiona? She didn't hurt you?"

"Yes. I mean no. I mean... I'm..."

The sound of rushing water drew Nyah's attention back to the flooded bayou. She stared for a moment until the harsh reality of what just happened, of what she'd done, overwhelmed her. Her legs grew weak and her stomach twisted in knots. From somewhere far away, she heard Danny's voice.

"Where are you, Nybear? I'll come pick you up."

Nyah dropped to her knees and began to sob.

"Nybear? What's wrong?"

"Oh God, Danny. I... I killed her. Fiona is dead. I could have... maybe I should have helped her. I don't know. But I didn't. I killed-"

"She's dead? For sure?"

Nyah closed her eyes and turned away from the water.

"Yeah. She's gone."

"Nybear, listen. Whatever happened, you did what you had to do. She would never have given up on hunting you. Hunting us."

Nyah tried to breathe. Slow. Calm.

"It's just..."

"Listen to me. You're not the bad guy here, Nybear."

"I feel sick, Danny. I feel like I should have done something different."

"Killing ain't easy. It never gets easy. But listen to me. She killed your dad. She tried to kill Quin. And she would have killed me and you and anyone else who got in her way. She was a monster. A rabid dog who needed to be put down."

Nyah said nothing. Danny said nothing. For a few moments, Nyah's breathing, slow and calm now, was the only thing filling the silence.

"Nybear. Tell me where you are. I'll come get you and we can make some tea and talk this all through."

"That sounds amazing," Nyah said, then slowly exhaled. "How do you always know just what to say?"

Danny laughed. "I learned it from your mom. I lost count of how many ledges she talked me down from."

"God, I miss her, Danny. I think I saw her tonight. Like a vision, you know?"

"I want to hear all about that. Now where are you?"

"Desi!" Nyah said, suddenly remembering her friend. "Sorry. I have to call Desi and let her know I'm okay. She's closer, so she can drive me home. I promise I'll be there soon."

Danny let out a long, deep sigh. "Sure, Nybear. Just get home quick." He hesitated, then added, "And we should talk about Jada."

CHAPTER
SEVENTY-ONE
LAST WORDS

Danny ended the call with Nyah and set the phone down on the counter. Some blood from his hand smudged the screen, but he'd clean that up later.

He picked up Jada's Glock and walked to where she was sitting on the floor by the counter, eyes red from tears, her knees pulled up to her chest with one hand holding a blood-soaked dish towel to her injured shoulder. Danny's favorite kitchen knife, also covered in blood, was resting on the floor by the stove where he'd tossed it after pulling it free from Jada's shoulder.

"I guess you were right," she whispered with ragged breath. "Never underestimate Nyah."

Danny stood over Jada, pointing the gun down at her.

"It's time," he said.

Jada closed her eyes. "I know. Just get it over with," she said, then added, "For what it's worth, I'm glad she's okay."

Jada kept her eyes squeezed shut, too frightened to look and see what was coming. What she knew she deserved.

A million thoughts filled her mind in those next few

seconds. The final few seconds of her life. She didn't expect things to end this way, but she should have known. Danny was a dangerous man on his own, but mess with Nyah and he becomes an unstoppable force. Now here she was, about to die in his kitchen. Fitting, she supposed, since it was Danny's favorite room in the house. They'd made good memories here.

Another thought. She wondered if the memory of her brains splattered on the cabinet would ruin the others or somehow bring Danny closu-

A bang. Jada jerked her body so hard, it sent another wave of pain shooting down her shoulder and into her chest. It hurt like hell, but she wasn't dead. At least, she didn't think so.

After a few seconds, she slowly opened her eyes. Danny still had the gun trained on her, but he hadn't pulled the trigger. Was he just toying with her now?

"Pick it up and go away." he said, then motioned to something next to her.

Jada turned to see a white box with a red cross on the top. That bang must have been from when Danny tossed it to the floor.

"A... a first-aid kit?" She shook her head in disbelief. "Why?"

Danny lowered the gun. "Get up and go. When you're far away, pull over somewhere, bandage up that wound and take a few Ibuprofen. Then get yourself to a hospital fast. Tell them you were mugged, or someone tried to rape you. I don't care." He waved at the kit with the gun. "Just pick it up, and go away. And if I ever see you again, if I even hear a rumor you're back in town, I'll hunt you down and put a bullet in your head."

For a few moments, Jada didn't move. Didn't speak. Didn't breathe. Didn't dare to tempt fate.

"Danny, I don't understand."

"It's pretty simple, Jada. Pick it up and get the hell out of my house," Danny said. "Consider this your second chance on life. But you better get moving, because I'm starting to remember how you almost got Nyah killed so you could get rich. You've got about two minutes before I change my mind."

Jada held up a hand to slow him down.

"Okay, okay," she said, then used her good arm to pick up the medical kit and set it on the counter above her head, then grab the edge of the counter to help herself up.

Danny offered no help as she took a deep breath and slowly pulled herself to her feet, wincing from the pain every few inches. It was a long and painful task.

Back on her feet again, she looked to Danny for more instructions, but he just waved towards the door with the gun.

She picked up the medical kit, then paused.

"Thank you, Danny. Thank you so-"

"Go," Danny interrupted.

Jada's eyes, already swollen and red from tears, grew moist again. She turned to leave with Danny following closely behind. She reached the door and put a hand on the knob, then braved another look back.

"Jada, you have about three seconds to-"

"My name is Vanessa," she said.

"What?"

"My name is Vanessa and I was a freelance cybersecurity expert before Fiona recruited me to work for the Montello family. I was in trouble. I needed the money. It's no excuse, but-"

Danny raised the gun and pressed it hard against her forehead. She tensed and closed her eyes.

"You think I care about any of that?" He was almost, but not quite yelling. "My patience with you is gone. I'm gonna to tell you one last time. Get the fuck out of my house!"

Jada, or was it Vanessa, couldn't leave without saying one

last thing. Something she'd known for a long time. Something worth risking a bullet to the brain.

"I... I love you, Danny."

Before Danny could respond, Vanessa turned, opened the door and darted out into the cool, damp air towards her car parked on the street. Danny grabbed the door and slammed it shut hard enough to shake the house.

He stood there for a few seconds, finally allowing himself time to breathe. Then he let out a long, deep breath, lowered his head and lightly pounded his fist against the door. It was a futile attempt to keep the tears away. He was a strong soldier, but his emotions would win this time. The tears came. Slowly moistening his eyes and streaming down his cheeks until he could fight them no more.

Jada's betrayal left him confused, hurt and filled with rage. He wanted to kill her. Should have killed her. But he didn't. Why? He knew the answer and he hated himself for it. He clenched his fist tighter, closed his eyes tighter and said it out loud.

"I love you too," he whispered, then hated himself all the more.

CHAPTER SEVENTY-TWO

NO MORE GOODBYES

Nyah needed a minute to breathe before she called Desi. A minute take it all in and get her head straight. She sat down beneath the bridge, pulled off her mask, closed her eyes and slowly inhaled. Calm and slow. Then exhaled. The storm was over. The rain was gone. Only the cool, damp air remained, soothing her soul and her bruised body.

Below, the water continued its hurried rush down the bayou, but Nyah was at ease. Fiona was gone. Really gone. For the first time in her life, she felt free. No more running. No more goodbyes.

She pulled her phone from her pocket to call Desi when the soft glow of another phone lit up near the pillar Fiona had been leaning against. She slid her phone back into her pocket, walked over and cautiously picked it up. No caller ID. She let it ring and considered whether to answer or toss it into the bayou. She answered.

"Did you get it done?" the person on the other end asked.

Bruno Montello. Had to be.

"Hi Bruno," Nyah said.

No response.

"Fiona is gone," Nyah continued. "And she's not coming back."

A pause, then, "Who is this?"

"Oh right. I should have started with that. It's Nyah, otherwise known as the girl who just ended your little sister."

"Bullshit!"

"I wouldn't lie to you about that, Bruno. What would be the point?"

Bruno's breathing grew heavy. For a few seconds, it was all she could hear on the other end.

"If you're telling me the truth, you're one dead bitch," he said finally. "No more holding back. The gloves will come off and I'll put everything I got into hunting you down and killing you."

Something occurred to Nyah. Why hadn't Bruno sent any of his guys to Houston? Why just Fiona? For a target this big, he'd no doubt send backup just in case. Could Fiona have been working alone? If true, there was something else she needed to know. Something that could give Nyah the upper hand.

"She never told you, did she?"

"Told me what?"

"Where she found me. Where I am right now."

Bruno's silence was her answer.

"It's over, Bruno," Nyah said after a pause.

"No, Nyah. It's not over. This is only just beginning for you. I'm coming for you, and I will find you. And when I do-"

"It's the Agojie," Nyah interrupted. "And now it's your turn to listen. You killed my dad and destroyed my family. But instead of hunting you down and ending you, I'm going to call it even. And hear me when I say this. If I get even a hint you're still chasing me, you won't have to search long because I'll come for you."

Without waiting for a response, Nyah reached back and tossed the phone into the bayou.

"Trust that!" she screamed into the emptiness.

For a while, Nyah stood there, searching for those all-too familiar feelings that usually overwhelmed her when she dealt with the Montello family. But she wasn't scared. She wasn't panicked. Hell, she wasn't even angry. She looked at her hands. Still steady. Not the least bit shaky. She clenched her hands into tight fists. She was ready. Ready to become the warrior she was born to be.

"No more running," she whispered to herself. "No more goodbyes."

Her phone buzzed, startling her back to reality. She pulled it from her pocket and smiled when she saw the name on the screen.

"Hey," Nyah said.

"Hey," Desi said.

Nyah read books about friends who didn't need words to communicate. Friends who got all they needed from a simple greeting. Desi was that friend. Her best friend.

"So, you good?" Desi asked.

"I'm good."

"Not gonna lie. I was scared."

"Me too."

Nyah could picture Desi standing there, pulling her long, curly blonde hair back with one hand while she held her phone in the other. A nervous habit of hers.

"You're gonna tell me everything, right?" she asked.

"Every detail. Can you pick me up?"

"On my way. But promise me something first."

"Anything."

"Promise you'll tell Danny you're not moving away after this. You're staying right the fuck here in H-town with us."

Nyah smiled and turned to walk back up the trail. Away from the water, away from the dark bridge, and most of all, away from Fiona. Forever.

"You got my word on that," she said. "Now get over here. We have a lot to talk about."

CHAPTER SEVENTY-THREE

THE RECKONING

Bruno tossed the phone onto his desk and clenched his fists. How many goddamn times did he tell Fiona not to go at it alone? How many times did he warn her? She was always so damn stubborn. He grabbed his whiskey glass and hurled it against the wall, shattering it into a thousand tiny pieces.

"Goddammit, sis! Why didn't you just listen to me!" he shouted to his empty office.

The sketch pad mocked him from his desk, so he swiped it to the floor with one broad stroke that took a couple books and a stack of papers with it, then pounded his fists on the desk hard enough to rattle the floor.

He took a few minutes to collect himself. To refocus. There was still work to do. He still had a business to run, after all. But now things were deeply personal. He would have his revenge. He wouldn't rest until he did. The little Agojie and the Army Ranger would die if it was the last thing on earth he ever did.

He grabbed a tissue from a box sitting on a credenza behind him, blew his nose, then reached over and pressed a button on his office landline. Someone answered on the first ring.

"Yes sir?"

"Is Dillon ready?"

"Another few months or so, but yeah. I'd say he's looking better than ever."

"I want to see him. Now," Bruno said, then ended the call.

Five minutes later, Matthew Walsh, Bruno's chief scientist, was standing in front of Bruno's desk, dressed in a white lab coat with an iPad in one hand and an energy drink in the other. He was twenty-six and didn't give a damn about his appearance. Underneath the lab coat he was wearing a worn-out t-shirt with some comic-book superhero Bruno had never heard of plastered on the front, and the same green denim jeans he'd been wearing for the past week. He disgusted Bruno, but the little guy was a genius. Light years ahead of people twice his age. The kind of genius that will either get you into the history books or on a most wanted list.

As it turned out, Matthew fell into the latter category, which is why Bruno was able to recruit him so easily. And unlike his last geneticist, Matthew had little chance of suddenly developing a conscience and trying to run.

"He's testing off the charts," Matthew said, handing the iPad to Bruno. "No signs of rage or loss of mental capacity. He's like a god, and he's only going to get stronger."

Bruno grabbed the iPad and tapped an icon. A video popped up. He clicked play, and an image of Dillon sitting in a metal chair in what looked like a large warehouse appeared on the screen. Dillon was perfect for the test. Average height, average build. A young thug with aspirations of rising in

Bruno's ranks. When the chance to help Bruno with his little experiment came up, Dillon was first in line to sign up.

Dillon's eyes were closed, and for a moment Bruno thought he might be sleeping. He almost said something when a loud buzzer, like the kind on a gym scoreboard but louder, blared out, filling the big room with an ear-deafening noise.

"That's Dillon's warning," Matthew said after the buzzer ended. "Any second now."

Bruno stared intently at the screen. Dillon continued to sit quietly, undisturbed by the alarm.

The camera view switched to a wide shot, revealing a large crate on one side of the warehouse.

The box began to rattle, then shake violently. Bruno turned up the volume on the iPad and heard scratching, clawing and what sounded like growling noises coming from inside the crate.

"The devil dogs," Matthew said.

The devil dogs. His father's failed experiment on a deserted island so many years ago. Strays taken and injected with a revitalized version of Nicky Junior's formula. Nicky shut everything down after things went haywire. Kept it locked up good until Bruno's dad took it on once again. He made some tweaks and tried again. This time on dogs. Everything was looking good until they started to lose their goddamn minds and attack anything that moved. Dogs stronger and meaner than a pack of lions and crazier than a grizzly bear on cocaine. His father ordered them all destroyed except for one last batch. This batch. Six devil dogs kept out of sight and out of mind for decades. Until now. Bruno spent his whole life trying to perfect what his father failed to do. After far too many setbacks, including the big one in Alaska with the Agojie, he was closer than ever.

"You're gonna like this," Matthew said.

A CHAIN ATTACHED TO A PULLEY SYSTEM RATTLED AND BEGAN LIFTING the crate door up. The devil dogs burst through the door even before it was fully opened, cracking and splintering the edges with their frenzied exit.

They were big, muscle-bound dogs. The kind always showing up on the wrong end of news stories. The formula didn't just destroy their mind, it made them unnaturally large. What was left of their fur was matted, tangled and blood stained. Most of their bodies were marked with deep scars, and at least one of them was missing an eye.

They spotted Dillon at once and charged. Lips curled back and teeth bared. The devil dogs closed the distance and the leader leaped into the air, jaws open wide, drool pouring from its mouth, a wicked, guttural snarl coming from somewhere deep within.

Dillon opened his eyes and reached out fast, grabbing the dog by its neck a split second before its jaws would have torn into his face. He stood up, gripping the dog tightly by its throat as it thrashed and clawed to get free, then hurled it into the remaining pack, knocking them aside like bowling pins.

A few dogs managed to maneuver past and lunge at Dillon. He side-stepped the first and brought a fist down on its head. The dog hit the floor hard enough to bounce back up into the air, then land with a smack on the concrete.

The second dog circled and tried to sink its teeth into the back of Dillon's leg. Dillon spun and grabbed the dog by the scruff almost faster than Bruno's eye could keep track, then flung it high up towards the ceiling where it ricocheted off two or three of the rafters before falling back down to the floor with a thud.

Bruno stared at the screen for a few moments longer,

watching as Dillon eviscerated the remaining devil dogs as easily as the first three. After it was over, he set the iPad down on his desk, swiveled around in his chair and gazed out from his high-rise window.

"Let me know the minute he's fully ready."

"Of course," Matthew said, then picked up the iPad and left the office.

After he was gone, Bruno swiveled back to his desk and punched another button on his phone. Again, someone answered on the first ring.

"Sir?"

"He's almost ready," Bruno said. "I want to fast-track the program. We'll move on the Agojie and Danny when we're up to speed and erase them off the face of this planet."

"Yes sir," the voice on the other end said.

"And where are we with Dr. Grady's kid?"

"We've got people watching him. If he recovers, we'll make our move."

"Good," Bruno said, then ended the call.

Bruno opened a desk drawer and pulled out an old photo. Two kids, a boy and a girl in big winter coats, stood in the snow next to a snowman. The girl was shielding her face from the boy, who held up a snowball in one hand, ready to throw. Happier times. Before they handed in their snowballs for bullets and made this life of blood and power their own.

He leaned back in his chair and stared at the picture a few seconds more, then tossed it onto his desk and wiped a tear from his eye.

"You wanted real power in this town, little sis? We're gonna get it. I promise you that."

EPILOGUE

BEN TAUB HOSPITAL, HOUSTON

"Hi, Mr. Grady." Dustin's voice woke Quin's dad, Dr. Darius Grady, from his trance-like state. He couldn't remember how long he'd been standing in front of the coffee machine, cup of coffee in one hand and staring at the bill acceptor's flashing, green light.

He turned to Dustin, happy for the distraction. Dustin was wearing dark jeans and a black t-shirt with a dark-red denim jacket and a thin, gold chain around his neck. Darius could tell he took time on the outfit, and he respected that.

"Hi Dustin," Darius said, then stepped aside to let Dustin get to the coffee machine.

He found a chair near the window and sat down. He told himself he'd come here to get a break from the constant beeping of the monitors in Quin's room, but deep down he knew it was to get away from his son. All those tubes and wires and mechanical sounds. The nurses coming in and out. He felt unsteady looking at his son like that. It wasn't right. He needed a break, and so here he was. And if the looks on the faces of everyone else in the waiting room was an indicator, he was in good company.

He was about to grab a magazine from the small table next to his chair to try and distract himself when he noticed Dustin still staring at the coffee machine, much like he'd been doing only moments ago. Looking without thinking, lost in a daze of events.

"Please, come sit," Darius said, motioning to the chair next to him.

Dustin thought for a moment, then pulled his hands from his pockets, walked over and sat down.

"Thank you, sir."

Darius took a long sip of coffee, holding the cup with two hands.

"Want some coffee? I'm buying?"

"Oh, no thank you, sir."

"No need to call me sir."

"Oh, sorry."

"It's Doctor Grady."

"Um..."

Darius smiled. "Just kidding."

"Oh, yes sir. I mean doctor."

"Darius."

"Right. Darius. Um, sir."

The coffee wasn't too bad for vending machine coffee. Darius took in another sip, thankful for the small comfort it brought in this crazy new world he found himself in.

Dustin shifted uneasily in his chair.

"Did you have something you wanted to say to me?" Darius asked.

"I mean..." Dustin wasn't sure what to say next.

"I'll ask you again. Did you have something you wanted to

say? This is the third time you've approached me since I arrived at the hospital. I'm starting to think it's not an accident anymore. You must have something to say."

Dustin thought for a moment, then leaned over and rested his arms on his knees.

"No. I just... I wanted to say we're all pulling for Quin."

"Thank you. Now if you don't mind..." Darius picked up the magazine he'd reached for earlier and opened it to a random page.

"Yes sir. I mean Darius." Dustin got up to leave, trying his best to hold back the tears until he was outside again, away from everyone. He'd almost made it to the door when Darius called out.

"Dustin."

Dustin stopped, his hand touching the exit door.

"Sir?"

"I'm glad you're here."

"Thank you."

"Come over here for a moment, if you don't mind."

Dustin looked around the room, then walked over and sat back down. Darius reached over and grasped his arm with a firm grip.

"Listen. When my boy gets better and gets out of this place, you be good to him. You hear me? Don't you dare break his heart."

Dustin's jaw dropped.

"Excuse me, sir?"

"Darius."

"Excuse me, Darius?"

Darius let go of his arm, smiled and took another sip of coffee, then pointed around the room with the cup.

"All these kids around here and you don't think I'd hear something?"

"Hear?"

When Darius didn't answer, Dustin closed his eyes and tilted his head back.

"Oh damn. I'm so sorry. Quin never wanted you to find out like that."

"It's okay."

For a few moments, they both sat in silence. Darius sipping his coffee, Dustin with his eyes closed, thinking of what he could possibly say next. Darius was the first to talk.

"I think he was going to tell me right before... Right before it happened," he said, closing his eyes for a moment to fight back a sudden rush of emotion. "He texted me to talk. I called, but he didn't answer."

"Sir... Darius. I know he thinks the world of you."

"Doesn't matter, does it?"

"I think it does."

"No. It doesn't," Darius said. His voice was shaky now. A tear made its way down his cheek. He set the coffee down and grabbed a tissue from a pack in his pocket. "I wasn't there when he needed me. I wasn't there at all." Darius sniffed and wiped his eye. "I've done some things I deeply regret, Dustin. And it's cost me dearly. But that's over, and things are going to change. I promise you. It's going to change."

"It's one thing to say it, sir. But..." Dustin cut himself off before he could finish his thought.

"What?"

"Nothing. Nevermind. It's good to hear you say that."

"No. Finish that thought, young man." Darius crumbled the tissue, picked up his coffee and turned to face Dustin with a look that made Dustin want to run and hide.

Dustin sighed, repositioned himself in the chair and thought for a moment.

"It's just that... Quin needs you, not your promises." Dustin turned to look Darius in the eyes, growing more confident as he spoke. “I know it’s not my place, but I’ve spent more time with him this past year than you have. And I’ve seen how your dedication to work beats down on him.”

Darius sat quietly, coffee cup in one hand, gripping the arm of the chair with the other.

“I’m sorry. That was out of place...”

“No. No,” Darius interrupted. “You’re right.” He looked down and took some time to contemplate, then turned back to Dustin. “You’re right. And you’re a brave kid to tell me that to my face. I can’t help but respect it.”

“Thank you, sir.”

“Darius.”

“Thank you, Darius.”

Darius sighed. “I just hope I haven’t messed things up too much. I hope it’s not too late to fix things. I... I hope-”

The clack of the waiting room door interrupted his thoughts. A man walked in. A doctor. Quin’s doctor. Darius and Dustin were immediately on their feet, searching the doctor’s face for any signs of bad news.

The doctor spotted them, nodded and motioned to the door.

“Dr. Grady, could you come with me?” A trace of a smile appeared on his face. “I have some good news.”

THE END

www.ingramcontent.com/pod-product-compliance
Lightning Source LLC
LaVergne TN
LVHW100507110826
845146LV00002B/551

* 9 7 9 8 9 9 4 3 2 0 6 3 1 *